NEVER TELL

Born in London with a love of all things dramatic, Claire Seeber began her career as an actress. Soon deciding she'd rather pull strings safely behind the scenes, Claire forged a successful career in documentary television, enabling her to travel the world, glimpsing into lives otherwise unseen. Also a feature-writer for newspapers such as the *Guardian*, *Independent on Sunday* and the *Telegraph*, Claire now combines (furious) scribbling with keeping a beady eye on her two young boys.

To find out more about Claire go to www.claireseeber.com or visit www.AuthorTracker.co.uk for exclusive updates.

Claire blogs at www.claireseeber.com/blog

Praise for Claire Seeber:

'An intense psychological thriller.'   *OK!*

'An absorbing page-turner.'   *Closer*

'A powerful and sensitive treatment of every parent's worst night-mare.'   Laura Wilson, *The Guardian*

CLAIRE SEEBER

Never Tell

AVON

This novel is entirely a work of fiction.
The names, characters and incidents portrayed in it are
the work of the author's imagination. Any resemblance to
actual persons, living or dead, events or localities is
entirely coincidental.

AVON

A division of HarperCollins*Publishers*
77–85 Fulham Palace Road,
London W6 8JB

www.harpercollins.co.uk

A Paperback Original 2010

2

Copyright © Claire Seeber 2010

Claire Seeber asserts the moral right to
be identified as the author of this work

Extract from *River of Time* is reproduced by kind permission of the author.
Published by William Heinemann Ltd, 1995

A catalogue record for this book is
available from the British Library

ISBN-13: 978-0-00-733467-4

Set in Minion by Palimpsest Book Production Limited,
Grangemouth, Stirlingshire

Printed and bound in Great Britain by Clays Ltd, St Ives plc

Mixed Sources
Product group from well-managed
forests and other controlled sources
www.fsc.org Cert no. SW-COC-001806
© 1996 Forest Stewardship Council
FSC

FSC is a non-profit international organisation established to promote the
responsible management of the world's forests. Products carrying the FSC
label are independently certified to assure consumers that they come
from forests that are managed to meet the social, economic and
ecological needs of present and future generations.

Find out more about HarperCollins and the environment at
www.harpercollins.co.uk/green

For Tiggy & Bethy
As the song says, We are Family…

Last year I read 'River of Time' - a family favourite - by renowned journalist Jon Swain who reported so bravely on Vietnam and Cambodia. I'm immensely grateful to Jon for allowing me to use his words in NEVER TELL; they help explain Rose's addiction to chasing a story.

I also owe barrister Rupert Bowers a great debt of gratitude (or maybe a bottle of wine or two) for all the court-room advice. ('That would *never* happen' - he said a lot: wherever fiction takes over from fact, I've chosen to ignore his tutelage). Thanks to Nicola and Matthew Sweet who really did make it to Oxford, and to all my mates who knew about guns and bombs. (Bit scary, really.) Thanks as usual to Flic Everett the 1st for speeding through the first draft and to Beth for taking it to the beach; to the Goldsmiths 4 for listening & commenting so constructively, especially when I was blushing in the more 'shocking' scenes! Thanks to Tim for letting me lock myself away.

Huge thanks as ever to all at Avon: especially Keshini Naidoo and Kate Bradley (and bon voyage, Max!). Sincere thanks to everyone who has supported me during the past year, particularly the last six months. You know who you are and I'm very grateful. Last but never least, thanks to my agent Teresa Chris for all the pep talks and the belief.

The desire to cover stories is sometimes irresistibly powerful;
this ruthlessness for getting the story over and above
all else, including love, has wrecked the personal lives
of many colleagues . . .

There was a restlessness in my spirit, added to which I didn't
know how to say no to a challenge . . . an irreconcilable
conflict of interest in my life.

River of Time, Jon Swain

PROLOGUE

All the way to London, the woman's words circled round my head like carrion crows. She'd hung up before I could ask more; that silky voice echoing down the years, a voice I was sure I knew and yet couldn't quite place. One more piece from the nightmare jigsaw the last year had become; one more piece nearly slotted back in.

Off the motorway, the traffic snaked back solid to the Blackfriars interchange. Frantically I watched the clock, creeping forward incrementally, until I could bear it no longer. Abandoning the car on a broken meter, I sprinted through the rush-hour fumes, dodging swearing cyclists and the motorbikes that sneaked down the middle, stumbling over the kerb on Ludgate Hill, until I was falling in panic, unable to right myself. A double-decker bore down on me, horn blaring; a builder in a yellow hard hat snatched me from its path in the nick of time, his warm calloused hand on mine. I was too stunned to do much more than blink at him and run on.

They were closing St Paul's Cathedral to sightseers as I finally reached the great stone stairs. For too long now my life hadn't made any sense; I had to know the truth. Someone, somewhere, had to know the truth.

3

Inside, the internal gate was shut.

'Please,' I gasped at the curate closing up. 'Please, I have to – I've come so far.'

That someone might be here.

'You look pretty desperate,' the jolly curate relented, waving me through with his walkie-talkie. 'Last one in. This one's on God.'

'How do I get up to the Whispering Gallery?' I wheezed gratefully, leaning on the barrier for a moment to catch my breath.

It took me ten minutes to climb up, and my heart was banging so hard by the time I'd reached the gallery in the huge dome that I had to sit down as soon as I got there. I'd passed a gaggle of Italian tourists coming down the stairs, but otherwise the space was empty. I thought he hadn't come, the anonymous writer – and I heard my name said softly, and I turned and saw him.

They say that when you're drowning your whole life flashes before your eyes – though it seems unlikely that anyone could confirm it. True or not, I felt like I was falling backwards now, splashing messily through my own life.

He walked towards me, thin and no longer elegant, wiry-limbed and crop-haired instead.

'Hello, Rose,' he said, and I tried to find my voice.

'I thought,' it came at last, 'I thought that you were dead.'

PART ONE

Chapter One

GLOUCESTERSHIRE, SPRING 2008

It wasn't turning out to be one of the good mornings. Fred had been up three times in the night simply seeking company, so my eyes now stung with tiredness. Alicia was in a foul mood because Effie had scribbled all over her new birthday sketchbook in purple felt-tip. Effie had insisted sweetly that she was *dying* for porridge until finally I caved in, and spent ten minutes stirring it like an automaton, whereupon she spat the first mouthful dramatically all over the floor and refused even one more try, citing the 'yucky bits'.

'Put your other slipper on, Freddie. The floor's freezing.'

'It's lost,' he announced dramatically.

'It's not lost. It's on the radiator there.'

He turned earnest eyes on me. 'Superheroes don't wear slippers, Mummy.'

'Well super-heroes are going to have horribly cold feet then, aren't they?'

I wondered plaintively for the three hundred and sixty-fourth consecutive day why James couldn't get up just once and make the struggle with plaits, porridge and a three-year-old's tantrums at least partly his own.

'I want my milk warm, Mummy,' Effie puffed, abandoning the

cornflakes and dragging the milk bottle towards her across the table.

'Just have it cold, Ef, OK?'

'I want it *warm*,' she pouted and promptly upended the entire pint over the flowery tablecloth.

'For God's sake, Effie,' my restraint deserted me. 'I *told* you not to do that, you silly child.'

'Shut up, Mummy,' she shouted back. 'You're *rubbish*.' Her little red mouth was wobbling.

A Ready Brek-encrusted Fred looked in wonderment at the raised voices and cross faces; Effie and I glaring at one another, me wavering between laughter and annoyance until Alicia turned Radio One up loudly. My pounding head pounded harder as Alicia pronounced, 'This is Fred's favourite song,' and jiggled so alarmingly at him that he fell backwards and promptly burst into tears. Finishing a complicated riff about some girl not knowing her name, she whacked her arm on the chair and burst into dramatic sobs that equalled her brother's. Soggy J-cloth in hand, I gazed at them, weighing up my options: opening the gin or joining them.

Into this chaos walked Mrs McCready, never more welcome, unbuttoning the shiny old coat that hid her ill-fitting velour tracksuit, a choice baby blue today. ('I think she sleeps in them,' James remarked at least once a week.) She took one look at Fred's furious red face and swept him off the floor.

'Come here, my precious,' she crooned, clutching his plump little body to her huge chest, his head half the size of one of her bosoms. 'I'll go and get him dressed,' she said. 'Won't I, precious? Come on, Effie.'

I turned the radio down, tossing the cloth towards the sink. It hit the floor with a soggy thwack, narrowly missing the cat. I kissed Alicia's arm better until her sobs eventually subsided, and retied her red ribbons before dispatching her to piano practice whilst I made a desultory attempt to clear up.

Waiting for the kettle to boil again, I gazed out of the mullioned windows at the cold March morning. It was crisp and clear now, the last tendrils of dawn mist dissipating under a slow-climbing sun. Two robins took a quick dip in the stone birdbath, flicking each other with something like affection. Below them a blackbird bounced along a lawn glistening with dew, hopefully pecking for a worm. It was chocolate-box perfect.

The kettle snapped off as I caught my reflection in the glass. I am in a stupor, I thought, I have been in a stupor for months. Not months, even – years. I move slowly, I have become plumper, my skin is soft and golden, the glow of repleteness is on me. And yet I'm not replete.

I shook myself from my self-indulgence. Things are good, I thought, trying to convince myself once again, and poured boiling water all over my hand as James appeared noiselessly behind me.

'Ouch!' I yanked my hand back quickly. Quickly, but too late.

'Careful,' James yawned, stretching, displaying a hairy stomach above stripy pyjama-bottoms. I ran my hand under the cold tap, the freezing water a new kind of pain on my scalded skin.

'Any coffee going?' J scratched his belly. 'Have you seen my phone?'

He rooted through the piles of paperwork I'd stacked neatly last night, through the old newspapers full of articles I kept meaning to read and never got round to, forms for Alicia's school trips and Effie and Fred's dinner money, bank statements that needed to go to the accountants, my notebook full of scribblings for ideas that I needed to write up properly. Scribblings that were decreasing in number.

'I need to call Liam. I've had a fucking blinding idea for Revolver. We've got to go all out on the VIP room. Marble, gold, the works. Seventies kitsch.'

I watched one pile slide dangerously to the right and bit my tongue.

'Where the hell's my phone? Did you move it again? I do keep saying just leave it.'

9

'Oh, J, don't mess it all up again,' I muttered, but my beautiful symmetry was already descending towards the floor.

'Don't fuss, Rose.' He found the phone in the pocket of his fleece. 'McCready can tidy it. She loves it.'

Ruined.

'Who's she?' Mrs McCready stomped back into the room, a beaming Fred beneath her arm like a small parcel. 'The cat's mother?'

'Oh, McCready, you angel.' James kissed her resoundingly on one thread-veined cheek. 'You're here to save us all, aren't you, petal?'

I couldn't help smiling. 'I thought *I* was your petal?'

'That's right, Rosie Lee,' my husband winked at me, 'you are. My one and only petal. Bring the coffee to the studio, would you? I've got to get on.'

I caught McCready's eye over his dark head. Obviously it was a good day.

'Liam, that you? All right, sir?' J winked at me again. 'Listen, my head's buzzing. I've had a fucking blinder of a plan. Think Joan Collins on a swing in *The Stud*, and forget all your troubles.'

McCready pursed colourless lips and released Fred from her grasp.

'So, sir, get your arse . . .' With a flurry of paper falling to the floor and a door slamming in his wake, J was gone. Troubles, I thought. The first I'd heard.

'I'll fetch him his coffee,' McCready said, as I'd known she would. For all her disapproval, she adored James. As she left the room, Fred in her wake, the phone started to ring.

'Thank you,' I called after her, adding milk to my tea and looking for the handset. Before I found it, the answer-phone kicked in.

'Pick up, Rosie, darling.' My heart jolted at the familiar drawl. 'We both know you're there.'

I finally spotted the receiver, tangled in a pair of small carrot-stained dungarees in the washing basket.

A deep sigh into the machine. 'There's only so long you can avoid me. I need you. And,' the voice dropped into a caress, 'you know you need me, darling.'

My hand hovered indecisively above the phone as I watched an image on the small TV in the corner – an image that I couldn't quite compute. The breakfast news: a man I hadn't seen for years, since university. He stepped down from a private jet, smiling for the cameras. Those pale glacial eyes. Escorted to Number 10, shaking hands with the Prime Minister. Easy to see he'd once been the most powerful man in Britain.

I forgot all about the phone and turned up the volume quickly, but it was too late to catch the full story.

A man I'd hoped desperately I'd never see again. Dalziel's father.

I dropped Alicia at school, Effie and Fred at nursery and then wandered absently round the supermarket. Amidst jars of apple purée and mountains of bright and shiny baby stuff, my mobile rang for the third time. Finally, I relented.

'What?' I muttered.

'Charming.'

'I'm really very busy, you know.'

'Very busy doing what? Comparing nappy brands?'

I looked at a stack of shiny green Pampers.

'No.' I turned my back on the nappies. 'I'm just going into a very important meeting, *actually*.'

Joyfully the Tannoy announced a large spillage in Aisle 4.

'Really?' Xavier sniggered. 'About what? Which tea-shop to hold the local mothers' meeting in?'

I smiled despite myself.

'No, Xavier. About . . .' I caught sight of Helen Kelsey studying nail polish in the beauty section. She really did look like a fox. Sleek, but a fox none the less. 'About – about the local fox hunt.' I

11

slunk back round the corner of the Pampers before she spotted me.

'I thought chasing foxes had been banned?' Xavier drawled. 'Don't tell me you're riding with those hounds.'

'It's still a point of serious debate in the countryside, actually.' I tried to sound convinced. 'There's a lot of tension still between hunt and saboteurs.'

Xavier yawned loudly. 'Oh, don't be so dreary, dearie. Come back to me. You're the best newshound I know,' he persisted. 'It's such a waste.'

'Flattery will get you everywhere,' I sighed. 'But I can't. The children, Xav. I'm not doing that whole nanny thing. And the team really need me here. I can't just up and—'

'Oh, please,' Xavier yawned again. 'It's hardly the *Wall Street* bloody *Journal*.'

'Stop yawning.' I chucked some baby-wipes in the trolley. 'It's so rude. The *Burford Chronicle* is a quality paper, I'll have you know.'

There was a long pause. We both dissolved into giggles.

'You silly cow,' he said fondly. 'Stop popping babies out and writing about giant marrows—'

'Er, I'm not sure I like that analogy, thanks, Xav.'

'– and cover this al-Qaeda story for me.'

I stopped laughing.

'What story?'

'New neighbour of yours.'

'Really? Who?'

'Hadi Kattan.'

'The art dealer?' Hadi Kattan was a regular face in the international media, from the *Financial Times* and the *Wall Street Journal* to *Hello!* magazine; patriarch of a beautiful glamorous family; contemporary of Al-Fayed, but shadowy and enigmatic where his peer preferred the spotlight.

'That's the one. Moved into a mansion in your neck of the woods.'

12

'Kattan is al-Qaeda? Pull the other one. It's Middle England, Xav, not Helmand Province.'

'So cynical. He was VEVAK for a while too apparently.'

'VEVAK as in Iranian Secret Service? They're nothing to do with al-Qaeda, surely?'

'Whatever. He's purportedly been involved with a smaller organisation, a branch of the tree. Al-Muhen, I think. Some Saudi Arabian mullah runs it from a *madrasah* somewhere outside Peshawar.'

'Everyone north of the equator's apparently got a link these days. Who's your source?'

'Guy in the Yard's anti-terrorism unit.'

'So well-connected, dear Xav.'

'Let's just say we share a sauna, darling.'

'Oh, I see.' I debated some sugar-free gingerbread men. '*That* kind of source. And he's straight up, is he?'

'Well, I wouldn't say straight, necessarily.'

'Hilarious! You know what I mean.'

'Check it out and see.'

'I can't.' Resolute, I picked up some over-priced organic crisps. The kids would prefer a lurid Wotsit any day. 'I've retired. For now.'

'It's time to come out of retirement. Christ, Rose, most people would be biting my hand off.'

'I appreciate it. I'm tempted. But it's not fair on the kids. You know that.'

'Rose, you had some babies, you didn't become Mother fucking Teresa.'

'She only had spiritual babies, I think you'll find.' I wheeled myself round to the Wotsits. 'Look, I'll consider it, OK?'

'Which means you won't,' he sighed.

'I will. I'm flattered, Xav. Thank you.' For a moment I caught a glimpse of the old me. It was strangely reassuring that someone else occasionally did too.

'It's a bloody waste, you rotting out there in the cow-shit. You were the best, Rose.'

'Thank you. Actually, talking about retirement,' I said carefully, 'I'm sure I just saw Lord Higham on the news.'

'So?'

'I thought he'd gone somewhere like Venezuela.'

'He may well have done, darling. I'm not his travel agent.' Xavier was snappy. 'Word is he's back on the political warpath. Officially he's come in some advisor role to the PM.'

My stomach clenched uncomfortably.

'Why the interest? Got a scoop?'

'I just – he's someone—' I was getting tongue-tied. I took a deep breath. 'Someone from the past,' I finished lamely.

'My dear! I've always liked an older man myself,' Xavier purred.

'Not like that. I knew his son, Dalziel.'

'The one who killed himself?'

The years rolled back like the tide.

'Rose?'

'Yes,' I mumbled. 'Yes, that one.'

'You have depths, my dear Rose, I've not yet plumbed.'

I jumped half a foot as a voice spoke in my ear.

'Rose!'

Helen Kelsey. I forced a smile. 'I'll call you back, Xav.'

'Before it's too late,' he drawled, and rang off.

Too late.

I summoned a smile for Helen; I wished my heart would stop beating so very fast.

Chapter Two

I arrived at the paper at eleven, which meant they'd all be on a fag-break out the back. I needed to busy myself: to stay in the present. Making myself a cup of strong tea, I checked the boards in the faint hope there might be a half-decent story for once.

'Edna Brown's prize-winning vegetables sabotaged.' Next to this someone had scrawled 'Watch out for her melons' in green marker.

'High School Musical comes to Cheltenham.'

'Five sheep savaged near Ostley Woods – return of the Burford Beast?'

The only story that looked remotely exciting was apparent police interest in a local MP and an allegation of bribery. I vaguely remembered him from Alicia's school fête, a sweaty, corpulent man more interested in the refreshment stall than the children.

Tina banged through the doors. Ex-Fleet Street herself, but sick of the horrendous hours and the in-fighting, she was happy and efficient running this little paper.

'Hello, stranger.' She slammed a pile of files down on her immaculate desk. 'How's tricks?'

'Tricks are OK, thanks, Tina.'

'How's the gorgeous husband?'

Everyone always loved James. The life and soul. 'Good, thanks. Pretty busy with the relaunch of the club.' I pointed to the board. 'What's Johnson being investigated for?'

'Not sure exactly,' she shrugged. 'Something to do with taking some kind of bung, I think.'

'Really?' I perked up.

'The by-election's coming up. All sorts are stirring.'

'Shall I take a look?' I said carefully. I didn't want to admit to myself how much I needed some kind of spur.

'I think Richard's on it, thanks, love.' She booted her old computer up. It made a sound like it was dying inside. 'Why don't you take a look at Edna Brown's lovely vegetables?'

'Oh, right.' I suppressed the sudden urge to scream. 'Yes, of course.'

Richard Sawton rushed through the door and scooped his car keys off the desk.

'Hey Rosie,' he winked, his long face almost excited, 'fancy a spot of doorstepping?'

'I was going to talk to Edna Brown about her—'

'Fuck Edna Brown.'

'I'd really rather not,' I grinned.

'Come on. The word is Johnson's going to get picked up again today.' He was almost out the door by now. 'I could do with a second opinion.'

I glanced at Tina; she waved us onwards with her trusty green Pentel. Grabbing my bag I followed Richard, feeling something I hadn't for the longest time. Adrenalin.

The Johnson story turned out to be a damp squib. Richard and I spent a chilly hour supposedly hiding outside his house, drinking stewed tea in polystyrene cups from the Copper Kettle, only for the wife to arrive at our window and bang on it with a cross be-ringed hand.

'This is private property, I'll thank you.' Her front tooth was tipped with fuchsia lipstick.

'It's not you know, love, it's a public highway, actually,' Richard pointed out affably. 'Have you got any comment on your husband's recent arrest?'

'He was not arrested.' Her soft chin quivered as she drew her camel coat tighter around her. 'He was merely 'elping the police with enquiries.' She'd got very grand, apparently, since her husband won his seat four years ago. A stone squirrel gazed at us from the pillar behind her, concrete nut held forever between his paws.

'Rightio. And why was that, then?'

She drew herself up to her inconsiderable height. 'I wouldn't know. You'd have to ask him. But, I might add,' she fixed us with steely little eyes, 'he won't tell you.'

'Rightio,' Richard repeated. 'Well, thanks for your help.'

I leaned across him, offered her my hand. 'Hi, Mrs Johnson. Rose Miller.' She refused my hand and glared at me instead. 'We will find out, you know, Mrs Johnson. It'll be in the public domain before long, so you'd be doing yourself a big favour by telling us your side of things now.'

'I have no interest in speaking with you,' she said stiffly. 'None whatsoever.'

'This is your chance to put your side of the story across. We could offer you an exclusive.'

'No comment,' she sniffed. The little boy statue peeing into the lily pond looked on languidly as she slammed the garden gate behind her and sailed towards her house.

Richard sighed, and started the car without looking at me.

'Richard, I—'

'What?' He concentrated overhard as he pulled out.

'I hope – I mean, you didn't think I was stepping on your toes back there?'

'Of course not.' He was obviously lying.

'I just thought – she needed some coercion, and—'

'Rose, it's fine really.' We slowed to a crawl behind an old red tractor. 'I understand, honestly.'

But he still stared straight ahead, refusing to look at me. My heart sank. I rarely mentioned my previous incarnation, and although sometimes they actually asked my advice at the *Burford Chronicle*, it was hard not to see how differently we had done things on the nationals. I was used to the pace of the major broadsheets, the fast-track of a story you had to turn around immediately. I was used to working alone, pushing on despite being told no, unrelenting when I was on the trail of a story. But in Burford they ran a polite ship – it was just that kind of operation. However welcoming they'd been since I'd joined their ranks a year ago, sometimes I felt they just suffered me because they were just – well, polite.

'So, what now—' I began as a shiny black Range Rover with partially-tinted windows swung into the small lane far too fast, ragga music pumping from it, narrowly missing our wing mirror. I ducked instinctively as Richard swerved into the hedgerow.

'Blimey!'

An indignant crow flapped out with a rusty squawk.

'Bloody idiots,' Richard muttered. 'Can't even drive the bloody things. I don't know why they bother.'

In the mirror I watched the Range Rover disappear round the bend. It was impossible to see who was driving.

'Stupid poser,' Richard muttered, reversing.

I thought of my husband's big car and cringed.

'It must be so annoying when you've lived here all your life,' I murmured.

'What?'

'All these fake farmers driving round in Chelsea tractors.'

'Or lived here since 'ninety-eight, any road.' Richard's face finally relaxed into a smile. 'Truth be told, I wouldn't mind having a go in one of them myself. I bet they're bloody powerful.'

We drove back to the office debating the finer points of Mrs Johnson's twee front garden. In the end, the pissing boy won genitals-down.

* * *

I was packing up to leave when Tina called me over.

'I have got one thing that might be more up your street. We want to do a kind of *Homes & Gardens* thing about the new guys up at Albion Manor. Bit of local glamour.'

'Oh?' I chucked my notebook into my bag, unenthused. It might be time to give up on the *Chronicle*. 'Who's that?'

'Hadi Kattan.' She stuck her pen behind her ear. 'I want to approach them about a lifestyle piece. It'd be quite a coup, wouldn't it? And I think they'll be quite keen because he's already involved with some community stuff. Word is he's helping launch his son's political career, so they're getting stuck in all over the place. And you're our big catch really, so he might buy it.' She looked up at me. 'Sound up your street?'

I had a chance to say no. I knew I should. But the part of me that had been chasing a story since I was twenty-one said yes.

'Sure,' I said quickly. 'Always. Let me know what you want to do.'

At bedtime I realised Effie's efforts at breakfast meant we were out of milk, forcing me to unearth a reluctant James from the studio. Leaving the kids glued to *Alice in Wonderland*, I drove to the garage at the end of the lane.

Pulling my cardigan over my head, I dashed through the driving rain to the kiosk, plucking a carton of milk from the fridge. As I joined the queue, there was a sudden screech of tyres on wet tarmac and a collective gasp. A small sleek silver sports car had taken the corner too fast, swerving to miss a motorbike, mounting the grass verge outside the garage and coming to a juddering halt inches from the Entry sign.

She looked like the mermaid from Alicia's book of myths, the young woman who flung herself from the car, and she was wailing. Her soaked green dress flowed round her body like seaweed, her face streaked with black kohl, her long hair dark and tangled under the fluorescence of the petrol station forecourt. The rain drummed down and the queue shifted and muttered as one organism, succumbing *en masse* to horrified fascination – for a moment, I couldn't drag my eyes from her either. I stared out of the kiosk window at this beautiful barefoot woman weaving unsteadily between the petrol pumps, the silver Porsche abandoned behind her, driver's door flung wide. In this light it was hard to see where the rain ended and her tears began.

I looked away, discomfort palpable in my chest, gazing instead at the damp and rather dirty neck in front of me, its owner now halted in her laborious counting out of coppers as she too stared, the silver raindrops on her beanie glistening.

'She's pissed out of her head,' the burly man in the next queue muttered. 'She don't know what she's doing. Look at her.'

'Someone should call the police,' an elderly woman said, her whiskers twitching, her face a sagging mask of disapproval above her ill-fitting mac. 'It's a disgrace.'

The mermaid raised her face to the heavens and howled into the night, her words incoherent. There was something so primal in her voice that all the little hairs on my arms stood on end. I pulled my old cardigan tight around me and willed the cashier to hurry up.

'You should call the police. They should, shouldn't they?' The man looked to me for approval as he folded his newspaper, but I found that I was speechless, as round-eyed as one of my own children.

When I looked back, the woman was falling. Her hands out before her to meet the ground, she crumpled like a wounded soldier until she was finally on her hands and knees, where she froze for a moment, head bowed. A car behind her sounded its horn irritably.

'Excuse me,' I said, pushing past a boy on a mountain bike gawping in the doorway. I hurried across the short distance to where she crouched, attempting now to pull herself up, doubled in half as if in pain.

'Are you all right?' I bent beside her. Her eyes seemed blind as she looked up at me.

A black Range Rover pulled up behind the Porsche, bumping up onto the grass, gleaming with rain and polish, braking just in time.

'I . . .' She wiped her face on her arm, smudging the streaming eye make-up further. She seemed slightly delirious.

'Can you stand?' I said, offering her my hand, trying quickly to assess what was wrong. 'Are you ill?'

I was half aware of the Range Rover's door opening, a tall fair man in a black windcheater jumping down now from the driver's seat.

'I – I'm not sure,' she mumbled. Her hand was ice cold. 'I don't feel – I'm not—'

'Maya,' the man behind me said.

I turned.

'Thank you,' he said to me, but he was looking at her. He spoke with a faint Celtic burr that I couldn't place. 'I'll take over now.'

Our eyes met briefly as I stood too fast, staggering very slightly. He put out a hand to me but I'd regained my balance so he turned back to the girl now, sliding his hand into hers, gently releasing mine. I stepped back. He had her now; supporting her, holding her upright. I thought I could smell lemon sherbet.

'If you're all right then . . .' I backed away, 'I'll just—'

'We're fine, really. Thanks a lot.' The fair man nodded at me. Under the artificial light, his eyes were frighteningly blue, his tousled hair sun-bleached like a surfer's. 'Ash is in the car, Maya. He's been really worried. Let's get you back home, OK?' His tone was soothing, like he was coaxing a nervous animal into a cage.

Through the open car door I saw the shadowed passenger lean forward and pull the cigarette lighter from the dashboard. I hesitated for a second, and then I ran back to the kiosk before I got any more wet.

21

The unnerved cashier was still muttering to her colleague about what to do and the burly man in his smelly red anorak was still loudly demanding someone call the police when another collective groan went up. I turned to see the girl collapse again, and now another man was by her side, dark-skinned like her, dressed in an expensive navy coat. The fair man stepped back.

The dark man pulled her up with gentle force and for a moment she hesitated, pulling away. He said something to her, taking her chin in his hand and making her look at him. Her make-up was streaming down her face in rivulets as she gazed at him, and she seemed to be listening. Eventually she stopped resisting and let herself sink into him, almost gratefully, her face in his shoulder as he guided her towards the big car like a docile child, ensuring she didn't fall despite stumbling several times.

The girl in front of me had finally pocketed her 10 Rothmans. 'Blimey,' she said, pulling her beanie down protectively, ready for the downpour. 'You don't see that every day.'

'You can say that again. Bloody foreigners. Just the milk?' My cashier held her hand out. 'Eighty-four pence, please.'

When I looked again, the girl like a maddened mermaid was being swallowed by the Range Rover. The dark man shut the door behind her and turned with a graceful movement to his audience in the kiosk. He smiled politely, bowed his head to us in a courtly gesture. Instinctively I stepped back.

He climbed into the Porsche. With a screech of tyres the Sweeney would have been proud of, both vehicles were quickly swallowed up by the night.

And then I went home, put the milk in the fridge, checked the children, fed the cat and finally went to bed alone again, I found that the woman's image was imprinted on the back of my lids. And even as I fell into sleep, I couldn't shake the uncomfortable feeling that the second man, the man called Ash, had been less guiding her towards the vehicle than forcing her.

And there was something else, something deeper down,

something clicking, whirring into place, like the levers on a dead-lock that are not quite true yet. Images from the day: the mysterious Kattan, the MP's wife so outraged, James, all newly tense. These images fought something I couldn't quite access, a memory buried deep. A memory fighting to the surface.

UNIVERSITY, AUTUMN 1991
FRESHERS' WEEK

The vague city . . . veiled in mist . . .
A place much too good for you ever
to have much to do with.

Jude the Obscure, Thomas Hardy

In the beginning . . .

In the beginning there was just me.

And then they found me.

Had I known I was being chosen for such immoral ends, I like to think I would have declined the invitation, that I would have made good my escape before it was too late – though I fear that my belief only comes from the beauty of hindsight – and anyway, theory is too hard now to distinguish from fact. But if I had ever guessed it would all end in tragedy and death, I would have stayed at home.

But I didn't know. I was a true innocent when I began.

Petrified and knowing absolutely no one, I arrived in the small soft-coloured city with my father's best suitcase, a dog-eared poster of the Happy Mondays and a box-set of Romantic poets that my grandma had bought me for my eighteenth birthday. I'd tried really hard to decline the green velvet lampshade my mother insisted I take from the spare room, to no avail; I planned to dump it at the earliest opportunity.

About to become part of an institution so venerable and famous, in the place of pride I felt fear, constantly wishing I'd gone with Ruth to Bristol to study drama with all the cool kids. I'd endured a painful Freshers' Week of starting stilted conversations with other monosyllabic teenagers, or worse, kids who wouldn't stop talking about anything elitist. By and large the beautiful crowd from Britain's public schools – Roedean and Eton, Harrow and King's – all seemed to know one another already and were imbued with the knowledge they needed no one else. Completely ignored, I felt adrift and friendless; overawed by the beauty of the city and the magnitude of history resting on its shoulders. Everywhere I walked were buildings so classical I'd seen them in books or on television; everywhere I wandered, the voices of students far more erudite than I echoed in my ears.

Eventually, sick of my own company, and with the vague hope I could win kudos enough to hang out with the 'journos', I wrote a ridiculously pretentious piece for the student newspaper (cribbed largely from library textbooks) on the Romantic poets, their denial of organised religion and how they would have loved the speed and freedom of motorbikes. To my undying amazement, it was printed.

On the Sunday evening, about to venture to the college bar for the first time, confident I finally had something to talk about of interest, I stacked my ten-pences up on the top of the payphone in my corridor and rang my parents to tell of my first success. My mother had just answered when I heard a snigger behind my back.

'Shelley fucked Mary on a Yamaha, didn't you know?'

'Yeah, but Keats preferred Suzukis, I think you'll find. La Belle Dame Sans Suzuki. Brilliant.'

Mortified, I banged the phone down on my poor mother and hid in my room for a week.

But boredom eventually got the better of me and I finally accepted an invitation from my sole acquaintance, a sulky girl called Moira, to go to the bar – where I drank two pints of snakebite ill-advisedly fast through sheer terror. Moira, who'd attached herself to me the previous week in the introductory lecture on Women's literature of the nineteenth century, was for some reason deeply bitter already, and I was concentrating hard on blocking out both her drone and her rather pus-encrusted chin when a dark-haired boy, who looked like he might be about to introduce himself, tripped over a stool.

'Watch out!' I shrieked, ten seconds too late. He'd deposited his entire pint in my lap, the cold beer soaking straight through to my skin. 'Oh God.'

'Very sorry,' he said, smiling broadly. 'I'll get you another one if you like.'

'I don't like, thanks very much,' I huffed, standing up, my smock dress an unpleasant second skin. I had an odd feeling he'd done it deliberately. 'I absolutely stink now. I'll have to go and change.'

'Oh, don't do that,' said the boy. 'At least you'll deter this lot.' He nodded towards a group of apparently giant youths whose ears stuck out at funny angles and who had just begun a round of indecent rugby songs. One of them winked at me and immediately began to sing, 'The girl with the biggest tits in the world is the only girl for me.'

'I doubt it.' I found I was emboldened by the alcohol. 'The smell of beer's probably a turn-on for them.'

The dark-haired boy laughed. 'You could be right there.'

'I'll come with you.' Moira shot to her feet, clamping my arm between slightly desperate hands as if she sensed she was about to be usurped. 'I need to start work on my Wollstonecraft essay anyway.'

26

'Oh dear, do you?' I looked at the boy's grin and then at Moira's yellow pimples. 'Look, actually, you go on.' I eased my arm gently from her hold. 'I'll have a gin and orange please,' I said to the boy with a confidence I didn't really feel. It was what my grandma drank; the first sophisticated drink that came to my slightly panicked mind. 'As long as you promise to stay between me and him.'

The rugby player's ruddy face was gurning scarily at me as he invoked the delights of the arse of an angel. Moira stomped off muttering about beer and Wollstonecraft and 'some people'.

'I'll see you tomorrow,' I called after her, rather too quietly.

The evening became a blur of alcohol and fags, and smoking a joint round the back of the bar, which was not as scary as I'd feared before my inaugural hesitant drag, though my head did spin a bit, and then going to someone's room in Jesus College, where someone else suggested a drinking game and we shared what they called 'a chillum', and I felt very debauched and grown-up until a plump girl called Liddy was sick in the bin, so we left. And frankly I was relieved, because my head was by now on the verge of spinning right off.

'I'll walk you back if you like,' said the boy, who was called James and had nice smiley eyes and freckles. He said his dad had been a butcher and he was the first in his family to go to university, which bonded us because I was also the first in my immediate family, though actually my uncle – the white sheep of the Langtons – had attended this college and I wasn't entirely sure that hadn't helped me a bit to get my place. That, and the fact that during my interview the white-haired professor had sucked a stubby old cigar throughout, most of the time gazing at the velvet smoke whilst I'd banged on about William Faulkner and the great American novel for fifteen painful minutes. Finally, as bored of the subject as the be-suited professor obviously was, I'd asked what brand he was smoking as my father imported cigars from Cuba to his little shop in Derby and loved a Monte Cristo

27

himself. After a discussion about the hotspots of Havana, where I managed to drop in mentions of both Hemingway and Graham Greene, as well as the delights of a daiquiri, the enchanted professor was happy to recommend I got an unconditional place.

On the way back to my room James and I passed a polished Ducati parked between two obviously student cars, one of them an Escort leaning dangerously towards the pavement. Drunkenly I admired the bike; my big brother rode one and there was nothing I loved more than getting a lift on the back – though my mother always went mad when I did.

James looked at me strangely as I kneeled down by the bike (wondering, actually, whether I could ever stand again). 'You're the girl who wrote that article in the *Cherwell*, aren't you?'

'My fame precedes me,' I agreed, too drunk to be embarrassed. The fresh air was doing nothing for my level of intoxication. 'I thought it was quite good when I wrote it, but everyone else thought it was terrible. It was terrible wasn't it?'

'Do you know Society X?' James said quietly. I could have sworn he checked behind him before he did so, but I was having some trouble focusing at all by now, so perhaps I'd imagined it.

'Nope,' I shook my head. 'Never heard of Society X.' I'd just attended the Freshers' Fair because frankly I'd had nothing else to do. I'd signed up to do Martial Arts because I quite fancied Bruce Lee and the idea of felling a villain with the single chop of a swift hand, and the Poetry Society because occasionally I wrote a few fairly dreadful stanzas myself, mainly about my dreams – but to be honest I found large groups of people rather shy-making. So instead I made a bad joke about X-rated films but James didn't laugh; he just looked at me strangely again before depositing me at the porters' lodge without so much as trying to kiss me. I was a bit surprised but actually relieved because that week I was still in love with a boy called Ralph whom I'd met in the summer holidays and who had promised to call me a fortnight ago. I was still waiting.

And to be honest I forgot all about James and Society X until I met Dalziel, the aristocratic Honourable who spoke like he'd stepped from the pages of Waugh but partied like a rock star in the making.

UNIVERSITY, OCTOBER 1991

The heavenly Jerusalem.

Jude the Obscure, Thomas Hardy

A week or so later Moira and I bumped into James on the Bridge after a tutorial, battered old guitar slung across his back.

'Come for a drink. I might even play something, if you're lucky.' James winked at me, dodging the bike-riders who sounded indignant bells. I didn't need much persuading; I realised I was pleased to see him. So far, university wasn't turning out to be the social whirlwind I'd imagined. As I followed James into the King's Arms, the pub where all the cool kids drank that term, I felt a quickening in my step. For the first time since I'd arrived in the city, I felt like I might actually be part of something.

I spotted Dalziel as soon as I walked in; it was impossible not to. His reputation preceded him; I'd heard a couple of girls whispering and giggling about him a few times in the bar or over coffee in the rec. He was apparently infamous, a third year known for his flamboyance, his looks and his charm. Lounging against the bar with an indolent grace, seemingly born of the innate knowledge that the world was his, he idly saluted James and then turned back to his friends. James bought a round of cider whilst Moira and I found a table beside Dalziel's friends.

I watched Dalziel hold court, laughing about something, blowing smoke-rings. After a while, I found I couldn't look away. I heard him mention a group called The Assassins.

'I've never heard of them,' I muttered to James. 'What do they sing?'

'They don't sing anything, petal,' James laughed. 'They're a group of supposed student dissidents who mess around with gunpowder, amongst other things.' He downed half his pint in one. 'Bunch of stupid schoolboys, if you ask me.'

'I got sick of blowing things up, to be honest,' I heard Dalziel drawl, and I felt a quiver of something visceral; a leap in my belly that I couldn't name. I stared at him. 'Pretty bloody tame.' He raised an eyebrow. 'Not enough banging.'

What did I feel then? Did I see a chance to be lifted from my so-far dull suburban life? The chance for the parameters of my life to be widened? Or did I just sense pure unadulterated danger?

Dalziel's group leaned together and began to whisper. A peroxided beauty, small and dark-skinned, lazed beside him, biting her nails in evident boredom and scowling at a taller girl with a funny angular chin, apparently called Lena. Lena was swaying at the table between the bar and us; talking very fast and with great animation to anyone who'd listen. I heard the words 'X' and 'commandment' and then she was told to keep her voice down.

'Is that the society – the X one?' I asked James. 'That you were on about before?'

'Shh,' he said nervously, sliding his eyes towards Dalziel.

'What?' I frowned at him. Moira came back from the loo and sat heavily between us. James looked even more worried.

'It's – I'm not – I shouldn't have mentioned it really.'

'What?' said Moira. James ignored her.

The peroxide girl sat at their table too now, very deliberately

31

kissing a beautiful Asian boy who had just leaned over her chair, her lithe body snaking round and up towards him. The tall girl had stopped talking and was staring at them aghast. After a few minutes, she slammed her chair back and flung herself out of the pub.

'Oh dear,' said James with glee. 'Lena's not happy.'

The other girl winked at him and turned back to the boy, but her eyes were on Dalziel the whole time.

'Why's it a secret?' I persisted, my second pint making me bold. 'What's the big deal?'

The boy slipped his hand into the peroxide girl's top. I looked away, embarrassed and, if I was honest, a little envious. I hadn't heard from Ralph again, which was rather mortifying as I'd spent the whole of August agonising over whether to give him my virginity. Finally I'd awarded him with it, sure it would be the start of something great. To my undying disappointment it had been painful and deeply unromantic, my head knocking against his mother's coffee table, fluff from her sheepskin rug tickling my nose, a carpet burn on my calf: all that, and I was *still* awaiting his call. Apart from the rugby players, I hadn't met anyone yet who'd shown any interest in me since I'd arrived. I was too quiet, I knew that; I hung back, too diffident, too shy.

'Just – please, leave it for now,' James shook his head at me. 'I'll – one day, you might find out. I just . . .' he trailed off unhappily.

'OK.' I was a bit hurt. I saw the inclusion I'd glimpsed slipping away. 'I get the message.'

'I think I might have to go, actually,' Moira slurred. She looked a little green.

'It's not like that, Rose,' James tried to explain. 'It's just—'

'I'll come with you, Moira.' I finished my drink and stood, noticing that Dalziel had broken away from his companions and was waiting to be served at the bar.

'Please don't get offended,' James was saying. 'It's just not my place to—'

On a sudden whim, I crossed to the bar, somewhat unsteadily.

'Hello,' I said shyly to Dalziel, and promptly dried up. His skin was like a girl's, so smooth it glowed, and he was the kind of natural blond people paid hundreds to simulate. I stared up at him, fascinated.

'Hello,' he replied, obviously amused, and offered me a hand. 'I'm Dalziel.'

'I know.' I took the hand. His skin was very cool.

'Right. And you are . . . ?'

'I'm Rose.'

The barmaid was there. 'A bottle of best white,' he informed her.

'Don't get the Soave.' I wasn't quite sure how to say it so I pronounced it 'suave'.

'I wouldn't dare,' he assured me. 'I said best – and anyway, I never drink Italian. Sancerre, please,' he said, flicking through the list. A dog-eared copy of Milton's *Paradise Lost* lay beside him on the bar.

'I'm studying that next,' I said shyly. 'It's difficult, isn't it? All the old language.'

'It's twenty pounds a bottle,' the barmaid sounded weary. 'The Sancerre. Are you sure?'

'Sure I'm sure.' He didn't bat an eyelid. 'Greatest text ever written.' He shoved the Milton in the back pocket of his tight black trousers. 'Darkness visible, and all.'

I was impressed. James appeared at my shoulder, and I found I was irritated. Surreptitiously I tried to turn my back on him, but he was persistent.

'Your friend had to go,' James said. 'She's not very well.'

'Ah, so you've met my old mucker,' Dalziel said. Next to him James looked like a burly farm-boy, I thought drunkenly.

'Have you read Scott Fitzgerald?' I was staring again. The heat of the pub was making me feel sleepy.

'Of course,' Dalziel shrugged languidly. '*The Beautiful and Damned*. Most apt.'

'You remind me of someone, you know.'

James snorted. 'Great line, Rosie.'

'It wasn't a line.' I was flustered.

'It might not have been, sweetness, but I could certainly do with one.'

'One what?' I was lost.

'One great line.' Dalziel took the money from the barmaid idly and then folded a five-pound note into her pudgy hand. 'Or more. For you, my angel.'

I gaped at him; not even my father tipped so extravagantly. Dalziel picked up the bottle and motioned for James to bring the glasses.

'So, Jamie, my love,' he threw over his shoulder, heading towards the table where we'd been sitting, 'what do you think?'

James looked unsure. 'About what?'

'A Rose between two thorns, hey?'

I looked into Dalziel's eyes. Later, I realised I'd never really known what colour they were. Amber perhaps.

'Another little convert for us? And an English student too. Are you well read?'

'Reasonably,' I mumbled. 'I'm getting there.'

'Perhaps you can help with my Union debate about God and the Devil.'

I was overwhelmed with gratitude and excitement; surprised because he didn't seem the godly type – but if it meant spending time with Dalziel, I would have converted to anything. For the first time since I'd arrived in Oxford, I was glad to be there. But then, I had no idea what was in store.

Chapter Three

GLOUCESTERSHIRE, MARCH 2008

The morning after I'd tried to help the wailing girl at the garage, I dropped the twins at nursery and drove homewards through the green Cotswold lanes, fighting a sudden longing for a cigarette. Xavier was still waiting to hear from me; and Lord Higham's face was staring at me impassively from the morning paper on the passenger seat. Images I'd blocked for years flickered remorselessly through my head until I had to pull onto a farm track. The rain had finally stopped during the night and the hedgerow sparkled with moisture, but I felt strangely bleak. I'd always known it was a risk coming here. It was too close for comfort; it always had been.

But during my last pregnancy four years ago, James had been recovering from a serious bout of depression. His record label had narrowly missed a takeover bid, thanks to his business partner's bad accounting, and the incident seemed to prompt the return of the nightmares from university days. He'd been haunted again, resulting in drugs and drink to counter endless sleepless nights. In the end he'd said the countryside was what he needed, he'd practically begged: and I'd craved peace myself, too exhausted to question his motives.

I sat in the car for a long time, thinking.

'Oxford 15 m, London 53m' read the quaint white fingerpost. Wearily I rested my head on the steering wheel as Mick Jagger bemoaned 'You Can't Always Get What You Want'. I felt utterly confused and suddenly torn. London and Xavier lay in one direction; my family and my home were in the other. And somewhere suddenly in the middle were these memories, the cold clamp of the past pressing around me, the hideous misadventure James and I had fought to leave behind.

I restarted the car, startling a lugubrious cow peering over the hedge, and I saw it was already time to collect the twins. They were so pleased to see me, running into my knees with euphoric cries of 'Mummy!' like I was the best thing since ice cream or Father Christmas, that the guilt I felt was savage. I shouldn't write about anything other than giant marrows: that much I owed my children. But my soul was aching for the thrill of the hunt. I took them home and kissed and hugged them until they told me to go away, and eventually deposited them in the garden sandpit with sandwiches and juice whilst I sat on the stone bench and watched them.

After a while I went inside and unearthed my notebook from the tidy pile, peeling an ancient half-eaten Twix from the front, and took it outside. Sitting on the bench in the spring sunshine, watching Effie's sand-cakes grow ever wetter, and Fred sampling some tasty mud, I scribbled for a while. When I'd finished, I closed the book and fished my phone out.

'So', I said carefully when he answered, 'if I do it, can I have *carte blanche*?'

'Don't be silly. You're not Kate bloody Adie, darling.'

'Not quite, no,' I said. 'I'm a bit Northern but not nearly as posh.'

'And you're prettier. Well, marginally.'

'Yeah, OK, Xav. Don't go overboard.'

'Listen, something else has just come through on the wire from Qatar about Kattan. It might be nothing. But I wanna be first if it's there. Specially after the fucking *Telegraph* stealing our ten-p tax thunder. I'll send everything over.'

'OK.'

'And, Rose, one thing. Be careful of interesting angles.'

'Funny,' I said shortly. I'd nearly been sued by the South African government the last time I'd written for Xav. Thankfully my instinct had been right, but it had been scary there for a while; the court costs mounting into six figures, me envisaging utter ruin.

'You've got a week.'

'OK.' I hung up. Effie looked up at me and then carefully poured some sand into her red plastic cup.

'Cup of tea, Mummy?' she asked earnestly, holding it out to me.

'Do you know what, my angel,' I lowered myself into the sandpit between them, 'I don't mind if I do.'

I had meant to discuss my plans with James that evening, though secretly I was dreading it. He was happy with me doing one day at the local paper: returning to a national would be entirely different.

But by the time the children were fed and bathed and I'd thought of all the right things to appease him with, James's partner in crime, Liam, had arrived for the night. Unsurprisingly, he had a new girlfriend in tow, a tiny jolly redhead with see-through skin and an over-inflated bosom.

Lord Higham was being interviewed on Radio Four when they arrived. I was desperate to listen but turned it down hurriedly as James walked into the kitchen. I knew he'd freak if he so much as heard the name.

'Hey, babe,' Liam kissed me. 'This is Star.'

'Wow.' I suppressed a smile. 'Hi, Star.'

'That's a funny name,' Alicia said. 'It's like being called Moon.'

'Or Bum-bum,' said Freddie with a joyful snigger.

'No it's not, silly,' said Alicia. 'It's not like Bum-bum is it, Mum?'

'No it's not,' I said, trying to keep a straight face. 'It's very silly, Freddie.'

'Bum-bum,' Freddie repeated, his eyes round at his own daring.

'Anyway you shouldn't say that, should he, Mum? It's rude.'

'No, he shouldn't,' I agreed solemnly. 'It is very silly, Freddie.'

'Bum-bum!'

'That's enough, Fred,' his father warned.

'It's not my real name actually – Star,' Star offered in rather vacant Northern tones. 'I wish it were, but it's not.'

'Oh.' Alicia, disappointed, took a moment to absorb this. 'What is it then?'

'Sarah. But you don't meet many film stars called Sarah, do you? It's dead dull.'

'Are you a film star then?' Alicia's eyes widened. 'A real live one?'

'No.' Star shook her head sadly. 'Not yet. I'm a podium dancer. But I will be one day.'

'What's a – a podion dancer?'

'Well, my darling,' Liam's eyes lit up, 'it's a lady who—'

'Alicia, have you finished your homework?' I cut across James's friend and partner, throwing him a warning glare. 'We should do your reading, shouldn't we? Do you need a hand?'

Liam was now swinging Effie wildly over his shoulder to screams of huge delight.

'My turn, my turn . . .' Freddie hopped up and down like a small jumping bean. 'My turn, Uncle Liam!'

James pulled a bottle of Jack Daniel's and three glasses out of the cupboard. 'We're going through to the studio.' He winked at me. 'All right, petal?'

It wasn't a question.

'Come on, Liam, put her down. You've got to listen to this new mix. And Don's sent the new plans through. They're fucking wicked.'

'James!' I admonished, but he just gave me a look.

'Why don't you all have some dinner first?' I offered hopefully. I could do with the company. I wanted to hear Liam's news and Star's views on podium fashion and world politics – anything, really, rather than be stranded high and dry with my own thoughts. The radio stared at me malevolently.

'You must be hungry. Did you eat on the way? I could knock up some pasta, if you like.'

'That'd be grand,' Liam began, but James glowered at him.

'No time to eat, mate,' he said. 'No rest for the wicked!'

Liam shot me a look that said he wasn't arguing. My heart sank. I knew this was the last I'd see of James till at least midday tomorrow. I made a final attempt.

'Oh, come on, guys. You must be starving after your trek up the M40.' I was almost pleading. 'It's no trouble. How about a nice carbonara?'

'Rosie, love.' James kissed me on the cheek, his voice dangerously low. I could smell whiskey on his breath. 'I don't think you need any more slap-up feeds right now. Know what I'm saying?'

I turned away quickly before they caught the glint of tears, knocking my notebook off the counter by mistake. I used to be at ease with my body, like Star seemed to be – once, before I'd had the children. James picked the notebook up. Idly he flicked it open at the last page, the page I'd scrawled on earlier, and began to read aloud in a stupid voice.

'"I feel savage, and I can't be, not here. I am confined by the honey-coloured stone, the sheer niceness of it all, the pretty houses, the postcard perfect village, the cricket green shorn to within an inch of its life, the twitching net curtains that are snowy white. It's all perfect and yet I am not. It is perfect and it's killing me."'

'James, please,' I said, trying to grab it back. Mortified, feeling like I'd just been horribly exposed, I couldn't bear to look at the others as James held the book out of reach high above his head; with sinking heart, I saw he was poisonous with drink.

'Oh dear, Rosie darling,' he pouted. 'Bit bored? Poor you. The perfect idyll and you're suicidal.'

'I'm not at all suicidal.' I was flushing violently now. 'It's just an idea for a story.'

James chucked it down on the side. 'Don't give up the day job,' he said with malice. 'Oh, that's right, you don't have one any more.'

'Come on, mate,' Liam muttered. Star seemed oblivious, thank God.

'James!' I mumbled. 'Please, don't.'

As quickly as he switched, he switched back again.

'I'm only teasing, darling,' he said, stroking my face. His eyes were black with something. 'Sorry. I didn't mean it. Come on, guys.'

'You're gorgeous, babe.' Liam squeezed my hand as he left the room. 'Ignore him. He doesn't know he's born.'

'I like your house,' I heard Star saying as they disappeared in James's wake, off to the studio built in the old garage. 'Is it real?'

As the door shut on them, I opened the biscuit tin and crammed two Jaffa Cakes down in defiance before sharing the rest with my delighted children. I wasn't gorgeous any more, if I ever had been. I knew that.

'Right, you lot. Bed.'

We'd moved from London just after I'd had the twins. I'd been in a stupor of sleep deprivation and cracked nipples, and possibly undiagnosed post-natal depression, worrying about Alicia and whether she felt pushed out, worrying that I didn't have enough time or love to split fairly between three children.

40

I did have enough love, it turned out – more than enough – but I didn't have enough time. That had become clear quite quickly.

My mother had come to stay for the first month, unpacking boxes, heating bottles and washing an endless rotation of small babygros. My father watched the golf; sometimes I slumped beside him on the sofa, wondering how a woman who'd once partied for England, ridden in army helicopters above battlegrounds and regularly flown into places like war-torn Sarajevo for work could be so utterly pole-axed by two tiny babies and a boisterous three-year-old. Occasionally I also wondered what the hell I was doing in the middle of the Cotswold countryside, pretty but reminiscent of the rural life that I'd left behind in the Peak District as a teenager – and far too near Oxford for my liking. But I was victim of James's whim after he'd shot a music video at Blenheim Palace and fallen in love with the place – apparently. Worried about the nightmares and the depression, I'd let myself be roller-coastered by his enthusiasm.

I'd given up everything for my kids, willingly; one of us had to and there didn't seem to be any question that it would be me. I'd certainly never argued. I'd simply switched off my computer and left the paper, my city friends and my beloved flat in Marylebone for my children and the country air they needed. There wasn't enough room for the pram on the pavement any more and, crucially, I didn't want to foist them onto a nanny whilst I continued tearing round the world unmasking controversy in often dodgy situations. It was time for domesticity, I'd accepted that quite readily. I was tired of running – that was the truth.

When the children were asleep, I sat at the kitchen table and poured myself a small glass of wine. I opened the laptop, attempted to write something about Edna's allotment – but giant marrows kept popping into my head. I saw myself through James's eyes: I was just like a benign shepherd. Not even that, a well-trained and obedient sheepdog. I rounded my children up and chased them gently through the day, and even when they or I were asleep, one ear was always cocked, one ear pinioned by my duty. Gone were the days when I went leaping to the challenge of a good story. Now my role was to stay close, although James was apparently still free to roam, and I was too exhausted to argue.

After about twenty minutes of desultory typing and deleting, typing and more deleting, I checked my emails for distraction.

There was one from Xav with biog details of Hadi Kattan, which I perused quickly. He was a fascinating man. He was born in Iran. His parents and sister had been incarcerated under the Shah's regime; he was the only survivor from his immediate family, thanks to being away at school in Britain. After their deaths he'd stayed here for some time, under an uncle's wing, educated first at Rugby and then Cambridge. He had famously denounced Islam in his thesis, part of which was published to great acclaim and controversy in *The Times*, after which he'd rejected the literary career so many had predicted and had gone on to make his reputation as a brilliant but ruthless trader on the London and New York stock exchanges. He briefly headed the Equities division of the World-Trident Bank before moving into the art world and retiring early with a huge fortune. His wife, Alia, had died five years ago, leaving him two children. The rumours of political intrigue, and an al-Qaeda connection seemed unlikely to me, given Kattan's political and religious background.

Below Xav's email was another, forwarded from Tina at the *Chronicle*.

'ASH KATTAN: HOPE FOR THE FUTURE,' the header said, and there followed a message from Tina: 'Hadi Kattan is hosting a party at his place on Tuesday to mark the launch of his son's political campaign: we're invited. Perfect opportunity

42

to ingratiate ourselves. Grab that lovely husband of yours and get a babysitter.'

I contemplated it for a moment. I felt the adrenalin begin to course through my veins, and I knew, as I'd known all day, that I wasn't going to be able to resist chasing the story.

UNIVERSITY, OCTOBER 1991

*Sweet roses . . . Of their sweet deaths are
sweetest odours made.*

Sonnet 54, Shakespeare

Despite Dalziel's apparent – if rather lackadaisical – enthusiasm
for my help in the pub that night, I didn't hear from him again.
I was hugely disappointed, but not that surprised. Along with
the realisation my brief encounter with him had been just a
drunken fancy of his, my nebulous hope of acceptance into the
upper echelons slowly died.

The Student Union put on a do on Saturday for Hallowe'en;
resolutely I bought my ticket. Moany Moira was going home for
the weekend, and I saw my chance. I had to make some proper
friends. The theme was 'Spooky '60s style'; I eschewed the normal
array of ghosts and werewolf costumes, and went for a pretty
spectacular multicoloured Mr Freedom jumpsuit I found in the
local Oxfam and some plastic fangs. After an hour or so of
pretending I was having a good time with a few people from the
Poetry Society, bobbing around to the Bee Gees and Mama Cass,
James arrived looking rather handsome as a be-fanged vampire

in a Beatles suit, a besotted freckle-faced girl dressed as Twiggy in tow. James waved but didn't come to say hello, and I felt a faint lurch as I watched the pair kissing passionately beneath fake cobwebs in the corner.

Surprised at myself, I drank too much cider, ending up cornered by an over-enthusiastic rugby player, a tall sandy-haired boy called Peter whose long hair had a nasty slick sheen, and who was so drunk he kept calling me Rosemary. Eventually I relented and let him kiss me outside the girls' loos, but when he started to paw at the zip of my jumpsuit with a large sweaty hand, I pushed him away gently.

'Com'on, Roze-mary,' he slurred, swaying dangerously. 'You know you want to really.'

'Actually, I *really* don't,' I insisted, but he was heavy and drunk, and horribly persistent. His breath a cloying mix of beer and peanuts, his wet pink mouth leered above my face before closing down on mine.

'Please!' I pushed him away harder this time, his lips leaving a trail of smelly saliva and peanut crumbs across my cheek. 'Get off!'

'Fucking Christ,' he snarled. 'You bloody plebs are all the same.' He lunged forward, slamming me against the wall as he pinioned me there, so hard that I hit my head on the skeleton hanging behind me. 'Little prick-tease.'

'Ow,' I clutched my head as the plastic bones rattled, a little stunned. Before I could move, Peter lunged forward again – and then, as if an invisible wire had pulled him, suddenly he flew backwards, landing on his arse on the beer-stained floor.

'Didn't you hear the lady?'

Startled, I gazed at a glowering James.

'Are you OK?' he asked.

'Oh yes. Fine, thanks.' Together we stared down at the crumpled Peter. Greying Y-fronts were visible above his ill-fitting brown cords, large sweat-patches staining the underarms of his striped shirt. I shuddered. I was drunker than I realised.

'I don't think she was enjoying that very much.' James was absolutely nonchalant, but his fists were both clenched. 'Were you, Rose?'

'Not much,' I agreed, nervously.

'Who the fuck . . . ?' Peter scrambled inelegantly to his feet, a mottled red suffusing his clammy complexion. 'Who the fuck asked you?'

'No one,' James shrugged pleasantly, turning away.

'Oi!' Peter pulled James round by the shoulder. 'I said, who asked you, you jumped-up little twat?'

'Let go, mate.' I could feel the tension rising in James as he stared at Peter's hand.

'You're one of those Society X morons, aren't you? Licking bloody St John's arse.'

James punched Peter square on the nose. There was a nasty crunch and an almost immediate spurt of blood. The taller boy crumpled forwards again, clutching his nose. James just stared down at him, and the blankness on his face chilled me.

'James!' The pale girl he'd been canoodling with in the bar stood in the doorway, her red beret pulled down over her curls, false eyelashes like spider-legs framing her huge shocked eyes.

'Yeah, all right, Kate.' James shook his hand ruefully. 'Ouch. His nose was harder than it looked.'

I gaped at him.

'You might want to think about leaving now,' James said softly, propelling me back towards the bar. 'We could walk you . . .'

'James!' The girl was scowling. She was very young, fifteen or sixteen maybe. Younger than we were. Peter groaned on the ground.

'I'll be fine.' I sensed her hostility. I'd had enough aggro for one night. 'Honestly. Thank you, though.'

As I left the bar, I glanced back at James. He was holding his companion's arm, apparently soothing her as they gathered their coats to beat a retreat themselves. Catching my eye, he held a hand up in farewell. I was utterly confused.

The following day was the anniversary of my French grandmother's death. I spoke to my mother on the phone in the morning; she tried valiantly to mask her sadness.

'Light a candle, love, if you get the chance. She'd like that,' she said, but I knew it was unlikely I'd be near a church. I mumbled something placatory, and promised to write soon.

Around four o'clock, after a day spent struggling with Blake's *Songs of Innocence*, I was desperate to get out of my stuffy little room. I grabbed my coat and fled into the fresh air.

The light was already dying in the chilly autumn afternoon as I walked aimlessly; my feet taking me across the Christ Church Meadow towards the old cathedral. The windows suffused with gold looked welcoming against the darkening velvet of the sky, and the choir were just finishing their rehearsals as I slipped into a pew at the back of the great building, listening to the last few beautiful lines of what I later learned was Handel's *Messiah*.

I waited as they packed up, calling to each other jovially, agreeing to meet in the pub over the road, and then I wandered down to the great table where the candles were kept.

The door slammed behind the last chorister. I put my money in the honesty box, chose a candle and then carried it to the wooden rack where the others flickered. I placed it alongside the others, some still lit, some melted to tiny jagged stubs, the flames shining bravely in the dim light.

As I picked up the matches I thought I heard a footstep, but when I looked round, the cathedral seemed deserted apart from me. I lit my candle and tried to focus my mind, thinking fondly of my grandmother, her funny Anglicisms, her boeuf Bourguignon that melted in your mouth, her horror when my mother cut my infant hair short. ('*Mon Dieu! So common, Lynette. Vraiment, tout le monde dirait qu'elle est un garçon!*')

Placing the matches back, I felt a draught down the back of my neck. A sudden scraping noise made my heart jump – and then a great gust of wind blew through the cathedral from nowhere. All the flames guttered. My candle went out.

I tried to stand but I had cramp in my leg. Limping, I hurried as fast as I could towards the great doors – which suddenly seemed very far. I didn't want to stay and relight the candle; I wanted to go now. But before I reached the door, a slim figure slipped from behind a pillar, framed against the stained glass like an unholy apparition. I blinked. It was Dalziel.

'Hello,' he said.

'Oh,' I stuttered. I gathered my wits. 'Hello.'

'Praying for redemption?' He arched an eyebrow. Wearing a long black Astrakhan coat, the collar turned up to frame his pale face, he looked otherworldly. 'Are you the religious type then?' He regarded me coolly. 'You don't really look it.'

'No. I – it was my grandmother. She died – just, a few years – well, I – I just came to remember her, I suppose.'

'Well, All Souls' Eve is past.' He flicked his blond hair back.

'So?' I didn't know what he meant.

'When, my dear, the boundary is open between the dead and the living. But perhaps she'll rise again tonight.'

'Oh.' I thought of how very sick and slight my elegant grand-mother had been at the end. 'God, I kind of hope not. I think she might be happier where she is.'

'Really?' Dalziel looked amused. 'Remind me of your name.' He took a step towards me. 'Something floral, wasn't it?'

'Rose. Rose Langton.'

'Ah yes. Rose. "Of sweetest odours made." Well, perhaps you can help me, now you're here.'

I blushed hotly. 'Help you?'

'Yes. Number Four.'

'You've lost me,' I mumbled. He was so beautiful, close up. Ethereal, almost.

'Never mind. No time to explain. Got to defile Sabbath's day before the protectors get here.' Dalziel picked up the bag at his feet. A bright pink feather boa protruded from one end. 'Jesus needs a little help with his outfit. He's been feeling a bit chilly.'

As I watched in amazement, Dalziel produced full suspenders and stockings, crotchless knickers and nipple tassels in red satin, a push-up bra in black lace and a bottle of champagne, still cold, all from his bag.

'You open the Krug.' He pressed the bottle on me. 'I'll dress him. And get a move on. This place is never empty for long.'

I didn't dare admit I'd no idea how to open a bottle of champagne. Like a lost puppy, I followed him as he carried the underwear over to the six-foot Jesus, who gazed sadly down at the floor near our feet.

'See.' Dalziel ran his hand lovingly down Jesus's torso. 'He's freezing, poor bastard. Where's Mary when you need her, eh?'

Our eyes met and I felt a strange heat suffuse me, somewhere in the very core of me. Quickly I looked away again, struggled with the champagne's foil, untwisting the metal. For some reason my hand was shaking.

'Tassels or bra?'

The cork popped suddenly, nearly taking my eye out. It hit the pillar and ricocheted beneath a pew.

'Oh, you bugger,' Dalziel was murmuring to himself as champagne sputum poured over my leg, the froth spraying Jesus's new outfit.

'The tassels won't stay on. His chest's too slippery. So that decides it.' Dalziel clipped the bra round the back of Jesus. 'There we go.' He took the bottle from my hand and toasted Jesus. 'Genius.'

'But . . .' I looked at the incongruous idol before me. The suspenders flapped in a slight breeze coming from somewhere. 'I don't understand. Why . . .'

Voices were audible from the back of the cathedral. Dalziel

took a quick slug and then shoved the champagne at me as he gathered up his bag. 'Come on.'

'You forgot the boa,' I whispered.

'Too late.' Dalziel grabbed my other hand, and we ran for it, giggling up the side aisle, dribbling champagne and pink feathers as we went.

Outside we kept running, expecting to hear angry voices behind us, through the grounds, past the porter in his bowler hat and Crombie, towards the Meadow, ending panting beneath a huge tree as it began to drizzle. Dalziel took the bottle and drank, long and hard. He looked at me.

'You know, you're more fun than I expected,' he said, and I felt my heart turn over. 'Little Rose.'

'I'm not so little,' I protested. 'I'm eighteen.'

'Are you?' He passed me the bottle. 'Very grown up. What's the time?'

I checked my watch. 'Six thirty.'

'Gotta go.' He leaned down and kissed my cheek. He smelled a little of something sweet; later I learned it was patchouli oil. 'Gotta meet a man about a dog.' He winked at me. 'See you around. Keep the Krug.'

He melted into the night. I stood for a moment under the tree in the Meadow, the city bright before me, the night dark behind me. In a window of Christ Church halls, a grinning pumpkin flickered.

I was more than a little light-headed. I was utterly intoxicated – and not just from the champagne.

GLOUCESTERSHIRE, MARCH 2008

James was shouting desperately in his sleep. As I came to, I could hear him moaning that he was being crushed.

'It's so dark,' he kept repeating. 'Let the light in, please.'

Befuddled with sleep, I pulled the curtains back although it was still night, and gently tried to wake him. He hadn't had one of the really bad nightmares for a while. Now he was sweating and gurning, his face pallid in the moonlight, thrashing across the bed like a fish in a net. I tried to hold his arms still but it was impossible, his desperation making him strong as Samson. As he flailed he caught me hard across the face – but it was only the next day I realised he'd cut my cheek.

In the morning he said he didn't remember the dream, but he looked unkempt and exhausted, as if he hadn't slept at all, huge circles beneath his Labrador-brown eyes.

'You're up early,' I said, plonking some toast in front of him that he pushed away. 'Are you all right?'

He didn't speak. He just sat at the breakfast table drinking black coffee and reading the *Financial Times* in sullen silence whilst the children ate cereal and bickered, and the *Today* programme murmured in the background. Liam and Star were still in bed; I didn't expect to see them before noon.

I was plaiting Alicia's hair when James ordered me to turn the radio up.

'News just in this morning: as feared, the Nomad Banking Conglomerate has gone down with the most devastating effect,' John Humphrys announced. 'A huge shock to all involved. What exactly is it going to mean for the investors?'

'Turn it off, for fuck's sake.' James stood up, his face horribly taut, a muscle jumping in his cheek. 'Christ, all this fucking doom and gloom. I thought this was meant to be boom-time.'

I realised it wasn't the time to reprimand the swearing.

'Mummy,' said Effie, 'can I have a cross hot bun, please?'

'I'm not sure how much more I can take actually.' James rammed his chair into the table. 'We'll be lucky if we're not out on the street soon.'

He was prone to exaggeration, but I wondered now if the warning signs of his former depression were rearing their head again. I thought rather nervously of the troubles he'd mentioned the other day.

'James, please,' I beseeched as Alicia looked at him curiously. 'Let's talk about it in a minute, OK?'

'Cross hot buns, cross hot buns,' the twins began to chant, oblivious.

James threw the paper on the table and slammed out of the room. It was obviously not the time to tell him I wanted to go back to work, although if the money worries were real, he might welcome it. I slathered my toast with marmalade and glanced at the front page.

'**Art Dealer's socialite daughter protests for Islamic Fundamentalism,**' the headline read. There beneath the print was a photo of a girl struggling with a policeman in Parliament Square, dark hair falling across her beautiful but angrily contorted face, a black boy with short dreds behind her, partially obscured. Licking marmalade from my fingers, I pulled the paper closer and looked again. It was the girl from the petrol station.

UNIVERSITY, NOVEMBER 1991

The River of Oblivion rolls . . . whereof who drinks,
Forthwith his former state and being forgets.

Paradise Lost, Milton

I didn't see or hear from any of them again until the middle of November. There were vague murmurings on campus about the incident in the cathedral, and one mention in the *Oxford Gazette*; and sometimes I wanted to shout, 'That was me' – but I never did. Life went on as normal. I immersed myself in my work, but I found myself searching streets, bars and crowds longingly to see if Dalziel was there. He never was, and there was a part of me that was relieved. Once I saw Lena and the beautiful dark girl in the King's Arms but they looked through me in a way that made me shrivel. I wanted to do well at Oxford and I had a feeling deep in my bones that these boys and girls, this group, were never going to be good for me. I asked a few people about Society X but no one seemed to want to talk about it. Some just smiled and looked away; lots had never heard of it – and a few looked faintly appalled when I mentioned it, so eventually I stopped; I started to forget about them all.

But one evening there was a folded note sealed with scarlet wax in my pigeonhole, my name in flowing black italics. For some reason, my fingers fumbled with the seal as I tried to open it.

'X MARKS THE SPOT' the note proclaimed, giving a time and an address, which later turned out to be one of the best streets in town, instructing me to 'dress dangerously and bring something intoxicating'. I wasn't exactly sure what the latter two meant – but I did as I was told, spending the last of my grant on a black velvet catsuit and the highest black heels I could find.

On the night in question I bought a bottle of Lambrusco for Dutch courage, and opened it in my room. I slicked my hair back, painted my eyes with kohl and my mouth with scarlet lipstick, splashing myself with Chanel No. 5 that I'd nicked from my mother. I was excited. Overexcited at the thought that I had an invitation into the elite.

And then I sat on my narrow bed and decided I couldn't possibly go. I was terrified. I didn't know anyone. They'd think I was an idiot; a country bumpkin. They'd laugh at me. I heard the other students on my floor come and go, the laughter of a Saturday night, music fading and increasing as doors opened and closed. Only I was alone, apparently. I reapplied my lipstick for the fifteenth time. I drank a bit more wine. I changed my mind, then changed it back again.

In the end I was there just before midnight, as instructed, clutching the Jack Daniel's I'd bought because I'd read that Janis Joplin had drunk it, at the door of the tall town-house on Lawn Street. My belly squirmed with nerves. The lights were all out as I rang the doorbell and I thought for a horrid second they'd forgotten me – or perhaps it was all a nasty joke to get me stumbling around town in killer heels like a drunken fool.

The door opened a crack.

'Password?'

'Pardon?' I said.

'Password,' the voice drawled impatiently.

'I don't know the—' I began, and the door started to close.

'No, wait.' I had a flash of inspiration. 'X?'

The door hovered – and then opened just wide enough to let me in.

'That'll do.' Black-tipped fingernails grasped my arm, and pulled me through. The door slammed behind me. I was in.

I followed the tall girl called Lena, whose hair was now pink and who wore nothing but a bra and bondage trousers, down a white hallway into a very minimal room. The floorboards were painted black, the walls red, and there was no furniture at all apart from a red velvet divan, a black granite coffee table and long white curtains. It all looked like a stage-set, particularly as a hundred candles flickered and guttered in the breeze from the French windows. The room was terribly hot and music swelled from the expensive stereo in the corner, some kind of opera I didn't recognise. A few people I didn't know stood round the corners of the room, drinking, smoking, mostly silent. Everyone seemed to be wearing black and it was clear everyone was nervous, although there was a certain loucheness to most of them. They eyed me with feigned disinterest and chose to ignore me. Lena lit a chillum and handed it around.

James appeared, and I headed towards him gladly. He was wearing a dinner suit that rather drowned him, despite his stocky frame, and he too seemed on edge. His nervousness surprised me, and made my own heart thump more.

'This is all a bit weird,' I whispered. 'What's going on? Where's Dalziel?'

'He'll be down in a minute.' He eyed me warily. 'You look nice.'

'Nice?'

'Good, I mean. Very good. You look like one of those girls in that Robert Palmer video.'

'Do I?' I was flattered. 'Just need a guitar to get me going.'

'You'll need a bit more than that tonight,' James said, producing a hip flask. 'Drink?'

'Thanks.' I took a swig and choked. 'God. What the hell's that?'

'Hell is right, you innocent,' he scoffed. 'Never tried the green fairy?'

'Fairy liquid?' I was confused.

'Don't be bloody stupid,' he laughed. 'Absinthe.'

I obviously looked blank.

'All the French Impressionists drank it.' He was impatient. 'Toulouse-Lautrec lived on the stuff.'

'Toulouse who?'

'Painter. Very short man, Paris, turn of the century. Dancing girls? Fucking genius.'

'Oh, I know.' I was relieved. 'Cancan dancers?'

A church clock nearby struck midnight. James took another swig and pocketed the flask. 'It's time,' he whispered reverently.

'Time for what?' I giggled nervously. 'Are you going to turn into a pumpkin?'

'Shh,' James's brown eyes were dilated in the candlelight. 'He's coming.'

The door opened slowly and Dalziel walked in. He looked ridiculously sophisticated in a tight-fitting black suit, a pristine white shirt, his blond hair sleek, his long bony face deathly pale apart from two spots of high colour on his cheeks, his eyes ringed with kohl. When he turned I saw he had attached to his back a pair of beautiful angel wings that looked like they were made from swan's feathers. He really was quite unlike anyone I had ever met. Five or six beautiful boys and girls, all wearing black, all in varying states of undress, followed him into the room. He regarded us all, then turned off the music and, placing a cigarette in an ebony holder, lit it languidly. He was captivating to watch; I couldn't tear my eyes away. We all waited.

'Good evening, my lovelies. It's wonderful to see you all here at the witching hour. Thank you for coming.'

We waited as he blew a perfect smoke-ring.

'Now,' we were treated to a smile, 'if you could deliver your intoxicating materials for the good of one and all, that would be much appreciated.'

One by one we deposited our booty onto the table. James had a whole bottle of absinthe, but I noticed he kept the hip flask well hidden. I looked around for the beautiful peroxide girl who had always been with Dalziel before, but she wasn't there. Lena put down a small plastic bag of white powder, another boy a couple of paper wraps, a tall girl a clump of straw-looking things, which I later discovered were magic mushrooms. More bottles and potions followed. Then Dalziel tipped a bottle of white pills into a small china bowl in the centre of the table.

'One for all, and all for one,' he murmured. 'Never say my love is not shared between you.'

James pushed me forward and shyly I placed my Jack Daniel's on the table.

Dalziel fixed me with a look. 'Displaying a distinct lack of imagination there, my dear Rose.' He inhaled through the ebony holder with wearied languor. 'But as you are a Society X virgin, we will forgive your misdemeanour this time, although I might have to smack your bottom later.'

Low laughter rippled through the room and I flushed scarlet, staring at my feet.

'Now,' he looked around, 'is that everyone?'

The room murmured assent. Dalziel whispered to Lena, who went to change the CD as he smiled slowly at us all. I had a sudden vision of us standing before him like lowly acolytes, mesmerised, a strange sense that we were all waiting to bask in his approval.

'So. It is Commandments One and Seven we'll be enjoying tonight. We've done Four most recently, we very definitely didn't keep the Sabbath holy. It was most amusing, wasn't it, Rose?'

I flushed under Dalziel's scrutiny, nodding fervently, aware of the envy of some of the others. Lena shot me daggers.

'Although the Bishop of Oxford clearly didn't think so.'

'No sense of humour, the bloody clergy,' Lena was keen to join in. 'Jesus in women's underwear was fucking brilliant, I thought—'

'Anyway,' Dalziel cut her off, 'tonight we will begin with Number One: *You shall have no other gods before me.*' He cranked the music right up and unveiled a statue under a velvet cloth of a man with an enormous cock, festooned with a garland of thorns. 'My dear friend Priapus. Let the party begin. Let us make darkness visible.'

Jimi Hendrix's guitar screamed through the room and I felt a great surge of anticipation and, frankly, terror. I wasn't sure that I wanted to be here any more but I couldn't drag myself away. Dalziel must have sensed my fear; he came to me.

'You look very beautiful, darling,' he said quietly, and he ran a finger down my cheek. 'Very curvy and delicious.' He put a pill in his mouth and then he leaned down and kissed me. I felt his tongue and then I realised the pill was now in my own mouth. For a moment I was about to protest but he handed me a glass and murmured 'Swallow. I always do.'

So I drank and swallowed. Then he leaned down again and kissed me properly, and I felt the lust lick through my body like forest fire, and I pressed myself into his tall form and held his snake hips and kissed him back. I couldn't believe this was happening to me: my wildest dreams coming true. Dalziel wanted me.

Abruptly he pulled away, grabbed the pink-haired girl and pulled her over to us.

'Rose, meet Lena,' and I smiled, and my legs felt a bit trembly in my very high heels, higher than I'd ever worn, and I went to shake her hand but Dalziel said, 'Don't be silly. Kiss her.' I hesitated because I really didn't like girls, not in that way, but Lena wasn't so reserved; she leaned in and kissed me, and I just thought her mouth was very soft where a man's is normally harder and there was no stubble, only soft skin, but it wasn't so bad. I was starting to feel very strange, like the whole room was moving away and I was growing very tiny and then big again and then Lena was putting her hand on my breast and I pulled away because I felt a bit sick.

'Don't worry,' Dalziel grinned; he'd been watching us lazily, 'you're just coming up. You'll be fine in a sec.'

I stumbled to the French windows to breathe in the cold autumn air and after a moment or two the music started to overwhelm me. It had changed from Hendrix to something tribal, the beat of the drums pulsing through my veins, and I was beginning to feel like I was flying. I was ecstatic, in fact I was surely about to lift off the ground like a bird. The music was inside me, and outside me and then James was there and he held me and we danced and he got nearer and I pushed myself against him and I never wanted to let go.

'This is amazing.' I smiled and smiled, feeling my limbs were like liquid and so strange. I tried to articulate it but I couldn't. 'I've never felt like this before,' I shouted over the music.

'No, well,' he smiled back, 'you've probably never taken Ecstasy before, have you?'

'God, no. Is that what it is?' I forgot even to feel fear; I just felt amazed.

'It is indeed. It's gonna break down society's barriers.' His eyes were slightly glazed. 'We will all love each other for ever and indiscriminately.'

And I felt decadent and cool and amazing, and then James was kissing me and I felt so odd, like I actually loved him and I kind of wanted to say that to him but I didn't, I just kept kissing him. The music had changed to banging house and I wanted to dance now. The beat was in me, I was the beat and I was dancing now, writhing and turning, and I felt like everyone was watching me.

And then Dalziel was talking, far more dishevelled than earlier, his jacket was off and his shirt was unbuttoned, flowing loose from his trousers, exposing his smooth chest, his ribs that jutted out. He stood on the small table and he was asking for quiet and people were complaining, 'Don't turn the music off' but he said it was time, time to do the seventh thing.

I didn't know what he meant and I didn't care.

A girl was led in wearing a strapless black dress, very fitted around her voluptuous curves. She was short, elegant, olive-skinned, with almond-shaped eyes, long dark hair in a French plait, a year or two older than us, perhaps. She was beautiful in a soft, rounded way. I smiled at her, but she ignored me, and I realised after a second that she was not quite here with us. Her eyes were unfocused and she stumbled slightly. At first glance she looked quite beatific but the longer I looked at her, the more it became apparent that she was in some kind of trance.

Lena stepped forward and blindfolded the girl, who appeared to acquiesce willingly, staggering slightly in her stilettos, a red satin scarf tied around her eyes. Lena ran her hands down the girl, slowly across her breasts, a lascivious smile spreading across Lena's face. The music was put back on and the girl was led to the divan, her hands held before her as if in supplication or prayer. I wanted to dance again and I grabbed James's hand, but he was distracted, I could feel that he was waiting for something. He watched Dalziel, who had a spray-can in his hand. In his great looping script he wrote on the wall. I thought that was quite amazing, writing on his own wall.

'*You shall not commit adultery,*' he scrawled, and then he turned triumphantly to us. 'This is Huriyyah. She is the lover of someone I know well,' he proclaimed, 'very well indeed'. He looked around at his minions, challenge in his eyes. 'And I have –' he paused momentarily – 'I have, let us say, *persuaded* her to help my fallen angels celebrate tonight. So – who will be the lucky taker?'

I was thoroughly confused.

'Or the first, should I say?'

'Christ,' James muttered beside me, and then the door was flung open and someone wearing a demonic goat-mask stood there, horns curling up to heaven like a devil.

'Azazel, my dear friend, come in,' Dalziel purred. 'Join the rest of your clan.'

'Who the fuck's Azazel?' a girl behind us muttered.

'Goat-demon, seducer of men and women.' Dalziel gestured to him. 'Cast out by the Archangels to abide in darkness for all time.'

Whoever he was, he stepped forward. 'I am ready,' he said in a gruff tight voice. 'Please.'

And he approached the young woman, who was being held down now, lying on her back, seemingly insensate, one arm thrown elegantly back, her suspenders showing. The smooth skin above her stockings glistened in the candlelight and on her inner arm were bruises and what I supposed could only be track marks from a needle.

'Is she up for this?' I asked James nervously, not feeling absolutely as high as I had moments ago.

'Looks like it,' James shrugged.

'But –' I licked my dry lips – 'but why would she be here if she's someone else's lover?'

'I don't know. Who knows what goes on between people?'

The girl was being helped by two of Dalziel's boys to peel her pink knickers off, raising her hips off the divan so a dark triangle of pubic hair was visible. Despite my misgivings I felt the excitement in the room, the murmur as the air thickened with lust, the music pulsating so I felt it in my breastbone, wreaths of smoke from cigarettes and joints and God knows what else hanging in the air around us, and the drug already in my veins surged through me again.

'Place her in the crucifix position,' Dalziel ordered. They did it. She was almost frighteningly floppy and acquiescent.

61

Azazel removed the goat-head and we saw it was a boy with a head like a bullet and hair like a brush; a boy who looked somewhat out of place amongst all the beautiful people. He was sweating and red-faced, and his eyes glinted with excitement as he undid his trousers.

'Form a queue,' Dalziel drawled from behind the divan where he was stroking the naked arse of a tall dark boy. Then the short boy was between the girl's legs and pulling her dress down, sucking on a dark nipple he had freed and fumbling with his trousers, and then with a great groan he was in her and she was turning her head back and forth as if she was indeed enjoying it, or perhaps she was just delirious. Then Dalziel and the dark boy were kissing and Dalziel bent the boy forwards over the divan and was biting his neck, grinding into him. Someone turned the music up louder still and couples were pairing off. Lena and another girl writhed against the wall together, and James took me by the hand and led me out through the French window.

He pulled me into him and kissed me again, and although the night was freezing I didn't seem to feel it and he untied my halter neck impatiently and pulled my catsuit down. He hiked me up onto a small wrought-iron table and we fucked right there in the garden. He was only the second boy I had ever had sex with but I felt so fluid right now, made of air, I might do it with anyone. At one point a light in the upstairs window of the house next door went on and I didn't even care.

'Someone's watching us,' I murmured in James's ear and he just thrust harder.

'Let them,' he whispered, and I moaned with pleasure.

Afterwards we went back inside to find the girl had gone. Only the silk scarf lying on the floor showed that she had been there. Dalziel and the boy were on the divan now themselves. They looked like they were sleeping, wrapped round each other, and suddenly I felt very cold.

'You're OK,' James said, 'you're just coming down a bit,' and he gave me his jacket; someone else offered me a line of white powder chopped out on the table but actually I didn't want it. Lena was so out of it she was crawling on the floor, laughing in her knickers and bra, occasionally barking like a dog, much to the hilarity of various bystanders.

'That was full on, wasn't it?' a dishevelled boy said to James, his eyes like saucers, his nose streaming from the drug he'd just snorted.

James lit a cigarette. 'Too busy having my own fun, mate.' He kissed my shoulder and I smiled decadently. 'What was?'

'When the girl started to come round.'

'What girl?' I said.

'The druggie. She was about to change her mind, I swear.'

My stomach plunged, and I felt icy. 'Change her mind?'

'Yeah. She changed her mind for a minute there.' The boy looked dazed, a little rueful, perhaps. 'But Dalziel soon sorted her out.'

'What do you mean?' I looked around for my coat. 'What does that mean?'

'He sorted her some more smack. She was OK in the end. Could have been ugly, though, couldn't it?'

'Ugly?' I intoned stupidly. I wanted to leave now.

'Yeah. Less adultery. More like . . .' He glanced round nervously.

'More like what?' James prompted.

'You know what I mean. More like rape. Specially with bloody Brian.'

'Brian?'

'Azazel. The goat-demon. Very apt. He gets out of control, that boy. Dalziel wants to watch that.' The boy zipped his trousers up. 'That's the trouble with oiks.'

I thought of the girl, all floppy and blank, and I winced. I thought of my little room in the halls of residence and all my things there, even the green lampshade from home, and I wanted to be there now.

'Do you think she's all right?' I asked the boy, and he shrugged.

'Happy as Larry last time I saw her. Once she'd stopped crying and the new smack kicked in.'

I grabbed James's hand. 'Can we go?' I asked him. 'Please. Now.'

We left.

'God, I'm freezing,' I said out in the street. 'I can't warm up.'

James put his arm round me, and we went back to my room and I stripped off and put on my pyjamas, socks, my warmest jumper, but still I was freezing. He held me as we listened to Massive Attack and got into my single bed, drinking tea and talking into the dawn. We didn't mention Huriyyah but I knew we were both thinking of her. And somehow, James never left.

In the cold light of day I didn't feel so proud of my behaviour, in fact I felt ashamed.

'So that was Society X?' I asked James as we walked into Brown's coffee-shop the next day.

'Yes, it was. Just for the privileged few,' he said – which apparently included me now. James explained that it was Dalziel's brainchild, his pet project. Was I a pet? I saw myself out in the garden half-dressed; I kept thinking of the girl's vacant face and her eyes that were so glazed and unseeing. I didn't understand what had got into me. Apart from James, and illegal substances, of course. I felt strange. Somehow different – and older.

It was all about breaking the Ten Commandments apparently, James explained, hence X, the Roman numeral for ten. Dalziel was writing a dissertation on it for his theology module, James said, and he apparently wanted to prove that you can have free will and choice and still live in the confines of civilised life but outside organised religion. It all sounded very peculiar to me – far more about decadence and doing exactly what you liked than any aspect of religion. And although there was a part of me that was hugely flattered by Dalziel's attentions, the truth was, last night was beginning to feel more than a little sordid. I had enjoyed the Ecstasy at the time but it scared me too; how consumed I felt whilst I was on it. Society X felt dangerous and exciting, but also out of my league entirely. Over the next few weeks, it began to feel nasty and puerile too.

I made a few enquiries about Huriyyah but no one seemed to know her. I scanned the newspapers, but I never heard anything about her. I started to forget: I busied myself with my new life at Oxford. My father sent me money for a push-bike and I marched against the Kosovan conflict.

I found that I was enjoying my lectures. I finally shook Moira and met Jen and Liz, who were more like me: we became inseparable. I got on with my work. And James and I were sort of dating; he was sweet and seemed keen, and I found that I liked sex, I liked it a lot – it was liberating. But I was worried by Society X and the lure it had for him. I tried to fight the feelings that were emerging for him, his big brown eyes, his funny smile, his protective air. I would not go to any of the X meets that he asked me to, and this annoyed him though he tried to hide it. I could see the attraction but it repelled me too. I was not that kind of girl. I felt very grown-up when I made this decision.

I read a lot of Hardy and I thought of Jude's words: 'this city of light and lore'. I worked hard and started to embrace the fact that I was part of this ancient institution. Some of the confidence of the kids there rubbed off on me; I became less shy and slowly I began to inhabit my own style. Occasionally I felt confined – the tourists in their cagoules and with their big maps, snapping us through the railings, like animals in the zoo – but mostly I just felt proud to be here.

I still found myself looking for Dalziel when I was out, but it wasn't with the same desperation of those first few weeks, and I was uncomfortable with the memory of Huriyyah, who

I never saw again. I resigned myself to the fact that the party was an amazing experience, but a one-off. I told myself that if she had been in any way unhappy about it, she would have come forward by now and I was content to leave it at that.

Chapter Four

GLOUCESTERSHIRE, MARCH 2008

As we rounded the bend in the long snaking drive, the floodlit manor house finally came into view between the great oak trees.

'Christ.' James stopped the car and, for a moment, we simply stared in awe.

For all my doubts about the Cotswolds, my own butter-coloured house was undeniably beautiful, the stone warm and inviting, a much-loved well-lived-in home. The great mansion that stood before us was not in the least inviting; majestic maybe, but somehow unsettling. Its dark stone spoke of antique grandeur rather than home and hearth. Gargoyles screeched wordlessly from the roof as we neared, the huge front door lit by flaming torches on either side, a line of expensive-looking cars parked neatly on the right.

'I like the flames. Nice idea for the club,' James said, driving up to the gatehouse, where a man with a clipboard stepped from the shadows.

James had only agreed to come because he thought there might be something in it for him. He always had an eye on the main chance, my loving husband, and I'd understood in the last few days that although the record label was still doing well, and his properties in New York and Europe were still ticking over nicely, the London club had just lost a major investor, meaning its relaunch was hanging in the balance. James was on the prowl for more backing, and fast.

At the top of the huge stone stairs we were handed champagne and shown through the dark-panelled hall, hung with tapestries of archers and deer, into a great drawing room, humming with polite conversation, the décor a peculiar clash of Gothic splendour and Arabic glamour. Small tables inlaid with gold sat between a leather three-piece suite and huge marble ashtrays festooned the antique sideboards, whilst the mantelpiece groaned with expensively framed photographs of family, a few of a grinning polo team and a huge white yacht in glittering blue seas.

The walls were hung with exquisite art that looked like it would be wasted on the majority of the guests, a mixture of portly middle-aged men and impeccable women with skinny ankles and expensive hair who basked in the heat of a great log fire.

'Fuck,' James muttered, downing his drink in two gulps. 'Wake me up when the party begins. I thought you said this would be fun.'

'Shh, J,' I warned. 'Be nice, please.' My heart sank as I spotted the local MP, Eddie Johnson, in the corner. Thankfully Johnson's wife was nowhere to be seen.

Tina and her bespectacled husband approached us now and they began to discuss the last series of *The Wire* with James whilst I eyed the photographs behind them. I'd just picked up a heavy gold frame housing the picture of a dark-haired doe-eyed teenage girl when a low voice made me jump.

'Mrs Miller, I presume?'

'Yes.' I replaced the photograph quickly and turned, composing my face as my brain caught up with fact. 'You must be Mr Kattan?'

'Indeed.' The elegant dark-haired man inclined his head politely. 'Charmed to meet you.'

Involuntarily I looked back at the picture of the girl. The water-logged girl from the petrol station, the girl from the protest in the newspaper. Kattan followed my eyes.

'I believe you met my daughter the other night.'

'Ah.' *The all-seeing eye.* 'Yes, I think I did.'

'She was having a very bad day.'

'A bad day.' *You could say that again.* 'She seemed a little – confused.'

'Yes. She was taken ill on her way home from London. A bad oyster, I believe.'

'Poor thing. Is she all right now?'

'Yes, thank God. Salmonella can make you quite delirious, her doctor tells me.'

'Sounds horrible. Is she here?'

He sighed. 'I was sincerely hoping that she would be, Mrs Miller, but . . .' His Middle Eastern accent was almost impercep-tible. 'The party would help her, I think. Meet some local people, make some new friends. But I am afraid she has gone – how do you say it? – walkabout?'

'I'm sorry.' The image of her wailing face spun through my head; the contorted face in the newspaper. 'Doesn't she like parties?'

'Usually. But she has had some . . . some trouble recently with a young man.'

'What kind of trouble?' I was intrigued.

'Oh, the usual, you know.' He inspected his fingernails briefly. 'I think the boyfriend is what the films might term a "heart-breaker".'

'Poor girl.' I was genuinely sympathetic. 'There's nothing more painful than love.'

He caught my eye. He had a neat intelligent face, dark hooded eyes. Not handsome but rather noble. 'That, my dear Mrs Miller, is undoubtedly true.'

'I hope she feels better soon. It's a lovely party.' I smiled again.

'Thank you so much for inviting us. I'm looking forward to meeting your son.'

'Thank *you*.' He bowed again. 'I'm afraid he is not here yet. I hope he will arrive soon.' Dressed in a grey suit, Kattan was the epitome of elegance, with a presence that pervaded the party, that drew the guests' eyes to him. His gestures were almost courtly, and his immaculate teeth, when he smiled, were a startling white against his olive skin. He might be renowned, but there was no doubt the man was also something of a mystery.

The heat of the room hit me and I fought a strange urge to sigh.

'It is wonderful to see so many people in my home,' Kattan said, beckoning a waiter. 'I fear it is often a little empty. And I believe you are not alone tonight?'

I shook my head. 'No. I must introduce my husband.' I caught James's eye across the room, he raised a hand in greeting.

'I hope you do not mind me saying, Mrs Miller, this colour red, it compliments you well.' His voice was like a caress, and I flushed, reminding myself I was here to do a job.

'That's a Stubbs, isn't it, Mr Kattan?' I indicated an old painting of a glossy racehorse on the wall behind him. 'It's beautiful.'

'It is indeed. One of my favourites for the line and realisation.' Kattan stood beside me now. 'I have some marvellous hunters here on the estate. I fear they do not get enough usage.'

'That's a shame.'

'Do you ride? You could borrow one if you so desire.'

'Thank you.' I shuddered involuntarily. 'But I don't really.' I would never ride again, I knew that much. 'Do you?'

A flicker of something indecipherable crossed his face. 'No. Maya does, occasionally, but it seems infrequent now.'

I had a sudden image of this man's hand on my bare arm. It was incredibly warm in here; the drink was obviously going to my head. James finally wandered over to shake hands.

'Great picture.' My husband helped himself to a canapé from

70

a tray, pointing at a Picasso next to an Emin. 'Think I prefer his earlier stuff, though. Not sure about all those weird-shaped women, personally.' He shoved the shiny caviar in his mouth inelegantly. 'Bit spiky for me. I like a boob or two.'

'James!' I reproved softly, embarrassed.

He rolled his eyes. 'So what exactly brought you to our neck of the woods, Mr Kattan?'

'This property came up for rental. I liked the countryside here. It is peaceful to me.'

'It is beautiful, isn't it?' James agreed.

I doubted James had noticed as much as a hedgerow since the day we left London. Very occasionally he ventured into the garden to kick a ball with Freddie, but he spent most of his time in the studio or rushing back to the city.

'Also,' Kattan stroked his beard lightly, 'I have some interests in the area.'

'Really?' I was curious. 'What kind of interests?'

'My son, Ash, wishes to run for Parliament in the next election, Mrs Miller.' Hadi Kattan caught my eye and held it. 'He is very fond of the area. He was educated nearby. This party is for him.'

Ash. The name was like a klaxon. The man from the garage, the man who dragged the girl back to the car.

I glanced around uneasily.

'Unfortunately he has been delayed. He's travelling back from Dubai. He has only recently returned to Britain after a few years abroad.'

'Why did he leave?'

Hadi Kattan sighed again. 'He became tired of people moving away from him on the underground trains, I believe.'

'That kind of prejudice must be very hard to bear,' I grimaced. For some reason, my internal alarm was ringing.

'It is the world we live in now, it seems,' Kattan said with dignity.

'Can you tell me about your son's political ambitions?'

'I'm sure he will be happy to tell you himself, when he arrives.'

I smiled. Thwarted. 'So I believe you're also a very important person indeed in one of the big banks.' I took a sip of champagne, relieved to look away from his intense gaze. I noticed that no alcohol had passed his lips yet.

'Briefly,' he acquiesced graciously. 'I was a director of World-Trident. But it was not for me. I do not particularly enjoy dancing to the corporate tune.'

'A man after my own heart. Impressive, though, Mr Kattan.' James raised an eyebrow. 'One of the big players.'

Kattan shrugged elegantly. 'Hardly. And banks are not the place to be at the moment, I think, my friends, as we are currently learning, no? I got out at the right time. I prefer the art in my home to the numbers on the screen.'

He gestured at the pictures; my eye was drawn to a diamond-encrusted skull in a glass case behind him.

'Damien Hirst?'

'Indeed. Are you a fan?'

'Not really, I'm afraid.' I went to take a better look. 'He pretty much stands for everything asinine about the past decade. Clever bloke, though, I guess.' I glanced at my husband. 'Tapping into hedonistic greed the way he did.'

James drained his champagne and winked at me. 'Another bloke after my own heart.'

As I straightened up, a silver Porsche hurtled up the drive and skidded to a halt in front of the house. I watched through the windows as a young black man flung himself out of the car and headed towards the house but he didn't get very far before he was halted by a tall figure, hood up against the wind. Hand on his arm, he was apparently trying to calm the shorter man, who gesticulated wildly at the house. Kattan glanced at them, and then turned me gently away.

'Anyway, I did not just mean business interests. I am more

keen on the recreational type now.' Heads had begun to turn at the commotion; both men were now getting into the car as I glanced round again. Kattan smoothed his lapel carefully with a flattened hand; he spoke a little louder. 'I am thinking of taking up guns, actually. I have quite a selection here.'

'Guns?' My ears pricked up.

'Shooting birds, you know,' Kattan smiled benevolently. 'Such a civilised part of your culture, I think.'

'Yeah, well,' James grinned and tossed an olive stone on the fire. The flames flared, 'more civilised than shooting people, I guess.'

I glanced out of the window. The Porsche had gone.

'Perhaps you would care to join me some time, Mr Miller. I would be honoured. We even have a hunting lodge on the estate designed specifically for lunch, I am told.'

'Don't mind if I do, Mr Kattan.' James toasted Kattan with his glass. 'Always up for a new challenge, me.'

'I always thought I might be a good shot, actually,' I interjected.

'I am not sure about women with guns, I must be honest,' Hadi Kattan bowed. 'What do you think, Mr Miller? It is not that fitting, I feel.'

'I don't know,' my husband smirked. 'Think of Charlie's Angels!'

I stared at James in disbelief. 'I think we're talking more *The Shooting Party* than Cameron Diaz, actually, James. Tweed and plus fours, not bikinis and bling.'

A thickset young Asian man with greased-back hair and small silver hoops in his ears entered the room now and hovered behind us, very still and straight, his hands clasped behind his back. The throb of a helicopter could be heard in the distance, above the sound of conversation.

'Zack. Please,' Kattan beckoned him over. The young man muttered something in his ear.

'Please, excuse me.' Kattan moved away from us. 'I have a small business matter to attend to.'

'What's *The Shooting Party* then? A porno about coming?' James muttered.

'Don't be so crude, darling,' I murmured back. 'It really doesn't behove one so well educated.'

'Don't be a bitch.' He glared at me.

'I'm not, really.' I felt exhausted suddenly. There was a criss-cross of tension in this house; not only between me and James, but the men arguing outside – and Kattan's own demeanour seemed rather intense. 'I'm going to find the loo.'

Crossing the panelled hall, I caught my reflection in a great ornate mirror as the door to the party swung shut, the noise quickly fading behind it. My eyes were glittering from alcohol, which I was unused to these days, and James was right: I defin-itely looked more curvaceous in my old velvet dress than I should.

Hand on the loo door, my heart jumped as I heard a thud from above. I hesitated. Checking behind me, I turned back and quickly headed up the huge oak staircase.

Door after door on the first corridor revealed nothing but empty rooms, a few with furniture shrouded eerily in dust-sheets, like small children playing ghosts. I paused again. In the distance I could hear the chop of the helicopter above – and something more sinister.

Somewhere not far from me, a woman was crying.

Hastily I opened the last door to reveal an ornate bathroom, and shut it again. I hurried back to the staircase and crossed to the opposite corridor, a slight sweat breaking out on my top lip as the crying got louder. The first door was locked. I rattled the door handle.

'Hello?'

I thought I heard a scuffle inside. Then silence.

'Hello,' I said more urgently. I thought of the wailing woman, although the crying had stopped. 'Maya?'

I heard the rasp and flare of a match and spun round. The fair man I'd met so briefly at the petrol station was leaning on the wall behind me, watching me impassively. I was struck by the incredible ease with which he held himself.

'Oh,' I said stupidly. 'You scared me.'

'Lost, Mrs Miller?' He chucked the match in the vase of roses beside him. 'The party's downstairs, I think you'll find.'

I realised he'd just used my name. 'I was just looking for the bathroom, actually,' I stuttered. The champagne had *definitely* gone to my head.

'Really? All the way up here?'

'Yes, really. Like you said,' I attempted a winning smile, 'I got a bit lost.'

He stepped closer to me, close enough for me to feel the warmth of his body as he reached down and circled my wrist with his fingers; I pulled back. I could smell lemon again. His eyes narrowed as he contemplated me. He didn't let go.

'What happened to your face?'

'It – it's just a graze.' I touched my cheek instinctively. I'd forgotten about James's scratch.

His expression was impossible to read, but his fingers round my wrist tightened and he pulled me along the corridor to the first door so I stumbled in my heels.

'What are you doing?' I mumbled. He didn't answer. He just leaned over me and opened the door, then turned me round.

'I'm showing you what you were looking for.'

His hand was in the small of my back now as he pushed me forward. I tried to turn back, anxious not to be shoved into this dark room by him – but he blocked the way with his shoulder so I couldn't pass.

'I hope . . .' my voice felt thick, 'I hope . . .'

'You hope what?'

'I do hope you're not threatening me.'

'Don't be so stupid.' He looked at me with those blue blue eyes. 'Why would I do that?'

We stared at each other. His eyes were blue as untroubled sky. Then slowly, very slowly, I backed into the bathroom and shut the door between us, leaning my cheek for a minute against the cool wood. The idea that he was there on the other side disturbed me intensely. I sat on the side of the bath and put my head between my knees for a while.

When I came out, he'd gone. I crept across the corridor and tried the locked door again. This time, it swung open. Behind it lay a pretty yellow bedroom, all sprigged wallpaper and a four-poster bed; in the corner, a Louis XIV chair with a woman's silk robe thrown carelessly across it. There was a silver hairbrush set on the dressing table and a bottle of Dior perfume, but not much else – apart from another door in the corner, behind which I thought I could hear movement. Taking a deep breath, I headed towards it.

'Hello?' I said again, and then I put my hand out and wrenched it open. A hiss and a squeal, and a ball of white fur launched itself between my feet and disappeared under the bed. A bloody Persian cat! I laughed tremulously at my own stupidity.

As I went to close the bedroom door behind me, I glanced at a portrait hanging on the wall. The sleepy brown eyes of a young woman gazed down on me and I froze on the spot. I felt the same icy sensation I'd felt in the office the other day.

I stared and stared up at her, almost expecting her to blink back – but of course she didn't.

I hurried down the stairs, back to the party, her eyes boring through the door into my back the whole way.

Downstairs, the party was beginning to thin out. Kattan's young henchman was gone; the MP, Eddie Johnson, was so drunk he was in danger of toppling over like a giant Weeble. Over by the fireplace my husband was deep in conversation with Kattan, both talking in low voices, Kattan smoking a cigar. The smell reminded me of my childhood.

'All right, my petal?' James kissed my head as I arrived at his side. I smiled weakly. My every instinct screamed that something was terribly wrong in this house, that the veneer of wealth and respectability covered up a darkness I couldn't yet fathom; that so far it was impossible to put my finger on it. I felt the strongest desire to run away – but a stronger instinct to know the truth.

'Yes, thanks,' I murmured, smiling at James, who looked like Lewis Carroll's Cheshire cat.

'I was just telling Mr Kattan about Revolver,' James said, pocketing something. My heart sank.

'Indeed.' Hadi Kattan, smiling pleasantly, exhaled a plume of blue smoke. 'Every man should have the chance to own a nightclub. Life would be so boring without a little fun, no?'

'I guess it's always good to let your hair down.' I took James's arm like the loyal wife I was.

'Here's my card,' James said. 'Let me know what you think.'

'I'm so sorry to drag him away, Mr Kattan, but I think – babysitters and all – you know . . .' I wanted to be home with my children right now.

'It's been fantastic to meet you, sir.' My fickle husband, so easily turned. 'Guess we're going to have to call a cab.' James looked ruefully at his empty glass. I bit my lip. He had promised he would drive.

'Please,' Hadi Kattan took my hand, 'Danny Callendar can take you home. I am sorry you did not get to meet Ash. Next time, perhaps.'

'Oh no, that's fine, honestly,' I said quickly. 'Thank you, but a cab's fine.'

'Please, Mrs Miller,' Kattan's voice was silky, 'I insist.' He pressed his warm lips to my cold hand.

Waiting on the front steps, I shivered: the sudden drop in temperature pervading my bones.

'Something's not right here,' I muttered to James. 'I can't put my finger on it, but something's not right.'

'Rubbish.' My husband shrugged himself into his leather coat and switched on his phone. 'He's a charming bastard, I'll give him that.'

I thought of Kattan's lips on my hand and shuddered. 'All that stuff about women and guns, for Christ's sake. It's like the bloody dark ages. It's like the bloody Taliban.'

'For Christ sake, Rose,' James's cheerful demeanour dissolved, 'you sound like that BNP bloke on the news the other day.'

'I don't.' I was appalled. 'I just – I don't trust men like Kattan, and I've met a few. All smiles on the surface and bigotry beneath.'

'You sound rather bigoted yourself, petal. You're always looking for the worst in people.'

'I'm not. I just look for the truth.' I thought of the painting in the bedroom; I remembered James's recent terrible nightmare. All these events were conspiring to bring back memories I'd suppressed for so long. I wondered whether I dare say it. 'James—'

'What?' He was more interested in his phone.

'It's very odd. I just saw a picture, a painting upstairs.'

'So? The whole house is full of bloody paintings.'

'It really looked like Huriyyah,' I whispered.

I definitely had his attention now.

'For fuck's sake!' His dark eyes were furious. 'I actually had a good evening for once. Don't ruin it now with your stupid imaginings.'

'I don't think I was imagining it,' I protested quietly. 'It really gave me a jolt.'

'Just shut up, OK.' He rounded on me. 'OK?'

'OK.' I was taken aback by the force of his anger as the Range Rover pulled up beside us.

Grit and cut grass stung my eyes, and my hair lashed my face painfully as the helicopter finally landed, great blades chopping the air. James shoved me into the car and swung in beside me. 'Cheers, mate,' he yelled over the din. 'This definitely saves us a wait.'

My heart sinking, I caught the fair man's eye in the mirror and looked away as he raised an eyebrow, a very faint grin playing on his face.

'Shame we can't jump in the chopper.' James stretched out his legs. 'Best way to travel.'

'It belongs to Ash Kattan,' Callendar said, pulling away smoothly. The helicopter blades were slowing as I turned to take a final look at the house.

I saw a face at an upstairs window; I figured it was about where the bedroom I'd been in was. Just in time, I suppressed the urge to shout 'Stop'.

'Where is Maya Kattan at the moment?' I leaned forward. 'Do you know?'

'For fuck's sake, Rose,' James hissed. 'Just leave it.'

'It's just that Mr Kattan said he wanted her to meet us,' I pressed on regardless. 'It was a shame she couldn't make the party.'

James took my hand and squeezed it so hard I winced. I glanced into the driver's mirror as I sat back. Danny Callendar looked at me inscrutably.

'I'm not quite sure where she is, Mrs Miller,' he answered easily. 'Perhaps she's gone up to London for a few days. She often does.'

'Why?' I wondered who the man driving her silver Porsche had been. I wondered if I dared ask.

'I wouldn't know.' His tone told me I would get no further tonight. He offered us a paper bag over his shoulder. 'Lemon sherbet?'

We both declined.

Silence fell across the car. One thing was certain: I knew for sure I couldn't do Xav's story now. However much my appetite was whetted, I had to stay home with the children. I'd sworn for their sake I'd never do anything risky again; motherhood had to come first now, and the atmosphere in the manor didn't bode well at all.

Leaning my head against the glass, I watched the tall hedgerows slide by in the dark, listening to the hiss of the tyres on the road. I was sitting beside my husband, but I was lonelier than I ever remembered being before I was married. I felt a strange longing for something I could not describe.

As we pulled into our drive, James's mobile rang. 'Cheers, mate,' he thanked Danny Callendar as he picked up the call, sliding out of his side. 'Good news, Liam. New backer in the offing, I do believe.' My husband disappeared through the studio gate.

Before I could open it, Danny was already at the door.

'I'm fine, really,' I insisted quietly, but he held out a hand. Eventually I took it and looked up at him as I jumped down. I found I couldn't smile.

'Thank you very much,' I said. My skin felt like it was burning where his hand touched me. For a split second his hand seemed to linger on mine, and then he was back in the car. I saw a flame through the dark window as he lit his roll-up, and then he was gone.

THE POST ON SUNDAY, DECEMBER 1991

THE GENTLEMAN'S DIARY: UP THE CREEK?

We hear that Dalziel St John, eldest son of Lord Higham, our current Home Secretary and John Major's great golfing buddy, has been living it up again of late. We all remember that St John Jnr went somewhat off the rails during his gap year: this kindly columnist will draw a veil over the episode. Suffice it to say that young Dalziel may have taken the 'high' in living the high life a little too literally down in North Cornwall's elitist Rock.

Now in his third year at Magdalen College, St John Jnr had apparently worried his parents again during the last summer holidays with talk of dropping out to model for Versace – amongst other 'keen' parties (homosexual French designer Gaultier famously called him 'truly divine inspiration', the fashion-conscious amongst you might remember). However, under the steadying influence of new girlfriend and sometime Sapphist Lena Holt (this lady is for turning obviously!), daughter of the late Marquis of Gloucester and opera singer Constantia Latzier,

*all has seemed well for a while: Dalziel has been safely ensconced
back at Magdalen finishing his theology degree, after which he
is expected to fly straight out to Argentina to manage the family
polo farm for a while.*

*So could the rumours be true that Dalziel has just this weekend
been caught defecating at the altar of Christ Church, the ancient
cathedral? Yes you did indeed read correctly: defecating, not dese-
crating, though some might argue they are one and the same. It
may yet turn out to be fortunate that his father is second cousin
of the Bishop himself, although my sources tell me both men are
very far from amused. Indeed, Lady Higham is so mortified that
she has retired to Barbados for a sojourn at the Sandy Lane spa,
citing 'nervous exhaustion' (something the poor lady has suffered
much of, apparently, for one so young).*

*We shall, of course, keep our trusty readers posted of further
developments – but let us just surmise for now that young Dalziel
is well and truly up the creek and in the 'proverbial' with his
folks . . .*

'Have you seen this?' James threw the newspaper on the
café table, spilling my tea. 'I can't believe that rag's got hold
of it.'

'Yeah, I've seen it.' I pushed the paper away and finished my
poached egg as James sat down. 'Me and the whole of college. I
can't believe you'd buy that rag, James.' I was only half joking.
I'd been discovering yet more political principles this term. 'I'm
shocked.'

'You're too liberal for your own good.' He shook his dark head
sorrowfully. 'Dalziel's old man did such a wicked job of keeping
it quiet. He's going to go ballistic. White coffee, please, love,'
James winked at the pretty waitress, who tossed her hair and
immediately turned her back on him.

'Who'll go ballistic?' I mopped up the last of the yolk. 'Dalziel's
dad?'

'No, stupid. Dalziel.' James pinched a chip. 'He's done a deal with his dad to keep this kind of stuff out of the paper.'

'How can he do that?' I was intrigued. 'Keep it out? He's not God. Or royalty.' I considered that last statement for a second. 'Or is he?'

'Not quite, but he's pretty well connected.'

'I never realised his dad was a lord. Or Home Secretary.' I wasn't quite sure whether to be impressed or contemptuous, given that St John Senior was such a dyed-in-the-wool Tory. My new worst enemies.

'Anyway, Lord Higham owns half of Wapping. And,' James lowered his voice, 'Dalziel's got stuff on his dad that would blow the government out of the water – and his dad knows it.'

'God,' I leaned forward, 'like what?' I was really curious now.

'I'm not at liberty to say, petal.' James stroked my cheek as the waitress brought the coffee. 'He'd have my guts for garters if I breathe a word. Let's just say it's in Daddy's interest – Daddy who likes lots of girls – it's in his interest to cover Dalziel's tracks. And anyway, he didn't do it. Dalziel. The shitting thing.'

I felt inordinately relieved. It seemed so crass somehow; below Dalziel. The young waitress was staring at James's fingers on my skin and shoved the cup down so hard boiling coffee slopped out, burning my arm.

'Ouch!' I looked at her reproachfully. She looked vaguely familiar, her hair pulled back tightly from her cross, freckled face.

'Bloody students,' she muttered, and slammed back into the kitchen.

'Friend of yours?' I raised an eyebrow at my some-time boyfriend.

'Possibly,' he grinned. 'Are you jealous?'

I thought about it. 'A little bit,' I said, truthfully.

'Don't be. She's just a skivvy.'

'James!' I was shocked.

'A bit of rough can be a laugh, I guess.' He raised his eyebrows at me, all arch. 'An experience.'

'For God's sake, James.' I took the bait. 'You sound just like him.'

'Who?'

'Who do you think?' I blew gently on my burned skin. 'Your great lord and master.'

'Don't be fucking stupid,' James bristled. 'I'm my own man.'

'Boy,' I teased.

'Man. No one tells me what to do.'

'Oh, really?'

'Yes, really.' James ladled sugar in his coffee, spoons and spoons of it. 'He's started talking about us all meeting again, actually.' He was casual as he stirred his drink.

'Oh.' My stomach tightened. 'Why?'

'Not sure. He's got some grand scheme up his ruffled sleeve. It'll be a laugh. Just think of last time.' He winked at me again, rather lasciviously for such a young man. It turned my stomach a bit; I was shocked at my own reaction.

'I'd rather not,' I muttered. I was still haunted by the vacant look on Huriyyah's face. The fact she hadn't really been present despite her body being in the room; the body that had been no more than a piece of meat. The vague rumours I'd heard since that both boys *and* girls had been lining up to take turns with her.

'Come on,' James persisted, 'we'd never have got together if he hadn't held that party. And it was a laugh, you've got to admit.'

'I suppose so,' I smiled weakly.

We both jumped as Jen knocked on the glass window, her short hennaed hair blowing upwards in the December wind, cheeks ruddy from cycling.

'Gotta go.' I gathered my things, relieved suddenly to be leaving the steamy little café. 'I've already paid for mine. See you soon, yeah?'

'Oh, right.' He looked put out. 'Like when?'

The bad-tempered little waitress was watching us. I realised with a jolt it was Twiggy from the Hallowe'en do. Instinctively I leaned over to kiss James full on the mouth.

'I'll be in the college bar later, I think,' I said. 'About six.'

'And what shall I tell Dalziel?' James swung back dangerously on his chair's back legs.

'About what?'

'He'll want to know who's in.'

'I don't know,' I frowned. 'I'm not that bothered, to be honest, J. I've got a lot on. I've just had another article actually commissioned for the *Cherwell*. It's got to be in by next week.'

Jen knocked again more urgently, pointing at her watch in elaborate mime.

'I'm going to be late for my seminar.'

'All right, Goody Two-Shoes,' James taunted.

I let it go. 'I'll see you later.'

Cycling through town, my fingers frozen round my handlebars despite my woolly gloves, my mind kept darting back to Dalziel and how I'd felt when he kissed me that cold winter night, and how I'd felt when I'd watched him kissing that boy. But most of all, to the face of the girl on the divan: how utterly lost she had been.

Leaving my tutor group later, I realised I'd lost my scarf; on the way home I popped into the café to see if it was there. The sulky waitress was cleaning the coffee machine behind the wooden counter.

'Haven't seen it,' she muttered, and I had no choice but to believe her.

'Really fancies himself now, that boyfriend of yours, don't he?' she said as I opened the door to leave.

I paused and turned. 'What do you mean?'

'You should have seen him last year.' Her pretty face was

flushed. 'He was like a – a lost puppy and he dressed like a right bloody spod, carrying that stupid guitar everywhere. Only too glad to mix with the likes of me then.' She wiped the steam pipe so savagely I thought it would snap. 'Not that I was interested in him.'

'Oh,' I said rather helplessly. 'I'm sorry.'

'Don't be. Much better fish in the sea.' She turned her back on me again before I could read the expression on her face. Her voice was strangely muffled. 'You're welcome to him.'

There wasn't anything else to say really. I saw her in town a few weeks later with another boy; she was wearing my scarf. I decided she could keep it.

Chapter Five

GLOUCESTERSHIRE, MARCH 2008

The morning after the Kattans' party, the taxi dropped me at the gates in the overgrown lane. I had a feeling of foreboding that I tried to dispel, but my stomach was churning slightly even before I began the long walk up the drive.

Last night it had been my turn to lie awake, sleepless beside a snoring James, recalling events I had blocked for years. And as I stared into the darkness, craving sleep and peace, I couldn't understand why all these events were conspiring to meet now. But whatever the reason, the past seemed to be travelling inexorably towards me – and there was nowhere to hide. All night I'd pondered the portrait in the bedroom, until finally I'd decided that James was right: that I'd been mistaken: that one sloe-eyed beauty might look rather like another. But still I couldn't quite push Huriyyah's face from my mind.

The gravel crunched satisfyingly underfoot as I set off, my hand clasped round the car keys in my fleece pocket. In the past few weeks the earth had yawned mightily and begun to waken, and I was flanked now by creamy yellow daffodils that flickered lightly in the breeze, the great glossy camellias behind them festooned with buds as big as my fist. The temperature at night was still close to freezing, but this morning had dawned fresh and bright – a mismatch for my sense of apprehension. I intended to fetch the car and leave the property as quickly as I could.

My phone rang. Xavier.

'Where are you?'

'Fetching my car from Hadi Kattan's house in Gloucestershire.'

'You got in there then? Good girl.'

'Yes,' I said. 'And now I'm getting out.'

'What do you mean?'

'It's not for me, Xav.'

'Don't be a pussy, Rose.'

'I'm not. Like I said, I'm flattered, and I think you should follow it up – but you need to get someone else to do it.'

'But you're in already. I've got more juicy stuff coming through; rumours that Kattan may have financed a training-camp from his home in Tehran. Plus he's been the subject of a CIA investigation.'

'Really?' I thought of the man last night at the party, of the helicopter, of the hysterical and now apparently missing daughter.

Detecting my hesitation, Xav pounced. 'Come on, Rose.'

'I've already been warned off by his laconic idiot of a driver.'

'A nice bit of rough? Right up your street.'

'Up yours, you mean.'

'Darling! All those coarse farmers are having a terrible effect on you.'

I thought of Hadi Kattan's firm handshake and the way he held back from the rest of the crowd; the assurance in his stance. 'Kattan's much more my type.' For all his inherent sexism, no man had smiled at me like that for years.

'You're a happily married woman, let me remind you, Rosie.'

A sudden breeze sent a flurry of blossom skittering before my feet.

'Not sure about the happily bit right now,' I muttered.

'At last she's seen the light,' Xavier drawled. He'd never bothered to hide his feelings about James.

88

The blossom whirled in circles on the ground before me.

'Anyway, Kattan's certainly a character. Very old-school polite, but a will of iron, I'm sure. And his son, Ash, is apparently disenchanted with Britain, and running for Parliament.' I was rounding the last bend in the drive now, heading towards a stable block and garages on my right, walking into shadow beneath great elms that blocked the sun from my path. The gargoyles on the roof were still screaming silently as I neared. I had the unnerving feeling that I was being watched and I felt a shiver of apprehension. 'But I'm sorry, I just can't do it, Xav.'

'Fuck, Rose,' Xav swore softly. 'It's not like you to wimp out.'

The great windows of the Gothic manor frowned down like huge unblinking eyes, and then something stopped me in my tracks. I wasn't sure exactly what I'd seen but it was like a flash of light, something white billowing in the window to the left of the great front door. Somewhere nearby the clank of metal on metal startled me. My own involuntary gasp made me laugh.

'Rose?'

'I'll call you back.' I hung up.

'Hello?' I called. Someone had been listening, I was sure.

Silence fell again; just the fluting of birdsong, and then the distant bleat of tiny lambs. It was an eerie sound; rather like my children crying. I took a few small steps towards an old cream-coloured racing car abandoned on blocks. Alongside the garage wall were stacked great canisters; presumably for petrol.

'Hello?' I steadied my voice. 'Anyone there?'

There was no response. A sudden gust blew through the branches like a great breath as I took another step and then the light from the window struck me again, flashing across my face so I had to shut my eyes. Not a light I realised, some kind of red laser. It swept the ground before me and then disappeared.

I contemplated turning back – and then I heard the metallic sound again.

'Hello?' I repeated, awash with adrenalin – and then Danny Callendar emerged from the garage, rolling a cigarette.

'You really made me jump.' I tried to stifle my nerves. Wood smoke hung in the air like a distant warning. Like an exhaled sigh.

'I'm sorry,' he said easily, and licked the cigarette paper. 'Can I help?'

I smiled politely. 'I've just come to collect my car.'

'Fair enough.' Callendar looked down to light his roll-up, then up again as he inhaled. 'It's still up at the house.'

He was so abrupt, it seemed peculiar after last night. So abrupt he was rude. I regarded him for a second. His eyes were uncomfortably blue, piercing even; his skin looked like it had suffered too many summers under hot sun. It was hard to place his age; somewhere in his mid-thirties, I'd guess; a year or two younger than me, perhaps.

'What exactly is it that you do here?' A sudden gust whipped my key-ring hard against my wrist. 'Ow.' I dropped the keys.

He bent down to retrieve them, handing the ring to me. 'Who wants to know?' His skin was hard and calloused, oil beneath his nails.

'Me, obviously.' *What a stupid thing to say*. 'I just wondered.'

'I drive for Mr Kattan.' He took another drag, eyes squinting against sun and smoke. He had nice hands, I thought absently. Long elegant fingers, despite the filthy nails. 'Amongst other things.'

'What kind of other things?'

'This and that, Mrs Miller, this and that.' He leaned against the old car.

'And is Mr Kattan here?'

'Dunno.'

'I see.' I tried another smile. 'Does he have many visitors?'

Danny Callendar laughed – but he was laughing *at* me, that was clear. 'What's it to you, honey?'

'I'm meant to be writing a piece on him for the local paper. Just interested. Professionally, you know.'

'Well, professionally,' he removed a bit of tobacco from his tongue, 'he has a few.'

'Right.' I was tired of smiling to no avail. 'So I'll just make my own way up to the house, shall I?'

His expression was unreadable. 'Were you expecting a lift?'

We stared at each other for a moment. A huge chestnut hunter whickered softly at the fence nearby.

'Beautiful horse.'

'Just for show really. Maya rides them occasionally.'

'Oh?'

'When she—' He stopped, ran a hand through his fashionably dishevelled hair. Was it affection I detected?

'When she what?' I prompted gently.

'Nothing,' he shrugged. 'I'm pretty busy actually.'

I'll bet. Cleaning cars. Flat out.

'So if you don't mind . . .' He turned away. Normally I found a Scottish accent attractive, but his annoyed me intensely.

'Of course. Thanks a lot for your help.'

If he detected the sarcasm he didn't react and he disappeared back into the depths of the garage without a second glance. I took a deep breath, and carried on up to the house.

I was like Catherine Morland from Jane Austen's *Northanger Abbey*, imagining ghosts and villains where there were none, always looking for drama round the next corner. I had to accept that my addiction lingered, despite my self-imposed retirement. Ridiculous, I told myself, unlocking the car door. I turned the radio on, clicked my seat belt in and began to reverse towards the fountain, where I could turn.

'*This is the sound of a bomb not exploding because the neighbours noticed the chemicals being stored in the garage,*' a male voice droned from the radio.

'Oh, for God's sake,' I muttered, putting my foot down. 'Bloody idiots.'

Suddenly a man was hanging on to my door, desperately trying to rip it open. I braked sharply.

'Call the police,' he was shouting, his thin blue-black face shiny with sweat, his eyes wide with fear. 'Call the police, tell 'em she's a prisoner and I—'

'Please,' I tried to keep calm, 'let go of the door.'

'Let me in.' He rattled the handle.

'I will. Just please, let go and – and we can talk properly.'

He wasn't listening to me; he seemed delirious with terror. There was spittle on his broad lower lip as he intoned, 'Call 'em now, call 'em now. Tell them the truth about this family, about that man.'

'Please,' I tried again, 'just calm down, OK?'

His face was pressed up hard against the car window, his nose flattened horribly against the glass, pupils dilated, the whites yellow.

I undid the central locking and he saw his chance. He tugged open the door and started to pull me out.

'Hang on,' I cried frantically. 'Just, please, let me—'

He was really hurting me, both hands on the collar of my fleece, pulling me against my seat belt until it cut into my neck, threatening to strangle me.

'Please,' I gasped for air. 'I can't breathe.'

When I was small, a boy at the local swimming pool had got into trouble in the deep end; as the proud owner of a Silver life-savers' badge, I'd dived in to help. But panic had made him mad and instead of letting me guide him safely to the side, he'd used me as a float, holding my head under water as he fought to stay alive, pushing me down until I thought I would die, my lungs exploding with the effort to get air.

'Please,' I gasped now, 'my neck. You're hurting me.' But the man was so frantic, he was deaf to my plea. 'Please stop.'

A pair of arms came around the man and he was pulled to the floor, hands forced behind his back.

Feet on the gravel now but still sitting in the car, I bent double, staring at my shoes, trying to get my breath. When I looked up, a young Asian man had one knee in the small of the man's back, and Callendar was sprinting up the drive.

'Are you OK?' he called as he neared.

I nodded uncertainly.

'Get off me, get off me,' the man on the floor was moaning.

'Are you sure?'

'Yes.'

Callendar and I stared at one other; a moment suspended in time. I looked at him and I felt nothing but confusion.

'You need to leave now.' He spoke first, breaking the tension. 'It's not safe for you here.' His tone was urgent.

'But . . .' I looked at the man on the floor, 'he needs help. The police, he said—'

'He needs locking up,' the Asian man spat, 'don't you, blood? Fucking nutter.'

I recognised him from the party; the man who had waited for Hadi Kattan by the door, now dressed in combats and a vest in place of the shiny suit he'd worn last night, a faded tattoo of a star and moon on his upper bicep. He pulled the black guy up by the hands and then dropped him again heavily so his face hit the gravel.

'Don't!' I shouted, wincing as I felt the thud of his torso smacking the ground. 'Please.'

Callendar moved between me and the two men, his jaw set rigid.

'Zack, take him up to the house.' From the corner of my eye, I saw him boot the man on the floor in the ribs.

'My pleasure.' Zack pushed the man's face into the gravel again. I winced.

'Your neck.' Callendar reached an arm out to me and I tried

not to flinch. 'You're bleeding.' He held his sleeve against the welts that were already rising there. For the first time, I felt frightened of this man.

'I'm fine.' I felt the pressure of his arm on my skin.

'Get it seen to, I would.' He stepped back now.

'But I think . . .' I began rather helplessly. I didn't know what to think, that was the truth.

'Don't think,' Danny said quietly, reading my mind. I saw blood on his sleeve. My blood – or older, darker – drying blood? 'Please, Mrs Miller, just get in your car, and go.'

'But . . .' I stammered. 'I'm more worried about him.'

'It's family business, love,' the man called Zack said over his shoulder, as he hauled the black guy to his feet and marched him towards the house, scooping up some tool box he had evidently been carrying under one arm. The black man's face was bleeding from the gravel, blood and stones speckling his face like some kind of unholy pox.

'Call the police,' he groaned. 'Call 'em before it's too late.'

'Shut it, you,' Zack snapped, giving the man a shove so he stumbled. Zack grabbed his wrist before he hit the floor again and manoeuvred him up the front steps.

'Danny . . .' I'd never said his name before. It sounded oddly intimate. 'Please, what's going on here?'

'Don't worry about it.' He pushed me inside the car again. 'It's not your concern.'

'Is that meant to reassure me?' I said.

Danny shrugged. 'Not really. Remember, Mrs Miller, too much poking around can make Rose a very dull girl.' His face was grim. 'Understand, pet?'

He shut my car door hard, and walked towards the house.

I sat there for a minute, my hands clammy on the wheel, watching as Danny Callendar disappeared into the house behind the other two men. I sat there, absolutely impotent, angry and shaken, unsure what to do. I cursed myself for ever coming here.

In the end, time decided things for me. If I didn't leave now, I'd be late for the twins. I turned the car back down the drive, my eyes fixed in my mirror as the house receded. It was finally quiet from the outside, but God only knew what was happening inside.

As I pulled into the lane, a prehistoric Jeep nearly took me out on the opposite side. I oversteered and rounded the bend too fast, then felt a lurch, followed by the awful crunch of metal on concrete.

'I don't believe this is happening.' I slammed the steering wheel with my hands. 'For God's sake.'

Somehow I managed to manoeuvre the wounded vehicle up onto the verge as a silver BMW, horn blaring, swerved round me, the driver mouthing obscenities through his window. I ignored him with what I considered to be great serenity, and debated my options.

As I fished in my pocket for my phone, a car pulled into the drive from the other end of the lane and I felt my mouth open in surprise.

I was sure my husband had just driven through the gate to Hadi Kattan's house.

UNIVERSITY, DECEMBER 1991

For he on honey-dew hath fed,
And drunk the milk of Paradise.

'*Kubla Khan*', Coleridge

Two nights later, I'd been studying in the library and then out for a quick drink with Jen. I'd cycled home, slightly drunk, pondering the essay I'd just started on Mary Shelley. My professor had suggested the great Percy Bysshe Shelley had actually written his wife's classic, *Frankenstein*, to the groans of all the girls present. I wanted something really fresh to say, but my research had turned up nothing so far.

At the lodge I chained my bike and clambered up the stairs to my room. The door was unlocked, which was odd, but I'd been in such a rush earlier, I must have forgotten to lock it.

Peeling a strand of hair away from my pink face, damp from the frenetic cycle home, I threw my coat on the bed and turned on the bedside lamp. The bulb blew with a loud pop.

'Shit.' I didn't have another one. I headed for the light-switch by the door. The door slammed shut in my face and as I moved quickly to open it again, an arm shot out of the shadows and grabbed my wrist. I shrieked in surprise.

'Don't scream, precious,' a low voice whispered. 'It's so Hammer House.'

Sweating, my eyes slowly adjusted to the gloom. A figure behind the door.

'My love is like a red, red rose,' he purred. Something glinted in his right hand. 'You look well, lovely.'

'You frightened me.' My heart was still thudding painfully. After a second or two, I moved to switch the light on.

'Don't, please,' Dalziel said, his hand tightening round my skin. 'I hate the light. Don't you have a candle or something?'

'Somewhere, I think,' I said, rooting around on the shelf above my bed. He sat on the bed and handed me a lighter.

'Sorry to have scared you,' he drawled, though he clearly wasn't. 'I missed you, Rose. Nice beads.'

'Oh,' I said, suddenly shy. 'Thanks.' I wasn't sure if he was teasing me. 'They're like the ones the Inspiral Carpets wear.'

'I see.' He was solemn. 'Nice picture too.' He pointed at the huge poster of Tim Burgess from The Charlatans above my bed. 'If you like that sort of thing.'

'And do you?' I asked.

'Not much.' He flipped the shiny thing in his hand over and again. I realised it was ten-pence coin. 'Nice lips, though.'

I had a sudden flash of him and the dark boy writhing on the divan.

'So what are you doing here?' I asked awkwardly. 'Not that – I mean,' I hesitated, 'I mean, you're very welcome.'

'That's kind, my love. I have to tell you, though, I'm very sad, actually,' he murmured. 'Since I heard that you're not my number-one fan any more.'

'I never said that.' I was embarrassed. I sat on the edge of my narrow bed. 'Who told you that? I haven't – I haven't even seen you for weeks.'

'No, well,' he pulled something from his pocket, 'I've been quite busy. Finishing my research for my dissertation.'

'The Christ Church thing, you mean?' I blushed. 'Is it true? Did you – did you crap in the cathedral?'

He shrugged, so relaxed I could imagine him slithering to the floor in one fluid move. 'No.'

'Who did then?'

'How the hell do I know? Someone who adores me, clearly.' He was only half joking.

'Why do they think you did?'

'Because they've got no imagination. They choose the obvious.'

'Oh,' I said, perplexed. 'Is your dad cross?'

'Don't be so naïve,' he snapped. 'I don't give a shit what my father thinks. Literally.'

'Sorry,' I stuttered. This boy made me so nervous, surrounded by his aura of expectation. He recovered, flicking his white-blond hair back, and smiled at me, winningly, his face lit as if from inside.

'Rosie, Rosie. It's just – I'm so very near. And now I need your help, lovely.'

'Really?' I stuttered. I'd forgotten quite how beautiful he was; those girlish dark lashes sweeping down onto porcelain skin, his face fine-boned and pure.

'We had fun, didn't we? With the silly underwear thing?'

'Yes,' I bit my lip. It *had* been fun. And harmless.

'Look, tails you help me,' he flipped the coin into the air, 'heads I'll leave you be.'

The coin shone as it spun through the candlelight.

'Tails it is, lovely.'

But I never saw if it really was. He was reaching into his pocket now, rolling something dark between his fingers, shoving it down into a small pipe and lighting it.

'Please say you'll help me, darling.' He reached over and took my hand, pulling back my sleeve and stroking the skin on my inner arm. I froze at the intimacy, and then I remembered the track marks on Huriyyah's arm. I laughed shakily.

'What?' He looked amused, but didn't stop stroking my arm. 'Is that nice?'

Slowly I relaxed, feeling catlike, as if I might start purring.

'You've got beautiful skin, Rosie. Smooth as silk.'

'I haven't,' I stammered. 'Have I?'

'Oh, yes.' He inhaled from his pipe. 'Try this, lovely.'

'What is it?' I eyed it suspiciously. I didn't recognise the sickly sweet smell. 'Is it dope?'

'Yes, it's dope. Nice bit of Moroccan hashish from a nice Moroccan boy I know.' He stood up, flipping through the books on my desk. 'I see you're studying the Romantics.'

'Yes.' I took the pipe. 'I love Shelley, don't you? He's so passionate, I think. I wish I could have met him.' I inhaled lightly. 'Can you imagine the conversations between him and Byron and Mary Shelley? God.' I stopped before I coughed.

'*In Xanadu did Kubla Khan a stately pleasure-dome decree*'. Dalziel threw a book down and turned back to me. 'Say you'll join me, Rosie,' he implored vehemently. 'I like you. You'd make me so happy.'

'Join you in what?' I said. The sweet smoke hit the back of my throat and despite my best efforts, I did cough. I felt gauche but rather elated.

'Take a proper drag, my love,' he insisted. 'You'll see. *For he on honey-dew hath fed, and drunk the milk of Paradise.*'

I took another big drag, down down into my lungs and it was both sweet and acrid, and then I contemplated the enormous world map on the wall above my desk, the candle throwing pools of light onto it, which moved endlessly. The map I'd bought from Blackwells on the High Street, the map I'd marked with pins for all the places I wanted to see, the places I needed to visit. I stared at it until it became all hazy and then I thought I really couldn't sit up any more, my body felt so heavy and soft.

I fell back onto the bed, thinking this wasn't like any dope I'd ever smoked before.

I closed my eyes; I couldn't keep them open. I felt sick briefly and then it passed and I realised I was having some kind of vision. The dreams came quickly until I didn't know if I was awake or sleeping. I dreamed I was Mary Shelley, running bare-foot by an Italian lake in a long skirt that swished around my ankles, with Dalziel sitting inside a villa, watching at a desk and he was smiling, iron bolts instead of ears just like Mary Shelley's monster.

At some point Dalziel fed me some more and then I thought I slept until I dreamed I was flying around the map of the world.

Much later I awoke, as if from the deepest sleep. The neon red of my clock radio said it was four o'clock and I couldn't work out if that was day or night. I was wedged in between the wall and a warm body; slowly I realised that Dalziel was lying beside me on the bed and I had no idea what had just happened. I gazed at him, almost unseeing, until eventually he opened one sleepy eye.

'All right, lovely?' he said. 'Enjoy the trip?'

'Oh God, Dalziel,' I mumbled. 'That was amazing.'

'Not bad, is it?'

'What was it?'

'Don't you know?'

I shook my head.

'God's own medicine.'

'Oh.' I was none the wiser.

'That, my precious, was the poppy. Coleridge and your friend Percy's favourite friend, to name a few fans.'

'Opium?'

He smiled beatifically, and shut his eyes again.

I lay on the bed and all I knew was I'd seen sights I'd never seen before.

* * *

For the next few days I spent every waking hour that I was allowed to with Dalziel. Sometimes he would just disappear and I would cycle past his house in the hope the lights would be on but they never were – until he would turn up somewhere unexpected to collect me, and my heart would leap with anticipation. Nothing sexual had ever happened between us and I didn't really care; I was attracted to him, undoubtedly, but in truth, I was happy just to enjoy his company. He radiated light a little like the sun; I was happy to absorb his warmth, although there were a few too many of us satellites to make it entirely comfortable.

At first the only place we went together was to my little room on the second floor, but after a while he took me back to his house, so unlike the digs of any of my other friends, and I imagined it was because he finally trusted me. It was less a theatrical set than the first time I'd been there, though still minimal in the extreme. The furniture looked expensive and the paintings on the walls by people I'd actually heard of. On the wall in the hall by the unused kitchen were two black-and-white photographs of a couple of beautiful children; I assumed they were Dalziel's siblings. But he refused to be drawn on his family and I soon gave up asking. I was simply happy to be with him, and deep down I felt like I was blessed to have been chosen. Jen and Liz thought I spent too much time with him, and James was constantly sulking whenever we all spent the evening together, but I didn't care.

How could I explain the grip Dalziel held me in? The long sleepless nights soaring above the planes of my imagination until I never wanted to return to earth. I loved him, I knew that. 'You have a sad mouth, Rose,' he said dreamily. 'That's why I knew we would be such friends.'

He told me stories of his childhood, about rowing on the lake in his father's grounds, and hiding in trees when his nanny looked for him, desperately calling his name until he relented. One night

101

when he was very stoned Dalziel talked about a puppy he once lost: he said he'd let it out at night; it had belonged to his sister and it had annoyed him, he said, for some reason, but he felt forever guilty when it disappeared. After that admission he fell silent and refused to talk again until the next day.

I asked him about Society X and he admitted it was really just a game that he had started because he was bored. 'I had a point to prove once, I think,' he said, 'but I seem to have forgotten what it is right now.' And we laughed, slightly feverishly.

I had accepted we would never become lovers – I knew deep down that he usually preferred boys – but he made me feel like I was different: special, intelligent – beautiful, even. 'Your skin is all creamy,' he whispered, stroking my hair as I lay beside him. And I had spent so long waiting to be accepted, and I knew now I was part of something great. Something the other students could only look on and dream of themselves, something they were not privy to. We were the lucky ones.

'Little dreamer', Dalziel called me when we were alone. 'You're always hoping to step outside real life, aren't you?' and he was right. The lure of the opium for me was finding myself in deserts with Byron or sailing the seas of Coleridge's Ancient Mariner. The world was opening up for me in more ways than one, and I wanted more.

Chapter Six

GLOUCESTERSHIRE, MARCH 2008

My poor wounded car just about made it back to the village after the incident at Albion Manor. I kept wondering if it had been James's Audi I'd seen at the gate, but then Fred and Effie were waiting at the nursery door, their chubby faces beaming, and some kind of peace settled over me like a thin blanket. I watched them padding across the grass with a huge drawing of superheroes fluttering between them, Effie's hat slipping over her face so she could hardly see where she ran.

'We thought you wasn't coming, Mummy,' Freddie said. 'But Mrs Foster said you'd only be a mimit.'

I gathered them to me. 'I'm sorry, baby. I won't be late again, I promise.'

'Mummy,' said Effie, freeing herself impatiently, 'I'm vegetarian, aren't I?'

'Are you now?' I kissed her cheek. 'That's nice.'

'I'm not vegetarian,' Fred said scornfully. 'I'm English.'

I laughed and kissed their shiny heads, tucking them into the car beneath the frosting of cherry blossom on the roof. I looked at them and closed the door, thinking of Danny Callendar's words, thinking uncomfortably of the man being marched to the house, the sly boot in the ribs. I had been warned off, and right now, it made absolute sense to stay away. I'd made a silent promise to the children, to the unborn Alicia after I was threatened in LA during my first pregnancy, that I'd never put their lives or my own in danger again; that I wouldn't choose the story over safety any more.

'I'm going to Vietnam next week,' James said, feet up on the kitchen table.

'Oh?' I put a plate of slightly singed macaroni cheese in front of him, which he ignored, flicking the television on. 'Get us a beer, petal, would you?'

'Why Vietnam?' I opened the fridge.

'To talk about opening a branch of the club out there. Saigon's the new Bangkok, didn't you know?' He wasn't looking at me, but at the screen behind me. 'Oh, goal!'

'Right,' I said, handing him a Becks. I picked up the salad and plonked it on the long kitchen table. 'Stay with me, J, will you?' I could tell he was itching to return to the studio but he did as I asked, forlornly abandoning his *Sight and Sound* magazine and taking his feet off the table.

'You know, it's funny.' Carefully I stuck my fork prong through a macaroni tube and cast a quick look from under my lashes at my husband. 'I'm probably going mad, but I suddenly thought I saw you out at Hadi Kattan's today?'

'You didn't.' He shovelled a bit of pasta into his mouth and pulled a face. 'Christ, Rosie! This macaroni's all crunchy.'

'Yes, well,' I jabbed at it, 'it might not be one of my absolutely best efforts. Have some salad.'

'It never is a best effort.' He pushed the bowl away. 'I hate bloody rabbit food, you know that.'

'It's good for you,' I said mildly. 'I'm sure I saw you there when I went to get the car, you know.'

'You didn't, darling, really.' James leaned over and kissed my cheek, and slowly I began to relax a little. I was about to tell him about the man up at Albion Manor, about my disquiet and the violence and whether I should report it to someone, when James stood, putting his plate in the sink. 'I'm not very hungry, actually. I had a burger in Oxford earlier.'

'Oxford?' I said warily.

'I had to go to the bank.'

'Oh?' Our avoidance of the place was unspoken – but we'd never once visited the small city since we'd moved out here.

'Yeah, it couldn't wait.' Was it my imagination or did he look a little sheepish? 'I just shot in and out again.'

'Everything all right?' I abandoned the macaroni myself now and attacked the lettuce instead. I pushed thoughts of Society X away; they were already too near the surface.

'Of course, petal. Never better.'

'And you definitely weren't up at Albion Manor earlier?'

'Rose!'

I recognised the warning signs; I raised my hands in supplication. 'OK, OK. I just thought, I could have sworn it was your car.'

'Everybody's driving silver Audis now. Where one leads, the others follow, eh, Rosie? Actually that reminds me. Have you seen the Beamer catalogue around?'

'Probably in that pile.'

I was sure he was lying about Hadi Kattan but frankly I didn't have the energy to argue with him now. If he had decided to deny it, the row could go on all night. I watched him rifle through the pile, dislodging the travel supplements stacked on the top. He came across an unopened bank statement and for a moment his eyes seemed to darken as he gazed at it. I had a sudden flash of inspiration.

'Why don't we all come?' I looked at him, light in my eyes.

'What?' He pocketed the statement quickly. 'Come where?'

'To Vietnam. I'm serious, J – I mean, it'd be amazing, wouldn't it? The kids would love it.' I felt genuinely enthused. 'It's good to do these things now, J, before Alicia gets too big to take out of school. It'd be brilliant. A real bonding experience. We could go back to Nha Trang.'

James and I had travelled all the time before we had the children, it was part of the glue that held us together. We'd had such adventures; we'd seen such sights. He would come and meet me when I finished foreign assignments and we would discover new places, basking in the sun, pottering round parts of cities that the tourists never saw, drinking the local hooch or playing cards into the early hours under star-studded skies.

'No way.' James finished his beer and threw the bottle in the bin. 'I'm flying in and flying straight out again. There's too much to do here to have a holiday.'

I gazed at him and I wondered when this huge gulf had opened up between us. I'd been staring down into it, teetering on the edge for too long now.

'It's quite, kind of – solitary sometimes, you know – specially when you're working all the time.'

'But you like your own company. Pottering around the garden and all that.'

I gritted my teeth. 'I do love the garden, yes, of course I do.' He'd been working on the super-club project for months now, staying up all night again, chasing sponsors and investment deals. I was trying to be understanding; trying so very hard not to feel ignored. 'But there's only so many plants you can talk to before you feel a little mad.'

'And only so many you can smoke.'

'Shut up, J,' I muttered. 'Just forget it, OK?'

James backtracked. 'Look, I wouldn't be able to spend the time with you I wanted to. Next time, petal, I promise.' He turned the football up. 'Let's book something nice for the summer. The Caribbean, yeah? Nice five-star all-inclusive, nanny service, all that malarkey. Just what the doctor ordered.'

I looked at him blankly. The old James would have rather

stuck pins in his eyes than go all-inclusive, hermetically sealed into a 'safe' environment for overprivileged tourists.

'Just no leaving the kids alone at night and going off for tapas, yeah? By the way, have you seen my phone? Oh fuck's sake, John Terry. You muppet.'

He lost his phone at least once a week.

'No I haven't, and that's not funny, James,' I said quietly. I retrieved the beer bottle from the bin and put it in Alicia's recycling box. 'Where's your spirit of adventure gone?'

'It's all used up in this bloody club, that's where it is. Stop bloody moaning, woman. Oh, come *on*, Cole – oh, you stupid twat.'

I picked up my plate and carried it to the sink where I ran the water until it was almost boiling. I held my hands under the water until I couldn't bear the heat any more. Outside was complete darkness; my beautiful garden was utterly veiled by the night. The foxes barked and screamed. I looked at James's reflection in the darkened window before me, and considered the tight layers of care we construct around ourselves, those nearest to us who supposedly protect and support us. I remembered the boy James once was; looked at him lounging in his chair, beer in hand, and I saw the man he had become. Not the man I had foreseen, somehow, a much looser cannon. And I saw the care I had for him, my fourth child almost, and then all around me I saw the cage I was in. But nowhere, nowhere – however hard I looked – could I see the care he had for me.

Stupid with sleep, I was woken at dawn by a tousled Alicia standing by my bed like a small wraith in her white nightie. James wasn't here, which meant he'd crashed out on the studio sofa yet again. I slept without James five nights out of seven these days. I blinked blearily.

'Climb in, baby.' I discovered a snoring Fred already curled up in the small of my back. I pulled back the duvet to let my daughter in, but she stayed standing where she was.

'There's a man in the garden, Mummy,' Alicia whispered. 'I saw him. He went like this.' She held a finger to her lips. 'You know, like "Shh".'

I sprang out of bed, and rushed to the window, my heart thumping. Alicia followed me.

'Get back, Lissie,' I ordered urgently. 'Get in bed now.'

I pulled the curtain back quickly and peered out into the gloom, but there was nothing.

'Are you sure you saw a man?'

'Yes,' Alicia insisted. 'He had sticky-up hair, like this.' She demonstrated with her own dark locks. 'And it was white.'

'You mean blond?'

'And he waved at me, and then I couldn't see him any more.'

'Get into bed. I'll be right back.'

I ran downstairs. In the half-light I made out a small flat object on the doormat. I picked it up. James's mobile phone.

I unlocked the front door, looking out at the break of light on the horizon, a pale sliver between dark sky and hill. The garden was empty, a quiet settled over it by dawn. I shut the door again, put the phone on the hall table and went back upstairs. I pulled the curtains tight and got back into bed between the two children, moving Freddie, who was sprawled in a diagonal across the whole mattress. Then I got out again and checked on Effie next door, invisible apart from a tuft of hair sticking out from under her duvet.

So James had lied, as I'd suspected he had, about being at Albion Manor. And Danny Callendar had been creeping around my garden whilst we slept. Nothing made sense, least of all the strange knot in my stomach.

Try as I might, I couldn't get back to sleep again.

UNIVERSITY, JANUARY 1992

I approach and ye vanish away,
I grasp you and ye are gone;

Longfellow

I was desperate to get back to college after the holidays; I was bored watching Christmas television with my parents, listening to my brother bang on about motorbikes and the assets of Sally from Accounts; eating endless turkey dinners. Worst of all, I was bored by my friends in the pub who suddenly all seemed terribly ordinary after Oxford. James came to see me just after New Year, and stayed in the spare room; chastely I didn't creep down to him in the night. We drove over to Chatsworth in his bashed-up old Renault, and drank tea, freezing out by the swans, and to my surprise, when he left, my mother said she'd really liked him. But I didn't care: I was just desperate to see Dalziel – and, if I was really honest, to get high. I missed the descent into calm; I craved the slow heavy hold the drug had over me as it entered my bloodstream. Our first Saturday back in January, Dalziel and I smoked yet another opium bong in my room. I'd been reading Longfellow all week and as we lay entwined on my narrow bed,

109

I told Dalziel of my dreams of the great white winged horse: that I had seen myself flying over the world on the mighty Pegasus. I stroked Dalziel's face and curled myself into him as he coaxed my visions on, until eventually my eyes fluttered closed against my will.

Already I loved Dalziel in a way I'd not known was possible. He made me feel alive and yet relaxed; protected yet exhilarated. It was like living on a knife-edge between reality and paradise. I adored him in a way I'd only experienced in the school playground aged five, perhaps, but never since. We didn't have sex; it wouldn't have seemed right, by now I was clear on that, and I knew that he didn't see me that way.

The next night I was asleep in my room when Dalziel woke me, his eyes shining strangely as I tried to focus on him.

'Number Eight,' Dalziel said, gazing at me as if in a trance.

'What?' I tried harder to focus through eyes seemingly sealed shut. He pushed my hair back from my face, gently he tucked a strand behind my ear as I tried to sit, cupping his hand behind my head. He'd taken something different from opium, that was apparent; what, though, I wasn't sure. As I hauled myself up on my elbows, he pushed something powdery into my mouth, something foul-tasting, holding a bottle of wine to my lips so I could swallow.

'Yuk,' I shuddered. 'What the hell was that? And what do you mean Number Eight?'

'Never mind. Put these on.' Dalziel chucked a pair of trousers on the bed. Blearily I pulled them on before he led me downstairs into the freezing night.

'It's so cold,' I moaned, shivering as he wrapped me in a fleecy jacket. I realised I was wearing skin-tight jodhpurs as he pushed me into the small cream sports car he hardly ever used. He drove us out into the Oxfordshire countryside, the lanes quickly turning black, no light apart from the moon dappling the road through the shrouded trees that leaned eerily towards us.

'You do ride, don't you?' he asked casually above the throb of the engine, taking a corner so fast and wide that the tyres screeched.

'Ride? As in horses?' I didn't really. I'd tried it briefly as a plump ten-year-old, bouncing round a paddock for a few weeks on a bad-tempered pony before it finally got so cross with me mauling its mouth it deposited me smartly in the nettles. But whatever Dalziel had given me now was beginning to buzz into my brain and suddenly I felt infallible, invincible, on top of the world. I could ride in the Grand National and no doubt I'd win.

'Definitely,' I nodded with enthusiasm. 'Love horses.'

We shot past a huge white gate and Dalziel swore softly, reversing so fast I felt breathless, too fast for me to read the sign above it, though I caught something about 'Royal' and 'Livery'. He parked the car practically in the thick hedge beside a great stone wall. His driving was atrocious at the best of times, but to be honest, I was surprised we'd made it at all.

Grabbing a rucksack from the back seat, Dalziel slung it on his back as we clambered over a stile into a muddy furrowed field. There, in the moonlight, a boy was waiting for us. Small, skinny-legged and sullen, his flat cap pulled right down over his face, he held two great horses by their bridles, one grey, one almost black in the moonlight.

'Wow!' Slowly I approached the grey, holding a tentative hand to his velvet nose. He snorted into the cold night air, his breath crystallising before him as he whickered softly. 'Beautiful. You're beautiful, aren't you, darling?'

In response he bumped my neck with his nose and I leaned into him for a moment, revelling in the warmth of him, the comforting pungent smell of horse, hay and dust.

The boy was nervous, though, checking his watch.

'You haven't got long,' he muttered to Dalziel, who kissed me quickly on the lips before giving me a leg-up into the saddle. It creaked satisfyingly as I sat down. I felt like my head was touching the sky and yet I felt tiny, tiny. I was one with the mighty horse, the power beneath me sending flashes of excitement down my spine. My teeth were chattering with cold and nervous energy.

'Ready, Rosie?' He mounted the other horse.

'Ready!'

Dalziel leaned down from the great black and handed something to the boy; money, perhaps, I thought. 'Meet us at the other end,' he said, and the boy nodded.

'Lot's field. I'll be there.'

'We can fly now, Rosie,' Dalziel drawled, his horse wheeling and snorting in the cold night air. And then he slipped a riding crop from his boot and gave my horse's flank a whack. 'Come on, Pegasus.'

'He's called Hooligan,' the boy called. 'Not Pegasus.'

The horse whinnied and bucked, and I clung on for dear life, charged with pure emotion, the adrenalin coursing through my veins to join whatever else I'd taken: the most amazing thing was that I didn't feel fear at all.

We galloped across the field, with only the moonlight to guide us; galloped until we were sweating and panting ourselves. The ground was flying beneath our feet, clods of earth thrown up in the first field, then through the next into the short January wheat as I clutched the horse's wiry mane, threading my fingers through the coarse hair, and leaned low over his neck. I thought I'd never felt anything so electrifying in my life as riding this horse beneath the stars.

Finally we stopped. Dalziel dismounted under a huge oak tree and held a hand out to me. The moon was a brilliant white orb in the black sky, the stars like a map of the world above us, and I was wide-eyed and childlike with the thrill of it all. I was the luckiest girl in the world.

As I slipped to the ground, legs shaking, the boy was climbing over the metal gate in the fence of the field we now stood in. An old Mini was parked on the other side, engine chugging.

'Are you ready?' Dalziel said to him as I stroked my horse's nose and whispered endearments.

'Are you sure about this?' the boy muttered. His accent was Northern, the vowels elongated. He looked nervous, his fists curled by his hips. 'I thought you was joking.'

'I gave you the money, didn't I?' Dalziel snapped. 'Hold him.'

I watched as the boy took Dalziel's mount by the bridle, crooning to the big horse. He wheeled him round, nudging the horse's shoulder to get him to move. Dalziel was delving in the rucksack.

'Number Eight, hey, Rosie!'

I racked my brain. 'What is Number Eight?'

'"You shall not steal" of course.' He pulled something long and black from the bag. 'And we have. Stolen well, my lovely.'

And I looked again and realised with a horrible squeeze in my belly that Dalziel was holding a rifle in both hands.

'What are you doing?' I stuttered. I suddenly didn't feel so high. The barrels of the gun glinted in the moonlight.

'Number Six too.'

'Mate,' the boy said, 'here, mate.' He stepped in front of the horse. 'I've changed my mind.'

'Good for you.' Dalziel was quite calm. He cocked the gun at the horse, at the boy. 'I haven't.'

'Dalziel.' My own horse was stamping now, walking backwards, pulling on the reins as if he recognised the danger. 'What are you doing? Put the gun down.'

'No, Rose. "You shall not murder", remember. And settle some scores as well.'

'What scores?' The leather was biting into my hand, chafing my palm.

'The horse ain't done nothing wrong, whatever your grievance with the boss.' The boy was small, but he pulled himself up to his full height. The black horse towered over him. 'Let him be.'

'What boss?' I was feeling increasingly frantic and sick. 'Dalziel, for Christ's sake.'

113

'Christ has nothing to do with it.' Dalziel levelled the rifle at the horse's great chest, the boy still between gun and beast. 'Step out of the way.'

'No.'

'Step out of the way.' I heard the tension in Dalziel's voice now. He gestured with the gun. 'Move – or I'll shoot you both.'

'Dalziel,' I stamped my foot desperately, 'put it down, now.'

'Or?'

'Or, or I'll –' I'd seen a phone box near the car – 'I'll call the police.'

Dalziel contemplated me for a moment, without ever moving the gun.

'I thought you were my compadre, Rose.'

'I am. But this is wrong, Dalziel. You know that. You don't need to kill him. He's so beautiful.' I edged closer. 'Please, Dalziel. Put the gun down.'

He stared at me as if he didn't know me. Then he raised the gun and fired in the air. Both animals shied, my horse rearing again so I was pulled almost right off the ground, my arm yanked almost from its socket, making me drop the reins as I did, my hand stinging wildly as the leather ripped the skin from my palm.

Dalziel levelled the gun at the boy's chest again; the boy pushed his cap back on his head.

'Go on then.' He stood firm, soothing the dark horse, murmuring sweet nothings to him.

For a moment Dalziel didn't move. None of us did. I held my breath, down on my knees in the mud. And then finally, he lowered the gun. Slowly I picked myself up off the ground.

'I was only joking,' he said, laughing a strangely tremulous laugh. 'You knew that, didn't you?'

'Some fucking joke.' The boy swore furiously and spat on the ground towards Dalziel's feet. Dalziel raised the gun again.

'You're mad, mate.' The boy stared at him. 'Fucking mad,' and then he vaulted onto the horse's back. He booted the

114

animal and they cantered off the way we'd come, stopping only to gather up the grey's reins, before kicking his horse on. I could feel the vibration of the great hooves through the damp ground as I tried to stand.

I'd rarely experienced so much relief as I felt in that moment, as I watched the horses turn to black dots beneath the moon.

Dalziel and I drove back to his sports car in silence. I couldn't trust myself to speak: I was still shaking, and when I got out of the Mini to change vehicles, I was sick into the hedge. Whatever he'd given me had worn off totally, and the opium I'd smoked earlier that evening had left me with a terrible headache.

As I straightened up, I read the glossy white sign above the gate. There was a flouncy black monogram that was hard to decipher, an H and an S; a J perhaps. I didn't care, frankly. I just wanted to go home now, to crawl into my bed and to sleep the whole nightmare off.

As we pulled up outside my college, Dalziel pushed his hair back from his face.

'Sorry,' he muttered, and I paused, my hand on the car door. I realised I'd never heard him apologise for anything before. 'I don't know what got into me.'

'What was that stuff you gave me?' I asked quietly.

'Just something one of the med students sold me.'

'What was it?' I was insistent. I was angry. I'd never really felt angry with him before, but now I was scared and ashamed.

'Methamphetamine.' It meant nothing to me. 'I thought it would be fun.'

I opened the door and staggered out. I just needed to lie down.

'It wasn't, though, was it?' he said sorrowfully. 'Rosie, I'm so fucking shit and useless sometimes.'

He looked bleak as he leaned over and pulled the door shut. Before I could reply, he was gone.

*   *   *

A week later it was my birthday, and I had dinner in a cheap Italian with Jen, Liz, James and a few others, glad to have some other friends, to be honest; aware I'd made little effort with them lately. Dalziel was still off the radar and I was finding it painful. I went to bed that night with James, a little tipsy, sad but resolute. The next morning, though, a huge bunch of white roses was waiting for me in the porters' lodge, the first flowers I'd ever received. The porter winked at me as I fumbled with the envelope.

'Let me take you out to apologise, dear Rose,' the little card said. 'Call me.' So I did, and we arranged to meet in The Turl.

Dalziel never drank in town; he said it didn't behove him to, as a third year. We met in the pub, where he gave me a first edition of Thomas de Quincey's *Confessions of an English Opium Eater*, inscribed from 'Your loving friend and fellow dreamer'.

'Rosie.' He kissed my cheek. 'You look lovely. Look, I've just got to meet a man about a dog in Jericho.'

'Dalziel—' I started to protest, but the glint in his eyes silenced me.

'I won't be long, I promise. Buy a drink. Buy three.' He gave me a twenty-pound note and was gone.

Clutching the book, I'd bought myself a gin and orange and was making my way back from the bar when a slender dark girl with peroxide hair blocked my way. She wore very high heels and a skin-tight black dress with a biker's leather jacket over it; in her perfect nose sat a tiny gold nose-stud. Yasmin – the girl who had been with Dalziel in the pub the first time I met him, and the girl I caught him with that night at the Oxford Union, I realised blushing now, in my first term. It seemed so long ago, but actually it was only a few weeks.

'I recognise you,' she announced. Her tone dripped with boredom but her stare was caustic as paint-stripper. 'You're this term's inamorata, aren't you?' Her accent was as refined as Dalziel's; it suggested years of easy privilege.

'Not really,' I mumbled, suddenly nervous. Next to her feline beauty, I was more carthorse than Joni Mitchell, in my leggings and beads. 'We're just friends, actually.'

'Really?' She raised a pencilled eyebrow. 'What are you reading?' She grabbed my book before I could stop her. 'Ha!' she said, flipping through it. 'One of *them*.'

'One of what?' I held my hand out for my book.

She shoved it at me. 'Tell me,' she scoffed, her red lipstick too thick over her luscious mouth, 'is he still banging on about his bloody Society X? So fucking infantile. I couldn't bear it any more.' She lit a Marlboro cigarette without offering me one; considered me for a moment before exhaling into my face. 'I tell you, he's damaged, that boy. I'd watch him, if I were you.'

'Why?' I shook my head, confused. 'What do you mean – damaged?'

'Positively curly-wurly cuckoo, my dear.' She tapped the side of her peroxided head with a red-varnished finger. Her nails were horribly chewed. 'Anyone who's sent away to school at five is fucked up, aren't they? Speciality of the upper classes, of course.'

I realised she was drunk.

'And even more fucked up if it's just so their dear mother can drink herself to death.'

'Five years old?' My heart went out to Dalziel. 'But – I thought his mother was alive?'

'His *third* stepmother might be, last time I looked.' She dragged hard again, scarlet staining the cigarette filter. 'Just about. But she hates him anyway. And then of course, there's Lucien and Charlie, not to mention Annabella and Rebecca, spoiled little cow.'

I had no idea what she was talking about. For some reason she was becoming agitated.

'Christ!' she expostulated with disgust. 'You want my advice –' I didn't but she was going to give it anyway – 'run a fucking mile.'

She threw the cigarette on the flagstone floor and ground it out with a pointy leather toe. Over her shoulder, I watched Dalziel walk into the snug on the other side of the pub.

'Nice to meet you,' I mumbled, banging against a paunchy drinker in my rush to get away.

'Just don't say no one warned you,' she shrieked after me.

I felt a little shaken as I joined Dalziel. 'Friend of yours?' I asked him as the girl provocatively wrapped her arms around a short black guy, watching us the whole time.

'I've known her for years,' was all Dalziel would say, and soon after that we left. But I saw him glance back as the street door closed behind us. For the first time since I'd known him, he looked visibly upset, his pale face flushed with colour. Worse than upset, in fact. He looked shaken to the core.

Chapter Seven

GLOUCESTERSHIRE, MARCH 2008

I was due at the *Chronicle* the next day, but I was so tired I couldn't concentrate, and I was conscious I was stalling Tina about the Kattan piece. Consciously I'd made the decision to have nothing to do with him, but I was aware that deep down I still felt more allegiance to Xav than the *Chronicle*, and that maybe I owed it to him too. And it was eating away at me; in honesty I was loath to give up the story entirely; it just wasn't in my professional nature and I thought Xav was right: there was definitely something going on. I thought of the man being dropped onto the gravel; the stacks of petrol canisters, the Islamic tattoos; the unmitigated tension. I made a few surreptitious calls to a few contacts from the old days: Louise at the Press Association, Guy at Reuters, just putting out feelers on the family; and then I wrote a review of the Cheltenham Players' rendition of *A Little Night Music* (truly dreadful, but the refreshments had been cracking, so I wrote a lot about them).

I stopped at the upholsterers on the way to collect the twins; they were re-covering our old divan with an incredibly expensive red velvet that James had left over from the Paris VIP room. As I entered the dark little shop, the quaint bell above the door jangled.

'Oh, Mrs Miller.' The salesgirl seemed slightly flustered as she emerged from her lair of fabric rolls and ribbons.

'Is it ready?' I smiled expectantly.

'Actually we haven't been able to finish the order yet because I couldn't process the credit card.' She busied herself refolding a bundle of golden silk. 'Mr Ballantine's such a terrible stickler, I'm afraid. Shall we just check we have the right details?'

Flummoxed, I gave her the card. It failed again. I found another one; to both our relief, this one worked. I'd have to remind James to top up the account. He was so slap-dash about money.

As I pulled up in the drive with the twins, dance music throbbed incongruously from the sedate old house, the naked rose tree creeping carefully between the rattling windows. In the kitchen McCready was hiding behind the ironing board, the cat hunched at her feet; her tracksuit a bright vermilion today, matching the thread veins in her apple cheeks.

'Awful lot of swearing going on,' was all she would say, her mouth a tight line. She took the twins out into the garden as I began to lug the Hoover upstairs, pausing in the hall as I heard raised voices from the sitting room. It was Liam and James, I realised, though it was hard to decipher the conversation over the beat of the music. I was about to open the door when Liam said, 'Don't fucking tell her.' I heard something else angry and incoherent, then I was sure he said, 'I'm warning you.'

Fingers on the door handle, my stomach rolled queasily.

James replied, but I couldn't hear him properly. After a few minutes, all I'd made out were James saying, '. . . too much money' and, '. . . asking for trouble, mate.'

I breezed into the room. James was facing the door and saw me first, but Liam had his broad back to me and he jumped when I spoke.

'Coffee, anyone?'

120

'God, you scared me,' Liam said guiltily as I went to kiss him. 'I'd love one, sweetheart.' He was particularly pasty-looking this afternoon, a great bear of a man wearing a red checked shirt that did nothing for his freckly complexion.

'Late night?'

'He's been shagging that bird all night,' James teased, who in comparison actually looked rested for once.

'Which bird? The lovely Star?'

'Who else?' James said, a flicker of something passing over his face. Jealousy? I wondered, eyeing him.

'Yeah,' Liam flushed. 'But not all night. Only till about four.'

'Oh, only four? You slacker. God, those were the days, eh?' I looked at my husband, but he didn't meet my eye. Our sex life was non-existent since the twins.

'He's got it bad,' James said, turning the music off. 'You know, I'm not sure about that last track, Liam. It hasn't got the – I dunno – the verve of the first few. What did Noel have to say?'

'He quite likes it. Don't love it, though.' Liam looked rueful. 'I think we all know it's not quite there yet.'

'Let's take it in the studio and have a tinker.'

'I wasn't expecting to see you today,' I said to Liam as he picked up his rucksack.

'Just come up to sign some paperwork before my trip.' James was nonchalant. 'Come and have a listen if you fancy it.'

'I'd hate nothing more, my darling,' I joked. 'Give me Fleetwood Mac any day.'

No one laughed.

When I took them coffee ten minutes later, the tension between them appeared to have diffused; they were happily hunched over the computer together, fiddling with the bass line.

'I dunno,' I said, 'I thought when you got this successful, I'd stop being a studio widow.'

Only Liam looked up. 'You know us, Rosie. Boys and their

121

toys.' He was joking with me, but he still seemed remarkably uneasy.

'By the way, James—'

He didn't look at me as I passed him the sugar. 'Yeah?'

'Your phone. It was dropped off by Kattan's driver, wasn't it?'

'Oh.' Now he did look up. 'Yeah.'

'So you *were* up there?' I was truly puzzled.

'Yeah. Sorry. It totally slipped my mind. I went to talk to Kattan about the club.'

'And?'

I saw Liam shoot James a look.

'And there's a chance he might invest. You knew that. A chance. Quite slim, though. He's got some funny ideas, that guy.'

'Oh?' I was curious. 'Like what?'

'Rosie,' James widened his eyes at me, 'please. We've got to get on. Talk about it later, yeah?'

The bass kicked in again, and I shut the door firmly behind me before I was deafened. But as I drove to collect Alicia, I couldn't free my mind of the feeling they'd been arguing about something serious. I hoped Liam hadn't messed up financially again; it had happened in the past when the label nearly went bust. At least it might explain James's recent stress. But I still didn't know why he'd lied about being up at the manor. A worm of discomfort curled into my gut.

At 5 a.m. the phone woke me.

'Yes?' I mumbled into the receiver, suddenly terrified. Despite all my years as a reporter, early morning and late night calls always boded badly for me. Since the implosion of Society X it only made me think of fatal news; more recently, of my father's heart attack.

'Morning, Rose.'

'Who's that?' My brain slowly cranked into life.

'It's Louise at the PA. Sorry to wake you,' she sounded impatient, 'but you did say to call you if I got any information.'

'Yes, of course.' I fumbled for my watch to check the time. 'What is it?'

'Just came through. There's been a death up at that house you were so interested in.'

'Albion Manor?' I sat up in bed.

'You got it. Sounds like something out of Agatha Christie, doesn't it? Body in the library and all that kind of thing.'

'Fuck.' Blearily I tried to compute what she was saying. I heard her keyboard rattle as apprehension crept up my spine. 'Who . . .' I cleared my throat, 'who's dead?'

'Young male. No name.' There was the rattle of the computer again. 'Early-to-mid thirties, no other details yet.'

'Right . . .' Fingers of fear clutched my neck. 'God. Foul play, presumably?'

'Definitely sounds dodgy. Not sure what the coup is yet. If I hear more, I'll let you know. Just wanted to give you the heads-up.'

'Cheers, Louise. I really appreciate it.'

I tried to ignore the tightness in my chest, easing myself over sleeping children, pulling my cardigan on to go to find James. He was snoring on the studio sofa, a half-empty bottle of Jack Daniel's on the floor, headphones beside it and an ashtray overflowing with spliff ends. No wonder he was having the nightmares again.

'James.' I shook him. 'James, I need to pop out.'

'What?' He was groggy, hardly awake, his eyes closing again immediately.

'Can you come into the house, please, James?' I shook him gently. 'I need you to listen out for the children. I've got to go out. Breaking news.'

I wanted to go before I had to explain, and dashed from the room as he started to sit up properly. 'The kids won't wake yet,

I'm sure. I'll be back,' I called, as I heard him grumbling behind me. 'Freddie's milk is in the fridge if he does, though. You'll have to warm it up in the microwave. Twenty-five seconds. Don't nuke it.'

I pulled on my boots and fleece and ran to the car. I wasn't sure how I would explain my presence; I wasn't even sure why I was going, but going I was. At this moment my main concern was who the hell was dead.

Dawn was breaking over the empty brown fields as I drove through the lanes, suffusing the sky with an unearthly light. A small brown rabbit froze between hedgerows as I braked just in time. Rounding the bend in the drive, I saw two police cars and an ambulance parked at the foot of the front steps. The front door was ajar, a uniformed PC standing in the porch. I parked my car by the stable block and pulled on my woolly hat and gloves.

'No press, love.' The policeman stepped down a few stairs and blocked my path, his breath crystallising in the dawn air. It was absolutely freezing.

'I'm not press, I'm a friend of the family. Who's dead?'

'I'm sure I recognise you.' He cocked a sandy eyebrow at me. His nose was red and dripping from the cold.

'I think my daughter goes to school with your son.' I smiled as becomingly as was possible at 5.30 a.m. 'Alicia Miller?'

'St Erth's? That might be it,' he said comfortably. 'Good school, that.'

'So . . .' I took a hopeful step round him.

'You still can't go in.' He held an arm out. 'The pathologist is doing his stuff.'

'Who's dead?' I repeated urgently. A cockerel was crowing somewhere insistently, over and over again.

'Not for me to say. No official identification as yet.' He was implacable.

I was about to start wheedling when the front door was flung wide. A young woman stood silhouetted on the top step.

Maya Kattan, at last.

She was wearing what looked like black silk pyjamas and was once again wild-eyed and dishevelled. Her face was as tear-streaked as the first time I'd seen her, and she staggered where she stood, as if it was too much effort to keep upright. And then she moved down the stairs in her bare feet, and she began to run. She ran straight past me, near enough for me to smell her musky perfume. I called her name but she didn't even hesitate, just kept going right past me towards the side of the house, across the gravel, despite her lack of shoes.

As I wavered there, two paramedics emerged from the house, stretchering a body, totally covered, down the stairs.

The wind sighed through the blossom trees as a human voice raised to join it in a chilling scream. I turned to see Maya falling, sprawling on the gravel, and I began to run towards her myself, driven by instinct, by her obvious pain – but someone else had materialised beside her. He was there, leaning down to pick her up, and I slowed, unsure what to do, filled with a sudden emotion I couldn't place.

The stretcher was down the stairs now, being lifted into the ambulance. I glanced back to Maya and I was halted by the look on Danny's face; the hairs went up on my arms as I read the expression of tenderness. I watched the way she placed her hand in his, rather like a child would. She let him pull her up, and he leaned down and said something to her, pushing the glossy black curtain of hair behind her ear very gently. I noticed that her hands were intricately tattooed with henna as she stood alone now and shook her head at something Danny said, and began to walk away, round the back of the house.

I stepped in her direction but this time it was Danny who blocked my way.

'I don't know why I'm not surprised to see you here,' he said, the Scottish drawl weary. He looked like he hadn't slept, his sun-bleached hair dishevelled, his black windbreaker zipped up to his unshaven chin. 'You're like a bad penny.'

'I got a call,' I said lamely. 'I thought perhaps I could help.'

Maya Kattan had vanished as the doors of the ambulance slammed shut behind us.

'It's a bit late for help, I'd say, wouldn't you?'

From somewhere came an almighty revving of a powerful engine. Danny glanced round and then back at me. 'I think you should go, doll. Go back to where you stay. Now. Before there's any more trouble.'

We locked eyes.

'This, Rose Miller, this is not a happy family to be around.'

'Who is that?' I gestured to the ambulance. 'Who's dead?'

'Maya's boyfriend, Nadif.'

'Oh God,' I said, but felt a surge of inexplicable relief. 'Boyfriend? The one her father called a "heart-breaker"?'

'When was that?' Danny Callendar looked down at me.

'The other night,' I said. 'He said she'd gone walkabout because she was miserable.'

'I see.' He was harder to read than Proust, this man. 'Like I said, not a happy family.'

'Was he –' I touched the welts on my neck unconsciously – 'Was it the man from the other day? The black guy?'

'Yeah, the Somalian. I wouldn't be too sad,' Danny said coldly, and fear licked me again. 'He was bad news all round.'

'How did he die?' I began to ask, and then Maya's car tore round the corner, skidding on the gravel, heading towards the fountain in the middle of the circular lawn.

'Christ, she's going to hit it!' I gasped, but Maya righted the wheel just in time, the back end of her Porsche swinging across the grass, tyres churning up the immaculate turf before she accelerated down the drive. A sleek black vehicle rounded the bend now, a Mercedes, heading straight towards her.

The cars were going to meet head-on.

I closed my eyes and waited for the crash – but it never came. The Porsche was almost in the hedge as Maya threw herself out of the vehicle.

'You murderer,' she screamed. 'You fucking murderer. You will stop at nothing, will you?' She kicked the tyre of the now stationary Mercedes with a bare foot, over and over again. She kicked it like a woman possessed.

Hadi Kattan stepped out of the car. 'Maya,' he said, extending his arms towards her. 'Please, Maya. I'm so sorry.'

'Get the fuck away from me,' she screamed. Blood was streaming down her foot. 'I never want to see you again,' and she stood very close to her father and stared at him. 'You just couldn't let me have my happiness, could you?'

'Maya lal,' he implored. 'Don't.'

He said something in Arabic. She considered him for a short moment and then she spat right in his face.

For a moment I thought he might hit her, but his arms remained by his side. Maya glared at him and then she turned and ran back to the Porsche. The gravel spun and flicked behind her, making the horses in the stable whinny in terror, and then she was gone.

'Callendar,' Kattan called. His tone was flat and hard as steel as he wiped the spittle off with a white handkerchief. 'Take the car up to the house. Now.'

Deftly Danny caught the key Kattan threw at him and then he went to obey.

I felt a surge of nervous energy as Hadi Kattan walked towards me. He crossed the small lawn that housed the fountain, flattening the tiny white crocuses scattered throughout the grass. For the first time I saw something in his face that scared me.

'What are you doing here, Mrs Miller?' he asked. He looked older than he had the other night, less noble, his face hawk-like in the early light.

I should have made good my escape while I could. I heard the cock crow a final time.

'Oh, Mr Kattan. I – I heard the bad news and—'

'I don't think you have been totally honest with me,' he interrupted quietly. 'Is there something you'd like to tell me, perhaps?'

My stomach lurched. 'Like what?' I smiled shakily. 'I don't have any secrets, Mr Kattan. Not proper ones.'

He stared at me until I wanted to hide my face like my children did when they thought I couldn't see them.

'But your husband told me, my dear.'

Betrayed by my own husband? My mind scrabbled like a rat in a trap.

'You are a writer, aren't you?' he persisted.

In the background, the ambulance started up.

'A writer?' I stalled. 'I write a few shopping lists, I know that much.'

'Oh, come on, Rose,' Kattan's voice was like a blade coated in honey. 'You write for that local rag, the *Chronicle*.'

Relief swept through my body until my knees actually felt like cotton wool.

'Oh, yes,' I said, and I actually laughed. 'I do. I'm sorry, I thought you knew. That's not a secret.'

'But you do have one, don't you, my dear Rose? A secret you have kept hidden as best you can.'

'What?' My legs still felt wobbly.

'I don't want you up here again, you understand?' Kattan took my arm and walked me towards my car. 'You have disappointed me.'

'Really?' I was confused, and his grip was firm. 'Why?'

'I don't want you anywhere near my daughter.'

'But why?' I protested.

'Listen to me, Mrs Rose Miller,' his face was grim, 'I know all about your sordid past. And let me tell you, not everyone thinks that blasphemy is a joke.'

'Blasphemy?' My skin was prickling. 'What do you mean?'

'You are an intelligent woman, I'm sure you can work it out. Some even call it a sin, you know. Whatever god you follow. Don't come here again, and please, don't cross me.' His hooded eyes were absolutely unreadable. He looked suddenly reptilian to me. 'It really would not be wise.'

UNIVERSITY, FEBRUARY 1992

*You shall not covet your neighbour's house; you shall not covet
your neighbour's wife, nor his male servant, nor his female
servant, nor his ox, nor his donkey, nor anything that is your
neighbour's.*

Bible, Exodus 20:17

Since the *Post* article about the defecating in the cathedral, there
had been some mutterings amongst the students that Dalziel's
exploits were going too far. To silence his critics, he organised
another Society X soirée on Valentine's Night, this time to celebrate the tenth commandment, the one about coveting stuff.
Only he asked Lena and James to help him arrange the party,
and not me. I wasn't sure what I was meant to have done wrong,
but I had a feeling it was something to do with the girl in the
pub. Dalziel had seemed so upset that evening when we left, and
even more so that I'd witnessed it. When I'd asked him later why
she'd been so cross, he simply cut me off mid-flow and refused
to talk about it again.

The anti-religion aspect of the party meant nothing to me; I
knew now it was just an excuse – Dalziel had admitted as much

130

– and I was unsure whether he'd put pen to paper for his dissertation the whole time I'd known him. And I wasn't sure how much I was looking forward to the night. Frankly, Dalziel's mood was scaring me a little since the Pegasus incident. He seemed increasingly desperate and wild, only calm really when we were in our opium trance.

I realised I was forgiven when he arrived at my room the night before the party. We got high together, and I was allowed to invite Jen as a special honour, and this time the evening was funny, people wore silly masks and came with real pigs and lambs. Lena and James went one better and stole a donkey from the sanctuary out by Woodstock. Dalziel had the bench from one neighbour's garden removed and put it in the neighbour's garden on the other side, and then rang the police to offer an eye-witness account. An extremely unamused WPC came to take a statement about what had occurred. When she left, Dalziel shut the front door triumphantly and turned to the inebriated crowd.

'Number Nine. *"You shall not bear false witness against your neighbour"*,' he crowed, and everybody whooped and clapped. It seemed so harmless and silly that the dramatic events of that January night melted into a distant memory. I watched him intently as he spoke; when I looked up, James was watching me. We'd been spending more time together as a group again in the past few weeks and it was a strange triangle Dalziel, James and I created, one that Lena sometimes barged into as well, though more and more often she was so wasted she was in her own world. James too was drinking all the time, Dalziel constantly plying him with whiskey and a new type of dope they called skunk, so strong it was hallucinogenic. James and I had stopped connecting properly a while ago, although we had never officially called it all off.

'I am the ultimate iconoclast,' Dalziel declared that night, standing in front of a print of the hideous green Grünewald Christ on the cross, pain and suffering seeping from every pore.

His eyes glittering dangerously, Dalziel held up a knife and slashed Jesus again and again.

'The ultimate twat aristocrat, doesn't he mean? Thinks he's fucking God,' someone muttered. 'Christ, this is embarrassing.'

'Perhaps God's fucking him – who can tell with this lot?' a female voice whispered back. 'What next, thou shalt definitely shag a sheep?'

Turning sharply, I recognised the female editor of the rival student paper, the *New Student*, standing behind me. A jolly Brummie with one long eyebrow and too many freckles, she winked at me.

'I thought von Bismarck's lot were bad, but this is bloody stupid,' she murmured to her companion. 'Someone ought to tell him this is real life, not fucking Brideshead Regurgitated.'

'He's certainly a vile body though.'

They both sniggered, and I felt a flush creep all over me. Was it for my benefit? I didn't know, but it was the first time I'd heard anyone speak out against Dalziel, and I realised I felt physically shocked, which later seemed naïve. I didn't know whether to say something to them – or what I would have said if I'd dared speak – but Dalziel was talking again now.

He turned back from the poster and toasted the room, unaware of his critics. 'Here's to nihilism,' he crowed, and we toasted him back – even the editor and her crony, with their cans of Stella.

People started pogoing to The Undertones' 'Teenage Kicks'; I could see that Jen was having fun, as she danced with Brian, the boy with the bullet head. I shuddered, remembering the last time I'd seen him – between Huriyyah's legs. Then Lena began an excruciating 'Dance of the Seven Veils' striptease, much to everyone's hilarity – and quite quickly I stopped enjoying myself altogether. Lena was more and more out of control these days, since she and Dalziel had stopped the pretence of dating. She seemed beyond reach.

Dalziel found me lingering in the corner, wondering whether

to leave. He kissed the top of my head lightly. 'Two birds with one stone, and another magnificent success,' he drawled. 'I just can't help myself.'

I smiled weakly. 'Congratulations.'

'Why don't you go upstairs?' he murmured. 'It's specially for you, you know.'

But suddenly I didn't believe him. Nothing was for me, it was all a charade, and I was stunned by a sudden flash before my eyes: as if I'd just experienced the beginning of the edifice crumbling and felt the urge to flee before it collapsed on me. I kept seeing the gun levelled at the horse's great chest; at the skinny little groom. I didn't understand what motivated Dalziel any more, I realised that now.

Soon after that the dark boy appeared and Dalziel vanished with him, so I went upstairs and had a pipe in the smoking-den that had been created in a bedroom, trying to curb my inexplicable jealousy. Dalziel would say it was so pedestrian – envy. But the bullet-headed boy had abandoned Jen now and had persuaded a ratty girl with train-track braces to give him a blow-job in the corner, and she was so drunk she was alternating it with being sick, so I left and went home with James, utterly confused.

That night James and I had strange disjointed sex for the first time in weeks, and it was like being out of body. I had felt so strongly about him at first, but now I watched us from the ceiling dispassionately, simply craving a return to my own private and romantic land, a land free of Society X's taint.

THE *NEW STUDENT* – FEBRUARY 1992

What fuels Dalziel St John's arrogant belief that his pathetic Society X holds any sort of allure for those with half a brain? We all know that Oxford is rife with societies, mostly for the rich and stupid. Piers Gaveston has celebrated actor Hugh Grant looking pretty in leopard-skin and God only knows what those boys got up to (anyone there, God?). The Bullingdon Club is of course for those male students with more money than sense – £1200 a tailcoat, people? Ex-chancellor Nigel Lawson's daughter Nigella even bravely tackled Sedan Chair Croquet in the Dangerous Sports Club (ooh, the danger). But the Honourable Mr St John prides himself in letting women into his marvellous society as well – how very modern – although I have a sneaking suspicion there is a very specific reason for this quaint anomaly. Yawn.

Having attended a meeting of the so-called 'Secret Society' the other night, I can safely say I was far from impressed. The evening was hardly challenging. Although St John chooses to surround himself with a group of easily-pleased suburban acolytes who apparently do whatever he suggests, this, I should point out, does not equate power. It just means he's choosing the weak. Suicidal ex-lesbians, drippy English students and music geeks who can't play a note are not the new élite, I fear.

Nor is it 'iconoclastic' to slash cheap pictures of Christ; St John calls it 'nihilism', I call it embarrassing. And as for the celebration of stealing farm animals, there's something deeply alarming in this practice. Far be it from me to suggest bestiality but really . . .

I would suggest that the Honourable St John take a leaf out of Daddy's book and keep his antics to the golf course. We have had one upper-class tragedy in recent years to tarnish the university's reputation: we don't need another one.

N.B. Can anyone actually remember a single important change brought in for the good of the nation by the senior St John, our current Home Secretary and at present, Britain's most powerful man? Answers on a postage stamp, please . . .

Chapter Eight

GLOUCESTERSHIRE, MARCH 2008

The day after Maya's boyfriend died at Albion Manor, my mother came to collect the children for the weekend and James flew out to Vietnam. I'd tried one final time to suggest that I might accompany him – my mother had even offered to babysit for the whole week – but James still rejected the idea. He was going earlier than originally planned, to 'see a man about some marble', as he put it, for his luxury chill-out room and for a meeting in Saigon. The reopening of Revolver in London was looming and he was determined that it was exactly what Britain needed. 'People need cheering up right now,' he said simply, and I had felt some affection for his black-and-white view of life; his optimism in frivolity.

The affection soon vanished on the way to the airport when I finally told James about Xavier and the Kattan story. I'd been nervous about mentioning it, but even I was shocked by the strength of his disapprobation.

'I can't fucking believe you never said anything.' James slammed his fist against his window as we joined the M4. My thoughts were speeding so fast I could hardly untangle them quickly enough to defend myself.

'But I tried to tell you days ago that Xav had called me. It's just – well, you never listen.'

James's face was deathly pale, the shadows huge under his eyes. 'You what?' His tone was quiet and menacing. I hadn't heard that tone for a while.

I clutched the wheel tighter. 'You weren't interested,' I said as blithely as I could, overtaking a caravan that rocked dangerously. 'And why would it have been such a bad idea anyway?'

'You know the answer to that, don't you, Rose?' His top lip had gone rigid as it always did in anger. 'Oh, it all makes sense now. For fuck's sake.'

'It's fascinating. He's fascinating. I've told Xav no, but you know, James, I've got a feeling, a sense, something big's happening out there.' I was gabbling with nerves. 'He's got his daughter practically a – a prisoner in that monstrous house, her boyfriend's dead, it's practically open murder. It's like bloody Jane Eyre up there, women locked in the attic, and you know, I think Xav might be right about the al-Qaeda connection.'

An Aston Martin tore up behind me and flashed its lights. 'Bloody idiot,' I muttered, but refused to budge.

'Rose,' James looked in the mirror, 'move over.'

'I won't be bullied by some stupid git, J. I'm doing ninety.'

The Aston inched nearer and flashed again.

Reluctantly I pulled into the middle lane. 'God knows what he's up to, or who is coming and going there. There's chemicals piled everywhere and that bloke Zack, who works for him, is a nutter. He's even got the Islam flag tattooed on his arm.'

I heard myself, too late. I thought of the terrible government adverts. I pushed the thought resolutely away.

'Hadi Kattan? Are you serious? Don't be so fucking stupid,' James snapped. 'Your imagination's running away with you. He's just a brilliant businessman. A wheeler and dealer maybe. Not a terrorist.'

'But you don't know anything about him, James,' I said. 'Just because you had a drink with him once and he asked you to shoot some birds, you think he's your best mate. And you told him about bloody X, didn't you? About Oxford? I mean, why would you do that?'

'I didn't.' James looked at me like I was mad. 'Don't be stupid.'

'He seemed to know about it.'

'How could Kattan possibly know about Society X?'

'He said something about blasphemy. He said something about – about you telling him stuff.'

'Rubbish. Why in God's name would I mention X? I was hoping he was going to give me money for the club. It'd be madness to tell him anything about our bloody sordid past.'

'He insinuated it.' I was sure Kattan had.

'Well you're wrong. And you're playing with bloody fire again, Rose.'

'Why? Look at it, J. Look at the facts. Henchmen, whispering, a politicised son who hasn't shown up yet. A daughter who's demonstrating for Islamic rights. And now her boyfriend is dead too. I mean, what else do you want?' Stubbornly I stared at the unfurling road. 'And why shouldn't I do the research, if I want to?'

'Because you agreed.'

'I didn't agree. Not really. I just said I'd give it a rest for a while. While the kids are small.'

'They're still small.'

'Oh, you've noticed, have you?'

'What's that supposed to mean?'

'It means, James –' *in for a penny, in for a pound* – 'that most of the time you hardly notice the kids, full stop.'

'That's bollocks.'

'It isn't bollocks, and you know it. You don't notice any of us these days, you're so caught up all the time.'

'I'm making money for the family.' This was his usual tactic. 'I'm earning our keep.'

'You're not making money drinking into the small hours and never coming to bed. You're not making money getting fucked and playing X-box with Liam, or snorting coke all night in London, pretending to make music with twatty popstars.'

'I'm not. I don't,' he muttered. His tone changed; he looked just like one of the children when they knew they'd done something wrong. 'Hardly ever.'

'Oh, come on, J. You promised to knock it on the head when we came here, but it's just got worse and worse. You're even having the bloody nightmares again. And you're arguing with Liam. Has he messed up again? You need to tell me. I can help.'

'No. It's all fine.' He stared out of the window at a field of seated cows. 'Must be going to rain.'

'James!'

'I've just . . . I've been really stressed with work,' he mumbled. 'This threat of recession isn't great for anyone. It'll calm down again, I promise.'

'Look, you know I love spending time with the kids – of course I do. But, you know . . .' There were sudden tears in my eyes. I blinked them away furiously. 'You didn't even want me to drop you at the airport today.'

'I just didn't want you to be bothered with it,' he mumbled uncomfortably.

I took another deep breath. 'I'm lonely, J.'

This would be the moment he turned to me and said, oh God, I'm sorry, darling, I love you so much, it'll be like it used to, I know I never see you, speak to you, pay you any attention, want to make love to you or even just cuddle you.

'So you thought you'd get all cosy with bloody Xavier again,' he snarled.

'Don't shout at me, please, James.'

'I'm not shouting,' he shouted.

There was a long pause.

'Sorry,' he said eventually. I could tell from his slumped bearing that he felt ashamed. 'I just – I thought you'd left all that behind you. You write your stuff for the *Chronicle*. Isn't that enough?'

I thought of Edna's marrows and smiled wryly. 'I suppose it's a bit like you not doing Revolver or the label but opening a disco in Burford. You might enjoy it, but it wouldn't be the same buzz.'

'I suppose.'

I ploughed on. 'The twins are in nursery every morning now. I just . . . Xav rang me, and I thought – I don't know – I just wanted to use my brain again, I suppose. And it's important people know the truth. That it's reported right.'

'You're addicted, you mean. You replaced one addiction with another.'

'I didn't.' But his words made me start. I *was* addicted – he was right – only I wasn't going to admit it now. 'I'm not really. I just miss it sometimes.'

'But,' James put his hand on mine. He touched me so infrequently these days the contact was almost a shock. 'But you know what happened last time.'

'Yes I know. But it was a one-off. I was unlucky.'

'And before that? You were nearly bloody killed in LA.'

I'd been following the Vice Squad out there; I was in the wrong place at the wrong time during a gangland shoot-out. A police officer and a fifteen-year-old boy had been killed, the boy lying in a pool of his own blood whilst his mother sobbed piteously, cradling his head in her lap.

'You're not doing it, Rose.'

I slid my hand away. 'What?'

'Don't be fucking obtuse. You're not doing the piece on Kattan for either the *Chronicle* or Xavier bloody Smith, and that's that.'

The slip-road to Heathrow was coming up.

'Well, I'm not going to, you're quite right. I'd decided not to already. But actually, I don't think,' carefully I indicated left, 'I don't think it's up to you.'

James left to catch his plane without so much as a backwards glance, without giving me a kiss or even saying goodbye.

I sat outside the airport in the fumes and endless stream of vehicles, the airport I flew from at least once a month in the old days, and I put my head in my hands and cried.

I cried for my new confusion. I cried for my children and the inadequate mother I often felt I was, and my guilt at wanting other things, old things, like work and the buzz that used to be the career I had loved.

And most of all I cried with relief that my husband had gone.

When I pulled away from the airport, heading not for home but for London, so did another vehicle, tight on my wheels, though I didn't know it at the time.

UNIVERSITY, MARCH 1992

I am reckless what I do to spite the world.

Macbeth, Shakespeare

After the scathing article about his exploits appeared in the *New Student*, Dalziel vanished. James said he'd been incandescent with rage; none of us was sure where he'd gone. For the first time this term, though, I felt relieved Dalziel wasn't in town. My own faith in him was less solid than before; I sensed he was walking a tight-rope between fun and hysteria, increasingly tense when we did meet. And crucially, I'd finally admitted I was in a spot of trouble myself. My new hobby was fast becoming an addiction. I'd even started to seek out the dealer when Dalziel was not around, and I recognised that it was a horribly slippery slope. I was actually looking forward to the oncoming Easter holidays so I could flee home to my parents. I needed to digest the crazy ride I'd been on this term; my tutors were not pleased and I knew I was already slipping behind with my studies. I needed some normality.

When Dalziel did return to Oxford a week later, good humour apparently restored, he asked us to meet, dressed for dinner. The esoteric elite, as he called us with a smirk, met in the pub nearest the city's grandest hotel, at 7.06 p.m. on Friday 13 March. Much later I discovered that he'd figured it was also 6.66 o'clock – the number of the beast.

James, Lena and I perched at the bar, and waited for the others to arrive. Dalziel and Brian walked in some time later, Brian sweaty and uncomfortable in his monkey suit, Dalziel elegant and at ease in his tuxedo, though his eyes were glittering rather manically and his pallor was obvious.

'Sorry I'm late,' he said, his pupils like pins. 'Family business.' He threw a car key on the table. His knuckles were grazed, I noticed, and there was a tiny spot of blood on his otherwise pristine cuff. 'And a challenge to meet.'

Lena gave a knowing smile. 'You did it then.'

Dalziel held a long finger to her lips. 'Shhh.'

He was on good form at first, cracking jokes and stroking us all, physically and metaphorically, telling us how pleased he was to see us. I, on the other hand, was not. Despite my new resolve, I'd spent the night before at his house smoking with him until we'd passed out again in the early hours; I'd woken irritable and headachey and telling myself this had to stop soon. But when Dalziel beckoned me over in the pub and kissed me full on the lips, my fears dissolved.

He bought a round of sambuca and continued to massage our egos, asking us questions about our courses, our plans for the holidays. Later I remembered that James was cross because Dalziel was paying me so much attention, and Lena too was soon sulking, her oddly squashed face all tight and annoyed, her fingers tapping incessantly on the table.

An ambulance screamed by, closely followed by a police car, sirens blaring. Dalziel stared out of the window at them.

'Big dramas, apparently.' The flat-faced barmaid passed a pint over to an elderly regular, her raisin eyes alight with gossip. 'Girl was in a car smash earlier over on the bridge. Hit and run, Michael said.'

142

Dalziel drained his glass and sent it sliding down the table. It would have fallen if James hadn't caught it. The blue of the police-car light was reflected eerily in his eyes as he turned back.

'One more?' Dalziel suggested, pulling a sheaf of notes out. We happily acquiesced, in no rush to leave the comfort of the pub. But now Dalziel's good mood vanished; he became increasingly distracted, edgy and distant. When I asked if he was all right he smiled and said he was just tired; but he kept checking his watch.

The bar was warm and comfortable with its smoky hop-smelling fug; it seemed a shame to leave. But we drank a final shot of sambuca and then Dalziel handed James a parcel and an envelope that he brought out from his inside pocket.

'This is for you, James. Don't open the parcel until you need to.'

'And how will I know when that is?'

'You'll just know. You can open the envelope when I leave.'

James shrugged. 'OK. You're the boss.'

I must have smiled inadvertently because James shot me a filthy look.

'Where are you going?' Lena moaned.

'I have things to set up,' Dalziel said enigmatically. 'I'll see you all very soon.' Then he kissed the top of my head and inclined his head to Brian, who leaped to his feet like an uncoordinated puppy and scampered after him. 'We've got work to do.' They vanished.

'You're very cosy,' James commented sourly.

'Don't be silly.' I smiled wanly at him. The truth was I was exhausted, hardly eating, hardly working right now.

'Better get going, I suppose.' James fiddled with the envelope. He looked vaguely menacing and rather handsome in his black polo-neck and tight black jeans, but his normally open face was taut and furrowed with worry. 'I wish I knew what Dalziel was up to tonight,' he muttered, tearing open the envelope. 'He's gone a bit weird, don't you think?'

Lena returned from the loo. 'He's settling debts,' she drawled, perusing the note. Her eyes were pinned now as Dalziel's had been earlier: her pupils tiny and black. She smelled of sick and Fracas perfume.

'What kind of debts?' James said. 'God, he'll be all night.'

'See the stolen chariot, dear boy,' Lena mocked, dangling the car key on her black-nailed finger. 'Guess whose it is?'

'How the fuck should I know, Lena?' James said. 'Why don't you enlighten us?'

'Actually,' Lena tapped the side of her nose, the left nostril of which was blood-encrusted, 'that's for us to know and you to find out.'

James laughed drily. 'You've got no idea, have you?'

'I fucking well do, actually, and you should keep your fucking mouth shut, dick-head,' she spat. 'Frankly, you should just be grateful you're invited at all. I've never known what Dalziel saw in you.'

'Likewise,' James retorted, but he was obviously shaken by her venom. 'Had a line too many, dear?'

'I moved on from charlie a long time ago, baby,' Lena said scornfully as she lit yet another cigarette. Her fingers were brightly stained with nicotine. 'Mind your own fucking business, anyway.'

'Yeah, yeah, OK, big girl,' James snapped. 'If you want to destroy yourself, Lena, that's fine by me.'

'Ditto,' she said unsteadily. Snatching up her bag she disappeared back into the ladies.

'That's what he likes to do, you know.' James looked almost angry. 'I've been so fucking slow.'

'What?' I was confused.

'Get 'em hooked and in his power. It's all about power with that bloke.' James drained his own drink now and read the note. 'He only wants us to go next door to the posh hotel. To the penthouse suite. Big fuss about nothing, after all that. And I tell you, Rose,' he stared at me with the brown eyes that had recently stopped smiling, 'one last blast and I'm done with all this.'

We shivered on the pavement, waiting for Lena. The sky was vast and the moon shiny and white. James pointed out Orion in the stars.

'He's the hunter, you know.'

I smiled at him. 'Yes, I know.' I looked at his freckled face lit up in the moonlight and thought what a nice boy he was, despite his sometime moods. Much safer than Dalziel. Therein lay the problem.

Lena stumbled out of the pub. 'Let's go, shall we?' she slurred.

'If you're sure you can actually walk,' James mocked.

'Why – did you want to carry me?' she retorted, but her vision was skewed and she staggered a lot.

We were like a bunch of shambolic squabbling schoolkids, I thought, hardly the elite society that Dalziel had envisaged. Without him, we fell apart immediately. I looked at us and for a moment, I saw what others might have seen. I thought of the scathing piece in the *New Student*. Not the sleek pack I believed I moved with, but a bunch of outsiders, lost and rather lonely. I shivered in the biting cold as James shoved Lena in front of him and towards the hotel. She was mumbling to herself; I was worried that she'd really overdone it this time.

We walked across the foyer as steadily and inconspicuously as we could and congregated outside the lift. As we waited, I looked through the stained-glass panes into the restaurant. And then I looked again.

'God, isn't that . . .' I poked James urgently. 'That's Lord Higham isn't it? Dalziel's dad?'

I recognised his face from the newspaper. A tall, smooth-haired man with a long rather benign face and wearing a heavy navy suit, he was sitting at a table with a group of others: a woman in cream with long dark hair with her back to us, a boy of about twelve next to her, and an older white-haired man. It appeared to be some kind of celebration. Bottles of champagne, bouquets of extravagant flowers, cards on the table. And at the end . . .

The lift bell pinged and the doors slid open.

'Come on.' James pushed us all forward into the lift.

At the end of the table sat the peroxide-haired girl who had accosted me the other week in the pub.

The doors slid shut on us.

'Who was that girl? Did you see her? Who is she?'

Lena leaned against the lift wall and, closing her eyes, slid slowly down onto the floor.

'What girl?' James nudged Lena with his foot. When she didn't stir, he picked up her cavernous bag and rifled through it.

'The dark one with the peroxide hair. On Lord Higham's table. I met her last term. She had a go at me about Dalziel. And then—'

The hazy memory of a lost night in the Oxford Union last term; the night they hadn't known I was there as I watched through the glass doors, aghast.

'And then what?'

'Nothing.' I shook my head.

James fumbled with the coke he'd unearthed from Lena's bag, scooping it straight out with his little finger and snorting it, and then offering a laden finger to me. I shook my head again.

'Go on.' He thrust it right under my nose. 'Don't be a wimp.'

'I'm not a wimp,' I protested. 'I just – I'm not sure it's my thing,' but the drink was in my blood and the cocaine was right there, so in the end I snorted it. James leaned back against the mirrored wall and grinned, wiping his nose.

'Just what the doctor ordered.'

'James,' I was shivering from anticipation and alcohol, 'who was that girl?'

'The beautiful one with peroxide hair?' The doors slid open and disgorged us. 'That's Yasmin. Dalziel's sister. He's been in love with her for years.'

146

Chapter Nine

LONDON, MARCH 2008

I spotted her straight away, sitting in the corner of the small restaurant by the window, Jackie O sunglasses shading half her face, a slash of dark red lipstick across the voluptuous mouth, an expensive green coat, thick wool despite the spring sun, collar turned up against a world she found grievous.

'Thank you for coming,' she said. 'I wasn't sure you would.'

'I was very pleased to.' I smiled at her, and ordered salami and cheese, olives and sparkling water. 'Though I don't think your dad would be. What would you like? Some wine?'

'I've already ordered,' she said. She crumbled bread from the basket incessantly as we spoke, the henna tattoos still intricate across her slim hands. On her left she wore a twisted diamond ring that flashed blue when the sunlight hit it.

'Were you engaged?' I was direct. From our phone call, I knew she was ready to talk, and she'd told me she wouldn't have much time.

She shrugged. 'I was about to be married,' she said, loosening her coat. 'For all that it matters now. Then my father found out.' She removed her glasses, and I was shocked at how sore her eyes looked. 'My father is a terrible bully, you know. He likes everything the way *he* believes it should be. He is a relic.' She spat the

147

last word. 'He is so old-fashioned, he refuses to come into this century.'

The waiter bought a carafe of red wine and Maya poured herself a large glass and drank half of it in one go. Then she offered to pour me some.

'Just a little, thanks. I don't really drink these days.'

'Oh?' She raised an immaculate eyebrow.

'Bit all or nothing, me, unfortunately,' I said, but she wasn't interested in me, and that was how it should be. I was never the subject – that was how I preferred it; how I worked best.

'So, why did you want to see me?' I smiled again. She was rather like a nervous thoroughbred.

'My father told me he was going to do an interview with you for the local paper. I want you to know the truth about him.'

I debated whether to tell her I wasn't doing it any more. In the end, I pressed on.

'Will you tell me about you first?' I coaxed her gently. 'It would help me. Why did he hate your boyfriend so much?'

'Because he was not of his choosing.'

'Not because he was a Muslim?'

'Maybe once my father renounced Islam,' she shrugged. 'But he's changed his views since 9/11. We all have.'

I sat up straighter. 'Really?'

'Everyone is so polarised today, don't you think?' She scratched her arm absently, trailing her fingernails up her smooth caramel skin.

'Perhaps.' I must not react. I must just listen.

'We all hate the atrocities carried out in Allah's name, of course. But that doesn't mean anyone should have to renounce him.'

'Of course not. So, did you grow up here?'

'I lived in Tehran until I was five and then we had to leave. For various reasons, it wasn't safe for us any more. I came to England and went to boarding school soon after. I didn't see my

148

parents for a few years. My father had angered the Ayatollah and he wasn't allowed to leave Iran for some time, and my mother . . .' she drank the rest of the wine in her glass, 'my mother was busy losing her mind.'

I picked at the plate of ham that had arrived. 'Why was that?'

'Because my father drove her mad, I believe.' A strange glassy smile appeared that tautened her face and never neared her eyes. 'Because men in his family believe, like so many others of Arabic culture, that women are to be seen and to serve and ornament them, but are not to be listened to. That is like Victorian children, no? Seen and not heard.'

'I don't think that's unique to Arabic men.' I grinned at her.

The waiter arrived at her shoulder to top up her wineglass and she smiled up at him, a proper bewitching smile – and I saw how very beautiful she was, the planes of her face melding together so it was hard to drag your eyes away from what was almost perfection. How beautiful – and how deeply troubled. She spoke of her family and her brother and the war and the Ayatollah's regime, and how when her mother died her father did not shed a tear. She told me of her teenage years after she left school and partied hard in London with the children of pop stars and politicians. Then she had left it behind, she said. Her diction was elegant and formal, her Iranian accent almost imperceptible, but she was edgy, nervous, constantly looking around. Occasionally she trailed off as if she couldn't quite remember what she was saying.

'I saw how empty and vacuous that world is.' Her bread plate was now a sea of crumbs, but not one morsel of food had passed her lips since I'd sat down. 'The world of nightclubs and celebrity and people who believe they are owed respect because their father once had a Number One hit or followed a fashionable cause like – like Live 8. It no longer interests me. In fact,' she drained her glass again, 'it disgusts me now.'

'So what do you do yourself?' I asked, and she gazed at me as if she didn't see me.

'I am retraining. I am more interested in the academic life now. The history of my nation, for example.'

She refilled her glass. I was alarmed at the speed she was drinking, but I knew it wasn't my place to interfere. I topped up my own glass of Perrier. I was finding it hard to get a real sense of Hadi Kattan from her; she was so angry and unhappy, but vague about his current pursuits. I touched gingerly on the recent CIA investigation that Xav had mentioned.

'Very likely.' She shook her head vaguely. 'But you must understand we don't talk of such things. All we have done for a while is argue.'

'Why did he move to the Cotswolds, do you think?' I asked, and a sneer caused her lovely mouth to twist downwards.

'Because he does not want people to see what he really is, and my brother persuaded him,' she said. She twisted her glass round and round. 'But the trouble is, Rose, the trouble is we do not belong anywhere. My family does not belong. We are neither one thing nor the other. And now this is what my brother, Ash, is trying to leave behind. He would like to be the consummate English gentleman. And what I really wanted to talk to you about was my own political beliefs. They are—'

She jumped as her phone rang in her coat pocket.

'You see.' Her hand was trembling as she showed me the display. 'It's him. He will want me to return home now. I will have to go.' She was suddenly in disarray as she started to pull her coat on, all anxiety. 'He likes to know where I am every hour of every day.'

I had one last chance to ask the questions I really needed to, and took a deep breath. 'Does he lock you in?'

'Who?'

'Your father,' I murmured. 'I thought – did I see you upstairs at the manor?'

She stared at me. 'Yes,' she whispered, 'yes, he does lock me in occasionally. And if I do not go home, he sends someone to retrieve me.'

150

'Who?' I asked urgently. 'Danny Callendar?'

She kept gazing at me until I felt an eerie chill.

'Danny,' she repeated. 'Yes, he sends Danny sometimes. Sometimes other people. Sometimes men or family from home.'

She stared at me. I saw a light sweat break out across her face. I couldn't tell if she understood what I meant; but I held her gaze. She was broken, like a beautiful vessel that had cracked fatally, but was still just about in one piece. Her phone bleeped again.

'I'm sorry, but I really have to go.'

'Can you – would you tell me the beliefs you just mentioned? About your boyfriend?' I said quickly. 'About what happened.'

Her almond eyes filled with tears. 'I can't speak of Nadif yet. It is . . .' she clutched the green coat shut across her chest, 'it is too painful. It is killing me.' She started to slide out of the booth, a waterfall of sleek hair falling across her pinched unhappy face.

I reached over and put my hand on her arm. 'Maya, I just want to know – why, why did you say your father was a murderer?'

'That's simple.' Maya Kattan put her dark glasses back on. 'I said my father was a murderer because he is. Because he killed Nadif. You ask him, if you dare.' She was standing now. 'I must go. Thank you for lunch.'

And she was gone, out into the bright sunlight of Marylebone High Street in her high heels and diamonds. I noticed she walked with a slight limp; I remembered her kicking her father's car outside the manor house. Her words rang in my ears: *Because he killed Nadif.*

I felt an urgent need to speak to my children. I phoned my mother from the table and spoke to Alicia and Effie. Freddie refused to come to the phone because he was 'busy, Mummy', drawing Spiderman, apparently. I told the girls I'd see them all tomorrow and how much I missed them; judging by the excited squeals it wasn't much reciprocated.

Hanging up, I delved in my bag for my purse, still thinking

about the children and the fact I should try to make up with James, if only for the children's sake, when I sensed someone watching me. I looked up sharply. Across the road I thought I saw Danny Callendar standing in the shadow of a shop canopy, leaning back against the glass window, hands in his pockets, staring right at me. My heart felt like it had just stopped.

But when I dashed out onto the street, looking desperately amongst the busy shoppers and the ladies who lunch, he was nowhere to be seen.

Chapter Ten

The house was so quiet when I got home, it was unsettling. I fed the cat, and then made myself some tea and took it out into the garden. It was chilly now, just before dusk. I sat on the bench beneath the magnolia tree that was about to bloom, its pale buds like hands tightly cupped in prayer.

I contemplated the past week's events. I couldn't see what the right thing to do was any more. I thought I should probably stop, not for James's sake or my own, but for the children. Who was I truly chasing Kattan for? I was lying to myself. But if I gave this last thing up, what was there left for me, apart from motherhood? Just James and I struggling to get through the days.

The cat came out for a while and made a half-hearted attempt to catch a couple of chaffinches on the bird table, but they were too fast for him. Despondent, he slunk back inside.

The sun set, sinking slowly into the wood behind our garden. James was right: I couldn't do everything, couldn't be all things to everyone. I was deeply intrigued by Maya Kattan and her father but I should turn my back on this life, at least for now. James's words in the car echoed in my ears and I remembered LA: the guns and the panicked yelling police and the grim-faced gang members cursing and sobbing over their baby brother, who'd died for a bag of heroin. I'd been eight weeks pregnant with Alicia without realising it at the time; I'd been racked with guilt when I discovered I might have risked my baby's life. I'd sworn then never to put any of us in any danger ever again, and up to now, I'd kept my word.

I sat outside for so long my tea grew cold and my fingers were blue around the cup by the time the weak sun had finally disappeared for the day. I went back inside and had a hot shower to warm up. Then I tried to ring James, thinking we should make peace, but his voicemail was on, though his plane must have touched down in Vietnam by now.

I went through to the study, switched the computer on to email Xav and looked for my diary to find the number for the Rex Hotel.

It wasn't in its usual place on the desk.

I'd scribbled Maya's number on the front leaf when she'd rung me last night; early this morning, just before we'd left for the airport, I'd run into the room to transfer the number into my phone. I knew I'd left the diary right there on the desk; it lived there permanently.

And the picture of the children had been moved. My favourite photo of the three grinning up at me on a Cornish beach last summer, Freddie's head turned towards his grinning sisters, his fat tummy swelling above little blue shorts, Effie's face pink from the sun, with ice cream on her chin, and Alicia straw-hatted, sticking her tongue out mischievously. The picture always sat in front of the printer so I could see it when I wrote. Only now it was slightly to the left, eclipsed by the screen.

Perhaps McCready – but it was Saturday. She never came in on the weekends unless I asked her to especially. I began to rummage on the desk, moving papers, going through the in-tray.

My heart beat a little faster; I knocked over a leaning pile of

New Yorkers that went tumbling, slapping to the ground. And then I stopped. *Come on, Rose.* I was getting paranoid. I'd probably left it in the car, or upstairs, or—

'Is this what you're looking for?' a low voice asked.

I screamed.

Afterwards I felt ashamed, but it was an animalistic noise that came instinctively.

'How the hell did you get in?' My heart was banging.

Callendar held my diary like a trophy, extending it towards me. 'You left the back doors open.' He actually smiled at me and I felt anger rise quickly now, replacing the fear. He crunched the sweet he'd been sucking.

'Well, you can walk right out of them again then, can't you?' The wash of adrenalin was making me shake. 'You really frightened me, you know.'

'I can see that.' He took a step towards me. 'I didn't really mean to.'

'Didn't *really* mean to?'

He shrugged. 'Didn't mean to, then.'

'I don't believe you.' I glared at him. 'What the hell are you doing here? What the hell are you doing with that?'

'Returning it.'

His nonchalance irritated me beyond belief. 'But you've just stolen it.'

'Stolen it?' He narrowed his eyes. 'No, Rose, you left it somewhere.'

'Somewhere?'

'The exact location escapes me.'

'Oh really?'

'Yeah, really. I'm just returning it. And I also came to ask you,' he stepped nearer to me, throwing the diary on the desk, 'what *you* think you're doing?'

'What do you mean?'

'You know exactly what I mean.' He rubbed his face wearily.

I pushed past him and into the kitchen, where I poured myself a glass of water and drank it in one. I heard him walk into the room behind me.

'Please, Mr Callendar.' I leaned on the sink and tried to calm myself. I was so angry now I was sweating; I'd become inarticulate in my rage.

'Danny.'

'Please, *Mr* Callendar, leave my property. Now.'

'I came to warn you, Rose. For your own sake.'

'Yeah, I got that bit, thanks.' I turned to face him. He'd laid his gun, a Glock, on the worktop. It lay there, black and silent. Vehemently I pushed down the fear rearing up inside; I'd be damned if I'd let him see it.

'This is what Mr Kattan pays you to do, is it, the "hired help"?' I stared at the gun and I felt hatred for Callendar's sheer arrogance. 'You must be very proud of yourself.'

'Maybe.' He shrugged again. 'I know what you're up to, by the way.'

'Oh, really?'

'I mean – I know who you are.'

We stared at each other for a moment. 'And who am I?'

'You're a journalist, an award-winning one,' he said indolently. 'But there's no story here, Rose Langton. Leave it alone.'

'I was only going to interview him for the local paper,' I protested.

'But you work for the nationals, don't you? The *Guardian*, *The Times*. He doesn't know,' he leaned against the worktop, lazily crossed his Converse trainers at the ankle, 'not yet. But I do. Like I know you saw Maya today.'

'I won't let you intimidate me, you know,' I said, but I was lying. I was already intimidated, gun or no gun. There was a quiet menace about him, the way he held himself, apparently so relaxed – all scruffy jeans and parka and messy hair, flecks of blond in his dark stubble – but it was all a front. I could sense the tension in him underneath the surface, like something pulled tight. Something about to snap.

'You don't understand what you're messing with,' he said quietly and before I could move he'd grabbed my arm, yanking me towards him. 'You really don't. Kattan's playing with you. And he will turn nasty. You need to keep away.'

'Get off me,' I hissed. He was hurting me. My heart was beating so fast now I thought it might actually become audible, and I struggled hard, trying to free myself but he was holding my arm so tight and he wasn't about to let go. I looked up at him, at his dark-fringed blue eyes and I was so near I could see the ring of black around the blue. Everything was flying around inside my head, banging off the sides of my poor brain.

'Is that why you were following me?' I whispered. 'I saw you, you know.'

'I wasn't following you,' he said, quieter still. And he looked at me and I looked back at him and something happened; I felt this surge from deep inside, a surge of something that I hardly recognised, that I had never really felt before, not in my whole life, and I was shaking now with fear but also something else. I tried to push it back down inside but he was too near and I stared at his mouth and then apparently he was speaking. I couldn't think, couldn't concentrate.

'For God's sake, Rose,' he muttered, 'you really don't get it, do you?'

'Don't get what?' I said, and suddenly I felt like crying, and thought, I'm probably just going crazy. That's all this is: I'm finally going mad. And then I said, I whispered, 'I do actually. I do get it. You're warning me off.'

He spoke, but I couldn't understand.

'What?'

'Don't,' he repeated. 'Don't cry.'

'I'm not,' I said, but my face was wet.

He laid one gentle hand down my left eye and cheek. 'You

just – you need to take care,' I thought he whispered then, and he looked different suddenly and I turned my head so I could hear him better, but his hand was still on my skin.

'Take care doing what?' I stared at him and his hand slipped down my face and perhaps I was actually drowning in the sea of that blue. And so I shut my eyes.

And when I opened my eyes again and looked into the sky, the sea in him, he looked back and I disappeared into the blue and then he bent his head and kissed me.

I couldn't suppress it, this feeling that had been growing in me since I first met him. It had grown bigger than me now and I didn't want to have to fight it any more. I didn't know until the second that he kissed me that he felt it too, the second he leaned towards me and I found myself kissing him back, and it was so natural, the most natural thing in the world like it was all I wanted to do.

We fell together. I didn't think of anyone else apart from him and me. I didn't feel guilt, I didn't feel anything apart from this instant, the here and now.

The here and now, this moment, this dark moment, the slamming, the harsh coming together, tearing at each other's clothes, his T-shirt off, the great dragon roaring on his shoulder, my shirt unbuttoned, my mouth on his, skin beneath my fingers, his hand tangled in my hair . . .

Oh God. We didn't make it to the bedroom.

And afterwards . . .

Afterwards he was so quiet I thought he must regret it. I could only hear our breathing and the tick of the kitchen clock, the hum of the fridge. And my heart racing.

I took his hand and we went upstairs and we fell asleep together. And then when we woke in the early hours we moved quieter this time and afterwards I found I was crying silent tears.

Because I knew this was wrong, but how could it be when it was absolutely right too?

158

Chapter Eleven

In the morning I woke early and alone, before the splinter of light around the curtains appeared. I felt tired and bruised, and I couldn't immediately think what was wrong.

It was too quiet: there were no children in the house. The rare peace unnerved me. Eventually I gave up trying to doze and went downstairs to make tea. I sat at the kitchen counter to drink it, and the Glock was gone – and so was Danny. I looked out at the light that sliced the grey morning sky and knew I should try James again. But his voicemail was still on, so I rang the Rex Hotel in Saigon.

'One moment please,' the singsong voice said. As I waited, I caught my reflection in the window. My eyes were swollen and there were bruises on my arm beneath my T-shirt sleeve. Fingermarks. I turned away as she came back on the line. The memory of Danny's skin on mine – but perhaps it had not been real.

'I am sorry. Mr Miller has not checked in yet.'

'Are you sure?' I was confused. He must have arrived last night. 'James Miller, from England?'

'I will check again. Excuse me one moment.' An electronic Vivaldi's *Four Seasons* chirped down the line; I wasn't sure which one exactly. *Autumn*, perhaps. 'No, madam. He has a reservation for one week but he is not arrived yet. I am sorry for your trouble, madam. Would you like to leave a message for James Miller when he does arrive?'

'Yes. No.' My mind was racing. 'Could you just say Rose – Mrs Miller – rang. His wife. And you're quite sure he didn't change his reservation?'

'Quite sure, madam. He was expected yesterday.' A crackle of static. 'Perhaps his flight was delayed.'

'Perhaps.' Perhaps the plane had crashed. No, that was ridiculous. I'd have heard something by now.

'We will hold his room for forty-eight hours – or until we hear from him. I will pass on your message when he arrives.'

The newspaper dropped through the letterbox as I hung up. James must have decided to stay somewhere else, though he was a creature of habit; we'd stayed at the Rex on our honeymoon and so naturally, he'd chosen it again. I tried Liam but it was too early: he'd still be in bed. Then I rang Xav and left him a message.

'I thought you'd like to know, I've been warned off Kattan again by him and his bloody henchman, and I'm sure you're barking up the right tree,' I said, pouring more tea, smoothing out the newspaper. Riots in London. Knife-crime statistics. Comment on Senator Obama's wife, Michelle's, wardrobe. Tightening of terrorism laws.

'Yesterday I met his daughter, the enigmatic Maya – at her behest, actually,' I went on. 'She's certainly got an axe to grind with Daddy. Call me when you get in.'

I checked the newspaper from front to back and then rang Xav back.

'And by the way, why are none of you running the death at the manor story?'

When I went upstairs to get dressed, I took my mobile with me. I was waiting for James to ring, I told myself, that was all.

* * *

160

My mother rings. They are enjoying having the kids so much can they stay another night. Fears that the visit would set my father's health back have apparently dissipated.

'It's giving him a new lease of life.' My mother sounds young and carefree for once.

'Please, Mummy, please, please,' Alicia pleads, snatching the phone. In the background I can hear Grandpa being a bear.

I laugh. 'Don't you miss me?'

'Gran let us stay up to watch *Doctor Who* and she's going to buy me a pink dress tomorrow. And she let us have a whole packet of Rolos *and* a KitKat –' a dramatic pause – 'each.'

Freddie comes on the line. 'Batman wants to stay at Gran's,' he says solemnly. 'And so does Under-woman.'

Only Effie seems to miss me, with a little sniffle at the end of our conversation.

'I'll see you tomorrow, Eff, OK, sweetie-pie?' I reassure her. I hang up and blow my nose. My emotions are all on the surface right now, my skin is off. I feel raw and available, like a peeled orange.

For once I have the time to choose what I wear carefully. I do my make-up very slowly. I play loud music in the bedroom and sing and feel like I used to when I was a teenager before a big night out. Before Oxford. The cat blinks at me from the bed as I shimmy around, and then yawns widely and goes back to sleep. I decide to walk to the village shop. On the way I pass a pheasant running out of the hedge; I smile at its silly run, like an old lady bent double. I sing Bob Dylan. I have stepped over the boundary into something new.

Outside the village shop, I see the Range Rover drive towards me. I stop singing. My stomach feels like lots of small things are rolling around inside uncomfortably.

Hadi Kattan opens his car window and looks down on me. His mouth is set and he is wearing expensive Ray-Bans that he doesn't remove when he speaks.

'Mrs Miller,' he says, 'I asked you not to go near my daughter, didn't I? But once again I find you have ignored my request.'

He stares at me blankly through the sunglasses. I feel small but I won't let him see that.

I consider the best tack. 'Really, Mr Kattan, we just had a perfectly harmless lunch. She wanted to talk. You said yourself she's lonely.'

'Why would she want to talk to a journalist? She is devastated, and you are trying to find out about her politics.'

My stomach plunges. Danny is sitting there in the driver's seat; he glances over. For an infinitesimal moment our eyes meet. I am pierced by those eyes – and then he looks away. I feel stung.

Instinctively I glance in the back of the car and there is Maya. It is hard to see her face clearly and she is still wearing sunglasses, but there is something so bowed and sad about her posture.

Then Kattan says, 'Please, Mrs Miller, this is the end of our dealings now.'

I am torn. Do I try to help her, or do I go quietly? I glance at Danny but he is fiddling with something on the dashboard. I start to turn away, then I turn back.

'Is Maya all right?' I ask boldly. 'Are you?' I say louder, so that she can hear too. She doesn't respond but leans her head back against the seat.

'Ah, your new friend, Maya.' Kattan takes his glasses off and looks down at me. 'Yes, Maya is fine.' There's a small mark across the bridge of his nose where the glasses have rested. His dark eyes are grave. 'Please, give your husband my regards.'

My husband, who has apparently disappeared.

And I smile at Hadi Kattan as best I can and then I walk away, and I know they are all watching me.

The big car passes by when I get to the end of my own drive, and when I stomp down to my house, I find that my hands are sweating where I've clamped them into fists.

*   *   *

162

I didn't want to return to my empty house. I despised myself suddenly for the Danny thing. How could I have been so stupid? I was already struggling with our worlds, our worlds that clashed, that did not unite. With my attraction to a man who did something I disagreed with so fundamentally – and worse, with my own morality. I had a husband, a family. And yet the part of me yearning so desperately recognised my deep and apparently insatiable predilection for danger – something my friend Dalziel had awoken in me, aged eighteen, and still something I couldn't seem ever to quash for very long.

I sat on the stone bench for a while in the back garden and deliberated. I decided I'd go to my parents and stay the night before bringing the children back with me tomorrow. It was funny, all this time I thought I'd enjoy the rest, the peace – but now I just missed them desperately: the twins' plump little bodies, Alicia's tuneless singing, the constant noise, banging doors, strident cartoons, even the fighting.

I'd pack a bag and drive straight to Derby; I'd be there by teatime. I couldn't sit around here waiting, and the Kattan thing was going nowhere.

Infinitely cheered, I unlocked the front door. Sunlight danced across the hall, the heady smell of the hyacinths in the kitchen pervading the air and—

There was an almighty crash from somewhere in the depths of the house.

'Hello?'

The cat screeched across the hall and I laughed tremulously. 'Bloody hell, Tigger. Take it easy, would you?'

He crouched with reproachful eyes beneath the kitchen table. I put the kettle on and thought about trying James again.

There was another crash from the direction of the studio.

I took a deep breath, picked up the nearest weapon – a rolling pin apparently – and made my way to the studio door. The light was on.

'Whoever you are, I'm calling the police,' I said loudly, and pushed open the door.

Liam was rifling through a box-file that he'd dragged from the shelf, his back to me. He jumped a foot in the air.

'Rosie.' He turned, flushing guiltily. 'Christ, you scared me.'

'I could say the same.' I sank down on a stool shaped like a pill bottle. 'Flipping heck.'

'I didn't think you were in.'

'No, well, I wasn't. God, I've had enough shocks to last me a lifetime this weekend.'

'What do you mean, shocks?' Liam put the file down and shut it. He was sweating, but it was cold in here, the radiators turned off whilst James was away.

'Nothing. Forget it.' I shook my head. 'What are you doing here?'

'James called me,' he muttered. 'He needs the details of the Barclays account.'

'Why didn't you just ring me?' I looked at him, puzzled. 'I could have found them for you.'

'I didn't want to bother you.' His big ruddy face was a picture of sweaty confusion. 'I, er, I thought you were away. I still had the spare key from Christmas. And we were passing.'

'Passing?'

Liam lived in East London.

'I'm taking Star away for the night. Swanky hotel with a spa up near Cheltenham. James recomm—' He stopped mid-sentence. 'Well, apparently it's meant to be very nice.'

'Did you get my message?' I asked. Outside I could hear a car pulling up in the drive and I felt a sudden leap inside, like a slippery fish in my chest. It was hope, I realised later.

'No,' Liam said, but I knew he was lying. 'What message?'

'I haven't heard from James since I dropped him at Heathrow. But *you* obviously have.'

'Yes,' he admitted carefully, 'yes, I have. He's fine.'

164

'But he's not at the Rex,' I said. 'You always stay there, don't you?'

The doorbell rang.

'That'll be Star.' Visible relief crossed Liam's freckled face. 'She went to get some fags from the shop.'

'So where is James?' I said, pressing him.

'He's going down to Vang Tau to meet the investors, I think. Seaside resort,' Liam muttered. 'Decided not to stay in Saigon. Too hot at this time of year.'

The doorbell rang again. 'Shall we?' he said with something like desperation, and we made our way down the hall, my brain whirring.

'You're not rushing straight off, are you?' I asked, opening the front door. 'Have a cup of coffee before you go?'

'I'd love to, but we're in a rush, actually.' Liam's discomfort was almost palpable. 'We've only got the room for one night. Sorry.'

'Oh,' I said, nonplussed. Star peered at me myopically from the doorstep, her fur collar framing her pointy little face, black leather boots up to her thighs, tiny frayed denim skirt.

'How do, Rose?' Her flat Northern tone was friendly. 'Nice to see you. I like your hair.'

I hadn't brushed it all day, but she was in earnest.

'Thanks,' I mumbled.

'Did you get it, Liam? Can we get gone now?'

'Yep.' He gave me a bear-hug. 'Got it. Thanks, Rosie. Sorry I scared you.'

'I've got a manicure booked at three,' Star said, turning back to the car. 'Wax hands and all.'

'Right.' I had no idea what she meant. 'Well, enjoy.'

'We will.' Liam beamed at me – a small boy off the hook. I grabbed his hand as he turned away.

'Liam.' I was starting to feel hurt. 'Why didn't James tell me where he'd be?'

'Dunno, Rosie.' He shrugged. 'Do you tell each other much these days?'

'Is that an accusation?' I felt a cold stone in the pit of my stomach, but his tone had been guileless.

'No. Just an observation.'

'Are you really sure you won't stay for a cuppa?' I said, suddenly loath to be alone.

'Another time, Rosie.' He glanced at the car. 'It's just – I don't want to blow this. I really like her. And you know me and women.'

'Er, yeah.' Liam was the archetypal Jack-the-lad. 'I do know you and women.'

We both looked at Star, busy redoing her dark lipstick in the car mirror, contorting her neat little face for the perfect pout.

'I'll try and stop by tomorrow on our way back, OK?'

'Not sure I'll be here,' I said, attempting a smile. 'Got to collect the three musketeers from my mum's. You go and have fun.'

'Well, I'll call,' he said. Star beeped the horn and then turned the stereo up. Dance music thumped through the chilly morning air.

'Time waits for no man, eh?' I said.

'Maybe, but with tits like that, I'd wait for her any time.' Liam's face split into a broad grin. 'By God, she's good in bed. Legs like a rubber—'

'*Liam!*' I pushed him in the direction of the car. 'Too much information, thanks very much.'

After they'd gone I felt desolate. I stared at my mobile, willing it to ring, but it didn't. I turned on the radio whilst I began to pack.

'Lord Higham arrived at the Tory Conference in Blackpool today,' Martha Kearney announced.

'Brilliant,' I muttered. I couldn't find my usual overnight bag. Perhaps James had moved it. I opened the cupboard and poked around.

'He is Cameron's guest speaker,' she was saying. 'And whilst Higham's aides are denying any rumours that he will try to make a leadership bid, some believe Cameron is keeping him firmly where he can see him.'

'Huh,' I muttered. 'Blackpool. Slumming it, poor thing.'

I spotted the black leather corner of my bag on the shelf above my winter coat; I tugged hard to free it. A big brown envelope of photos fell to the floor, the images scattering at my feet. I bent to pick them up. A town-house at night, a smart town-house, Georgian probably, with shiny white pillars and clipped topiary. People coming and going out of the front door; no one I recognised. I realised they were all men. Then an earlier photograph, dated the same November night last year as the others, but this one taken before midnight; a group of young women, high-heeled, long-haired, trench-coats belted tightly, a couple in fur coats, probably fake, pulled up around hard little faces, the lights from the streetlamps bleeding into the night.

And then finally, someone I did know. Lord Higham, walking down the front stairs of the house, talking on a mobile phone, shirt unbuttoned, his jacket slung over one shoulder. Three o'clock in the morning.

UNVERSITY, FRIDAY
13 MARCH 1992

O, thou bewitching fiend, 'twas thy temptation,
Hath robbed me of eternal happiness . . .
What, weep'st thou? 'Tis too late; despair. Farewell.
Fools that will laugh on earth, must weep in hell.

Doctor Faustus, Marlowe

James was still close behind me as we stepped from the Randolph's lift, my nose running from the cocaine. When Dalziel opened the penthouse door and took my hand to pull me inside, I could feel him trembling, his skin glossy with sweat, his hands clammy. Paler than I'd ever seen him, he was obviously wired, his teeth grinding, so high that he was almost rigid, though it was unclear exactly on what.

'Nice pad,' James said, peering into the suite. 'What've you been up to then? Your dad's downstairs, isn't he?'

'Yes,' Dalziel snapped. 'Celebrating his poxy wedding anniversary. A treat for all the family, I don't think. For Christ's sake,' he'd spotted Lena now, who could barely stand, 'I told her not to get too fucked, stupid tart.'

'Yeah, well,' James stared at Dalziel, 'maybe you should have told her that six months ago.'

Dalziel turned his back on us and stalked into the suite. 'Wait there,' he muttered over his shoulder.

I'd never seen Dalziel lose his cool properly before; the nearest he'd ever come was at the pub that night when Yasmin had railed at me. His sister Yasmin. I glanced down at my hand where he'd been grasping it. Something dark and sticky had marked my palm.

The boy with the bullet head was waiting at the foot of the stairs. He looked petrified. 'You heard him,' he whispered urgently. 'Wait there.'

'Keep your hair on,' James retorted. 'What's all the bloody secrecy about? Satanic rites?'

'I thought this was meant to be fun,' I agreed. The coke was such a brief buzz, and I was freezing and doubtful. I yearned for the numbing bliss of my opium.

'Fun?' Bullet-boy stared at me. 'Did you? Did you really? It is not fun, it is our mission.'

A handbell rang somewhere. I realised then, following James and a still-swaying Lena up the stairs of the penthouse, that I hadn't thought much about it at all; I'd just thought about Dalziel and where my next hit was coming from. Only now I felt an increasing sense of dread.

Music was playing – Handel's *Messiah*, which I recognised from the cathedral: that Dalziel often played at home, a soprano singing 'I know that my Redeemer liveth'. The entire room was candlelit and the thick carpet had been slashed and pulled up. Strange chalk marks and circles were drawn on the floorboards below.

'Christ,' James laughed nervously, 'this is going to cost someone a fucking fortune.'

A huge ornate four-poster bed squatted at the back of the room, entirely curtained in thick red brocade. In front of it, someone had constructed a makeshift altar on which sat a bottle of golden liquid and a cup.

'Don't mind if I do,' James said, moving towards the bed, and poured himself a drink – but Lena was too fast for him. The bottle went flying and smashed on the floor. She had possession of the cup; she drank it down in one.

'Greedy bitch,' James muttered. For a moment, Brian looked furious. Then he shrugged. 'She'll be sorry,' he murmured.

The room was stifling and I recognised the smell of incense from the Latin Masses my grandmother had taken me to in France, and something else, something sweet – which I later realised was chloroform.

And then a door opened behind us and we turned our heads to see Dalziel saunter into the room, chest bare and a pentangle painted on it, his hair greased back, his eyes painted black again. He smiled at us and it was a truly frightening smile, his teeth bared – and I saw it was because his soul was not present any more. He was empty and fearless with hatred and amphetamine.

'Welcome to Pandemonium.' He stalked to the bed and pulled the front curtain back. 'Welcome to Hell.'

There lay a sleeping child, hair dark as night on the snowy pillow, face pallid as marble.

And in Dalziel's shadow Bullet-boy walked, and he held before him a coiled rope.

My stomach plunged.

'What the fuck's going on here?' James demanded.

Lena staggered where she stood. 'Christ's sake,' she moaned. 'I think I'm going to be sick.'

'Christ won't help you now, my dear,' Dalziel deadpanned, and he turned to face us. 'It's all Christ's fault in the first place, you could say.'

'He's unconscious, isn't he, that kid?' James accused, staring at the motionless form. 'What the fuck are you doing, Dalziel?'

'What do you think?' he sniggered and his eyes were wild and dark in the candlelight, two spots of colour high on his chiselled face. 'Merely honouring my father and my mother.'

I looked at him and for the first time I was utterly repulsed. 'What do you mean?' My voice was high-pitched with stress.

'The final commandments, of course: Five and Six. "Honour your father and mother", and of course, the key. The one you must have all been wondering about. *You shall not murder.*'

'Murder?' James and I said in unison.

Lena bent over and threw up.

'This is my half-brother, Charlie.' Dalziel gazed down at the child and then pushed the dark hair back from the little boy's face almost tenderly. 'I don't like him very much; I don't think the world would be a worse place without him. My father probably won't even notice, he's got so many kids, and his mother – well, his mother is a whore.' He looked up at us and I saw that he was mad now, that he obviously had lost all sense of reality, his eyes flicking round the room nervously, starting at shadows and daemons. 'Just like his big sister Yasmin. My stepsister.'

Or not mad, perhaps. Maddened. I thought of the failed attempt with the horse. I stared at my friend.

'He's my twenty-first birthday present to myself. But,' he looked round at us again, his smile stretched taut, 'as usual, I'm happy to share.'

'Dalziel.' I reached my hand out to him. 'You're joking, right? He's only a little boy.'

'And if he was a grown-up, that'd make it all right, would it?' Dalziel giggled and my skin felt icy.

'No, of course not.' I was confused, the brandy and the sleepless nights and the stress snarling up my weary brain. 'But you don't want to hurt anyone, do you? Not really.'

'How the fuck do you know that?' he hissed. 'How the fuck do you know anything about me, any of you? You're all fucking stupid, the lot of you. God, you make me sick, you stupid, stupid fucking idiots.'

171

And with a plunging feeling, a feeling of despair, I remembered what Yasmin had said in the pub that night. I realised that if you feel you have nothing to lose, you are genuinely lethal.

'Well, I care.' James was speaking very fast. 'You're not going to hurt anyone, not when I'm around.'

'Oh, good, James,' Dalziel smiled at him. 'I thought you were too weak to act – but perhaps you're not, after all. I thought I had chosen you for nothing, but perhaps I was wrong. I do hope so.'

'What is this – some kind of warped challenge?' James asked. 'You're fucking insane.' Sweat was running down his face and he stepped nearer Dalziel until he was standing almost beside the bed. Lena was groaning on the floor and I looked at Brian and started to move forwards and then he threw Dalziel the rope and grabbed me, restrained me. I could feel Brian's hands were shaking, really shaking, and I thought I could probably overcome him. And all the time I kept thinking how could I have been so stupid, how stupid, how stupid . . .

'Perhaps I am.' Dalziel stood now so he was face to face with James, and in his hand he held a knife. 'You'll have to decide now, won't you, James? You'll have to make your own decision for once in your life, without me leading you.'

James put his hand inside his jacket and brought out the brown paper parcel that Dalziel had given him earlier, and in one fluid move unwrapped it. A stiletto knife in an ivory sheath. He stared down at it as if it were alive, as if it might rear up and stab him in the face. It was identical to the one Dalziel held.

'Kill me or I'll kill him.' Dalziel smiled beatifically and I thought that I might be sick now myself. 'It's up to you.'

Lena was crawling towards the door, crying and retching.

'Don't bother.' Dalziel laughed a strange reedy laugh. 'It's locked, loves, it's locked – and I threw away the key.'

'I don't feel well,' Lena moaned. 'I don't feel well at all.'

'Well, you shouldn't be so greedy, should you, love?' Dalziel taunted her, but his beatific smile was fading. He looked unsure suddenly, as if he might be coming round from whatever madness, whatever drug held him in its grip. He put an unsteady hand out, held on to the bedpost.

'Dalziel, please,' I implored. When he looked at me I saw there were tears in his eyes.

'Why not?' he said, and I saw he was crying. 'It's an eye for an eye, my love, isn't it?' The tears ran down his face, tracking through the smeared pentangle. 'My beautiful Rose. My morning star.'

And then the child on the bed stirred and moaned in his sleep, and I struggled desperately for a moment and I felt Brian's hands still shaking although his grip was like steel. I looked at James across the bed and we stared at each other for a second or perhaps it was an hour, it was too hard to tell, and adrenalin and fear took over. I sort of threw myself out of Brian's grasp with the vague idea of bringing him down, only he was too quick, and he picked up something from the sideboard. I didn't see exactly what but I thought it was a crystal vase, and he brought it down over my head – and for an instant the pain was excruciating. My eyes were swimming with water from the vase, or perhaps it was blood, and then I was falling down, down, down and I hit my head on the floorboards. I lay there on my side and I thought I heard someone screaming and—

And then all was darkness.

Chapter Twelve

GLOUCESTERSHIRE, MARCH 2008

Before I left for my parents', I locked the house up carefully, checking every window, every door. I'd just reached the junction for the motorway when my phone rang.

'Rose,' a desperate voice whispered, 'Rose, I don't have much time. I need to talk to you – now.'

I knew it was madness going back, but everything that had forced me to seek out the truth in my work felt heightened; I was compelled to follow the story until the facts became completely clear. I squared it with myself: the children were safely out of the way; I was still a free agent for the next twenty-four hours and I was determined to do something right.

My phone bleeped again. A text from Xav.

'*Call me: I'm in a meeting but I'll come out. Do not go near Kattan again. We need to speak NOW.*'

I threw the phone back on the seat beside me and put my foot down.

Rain clouds were travelling fast across the horizon, gathering darkness as they moved nearer. Verdi played on the car radio; something dramatic and tragic that I didn't know. It suited my mood.

The housekeeper answered the door.

'I've come to see Maya.'

'She's not here.'

'I'm sure she is. I just spoke to her.'

'I think you'll find—'

Maya ran down the stairs. 'It's all right, Miss Ellis, she's a friend.' She suddenly looked dubious. 'You *are* a friend, aren't you?'

'Of course.'

A doubtful Miss Ellis retreated reluctantly. Maya, it had to be said, looked slightly deranged: barefoot, in a white vest and jeans, her arms tattooed with unicorns on one side, a rainbow and what looked like a pentangle on the other. She presented a completely different picture from her previous glamour.

'I don't have much time,' she said, dragging me into the house from the doorstep, peering over my shoulder anxiously. Her face was free of make-up for the first time, huge shadows beneath her limpid eyes, her hair wavy and mussed. The wind moaned through the great oaks behind us and I stepped inside, pulling my jacket tighter. None of the lights were on and the old house was dark and gloomy.

'Look, I was worried about talking about Nadif yesterday.' She led me into the vast drawing room, speaking quickly, frenetically even. 'But I'm a virtual prisoner, and I want people to know the truth about my father before it is too late. He is a tyrant.' She lit a cigarette with a gold lighter; there were scratches on her shaking hand. 'He is a tyrant and a murderer. But you, Rose,' she looked at me and her bloodshot eyes were blazing, 'you can tell the world the truth.'

I had found my old dictaphone in the glove box; Alicia used it sometimes for her singing. I pulled it out now, placed it on the coffee table between us. Maya eyed it suspiciously and then shrugged elegant shoulders. She seemed slightly glazed by her obvious misery.

'Nadif had such ideals. No one understood. They didn't understand.'

'Who?'

'My dad. His yobs. They just used him until he couldn't say no. And then they tried to use him to get to me.'

I was lost.

'Maya, hang on. Can you slow down a sec?'

'You know my father has been hoping to be awarded a peerage?' She slumped on the sofa, ash dropping onto the floor. 'It looks doubtful now, but he thinks there's a chance he might have a seat in the House of Lords soon.'

'Really?' I was fascinated. I saw the headlines now: 'Peer locks up his daughter.' 'Does he have British citizenship?'

'Yes,' she nodded. 'Dual citizenship.'

'What's his connection in the Lords?'

'Never mind,' she said. She seemed slightly hyper, her mind skittering from topic to topic. 'That's not important now. Rose, he has made me a prisoner here again to stop me speaking out.'

'Again?' I leaned forward. 'Speaking out about what?'

There was a knock on the door and we both jumped. It was the housekeeper.

'Would you like some tea or coffee?' she asked, her small pebble eyes scanning the room quickly. Maya waved her away impatiently. 'Not now. Please, leave us.' She ground out her cigarette in the ugly marble ashtray and then immediately lit another one. Her French manicure was chipped. 'He did not like my boyfriend. Amongst other things, he was a black man, he was African. My father doesn't believe in mixing cultures or religion.'

'And what religion do you follow?'

'That doesn't matter, does it?' she laughed rather hysterically. 'I follow my own god.'

My heart sank. I'd hoped I'd been wrong about some of my assumptions, about facing the facts that seemed obvious about Maya.

176

'I saw you on that march in London,' I said. 'The pro-Islam one. With Nadif, weren't you? There was a picture in the paper. Were those his ideals you mentioned?'

She looked confused for a moment. 'Ah, yes,' she said. 'Yes, I remember now. He wanted to go. I was there to – it was—'

There was another knock on the door and a rather stooped middle-aged man in a slightly threadbare suit entered the room. He was paper-thin, a shadow of a man.

'Hello,' he said politely. 'Excuse me, but, Maya, I think you should come with me now.'

'I won't,' she said rudely. 'Go away.'

'It's time for your medicine.' He smiled apologetically at me. 'Do excuse me, Miss—'

'You can't make me take that poison.'

I didn't know what to do. I stood up, quickly pocketing the tiny tape recorder. 'Please, Mr—'

'Dr Fisher,' he smiled again, stepping towards Maya. 'Come on now, Maya. Be a good girl. Your father is so worried about you, you know that.'

'Rose, please,' she said, staring at me wildly. I was starting to feel like I was trapped in some sort of Victorian melodrama. I thought of Mrs Rochester locked in her husband's attic. 'Please help me.'

'I really think –' I said rather helplessly to the doctor – 'I think you should do what Ms Kattan—'

'And I think you should go now, don't you, love?' a voice interrupted. I spun round. The young man called Zack stared at me from the door. 'In fact, you were just leaving, weren't you?'

I gaped at him stupidly whilst the doctor moved towards a now sobbing Maya, and then Zack took me firmly by the arm and marched me to the door, down the front steps and to my car.

'Help me, Rose,' I could hear her calling pathetically. 'Please, help me.'

'You're hurting me,' I complained. 'That girl needs help. Let me go.'

'Do us all a favour, love. Get in the car and go now,' he said. He smelled unpleasant, of stale sweat and something I couldn't place. Something like ammonia. Something chemical.

'Is – is Danny here?' I said.

'Danny?' He stared at me like I was stupid. 'He won't help you, love. God, you're all the same, you bloody birds. See those blue eyes and think he's come to save you.'

He took my car keys from my pocket, opened the door, thrust me into the car, put the key in the ignition and turned the engine over.

'But I tell you what, love, he's worse than me. He's dangerous. He might be a good fuck, and believe me, he'll fuck anything, but he'd sell his granny for a quid. OK?'

He was so near I could smell his dinner on him, fighting with the chemical stench. I felt nauseous.

'Go home. Be a good girl, OK? Go home, and stay there.'

By the time I got to the road I was shaking with rage and anxious indignation, and I did what Zack told me. I went home. I went home and I called the police.

Chapter Thirteen

I thought they would send someone but they didn't. They took details and they knew who Kattan was – but they didn't seem unduly alarmed or surprised by my call.

'Are you making allegations of domestic abuse?' they asked, and I couldn't really say yes, because I had no evidence.

'Just talk to her,' I implored. 'There's something very odd going on.' But they said they already had interviewed Kattan and his daughter in connection with Nadif's death, and that unless I had evidence of any sort of violence, there was nothing they could do.

'What is the conclusion about the death?' I asked casually before I hung up, but the policewoman told me that was undetermined still.

'The inquest is scheduled for some time next week,' was the most I could wring from her.

When I hung up the phone rang again. It was James – finally.

'All right, petal,' the line was terrible, 'sorry I've been—'

'What?' I found I was yelling. 'I can't hear you. Where are you?'

'The mobile doesn't work on the—' Another massive crackle. 'No signal this far south. I'll be in Ho Chi Minh by tomorrow night. I'll call then.'

'OK,' I said. I could hear my own voice echoing down the line. 'Have you got a number where you are? At your hotel?'

'What? It's so hard to . . . Kids all right?'

'They're at my mum's if you want to ring them there direct.'

'It's not worth it. I'll speak to them tomorrow.'

'OK,' I repeated. I felt an almost nauseous sensation deep in my belly. 'James, Liam was here, he—'

'What? I can't hear you. I—'

The line went dead.

I paced the house, thinking. I turned the computer on and searched Maya Kattan again, but there was nothing apart from the picture on the London march, and a random shot of her with Paul McCartney's daughters and a small Geldof at some nightclub two years ago. Then I looked for Hadi Kattan again. His handsome face on the computer: his achievements, his family, his polo team, the possible al-Qaeda allegations that had come to nothing. I searched every article I could find. What was I missing? My brain felt like some old-fangled machine, the cogs grinding uncomfortably against each other.

I tried calling Xav, though I just got his voicemail, despite his earlier message. On Sundays he usually went to ground; we rarely talked about where he disappeared to, but he'd obviously gone there now.

I rang the kids again. My mother sounded surprised – they were still all fine. I paced the house.

I stared at my mobile phone, willing it to ring. It didn't.

When he came back, my hands shook on the latch as I tried to open it. I looked up into the blackness behind him, and there was a shadow on the half-moon suspended in the sky.

'I can't stop thinking about you,' he said, and he tried to smile, but I saw he couldn't.

And when he pushed me gently against the wall and kissed me, I felt that great wash of feeling again like a tide, like a wave that has been coming over the sea all this time; it is gentle as it picks you up and you don't want to fight it, you surrender to the inevitability.

The wave that brought me home.

Afterwards we lay in the darkness, and he said quietly, 'This isn't meant to be happening,' and I said, 'No, I guess not.'

I thought of Zack's words. 'Is there – do you – is there anyone else?'

'No.' He was almost vehement. 'No, there isn't.'

Neither of us moved. We talked quietly for a while; he asked me about the children, and I thought I detected a yearning in his voice.

Later, when all I could hear was his steady breathing and the silence stretched loosely across the room, I asked, 'Do you regret it?'

'What?'

'This.'

'No. The opposite.'

I felt relief flood over me for the second time. For a while neither of us spoke.

'I just wish—' He stopped.

'What?'

'I just wish you weren't married,' he muttered into my hair. His voice was so quiet I could hardly hear him.

For a moment, a very short moment, I considered his words. 'So do I,' I murmured.

Then he turned over and he laid his mouth on that part of my neck above my collarbone and I thought, I could stay here for ever.

Then the wave finally hit the shore.

Chapter Fourteen

I tried my best to avoid her, but to no avail. Dashing out of the village shop with water and badly needed headache pills, I saw she'd spotted me already.

'You're out early,' she cooed, checking her gold watch, her perfect bob swinging like a shampoo advert. Helen Kelsey – the summation of all I loathed about the Cotswolds, the twee main street, the shops that sold too much sickly fudge and pastel tea-cosies and nothing real; the unsmiling shopkeepers who eyed my noisy children suspiciously each time we entered.

'Going up to town.' Subtly I backed away. 'In a bit of a rush, actually.'

'Ooh, lovely,' she purred. 'Meeting James there? Nice bit of lunch?' Coyly she raised an overplucked ginger brow, insinuating a friendship we didn't have. 'Or perhaps a night alone for the grown-ups?'

I stared at the stubbly regrowth of her eyebrow. 'He's away on business,' I said, inching towards my car.

'Gone on ahead? I saw him last night in Oxford, actually. Frank actually took me out for dinner.' Badly she attempted self-deprecation. 'Lucky old me!'

I looked at her. 'You can't have seen him. He's in Vietnam.'

'I'm sure it was James's car.' Her frown was almost studious, her pink lipstick like it had been sealed on with varnish. 'I remember because he was going so fast, silly boy, and talking on his phone at the same time. A girl beside him.'

'Can't have been James,' I said, grasping my bag. 'Sorry, Helen, but I've really got to get going. See you soon.'

She was poisonous, reputation apparently well-earned as the local gossip, according to the few school mums who had befriended me; she took pleasure in malice and spite, they said. Deep below the surface there must be some terrible insecurity, some reason she was so odious. But I hadn't seen it yet.

Why then did I feel shaken as I swallowed my aspirin and turned my own car towards London?

I had such mixed feelings about going to the newspaper that at the last minute I slunk up the fire stairs to avoid the busy lift. Xavier was looking at the page layout on his desk when I stuck my head around his door.

'My my, it's Mata Hari,' he drawled.

'Ha blinking ha.' I took my sunglasses off.

'Why, pray, are you wearing a not very good disguise?'

'I'm just feeling shy. Pour us a coffee, please.' Peeling off my woolly hat, I slumped on the leather sofa. 'I'm absolutely gasping and I've just done 100 m.p.h. the whole way down the M40.'

'Hungover?' Xav eyed me suspiciously as he reshuffled the headlines.

'I wish. I slept so badly last night I'm practically tripping now.' I thought of Danny's mouth on my neck. I felt heat suffuse my body.

'I thought you'd given up illegal substances for Lent.'

'Funny. I couldn't – I couldn't sleep actually.' I pushed the memories down. 'This Kattan thing's really beginning to bug me. I wish you'd never mentioned it, you know.'

'Right . . .' His desk phone rang. 'Well, I've got some news for you.'

'Brilliant.' I sat up, alert for the first time that day.

'It's not brilliant, actually.' He picked up the receiver.

I poured us both coffee from the percolator in the corner whilst Xavier harangued whoever was on the end of the line. His office was as immaculate as ever, his stereo gently playing Bach, his reference books neatly ordered, magazines stacked in date order, all belying the frenetic nature of his job. Behind his sleek head hung a framed picture of a younger and more carefree us in evening dress, laughing at the Journalism Awards the year before I married; beside it a picture of the photographer Dean Harding in a flak jacket, taken just before he was killed in Afghanistan last year. Much loved, much mourned.

'Get Johnny Field on to it, now,' Xav snapped into the phone. 'Cherie Blair might be fucking litigious, but I will not go down the whole fucking Caplin route again and get shot in the arse with no story to show for it.' He dropped the phone into its cradle with disdain. 'Fucking *Telegraph*. Stealing our bloody thunder a-fucking-gain.'

'Kattan . . .' I began.

'The Kattan story is going nowhere,' Xav said flatly, adding four sweeteners to his coffee.

'Look, I know I've been a bit flaky about it all,' I soothed. 'But give me a chance.'

'I mean it's going nowhere because it's a dead end.' He studied his manicured fingernail as if it were the most interesting thing he'd ever seen. 'It's not you, darling. It's me. I'm pulling the plug on it.'

'But I am finally getting somewhere.' I put my coffee down and leaned on the desk. 'There's a story there, Xav, I know there is. Maya Kattan is a haunted woman with what I reckon are some seriously dodgy politics. She's all over the shop. I think she might have been radicalised by her Somalian boyfriend. Just let me—'

'Rose, I admire your passion, as ever. But you're not listening. I said it's a dead end.'

'But why? I don't understand.'

'Just accept it, sweetheart. I'll give you something far better. How about the front row at London Fashion Week?'

I stared at him, appalled. 'Is that a joke?'

'No. Perfect if you want to get back into the game.' He met my eye coolly. 'Rose, you have to accept things are not the same since you had the kids. You haven't worked for over four years, not properly. You turned down Basra, you—'

'I was five months pregnant with twins, Xav,' I protested. 'Even journalists have kids. I could never have been embedded then. It wasn't fair on anyone.'

'True. But male journalists don't have to pop 'em out,' he said. 'It's just fact, darling. Brutal, perhaps, but fact. You made the choice, not me.'

'You bastard.'

He raised a lazy eyebrow. 'I've been called worse, angel.'

'I don't doubt it,' I muttered. 'But you still haven't explained why.' I was increasingly frustrated. 'I think Maya Kattan is seriously in danger. I think they're doping her up to keep her prisoner.'

'Well, call the police then.' He stood up and walked to the window.

'I did. But we don't just call the police, do we? I mean, that's not our job.'

'This is dead in the water.' His McQueen suit hung beautifully from his short slim frame as he stared down at the busy road. 'Let's just say it's in the paper's interest to drop it.'

'Since when have you worried about the paper's interest?'

He just kept staring out at the grey sky, and I noticed for the first time how gaunt his clever face was, and realised he was deadly serious.

'Our job is to uncover the bloody truth,' I said slowly, computing the information. 'Which is in the public's interest, isn't it?'

'I can't go into more detail now, Rose. Just take no for an answer.'

'Has Kattan warned you off? Has that bloody—' I clenched and unclenched my fists. 'Has Danny Callendar been here?'

'Who?' said Xav unconvincingly.

'Danny Callendar. Tall, Scottish, taciturn. Works for Kattan. I think,' I took a deep breath, 'I think—'

'What?' For a second I had his attention.

I think he might have had a hand in the death up at Kattan's house. I think he might be a murderer.

'I think that anyone who employs a – a bodyguard is suspect, don't you? Anyone who isn't Britney.'

I know I can't get him out of my head.

'Do you really think I'd bow to the whim of some oik? Be careful not to see what you want to see, Rose.' Xav snapped the Venetian blind shut. 'Two plus two make five if you do the maths wrong.'

'Really?' I retorted. Something was most definitely not adding up here. 'So why the hell hasn't anyone covered the death at the manor? There's not been a whisper outside bloody Oxfordshire.'

'Like I said, Rose,' Xavier turned back to me, 'it's not in our interest right now to investigate Kattan. Should there actually be anything to investigate.'

'You thought there was a few days ago.' I could feel my blood pressure rising.

'I changed my mind.'

'Well, change it back. I think there could be a major scoop here, Xavier.'

He took his jacket off and hung it on the chair. I could see from his pristine shirt that he was sweating lightly. 'Write it if you like, but I can't print it.'

'Can't – or won't?' My anger spilt over now.

'Can't, won't – it's all the same,' he snapped.

'Xavier, this isn't you talking, I know it isn't.' I was thoroughly confused. 'Look, Maya Kattan says her father might have been looking at a peerage, but he's—'

'For fuck's sake, Rose,' he howled. 'It might be fascinating but just bloody well forget it.'

Rarely had I seen him so ruffled. My fists clenched defensively by my side again. 'Don't shout at me, Xav, please.'

'Well, just bloody take no for an answer.' He looked ill, I realised. He never sweated normally; he was far too self-possessed.

'But you're –' my voice was rising – 'you're not telling me—'

There was a knock at the door. Xav's assistant, Joy, stuck her head round it nervously.

'Hello, stranger.' Beneath her neat afro her friendly face broke into a smile. 'I didn't know you were here.'

'Hi, Joy.' I struggled to regain my composure. 'How are you?'

'Fine thanks. Sorry to interrupt, Xav . . .'

I shot him a look. He'd probably primed her.

'. . . But Lord Higham's office is on the phone. They really need to know if you're planning to attend the lunch on Thursday?'

'Tell them,' and this time Xav avoided my stunned gaze, 'tell them I'd be honoured.'

'Come and say hello before you go, won't you?' Joy said as she quickly shut the door behind her, escaping the atmosphere inside the room.

'Lord Higham?' I felt the old fear well up.

'Yes, bloody old Higham,' he snapped again. 'I don't know why you're so obsessed.'

I felt like I didn't know my old friend at all. 'I didn't realise – is he courting you now?'

'No, you dunce.' Xav opened the jet cigarette-box on his desk wearily and pulled out a packet of nicotine gum. 'He's just bought the bloody paper.'

UNIVERSITY, MARCH 1992

Shame is the shawl of Pink
In which we wrap the Soul.

Emily Dickinson

I wasn't sure what was worse. The disappointment and confusion in my parents' eyes when I woke up in the hospital, or the sadness I caught on the face of Dalziel's father the next day as he walked past my room with the third Lady Higham, Charlie's mother. They looked so bowed in grief, I had to turn my head away.

I was truly ashamed. I hid my face from the nurses, the doctors, the porters and the cleaners. I refused to see my friends. I thought everyone was judging me. I was glad to be in my tiny room, away from the rest of Oxford. I thought everyone knew what I'd done; that they could see my stupidity.

One night the jolly Brummie from the student paper came to see me, the girl who'd written so scathingly about Dalziel. Only she wasn't so jolly any more.

'Did you know he tried to kill me?' She sat beside me on the brown hospital chair, stiff and upright, her left eye almost entirely closed, a rainbow of bruises around it, one cheekbone bandaged.

I stared at her. 'No, of course I didn't.' From her tone it was obvious she believed I was somehow complicit. 'How would I know that?'

'Because you were his best friend.'

I weighed up her words for a moment. I thought how ironic it was that two months ago I would have been ecstatic to hear those words, to hear our relationship validated by an outsider, but now, now I was simply embarrassed.

'I had no idea, I promise you,' I whispered, tears springing to my own sore eyes. She looked at me and then she shook her head.

'You idiot. You bunch of arrogant idiots. Did you not see what you were doing? The sheer futile stupidity?'

'If I had,' I gazed out of the window; the dusk sky was choppy with cloud, 'if I had, do you really think I would have continued?'

Apparently Dalziel had been waiting for her as she left the newspaper office. He had promised her a story she couldn't refuse and the pair of them had walked to her car, where somehow he had persuaded her to let him drive. It wasn't until he was behind the wheel, she said, that she realised he was out of his head. It wasn't until he aimed the car straight at the wall of Magdalen Bridge that she realised his intentions; that he was apparently trying to kill her. To kill both of them, perhaps. She had broken her cheekbone in the impact, knocked unconscious, whilst, typically, Dalziel had walked away almost unscathed. Physically unscathed, anyway.

I remembered the ambulance racing past the pub. I remembered Dalziel's glittering eyes, the spot of blood on his white cuff. I clutched the blanket with both hands. How had it come to this? How I had not seen Dalziel's madness? I had been blinded by his beauty and his love – his apparent love – that was the truth. Blinded by the apparent aura of certainty and strength – and the opium haze I'd lived in for the past few months.

'He's offered me money, you know,' the girl said, 'Lord Higham. Blood money, to keep quiet.'

'Are you going to take it?' I asked.

'Well, he's offered me a job too, on the *Sun*.' She looked away, out of the window. 'I haven't decided what to do yet. But you –' she looked back at me – 'you should write about it.'

I stared at her blankly. 'Why?'

'Because it's a fucking exclusive, that's why. The inner workings of a megalomaniac's mind. Every journalist's dream.'

'But,' I said, 'I'm not a journalist – and he wasn't that.' And I felt the tears pool in my eyes. 'He was just my friend.' My hands plucked the blanket. 'My very very good friend.'

'Obviously,' she said drily.

I saw her once years later in a Clerkenwell pub when I was working at the *Guardian*; we nodded at each other but we didn't speak. She did take the job at the *Sun*, though, that much I knew; she became very famous as a right-wing columnist.

When I was discharged from the John Radcliffe Hospital after a few days, I went home to my parents' house. We drove out of the small city that had seen such sights, through the meadows and the modern toy-towns laid out so neatly by planners. Nothing felt real any more.

To everyone's relief and my eternal shock, the college authorities managed to hush the whole thing up, along with the Randolph's management and presumably Lord Higham's influence. There was only a very small piece in the papers about the deaths.

James had dropped out immediately. He had a massive breakdown and never finished his degree. Like me, he went home to his mother, but when she died a year later, he left the country for good, travelling to Australia and the Far East to recover. He sent me the occasional postcard, but even those stopped after a while. I missed him at first, but it was as if we couldn't bear to see each other; to admit our shame.

I returned to college in the autumn term. I worked hard and made up the time I'd lost. I avoided the funny looks I sometimes got. I didn't party any more. I hung out with Jen and Liz, thankful for their refusal to pass judgement on me: I got a Saturday job in the Botanical Gardens and sat under Tolkien's tree in my tea-break. I wrote for the *Cherwell* and then the new paper the *Oxford Student*; I drank occasionally in the King's Arms – never in The Turl – though my taste for alcohol was largely gone.

Two years later, I graduated with a good degree and after travelling round India, I joined a broadsheet as a trainee. Eventually I travelled the world as a reporter. The dreamer in me had been crushed by the disaster. The naïve teenager from the provinces was dead: now I had a thirst for truth; putting things right wherever I could by reporting the news people needed to know. Intensely grateful that the final antics of Society X had been kept from the press, thanks to Higham's omnipotence, I turned my back on the whole episode, never tempted to reveal the sordid facts to anyone. Only somewhere along the way, I had acquired a new craving for risk and danger that I could never quite suppress. And I never spoke to anyone in Society X again, until I met James years later.

A warm summer's afternoon, July 2000. I was at the Gare du Nord in Paris nursing a hangover and an aching heart, staring dispiritedly at the dry old chicken baguette I'd just bought as I waited for the Eurostar after a disastrous and unusually alcoholic sojourn in Paris with yet another unsuitable boyfriend. My mobile rang: I hoped it might be him, phoning to explain, but actually Concorde had just crashed fatally outside the city.

The World Service asked me to file an on-the-scene report,

which I did. Later that evening, sad and exhausted, I flopped alone on the huge and empty bed at my hotel in St-Germain. I tried to ring my old friend Jen, hoping she might be in town with the French Ambassador, but her voicemail was on. I chucked the phone on the bed, where it promptly rang again.

'Guy on the other line says he is your friend. Saw you on the news apparently. Wants your number, *chérie*. He's in *La Ville Lumière* too,' my old colleague Bernard at the Paris bureau sounded world-weary. 'Shall I tell 'im where to go?'

I tucked the phone beneath my chin and kneeled in front of the mini-bar, debating vodka or gin. Alcohol might be no longer my thing, but I felt I was going down tonight: the grief of the Concorde tragedy; my own disillusionment with the lover whom I'd just discovered had a wife he hadn't yet divorced, and two small children. His protestations about not being able to keep away from me, my irresistible sex appeal et al. simply weren't soothing the heartache I now felt. Yet again, I'd chosen wrongly.

'What's his name?' I broke the seal on the vodka. In for a penny . . .

'James something. From your college, he said.'

'James?' I put the bottle down. 'Not James Miller?'

Nervous but oddly exhilarated, we met that night for dinner on the Left Bank. It was a small Moroccan restaurant lit by a hundred tiny flickering candles; we sat on silk cushions beneath stained-glass lanterns and they served couscous from brightly coloured tagines.

James looked well. He was tanned and toned, dressed in a pale blue cashmere jumper and jeans. He was relaxed and charming, and full of funny stories about pop stars and actors he'd met in LA.

'I miss England, though,' he said as he topped up my glass of red. 'I've been away so long. I miss the greenness.'

'Yeah, I know what you mean.' I thought of all the deserts I'd seen, the collapsed cities, bomb-torn buildings, ramshackle poor suburbs, half-naked kids in the slums.

'But you know, Rose, most of all I miss the – familiarity.'

Something in his voice made my stomach lurch slightly. 'It's so nice to see you,' I said quietly and, at the time, I meant it. He put his hand over mine.

'Do you ever – have you ever seen anyone . . .' He trailed off.

'No.' I shook my head vehemently and picked up my wineglass.

'Rosie. Petal.' He put his hand out for a moment and I felt myself start to exhale. As if I'd been holding my breath for eight years.

'Do you feel like – do you feel like it changed you? For ever?'

'Society X?' He pushed away his plate and refilled his own tumbler. 'Yeah, of course.'

'We were so stupid, weren't we?' I said, shocked to feel tears spring to my eyes.

'We weren't stupid, Rose. We were just young. Young and incredibly naïve.'

'I loved him so bloody much, you know.'

'Yeah, I know,' he said ruefully.

I smiled. 'I loved you too.'

'Did you?' He looked so dubious I felt a latent stab of guilt.

'Yes, of course. It was just – well, you know. He was so – charismatic. I got . . . I got . . .' I sought for the right word.

'Side-tracked?'

'Yes, side-tracked. He was so charismatic – and so bloody mad in the end.'

'Well, I'd certainly never met anyone like Dalziel before.'

'Nor had I.' I grinned wryly. 'I went to a comp in Derby, for God's sake.'

'So, then. He was from a different world. You were over-whelmed.' He put his hand over mine. 'Don't beat yourself up about it.'

193

'It's hard, though, isn't it? You know,' I fiddled with my wooden napkin ring, 'I did a report in Rwanda a few years ago, about survivors guilt.'

'I definitely feel guilty.'

'So do I. I think it's kind of driven everything I've done since then – what happened in that hotel room that night.'

'Are you saying we're survivors?'

'Well, I'm not equating us to the poor bloody Rwandans, if that's what you mean, but still – I don't know. It definitely left me – different.'

'I don't understand.'

'Like, I was lucky to get out of it all unscathed.'

'And?'

'And now I have a – a kind of duty.'

'What kind of duty?'

'It's hard to explain.' I felt slightly abashed. 'To help others, I suppose. It's focused my career, definitely.'

'Well, it's left me –' he drained his wine and grinned – 'it's left me with a duty to get drunk.'

I gazed at him, meeting the kind brown eyes that I remembered so well now. 'Oh, James.' Only later did I regret not heeding his oblique warning.

He held his hand up to my face, and slowly I felt myself start to relax in a way I hadn't for years.

'Shall we . . . ?' Why did I feel suddenly shy? 'Shall we go?'

We paid as quickly as we could. We walked back through the streets of St-Germain, past the brightly lit cafés and bars, crowds on the pavements in the sultry night – but we didn't stop for a last drink. We went back to the hotel and we fell into bed. We didn't get out for two days.

I couldn't explain it at first.

We met and we reconnected. It was as if our secret held us together; as if we were the only two who could understand. Perhaps we remembered why we'd loved one another as teenagers, or maybe we just clung on, looking for something good to come from something terrible. And we shared a love of adventure, a thirst for new experience that perhaps Dalziel had taught us. Our reward from Dalziel: that, and a sense of guilt. Whatever the truth, the rest, well, the rest as they say, was history. Until today.

Chapter Fifteen

LONDON, MARCH 2008

I walked through St James's Park and I felt like I'd drunk too much coffee, which I probably had. I also felt exhausted and a little mad, to say the least. Nothing quite added up and every lead swerved off, with nothing coming back to tie up neatly. But what I couldn't decipher was, was there really no story worth covering – or had I simply lost my ability to follow a trail?

On the little bridge over the lake I stopped to watch the pelicans, who looked so venerable out on the fat rocks, bills resting on their plump chests. A tall couple in crackling anoraks handed me their camera, thanking me profusely in broken English. I took the picture and walked on, pausing beneath the frothing blossom trees in the sweet-scented air, in this oasis in the midst of all the fumes of London town. My mind was spinning fast as a Catherine Wheel.

If Xav refused to print it, perhaps I should write the story anyway: someone would want it, surely. It was my duty now to discern the facts – that's all I could see. But I knew I was playing with fire. I thought about the children up at my mother's house. This was the longest time I'd been away from them.

My phone bleeped. I didn't recognise the number; the text

message simply named a London hotel and asked me to come there in an hour, to tell Reception I had arrived.

I thought about how one day you don't know someone and then the next, you meet and you can never go back, can never unknow them. I thought about the point at which our lives collide, like a great comet speeding across a huge sky, touching first one star, then immediately the next, connecting momentarily, arbitrarily – and then moving on. But that connection is indelible, even when it's lost. It's there for ever. Danny was in the forefront of my mind, but Maya and James were there too; and the tendrils of Society X were pushing their way up through the foundations of my life again.

I put the phone away and I walked on and on and on. The sky was so blue, a true blue, the clouds stacked and soft. I wanted to reach up and pull them down around me, hide away inside.

The past twenty-four hours had changed my life irrefutably, I knew that much. I couldn't go back to how I was before. And I was too exhausted to go home.

I walked on into town.

The hotel on Charlotte Street was discreet and green, with flags waving gently in the breeze outside, a shiny receptionist and a busy restaurant full of women who wore sunglasses on the tops of their coiffured heads, and men in chinos. A note at Reception asked me to wait in the restaurant; I was shown to a table in the corner where I ordered juice and, realising I hadn't eaten for a while, a scone with cream and jam.

I'd just finished it when a young slim girl wearing a beige headscarf and black trousers arrived at my elbow.

'Rose Miller?' She had a familiar look but I didn't know her. 'Please, would you come with me?'

I followed her to a suite upstairs. She wore no jewellery and no make-up, and her hair was pulled back tightly under the hijab.

'Please, have a seat,' she murmured, taking off her jacket, and I perched on the edge of the armchair, waiting. Her skin was fascinating: smooth and shiny like marble. 'Can I get you a drink?'

'I'm fine, thanks,' I said. The sitting room of the suite was understated and furnished beautifully for a hotel, the smell from a huge vase of pink roses pervading the air; the door to the bedroom shut tight.

The main door opened and a suave man walked in; the girl immediately slunk into the background. I recognised him from the petrol station the other night. Only, when I looked closer, there was something familiar about his handsome face – something that still eluded me.

'Mrs Miller?' He extended a hand. 'Ash Kattan.'

We shook hands.

'Who – was it you who contacted me then?'

'I believe you met Maya again yesterday. Maya and her doctor.'

Ash resembled his sister, tawny-skinned and sleek, though he looked more like his father than she did, perhaps. Only his round eyes were very different, more protuberant than Hadi's, less veiled and far lighter. Reminiscent of someone else. I just couldn't think who.

'Yes, I did, very briefly.' I wondered uneasily if the family also knew I'd called the police yesterday.

'I think my father was surprised that you returned to Albion Manor when he had asked –' he smiled – 'well, you know.'

'Asked me to leave?' I helped him out. I thought I heard a noise from the other room, but he didn't react. My heart beat a little faster. I wondered whether anyone was in London with them, and then I despised myself for hoping it might be Danny.

'Yes. He can be quite – formidable, my father.'

'Well, the thing is – Maya, she—' I didn't want to get his sister into yet more trouble. Quickly I backtracked. 'I went to the house because, well, I thought I should make sure that your dad really didn't want to speak to me again. I was hoping to write about

198

him, you see. He's such an interesting man, and the local community would be so fascinated by his life.'

Ash stood and walked to the flowers, which he studied for a moment. Flattery was getting me nowhere, that was obvious.

'Mrs Miller.' Ash Kattan had a low attractive voice, a voice that was used to speaking and being heard. I wondered how his political campaign was going, if he was after Eddie Johnson's seat. Something told me he had bigger ambitions.

'I'm very worried about my sister.' Ash turned. 'I will be frank. Maya is not a well woman, you must understand. She is devastated by the death of her boyfriend. She is not –' he paused, searching for the right words – 'she is not in control, I think would be the most true thing to say.'

'What do you mean, control?'

'She – she has some habits that are not good for her. That is why we have asked Dr Fisher to stay at the house for a few days. To observe her.'

'And the medicine that she takes?' I asked.

'Maya is – she has had some mental health problems, Mrs Miller. She is of a – of what you might call a nervous disposition.'

'I'm sorry to hear that.' I thought of Maya's words about her own mother. *Busy losing her mind.* 'Could you be a little more . . . expansive?'

'My father would be upset that I've told you. He is very ashamed right now, ashamed and worried. But the truth is, Maya is an addict, Mrs Miller.' For a second I thought Ash's face might actually crumple. 'My sister is truly addicted.'

The room felt stifling hot suddenly. 'I see.' My mind raced back to the times I'd met Maya. 'I hadn't realised that, I have to say. I thought she was . . . just broken-hearted, really. Broken-hearted and frustrated . . .' I trailed off. I looked at Ash. He smiled back. He had a small black mole, almost like a beauty mark, by his mouth. He reached in his pocket, pulled out cigarettes.

'She is broken-hearted, yes. Her boyfriend died.'

'I know,' I said carefully. 'Poor Maya.'

'But he was also the problem when he was alive.'

'In what sense?'

'He was also her dealer.'

'I see.' I considered what he'd said. 'To be honest, I wondered if Maya had some strong political beliefs too,' I said as casually as I could.

Ash Kattan lit a cigarette and exhaled through his perfect white teeth. 'Such as?' He raised an eyebrow.

'I saw her picture, on that Islamic march in London a few weeks ago. She was on the news, wasn't she? And she said she was . . . learning about the history of her country. I wondered what that meant.'

'You wondered if that meant she might be a potential terrorist?' Ash Kattan laughed drily. 'Well, why not? We all have brown skin; we were born Muslim – although actually my mother was a Christian. We are the infidels, no? And I expect Maya said my father's politics are dodgy?'

My mind was reeling back and I tried to concentrate. The levers of the deadlock were starting to slide into place – but they weren't there yet.

'Maya was a little . . . lost a few years ago and she did turn to religion. My father tried to help her; he introduced her to what he calls the jet-set, the children of his business colleagues, the good-time gang. He thought it would distract her from her unhappiness. He does not believe in Islam any more; he lost his faith many years ago. Only unfortunately, she met Nadif.' He turned to his assistant. 'An ashtray, Taalah, please.'

The girl jumped up at once. She was in awe of him; I could see that much.

I cleared my throat nervously. 'But Maya said – she said your dad, after 9/11, that he reclaimed his faith.'

'You can't believe anything she says at the moment. She is a very mixed-up girl. My father was angry that all Muslims were tarred with the same brush, that's true to say. But it didn't mean he wanted to blow up the world, Mrs Miller. It didn't mean he began to follow bin Laden or any other mullah.'

'I see,' I said quietly. I studied his face again. Handsome, smooth. Too smooth really. Pretty almost.

'And personally I see myself as British, first and foremost. All I want is to iron out Britain's future. The rise of the BNP, that idiot Griffin, the English Defence League, the integration of the far right into Europe's major political parties, it's all a disgrace in the twenty-first century, don't you think?'

'Yes I do. Absolutely.'

'So, Mrs Miller,' he switched tack, 'I would ask that you understand Maya's sad predicament. And that you trust her family know what is best for her.' He held my eye and I felt a strange hypnotic quality about him, a trait that would make Ash Kattan quite brilliant as a politician. Like his father, he was mesmerising.

'Of course.' I thought back to the death at the manor. To Maya's glazed eyes yesterday. 'So what was the doctor giving her?'

'Methadone. She is withdrawing from heroin, Mrs Miller. That is our painful truth.'

I felt a rush of embarrassment. I thought of the addicts I'd met before; of Maya's glazed eyes. How could I have been so dense? I thought of Oxford and the Society, of my own guilt at the part I'd played. I felt old and tired; weary of this mess. I just wanted to go home.

'I'm so sorry.' I stood to leave. 'It must be very difficult for you.'

'Maya has been weakened, that is all. She has lost her way but her family are there for her.' Ash smiled his enchanting smile again. 'We are there to help her back on track. The devil is within us all, but we need to learn to subdue him.'

I stared at Ash and he looked back at me. *The devil is within us . . .* Of course! I'd heard those very words in a previous lifetime. I felt a light sweat break out on my brow as it all came back to me in a flash. How could I have been so incredibly stupid?

He looked like his father as he stood now, taking my elbow lightly. 'I'm so sorry, Mrs Miller. It has been a pleasure to meet you properly, but I have another meeting soon at the London Assembly.'

'Of course.'

'Thank you for your understanding.'

By the door I took a deep breath. 'I wondered – did you go to Oxford?'

'To the university?'

'Yes.'

'I did indeed. Oriel. And you?'

I didn't know whether to feel relief or incredulity that he didn't remember. 'Yes,' I mumbled. 'Magdalen. I came down in 'ninety-four.'

'A little younger than me then.' He bowed politely. 'Amazing place, Oxford. Very – esteemed. What a shame our paths did not cross.'

I nodded, my mouth dry. The memories of that cold November night came flooding back: the debating chamber at the Union, denouncing Lucifer and the idea of fallen angels. How young I'd been, how utterly naïve.

'Yes, it is a shame,' I mumbled.

He didn't seem to notice my disquiet. 'I miss my time there, I must say. Such freedom. Such opportunity.'

'Yes. Wasted on us when we're so young, I sometimes think.'

'And, please, can I ask for your discretion?' He escorted me to the door. 'I know what you journalists are like with a story, like a dog with a bone. But it will only bring shame on my family, you see.'

'Of course.' I glanced back at the bedroom door, still shut. 'I'm not interested in shaming anyone, really.'

'Good.' He half-bowed. 'Thank you. We have suffered enough, I think.'

'Where's Maya now?' I asked casually.

'At my father's house, I hope.' He extended his hand. I took it. His skin was hot. 'Being cared for.'

I didn't doubt that if they wanted to keep Maya locked up at Albion Manor, they could. But maybe, with her history, it was for the best. I cursed my journalistic greed for misreading the story; for believing the words of a junkie. But as I closed the door quietly behind me, I remembered the words of my first ball-breaking editor at the *Guardian*. 'Follow your gut – ninety-nine per cent of the time it'll be right.'

Something here still didn't quite add up. Someone was lying.

UNIVERSITY, MICHAELMAS
TERM, NOVEMBER 1991

Brighter once amidst the host
Of Angels, than that star the stars among.

Lucifer, *Paradise Lost*, Milton

I was late for the debate. I'd been immersed in writing last-minute notes for Dalziel, who'd finally summoned my help after I'd helped him dress Jesus in the cathedral, and my watch had stopped so that I'd run like crazy through the chilly November streets and still I was late. By the time I'd slipped into the heaving room, Dalziel was already speaking on *Lucifer: fallen Angel and misunderstood hero – or God's worst enemy?* He was surrounded by his adoring entourage, the girls all dolled up in flicky black eyeliner, most of the boys in velvet trousers like Dalziel's own.

My own churchgoing experience had been limited to once a year at Christmas, when my father, usually after half a bottle of sherry, made his annual attempt to ensure everyone in town knew he was a 'good bloke' and therefore 'very generous' (his words), which involved marshalling the whole family into a pew for an hour and a half of carols and alerting everyone loudly to the fact he was sliding a crisp fifty into the money bag they passed round. Occasionally, if my mother had a new outfit she fancied airing, we went at Easter too; and my Catholic grandma had taken me to Mass a few times in Rouen during family holidays, mainly to adore the priests. These inauspicious occasions, plus the rather desultory attempt my school had made to foist some kind of religious education onto largely uninterested adolescents, were about the sum of it.

The few debates I'd attended so far at the Oxford Union had been rather dull – over my head, to be honest. I'd been to one unimaginatively entitled *State or Public: Which education serves you best?*; and also heard Vanessa Redgrave be terribly serious and starey-eyed about communism. Frankly, I found the place intimidating, the confidence of the student speakers alarming, a confidence I couldn't possibly rival. But tonight I had a vested interest.

Arguing for Lucifer, the fallen angel and hero was Dalziel. I willed him on mentally but although his argument was interesting, even I could tell it was somewhat confused. Too late, the notes from my own reading of *Paradise Lost* sat wasted in my bag.

'Sure Lucifer missed his way for a while, and boy, didn't he pay the price. But he was the ultimate bringer of light,' Dalziel rounded off calmly. 'The morning star. He just got a bit big for his boots, therefore I'd argue that no one can say he was evil. He only wanted what everyone wants: a fair democratic system, not one where someone is better than others. So Lucifer didn't want to bow down to Adam; well, why should he have done? He was around first. And he was a lot more cool. I rest my case.'

The dark-haired young man who opposed him stood now, wearing a suit cheaper than he made it look. I missed his name as Dalziel's groupies were whooping loudly, but his case was compelling. Succinctly he argued for a Devil who wanted too much, who introduced the selfish 'I will' into the world as he refused to bow to God.

'The devil is within us all,' he suggested with silky persuasion, smiling an elegant smile that never quite reached his protuberant light eyes. He spoke with an almost imperceptible accent I wasn't well-travelled enough to place. 'But so is God, and not just because you go to church on Sunday or pray to Mecca every morning or don't play on the Sabbath. God is in here.' He tapped his chest. 'Satan or Iblis, or however you name the devil, is in here.' He tapped his head. 'But it is up to us to fight the temptations. And I suggest that if we fight them, it's far more heroic than descending into Chaos and Pandemonium, as Lucifer and his fallen angels chose to.'

'Really?' Dalziel yawned with feigned boredom. His cronies laughed appreciatively.

'Yes, really, my friend,' his opponent answered calmly, but undisguised frustration blazed across his face.

'The thing is, old stick, I think God sodded off a long time ago. Just take this century, for example. A couple of world wars, Hiroshima, the Holocaust, Pol Pot – where was he then? So Lucifer can hardly be blamed for getting fed up.'

'Didn't Lucifer who became Satan bring these things? Your God perhaps is gone. Mine is still here.' The dark-haired boy closed his fingers into a fist over his heart.

I felt a stab of annoyance at his conviction – and the fact that Dalziel was clearly about to lose to a better, more articulate speaker.

'Marvellous, *my friend*. So,' Dalziel batted his lashes at the President; she flushed unbecomingly, 'is it time for the vote? I've got some very devilish drinking to do.' He resisted winking at the audience, but was greeted by cheers and catcalls anyway.

The vote was close, but as I'd predicted, Dalziel lost. Despite his supporters, the other argument had been far more compelling – and watching him closely now, I saw the anger blaze up inside. It was almost tangible, the fury, like a virtual life-force stippling him; I felt him struggle to push it down again as the beautiful

206

dark girl called Yasmin slipped a comforting hand in his. He managed to smile elegantly as the other boy bowed to her and then departed, his largely male entourage following.

I spent as long as I could fiddling around with my bag while Dalziel flirted with the President but his humiliation was obvious, and he soon disappeared with the beautiful girl and the tall clumsy one in tow, the girls he'd been with in the pub the first night I'd met him, without so much as a backward glance at James or me.

'Why's he so angry?' I asked James, fighting my disappointment as we headed for the bar. 'He didn't look like he was taking it very seriously.'

'Dunno. That was some sort of grudge match, I think. And he hates losing anything.'

'What grudge?'

'Not sure. Dalziel doesn't give much away. Think that bloke and Dalziel went to school together or something. Don't like each other much, that's clear.'

We had one drink, but neither of us was really in the mood.

'Come on, I'll walk you back,' James said, retrieving his guitar from behind the bar. I realised I'd left my umbrella in the Debating Chamber and trotted upstairs to fetch it.

Passing the darkened pool room, I thought I heard a murmuring and a moaning. I peered through the glass door.

I couldn't be sure but I thought I could see Dalziel, his hair ghostly white in the dim light. In the corner, someone else sat smoking. The tall girl, Lena. I blinked. Dalziel was bending something over the pool-table before him. As my eyes got used to the dark, I realised his trousers were unbuttoned.

Accidentally I nudged the door with my shoe as I craned to see, and it swung open a tiny bit. Dalziel turned and smiled over his shoulder at me, a triumphant kind of smile, and I saw that he was rhythmically screwing whoever was before him, holding their head down as they sighed, their arms splayed across the green baize. I realised it must be the other girl, the lovely dark one with the streaks in her hair. And for a moment I thought he looked like the devil he had just revered, that beautiful angel Lucifer, fairest of them all, bathed in unearthly light: the morning star.

The portraits of the robed men who'd hung on the Union walls for ever watched unperturbed as I ran down the stairs, my cheeks scarlet with shame.

'Let's go.' I shot past James and ran out into the rain.

At the porters' lodge James tried to kiss me for the first time, but I ducked his attempt and dashed inside, utterly confused. I was frightened by my futile desire to be near Dalziel. I was frightened by how much I was attracted to him – an attraction I felt in my very core, despite the fact I knew he was dangerous. I saw the power he had over people, a power that I could not pinpoint properly, and it filled me with a kind of terror. It filled me with terror because it made me want to abandon myself; it made me want to fling myself at his very feet.

Chapter Sixteen

LONDON, MARCH 2008

Somehow I had known he would be there as I left Ash's hotel room and walked out onto Charlotte Street.

'Don't make that joke about a bad penny, please,' I said tiredly, but my heart was banging at the sight of him.

'Not fond of jokes really, Rose,' Danny said in his Scottish drawl. He was chewing a matchstick that he moved lazily to the other side of his mouth. 'I thought you'd have known that by now.'

'I just want *you* to know, I was invited this time.'

'Aye, I do know.' Danny yawned lightly and pulled his tobacco out of his pocket.

Something strong and painful filled my veins. Humiliation. Anger with myself. 'Don't you get bored of being their guard dog?'

'It's my job,' he said, removing the match and rolling a cigarette. 'Just doing my job, see, doll.'

'Right,' I said. I looked up at him, into those inscrutable blue eyes. 'And how do you square this with yourself?'

'What?'

'The violence up at Albion Manor, the heavies, beating people up – men who die, for Christ's sake – guns, the drug-addicted daughter – shall I go on?'

'Please don't.'

'But, Danny—'

He put a finger on my lips to silence me. 'I sleep easily enough, Rose,' he said quietly, and then he just started whistling – right into my face. A taxi pulled up in front of us and a stunning girl in a leather coat got out. He watched her impassively, shrugging down into his parka as he lit the roll-up.

I felt a curious stab of something in my gut. 'Could you . . . ?' I faltered. Our eyes met.

'Could I what?' He resumed the whistling.

I could see the freckles on the bridge of his nose. I suddenly wanted to punch him square on it. 'Could you not whistle in my face, please?'

He just winked at me. I shouldered my bag, making my way down the front steps to the street to the tune of 'My Bonnie Lies Over the Ocean', gritting my teeth. Then it stopped.

'Rose,' he called after me softly.

I turned back. 'Yes?'

The smoke from his cigarette was a haze between us.

'Remember what I said. Go home.'

Flushing furiously, I walked towards Tottenham Court Road and the car park. I'd be damned if I'd let them all tell me what to do. And I knew one person who might be able to help me reveal the secret I couldn't work out. It seemed I wasn't going home quite yet.

I had half an hour to get to the cuttings office, Cutting Out, before it closed for the day. Naturally I got stuck behind a pathetic procession of anaemic-looking Hare Krishnas banging their drums and ringing their bells down Euston Road. Then a police van screeched past us and blocked off the turning to Camden.

'For Christ's sake,' I muttered, trying to reverse. A surly cab driver was refusing to budge and I was about to get wedged in.

In dirty Kilburn I parked the car on a meter and ran up the road. I found a shop and bought a packet of Bourbon biscuits and a bottle of Pernod. Then I jogged down the stairs to the basement door of the town-house.

'Please,' I buzzed the door, 'please, it's Rose Langton. I used to work for Xavier Smith.'

'I'm shut,' a disembodied voice said. 'Go away.'

'Please, Peggy. It's so important. I wouldn't bother you, but this one's a winner. I swear.'

She opened the door a crack. I shoved the Pernod round it.

'And I've got biscuits,' I said, placatingly.

'And hard cash?'

'And hard cash.'

Muttering, she let me in. She was more blind than the last time I'd been here, and her glasses were milk-bottle thick, magnifying her grey eyes alarmingly.

'Remember me, Peggy?' I smiled as I pressed the Bourbons on her too. 'Haven't seen you in a while.'

'They all come back,' she said, seeming both cross and triumphant. The smell of cats in the warm basement was ferocious. 'They realise the damned computer won't reveal everything like some damned crystal ball, and they come sloping back.'

'Of course they do,' I soothed. 'How else would we get to the bottom of things?'

'No need to butter me up, my girl,' she sniffed, but a small smile played round her wrinkled old mouth. Her lipstick was a startling orange. 'I'm making chai. Want some?'

'Love some.' It would be undrinkable but worth it. 'Thank you.'

'What do you want?'

'I'm looking for anything you've got on a man called Hadi Kattan.' I headed to the end of the room that housed the 1990s through to the seventies. 'Hadi, Ash and Maya Kattan – do those names ring any bells? London society pages, Iranian and possibly Saudi connections.'

'Not off the top of my head.' She put the Pernod on a shelf and pulled open a drawer. 'But look in there. If it's not in there, it didn't happen.'

'And I was also looking for a girl called Huriyyah something. Possibly the same family. Probable Oxford connection. I don't know her surname, though.'

The kettle was whistling as I went through file after file, my hands shaking. I cut my finger on a piece of paper. Eventually I found Hadi Kattan. There was a piece on his rumoured involvement with the Iranian Secret Service, MOIS or VEVAK, from 1989 but it was largely unsubstantiated.

And then finally, I came across what I was looking for.

A picture of Hadi's wife, Alia, from the late eighties. Her photo stared out at me; a picture of the two of them at a polo match at the Royal Berkshire Polo Club. She looked a lot like Maya. And she wasn't who I'd feared; she looked nothing like Huriyyah. Of course she didn't – Huriyyah was far too young to have been Ash or Maya's mother. I felt a rush of relief. I didn't recognise her: thank God, I'd been wrong.

And then another cutting, much earlier, from *Tatler*, 1972, preserved in a plastic sleeve. Alia was so young, pregnant, beautiful and glowing in an ice-cream-coloured dress. I looked again at the photo. Behind the elegant couple stood a tall imposing man. Lord Higham. Was it my imagination – I craned forward in the harsh light of Peggy's basement – or was Higham's hand almost clasping Alia's?

Silently Peggy passed me one last file. A small article about an oil company, a subsidiary of Shell, franchised by an Iranian-based conglomerate. There was a small photo of two men shaking hands at a do in Kuwait.

'I always suspected that Higham was not to be trusted,' she sniffed, pushing her glasses up her nose. 'His own agenda and all that. The posh ones are never much good.'

212

'British Government steps into oil crisis: Allies for the good of British industry,' the headline said.

Beneath it, a few lines about how the pair were allies not just on the polo field, but also in politics and oil.

I looked closer. Higham and Kattan, shaking hands over a huge vase of lilies.

Ghosts whom I thought had been at peace were back walking the earth – images I'd buried after university back in the forefront of my mind. For the first time in a while, I found myself craving a drink.

Standing beneath the sprawling sycamore outside Peggy's house, I called my dearest friend.

'Take me for a cocktail? No work talk, I promise. No pressure.'

He took me to his club in Shoreditch. It was full of young girls in long T-shirts and leggings, and men who'd snorted too much cocaine and talked too loudly about it.

We didn't discuss work. We talked about him, about his constant exhaustion at the moment. And then we ended up on the subject of my marriage. Hardly the lesser of two evils.

'What's going on, Rose?' Xavier sipped his martini. 'You seem – distracted.'

'What do you mean?' I was defensive.

'Distracted by your life. By it not being what it should be.'

'That's you talking, Xav, not me.'

'You had so much promise, darling.' He looked positively maudlin. I could see the grey in his cropped hair.

'Christ, Xavier,' I pushed my straw very hard into the tiny shards of ice at the bottom of my glass, 'you sound like my obituary or something.'

'I meant I didn't think you'd plump for this.'

'For what?' I felt horribly raw and defensive. 'Three beautiful children and a million-pound house in the Cotswolds?'

'Oh, do me a favour, Rose. You were never about the money. You were about the ambition, the story and the . . .' He was distracted by a beautiful mixed-race boy in jeans so low-slung the shadow of his arse was visible. 'The kill.'

'I'm really happy being home with my children, thank you.' It was true – most of the time. 'What you mean, Xavier, what you really mean is – you don't like James.'

'You said it, darling, not me.'

'You might as well have done.'

'And you married him, not me. Thank God.'

There was a long pause.

'You know why I married him,' I said quietly.

'But it's not enough, is it, Rose? It's not enough being his nursemaid.'

'I'm not.' I was furious.

'Or, dare I say it, darling—'

I held a hand up in protestation. 'So *don't* say it, Xavier.'

'His mummy.' He ignored me, stretching with nonchalance, looking out at the high-rises that encroached on us. Canary Wharf blinked blindly.

'Shut up! James is a good father,' *when he feels like being,* 'and he's very talented. He's passionate about his work. He's made some brilliant music.'

'If you like that sort of thing. But does he love you?' Xav removed something from his back teeth with great delicacy. 'I mean, really love you? Like you deserve to be loved?'

'Don't mince your words will you, Xavier? Christ, it's not *Brief* bloody *Encounter* or something. It's real life.'

'I'm nothing if not a mincer, darling, you know that. So why do you stay with him?'

'Because.'

'Because?'

'Because I want to give my kids a chance. Because I want them to have what I had.'

'Which was . . . ?'

'A stable home,' I said rather helplessly. 'A normal loving home. Parents who liked each other.'

'Rose,' he said gently, 'you can't fake that type of thing.'

'I'm not.'

But we both knew I was lying. 'I think I'll have another one.' I drained my drink.

'That bad, eh?' He waved at the waitress. 'I just worry that your dear husband's the kind of arsehole who hangs out here with his baseball cap on backwards aged forty, boasting to a couple of tarts half his age that he once took an E with the Chemical Brothers and stayed up till Wednesday.'

'So what kind of arsehole are you, Xav?'

'The kind who can't resist one,' he drawled. 'Excuse me one moment.' He slid off in the direction of the boy.

I checked my phone again. Nothing. Funny how suddenly I was wedded to this bit of plastic. Like it was my lifeline.

Xav slid back.

'Blimey, that was quick,' I marvelled. 'You didn't just—'

'What do you take me for, Rose?' He lowered his lashes. 'Even I'm not that swift.'

My phone bleeped. I read the message; my hand shook a little.

'Who's that?' Xav narrowed his eyes. 'Rose Langton. I recognise that look.'

'No one,' I said, but I was blushing. I found it oddly comforting that he knew me so well.

'Rose,' he sighed. 'For Christ's sake, be careful. You don't need to get hurt now.'

It was late, it was dark, London throbbed around me. Full up with adrenalin and nerves, I left the club.

The moon was full, but the dim little street near Paddington Station was too narrow to absorb its light. A hanging-basket full of dead geraniums hung by the peeling front door of the

B & B, half a bicycle with no seat chained to the railing. Somewhere inside, a couple argued in an African dialect, Yoruba perhaps, their voices floating out angrily from the ground floor, the smell of curry and rotten bins mixing in the chill spring night. I paused, unsure whether this was the right place. And then I heard a low tuneful whistle. 'My Bonnie lies over the ocean . . .'

The front door was open. I ran up the stairs.

He was lying fully clothed on the small double bed, on top of the candlewick bedspread, smoking, the ashtray on his chest, the only light in the room the streetlamp outside. I stood nervously at the door, my back pressed tightly against it.

The net curtain blew in the breeze from the half-open window, and I shivered in the chill. I was frightened. I didn't remember ever feeling like this before. Happiness; excitement, perhaps. No, not so pure as happiness. Absolute anticipation.

'Why are you over there and I'm over here?' he asked, stubbing out his cigarette. I walked to the bed, and looked down at him. At his thick tousled hair, at the sharp freckled nose, the veiled eyes, the blue dulled by the dim room. The blue I kept falling into time and again.

I wavered there above him, unsure – and then he sat up, put out a hand.

I'd forgotten what it was to be wanted.

He pulled me down to him. 'Rose,' he murmured into my hair and I breathed him in. The grotty room, the noise from the street, the sirens in the distance faded until there was just us. Us – and time.

He pushed back my shirt and put his lips against my collarbone. Never enough time, I thought, dazed, and then I stopped thinking.

Afterwards.

I slept for a while. When I woke, he was watching me, and I smiled, suddenly shy, pulled the sheet up around me self-consciously.

216

We gazed at each other, the street-light dimly orange behind the nets.

'I don't know anything about you,' I said. 'It's really odd.'

He rolled over and away from me. 'There's nothing *to* know.' He sloshed whisky from a half-bottle into a stack of plastic cups with Mickey Mouse on the side, and handed the top one to me.

'I'd like to know *something*.' I sat up a bit. 'Where do you live, where do you come from, why do you do this strange job?'

I wanted him to say something that made it all right; that made what he did acceptable in my eyes.

'You don't need to know, Rose.' He stared at me and I could see myself reflected in his eyes. 'Really. I've done some things I'm not proud of, and I'd rather not share them.'

'All right.'

There was a pause.

'I don't normally behave like this,' I said eventually, sipping at the whisky. 'I'm not – this is the first time – I mean—' I choked on the fiery liquid.

He grinned. 'I'd never have guessed.'

I liked the laughter lines around his eyes. Lots of laughter lines; lots of laughing at some point. Only not with me. He was still and watchful. Like a cat, waiting for the mouse.

'Silly.' I tried to smile. 'You know what I mean. I mean, the first time – I mean, I'm not a bad person, you know. I don't – I haven't made a habit of this.'

'You are very unhappy, that's what I know.' He took the cup from me and put it down. 'It's obvious.'

He rolled me over gently and he traced my skin, my naked back with one finger and I shivered.

I was terrified. Terrified by what I was starting to feel so damn fast, so fast I was winded by it. Terrified by what I might do. By what he might be able to make me do.

* * *

217

Later he asked me about my husband. I was reticent: it wasn't part of this; of us. I didn't want it to be. Thinking about James brought me back to the children – and then my guilt began to kick in.

We lay tangled on the bed and he asked me other things: about my career, my times abroad. And for some reason, I believed that he was truly interested. I'd break off, embarrassed, and he'd prompt me on again. It felt like a luxury to be listened to this way.

My husband didn't want me, that was the truth. This man did. I was falling deeper, too quickly, I could feel it.

And afterwards. This man pushed me backwards on the bed and held my arms hard above my head. This man kissed me like I hadn't been kissed since I could remember. Since—

Ever.

Chapter Seventeen

Lust is not a noble emotion. I drove home at dawn, sick with a new feeling I couldn't admit; sick with missing my children. In the fast lane of the motorway I opened the window, in need of fresh air. Sunlight slid down the sky before me; the watery golden shafts disappeared into the trees and I had a sudden vision of walking up them, escaping into the clouds through that letterbox of light.

Lust may not be noble – but it was quickly turning to something else. Something I couldn't seem to rein in.

I shook my head. I needed coffee.

All the lights were on in the house.

'Hello?' I called.

There was a thump from upstairs; the old floorboards creaked.

'McCready?' I was confused. The cat shot through the banisters, making me jump. McCready must have arrived early.

A door slammed shut.

'Where the fuck have you been?' My husband stood at the top of the stairs, hair on end, in his pyjama trousers.

My mind began to bang down dead ends like a fly against glass. 'God, you scared me,' my voice sounded hoarse. 'I thought you were in Vietnam?'

'I was. It went so well, the deal was done – I came home again to celebrate. You said you didn't want to be left.'

I'd never said that.

'Only you weren't here.' He looked down reprovingly.

'I went to see Xav about the Kattan story.'

'Not that again,' James snarled, starting down the stairs. 'I told you to leave it, didn't I?'

'What are you so cross about?' I walked away from him, thinking, trying to make it add up, into the kitchen. I put the kettle on, throwing my coat onto a chair, checking myself quickly in the mirror. I was pale, my hair tangled and messy, last night's make-up smudged beneath my eyes. 'Xav and I went for cocktails last night. It was too late to drive back, and I was pissed.'

James followed me into the room. 'You don't get pissed.'

'Not often, no.'

'You never get pissed,' he repeated, staring at me. 'Not since—' He stopped. We eyed each other like boxers in the ring, waiting to see who would take the first jab.

'Well, I just felt like it for once,' I shrugged. 'No kids, no husband. Why not?'

'And where are the bloody kids? I've been looking forward to seeing them.' He was petulant as a small child.

'They're at my mum's. You know that. She's bringing them back this afternoon.'

'How convenient,' he muttered.

'What's that meant to mean?' I asked, chucking PG Tips into the teapot. I would not lose my temper. 'It's the first time since the twins were born that they've stayed there without me. It's a treat.'

'For who?'

'For all of us. A breather. It was you, James, who didn't want any of us to come with you to Saigon, I seem to remember. So,' I changed tack to deflect the inevitable row, 'did it go well?'

'Yes,' he said shortly. 'I got everything I needed. It's all on.'

'Brilliant.' The kettle snapped off. 'Listen, I'm knackered. I'm going to have a kip. That last margarita didn't go down very well, I have to admit. Tea's in the pot.'

'OK.' He'd started rifling through the post on the table.

'You can tell me all about Vietnam later, yeah?'

'Not much to tell,' he shrugged indifferently. 'Got what I needed, that's all. We can relax again.'

Upstairs I got straight into the shower, as hot as I could bear it, and scrubbed myself from head to toe. Then I drew the curtains and got into bed, but I couldn't sleep, despite my exhaustion. I just wanted my children – wanted Effie's plump little arms, and Freddie's fat tummy, Alicia's skinny frame – all in bed with me now. I couldn't wait to see them.

I'd just dozed off when the doorbell rang. I checked the clock; it was still much too early for my mother to have made it all the way from Derbyshire. I got up anyway, disappointed, and walked out onto the landing in my dressing gown.

'Who was it?' I called to James.

'What?' His voice was distant.

'Who was at the door?'

'I thought you got it.'

'Oh, for God's sake,' I muttered. I went down to the kitchen and rang my parents' house. My father answered.

'Hi, Dad,' I said jovially. 'Just checking what time Mum left.'

'She's here,' he said.

'Running late?' I said, my heart sinking. I'd never craved my children's presence more than this second. 'Can I talk to the kids, please?'

'What do you mean?' my father said. I heard my mother enter the room behind him. 'Hang on, Rose. Speak to your mum.'

I doodled a heart in two halves on the pad by the phone. A dead fly twirled on a thread from the windowframe.

'Hello, lovey. Had a good break?'

'Sort of,' I mumbled. 'Looking forward to seeing my monsters, I must say.'

221

'I'll bet. Sorry we're not going to see you today, but actually it's worked out quite well. It means I can play bridge with Marge later.'

'What do you mean, not going to see me? Can I speak to Alicia, please?'

'They've gone already,' she said brightly. 'They left about half an hour ago. They were so excited to go in that big car. And what a lovely man. So good with them all.'

Cold sweat broke out on my upper lip. 'What?' I croaked. 'What are you talking about? What man?'

'James's driver collected them. James's assistant left a message with Dad this morning.' But she sounded unsure now. 'Derek? She did, didn't she?'

'James!' I was screaming his name, 'James, come here now.'

I dropped the receiver as my husband ran into the room. 'Rose?' I could hear my mother's frantic voice, tinny, suspended in thin air as the phone dangled, futile on its lead. 'Rose, what's wrong?'

'What?' James was staring at me.

'Who did you send to pick up the kids? Tell me you sent someone?' I grabbed his top. 'Who did you send?'

'What?' His face was very pale. 'Rose, calm down. I don't know what you mean. I didn't even know where they were.'

'You did know,' I was shrieking like a banshee, shaking him fruitlessly. 'You knew they were at my mum's. Who did you tell? Who's got my kids?'

He picked up the receiver that was still twirling as uselessly as the fly.

'Lynn, it's James. Can you explain what's going on? Where are the children?'

This then, this was my punishment. I could not possibly hope for a life outside motherhood – but I had – and so this was my comeuppance.

I ran to the sink and retched violently.

* * *

222

We called the police. My mother had no details, she didn't even know the make of the car, but she'd thought it was James's, she was sure she'd seen him driving it before. Something big and grand, like the Americans drive, she kept saying. And the man, the man seemed so friendly, she kept saying. He wore sunglasses and a dark coat with a hood, and she didn't know what colour hair he had because he had a beanie hat on pulled down low, but he definitely wasn't dark. Well, she didn't think he was. Perhaps he was a bit dark – but she'd been running round fetching the children's stuff and making sure they had their sandwiches and done a wee and she just couldn't think straight, she was so panicked she couldn't think straight. He had an accent, maybe, she thought, some kind of accent. He knew James, she was sure of it; she'd met him before, she knew she had, she just couldn't remember where, but she was sure he was James's driver. He said he was. And the kids seemed happy to go with him, they knew him, they even kissed him hello – but she just couldn't remember his name, or if he'd said it at all. My father had deleted the message from the answer-phone and so there was no way of hearing it back. I tried not to shout at my parents for being so careless; I knew it wasn't really their fault. It was mine. I should never ever have left them. 'They knew him,' my parents kept saying, bleating in terror. 'They definitely knew him.'

How could they know the thoughts that filled me full of terror now? My mother just repeated helplessly that she didn't know cars, she didn't know the make, whilst shiny black Range Rovers kept careering through my head.

The police promised they would send someone round to interview her. Were we sure it wasn't a family member, though, they kept asking.

I slumped on the sofa and James put his arm around me. Momentarily I was grateful for the contact, but I was soon up again, unable to sit still. I'd rung Hadi Kattan's house immediately after we'd spoken to the police, but there was no answer.

223

And then when James went to make more tea, I found Danny Callendar's mobile number from the text he'd sent last night and I rang him. He didn't answer either, but I left a message asking him if he knew where my kids were.

An hour or so later, the doorbell rang and I ran for the door, skidding on the rug in the hall. As I plucked it back, I had never been so eager to open a door in my life. But it was only the milkman, come to settle his bill.

'Who is it?' James appeared behind me.

'No one,' I said. 'Just Bob from the dairy.' My voice was unsteady.

James walked down the hall away from me. 'I'll put the kettle on.'

I didn't want tea; I just wanted my children. Crouched down in the corner of the hall like a wounded animal, I promised God, I promised everyone and anyone who came to mind that I would stay at home for ever, never let the kids out of my sight, never stray from the house again, never crave anything else, if they could just come home safely.

'Please, please,' I intoned, 'please let them be all right.'

Danny's words kept ringing in my ears; his warning that Kattan would turn nasty. But the kids had kissed the man, my mother said, so it couldn't have been Kattan – could it? Why hadn't I listened? Why hadn't I been more sensible? I cursed myself, over and over again; I cursed myself.

James came back out into the hall and I realised I'd been talking aloud, mumbling like a mad old woman, rocking back and forth where I sat.

'Leave me alone,' I said, refusing to let him pull me up. 'I'm staying here until they come home.'

I was almost dozing, my head on my knees, the phone by my feet, silent now, despite having rung every person in the world I could think of that might possibly be able to help. Outside, the afternoon was drawing in, the March wind buffeting the windows without mercy. The magnolia tree had bloomed, but the flowers could never withstand the severity of the weather: the petals were already scattered on the grass.

As the church bell chimed four, I thought I heard something. My head shot up and I stood as quickly as my stiff legs would let me, my freezing feet all pins and needles. A vehicle was pulling into our drive as I tore open the door again.

'Liam.' I saw him striding across the gravel from the big Hummer. 'Liam!'

I felt the most almighty stab of disappointment and then, as if in a dream, I saw my eldest child's head pop up from the back seat and wind down the window.

'Alicia!' I yelled.

'Shhh,' she gestured, pointing at something and giggling. 'The twins are asleep.'

I ran across the gravel in my bare feet, dressing gown trailing, and scrabbled at the car door, breaking my nails, sweeping my eldest daughter down from the back seat and into my arms. Effie opened one eye groggily and I leaned over and unfastened her baby-seat, squashing Alicia's head in the process. Fred was fast asleep on the far side, thumb in his mouth, slumped over the seat belt, head lolling uncomfortably.

'Ouch, Mum, you're hurting me,' Alicia said, wriggling crossly. 'Mum! Get *off*.'

James was there now on the doorstep behind us, talking tersely to his partner in a low voice.

'Come and get Freddie, please, James.' I carried Effie towards the house, Alicia twirling across the gravel beside me, her pink dress bell-like as a fuchsia flower.

'Look what Gran bought me,' she crowed proudly. 'It's awesome, isn't it?'

'Awesome, sweetheart,' I said. 'Get Fred, James, can you?' I drew level with the men. Liam glanced at me.

'What the hell were you playing at?' I hissed at him over Effie's wispy head. 'Are you mad?'

'What do you mean?' Liam was calm. 'James asked me to collect the kids.'

Astounded, I spun round to my husband. 'James?'

But he was already crossing the drive to the car, unbuttoning Fred's seat belt, kissing his ruddy cheeks. Avoiding my gaze.

'When did he ask you?' I stammered. Helen Kelsey drove past the end of the drive and slowed, waving like a jolly schoolgirl. I hid my face behind my daughter's plump body.

'Ask him,' Liam muttered.

'I will.' I was incredulous. 'I can't – I don't—' I gave up, began to walk inside. 'I assume you're coming in this time?'

'I can't.' Liam shook his head. 'I've got to get back to London.'

'Really?' I stared at him. 'Why the constant rush?'

'No rush,' Liam said. 'It's just I spent the whole day collecting your children from Derby. I've got so much on. The club opens in three weeks.'

'Right.' I was nonplussed. 'Why did you collect them, Liam?'

Liam dropped his chin onto his jacket for a moment, his short sandy lashes masking his eyes. 'Ask your husband.'

James was by my side now, holding a grumbling Fred.

'James—' I began, but he looked at me imploringly. I realised with a jolt that he might have been crying.

'Can we talk about this later, please, Rose?' he muttered, so only I could hear. 'Take Fred in, can you?'

I put Effie down and took my son from his father; I clutched the twins tightly to me and hurried Alicia into the house as I heard the men's voices start to climb behind me.

'So,' I said as cheerfully as I could muster, watching my eldest child pirouette down the hall as I drank in the smell of Freddie, burying my nose in his silky hair, 'how about fishfingers and chips and Fab lollies for tea?'

* * *

226

Clamped to the phone, James studiously avoided me whilst I fed and bathed the children. He and Liam had argued out on the drive for a while, and then they'd disappeared briefly into the studio. By the time I'd sorted everyone out, Liam had left.

I'd just put the twins to bed and was about to curl up with Alicia and watch *The Sound of Music* yet again when the door-bell rang.

It was dark now and the porch light had blown but I recognised the figure standing in the drive, the Range Rover behind him.

'Thank you so much for coming,' I said shyly, relieved I was no longer in my dressing gown. The night we'd just spent together seemed so long ago already. 'But it's all OK. The kids are back safely, thank God.'

'Oh?' Danny looked at me quizzically. I was so pleased my earlier assumptions had been wrong.

'It was all just a hideous misunderstanding.' I smiled at him, pulling my cardigan tighter against the cold evening. 'I really appreciate your concern, though. Thank you. God, it's cold tonight, isn't it?' I peered up at the great sky. I knew I was babbling with nerves. 'Do you think it will snow?'

The night was colourless, full and heavy with the silence that always foretold snow.

'I think you've got the wrong end of the stick actually, Mrs Miller.' Danny looked down at his feet for a second. 'I've just brought a message, that's all.'

'Really?' I said slowly, my heart sinking.

'Aye, really.' Danny's voice was low, his hands shoved deep in his pockets. 'I can't spell it out any clearer than this, Rose. If you don't stay away, OK, if you don't leave Kattan's family well alone, your weans will be in proper danger. Don't ring, don't speak to them, don't do any research. Just leave everyone be.'

For a moment I was speechless.

'Do you understand me?' He looked up now and held my gaze.

227

'Not really. Is Kattan threatening me?' I held on to the wall for a second. It felt rough beneath my fingers. 'Threatening my – my "weans"? Seriously?'

'Maybe.' He shrugged with what seemed like utter indifference.

'Or sorry, perhaps you are?' I found my voice now. 'Is it *you* who is threatening my family?'

The blankness of his face bit into my soul as he shrugged again. 'Not especially me.'

'You bastard.' I made to shut the door in his face, but he stopped it with his booted foot. He took his hands out of his pockets and I realised with horror he was holding the gun I'd seen the other day. He folded his hands behind his back. My heart was pounding; I could feel myself start to shake.

'Listen to me, Rose.' His tone was urgent now. 'I don't know where the bairns were earlier, but I do know this is deadly serious. I warned you before this is not a game. Stay away, before something really bad happens.'

We stared at one another for a moment. Then Danny stuck the gun in his waistband, zipped up his jacket so that it covered his mouth and chin, and he walked away from me, towards the great blank-eyed car he drove.

With a bang I shut the door, bending double in the hallway as if I had just been winded with a gut-punch. In the thick rug I caught the glint of green glass.

'What did he want?' James said, a shadow in the kitchen doorway. I didn't know how long my husband had been there; I blinked down the tears that smarted, and reached down for the green thing that had glinted. A plastic jewel from a toy crown.

'I wish I knew, James.' Still clutching the jewel, I looked at my husband's ashen face. 'What the hell's going on?'

Chapter Eighteen

The next morning the snow had come, sealing us off into an impenetrable white world. I sat at the kitchen table and drank tea, looking at the soft branches bowed down with their new weight, listening to my children's incessant chatter.

'It's not, Mum, is it?'

'It is.' Freddie's bottom lip trembled and I gathered him up onto my lap. 'It *is* Harry-potamus, isn't it, Mummy?'

'Durrr,' Alicia scoffed, waving a book in his face. 'It's Harry *Potter*, you idiot.'

'Alicia,' I reproved mildly, 'don't be horrid. He's only three.'

A doleful James sloped into the room and smiled pathetically at me. Almost worse than angry or sullen James was contrite James.

'Stop it,' I snapped. 'You look ridiculous. You're far too old for puppy-dog eyes.'

'You used to like them.' He put his hand on my shoulder. I forced myself not to shrug it off. 'More tea, vicar?'

Silently I pushed my cup towards him as Fred jumped off my knee. I had the sudden inclination to fall in a heap on the floor, a suppurating, slowly dissolving mass of wet tissue and no hope. A heap of despair. But I didn't. I couldn't allow myself to. I pulled a silly face at Effie instead.

Last night James and I had argued until I'd finally given in to exhaustion. Hair on end and Jack Daniel's in hand, James had sworn that if he *had* asked Liam to collect the kids, he had totally forgotten. He had drunk too much on the plane coming back, he said, celebrating the deal, and he had to admit there were a few lost hours at Singapore airport. Perhaps he'd spoken to Liam then, perhaps he'd told Marsha who ran the office at Revolver, to call. He was very sorry, he said, so so sorry. He'd make sure it never happened again. He would make it up to me. How about that spa break he had promised me?

He was lying. But in the face of my cold disbelief and fury, he lost it altogether. At one point he hurled the vase of blue-bells I'd picked from the front garden onto the floor, crushing the delicate flowers underfoot. Later, contrite again, he couldn't understand why I wouldn't just forgive him immediately. And there was something else, a tense knot of something in my stomach, something I couldn't – or wouldn't – unravel, that kept me from forgiving him. That kept him at arm's length.

In bed he had wanted to have sex, but I didn't want him anywhere near me. I was still so cross, and it was so rare to feel desired by him that it confused me. The truth was we had lost our real connection years ago.

As he began to snore I lay wide-eyed, staring into the dark-ness. I heard the church bell chime the hour, and chime the next. I felt crippled with longing; but overwhelmed with sadness. I couldn't get Danny's face out of my mind; I couldn't get his betrayal out of my head. I had seen a glimpse of happiness and I had reached out to it. I knew I had started to fall, but I hadn't realised how far. I didn't understand myself.

Eventually I got out and crept into bed with Freddie, removing a small rubber lizard from beneath my left ear as I lay down, listening to his peaceful breathing.

When I woke in the morning, I was clutching my son like my life depended on it.

I looked out at the cat delicately picking his way through the pristine blanket of snow. I remembered a freezing January day in Oxford in Christ Church Meadow, where Alice had so famously fallen down the White Rabbit's burrow. Dalziel and I had lain on our backs after tripping all night long and made angels in the new-fallen snow, laughing, giggling together like kids. We'd swept our arms out and above our heads through the thick soft drift, creating wings like the archangels might have had.

'James,' I said slowly, 'why did Helen Kelsey think she saw you driving the other day?'

'When?'

'In Oxford. The day after you left?'

'She can't have.'

'She seemed pretty sure. And she said you were with a girl.'

James looked over at the kids, who were busy drawing snowmen, and then he sat beside me, lowering his voice theatrically. 'Look, I didn't want to have to tell you this, but . . .' He paused.

'What?' I felt a clench of something.

'I'm – a little worried . . .' he faltered.

'Just say it, J, for God's sake.'

'She propositioned me at Karen's Christmas party.'

'What?' I stared at him.

'Helen cornered me upstairs, by the bathroom. Her shirt was all undone. I was really embarrassed. She's got it bad, Rose. I think she's a bit obsessed with me. I think –' he paused again – 'I think she's started stalking me.'

I looked into his woebegone face and I began to laugh. I laughed until it actually hurt my sides.

'Why's that so funny?' he said, all hurt. 'I'm not that hideous, am I?'

'No, of course not,' I said, wiping the tears from my eyes. I didn't know whether to believe him and frankly I was beyond caring. 'I can just picture her trying it on, that's all. I bet she wears beautifully matched underwear.'

'I wouldn't know.' He looked uncomfortable. 'She didn't get that far. Thank God.'

'And what did you say?'

'I said thank you very much but, you know, I was happily married, et cetera.'

But he looked away when he said the last part. I began to gather the cereal boxes.

'Shall we go and play snowballs?' I said to Effie.

James stood and stretched.

'Now I've got that off my chest, I've made a decision,' my husband said. 'It's time for a party.'

'A party?' I repeated dully. Never had I felt less like celebrating.

'Liam and I need to announce our latest endeavours to the world. And we deserve one. Too much doom and gloom in the world right now. But things are on the up for us now, my petals.'

'I'm surprised you want to do anything with Liam right now,' I muttered. I'd tried to ring him a few times this morning myself to demand an explanation, but his phone kept going to voicemail.

'Well, he made a mistake,' James said, 'but he knows that now. He won't do it again.'

'Can we have balloons, Daddy?' Effie asked, her tongue curled up onto her upper lip as she concentrated on adding eyes to her snowman's face. 'And cake and party bags?'

'You, my darling,' James swept her up into his arms, tickling her until she giggled helplessly, 'can have whatever you so desire.'

'Can I? Can I?' Freddie hopped up and down. 'Can I have a Batman mask and a Harry-potomus and a – and a . . .' he couldn't think of anything else he wanted, '. . . another Batman mask?'

I looked out at the snow and I felt like my heart was cracking.

* * *

As quickly as the snow came, it disappeared again, leaving a dirty slush in its place, but slowly, spring returned. I got on with life. I went back to the *Chronicle* and wrote about Edna Brown's vegetable patch and the like. I avoided calls from Xav though I invited him to the bash; I tried not to buy his paper but I couldn't quite resist the temptation of keeping tabs on Ash Kattan or Lord Higham. I didn't go anywhere near the Kattans, although once I saw the silver Porsche parked in town. I lingered for a moment looking for Maya, but she never appeared.

At home I helped James arrange his party. I finally remembered about the photos in the cupboard, the one of Lord Higham, but when he asked me to show him, I couldn't find them, and James just laughed, and looked at me as if I was mad. And maybe I was. I remembered the images of Kattan and Higham I'd seen in Peggy's basement and I felt like my judgement was utterly off. I'd been too busy reading things into places there was nothing to be read.

I cooked the meals (not very well, admittedly), I smiled dutifully, I played with my children, washed them, brushed their hair and cuddled them, tried not to snap at them too much when they woke me in the night or fought and argued, drove them from A to B – but inside, inside I felt cold and, if they hadn't been there, not much better than dead.

I rang my friend Jen in London.

'Will you come to the party?' I said, and she whooped with pleasure.

'Just try and stop me. Will there be any nice men there? Please say yes. My sex life's like the Sahara.'

'I doubt it. They'll all be wankers from James's club or married stodges from round here. Or beautiful – and gay.'

'Great.' She sounded less enthused. 'I was hoping more Kings of Leon than George Michael. I'll bring my Barbra Streisand outfit then. How are you, anyway? You sound a bit weird.'

'Weird,' I intoned, zombie-like.

233

'Rose?' she said, worried. 'What's up?'

'Something. Nothing. Everything.' I felt my eyes fill. 'I've done something really really stupid.'

'You're not pregnant again?' She sounded horrified. Jen had a high-flying job as an interpreter for the government; babies were low on her agenda.

'No I'm not. That'd be better than this, I think.'

'Really?' She lowered her voice. 'God. It must be bad.'

'Jenny!' But I knew what she meant. 'I'll tell you when you come up.'

'Is it James?' she whispered.

'No. It's me. It's me and—'

'Oh God, Rose. You've slept with someone else.'

Blood filled my ears. 'I haven't,' I panicked.

'Yeah you have.' She knew me too well. 'And you're so bad at sex without love.'

'I'm not,' I squeaked. I wished I'd kept my mouth shut now. But it was killing me.

'I'll come up early. You can tell me all about it.'

'OK,' I said in a small voice.

'Oh, Rose. You've fallen for him, haven't you?'

'No,' I lied. 'Of course not.'

I hung up quickly.

In truth, of course, I was immobilised by the onslaught of such unexpected feelings. Mostly I just despised myself for falling so quickly. I told myself it was just the glimpse of escape Danny had afforded me, the stupid thought that he would accompany me on some kind of adventure, the kind I used to have before marriage and my children. But it wasn't. It was him. I had recognised some kindred spirit in this man. But I couldn't have him. It was all right and yet so wrong.

And this – this was the punishment for my infidelity. This pain. The fact that I was lower than when I began.

I was not a good woman any more; I had left the moral high ground.

The day before the party, Liam and Star arrived to help us prepare. There appeared to be an uneasy truce between my husband and his partner. A tension stretched between them I hadn't ever known before and that I didn't yet understand. I was still fuming with Liam and I avoided being in the same room as him because I didn't trust myself. In the evening Star's friend Katya arrived – a trapeze artist who would perform tomorrow night.

After supper James and Liam ensconced themselves in the studio; Star and Katya were playing dress-up with the children, painting Alicia and Effie's faces like beautiful gaudy butterflies, Freddie's like a tiger.

I took my cup of tea and slipped off to the marquee that was to pose as a chill-out space; I sat amongst the crates of wine-glasses we had hired, and I finally made the phone call that I'd thought about for days, my fingers clumsy on the mobile's keys. My stomach churned as I waited for it to connect, but there was no answer. I suppose I hadn't thought there would be.

I took a deep breath, and I left a message.

'I just wanted to tell you what I thought of – of what you said. All things considered.'

There was a noise behind me. The delivery men must be arriving with the sofas and the star-cloth. I spoke faster and quieter. 'I am used to being in dodgy situations, but no one has ever threatened my kids. I've done what you asked. I've kept away. But I just wanted to tell you that no one, no one has really ever managed to make me feel quite so, quite so—'

James pushed his way through the marquee flap. I hung up quickly.

'Who was that?' he asked.

'No one,' I said.

'This no one?' he said. He threw my notebook on the table

in front of me. 'This is real, isn't it, Rose?' His face was taut with anger. 'It's not bloody fiction, is it?'

It was inevitable, that was the terrifying thing right from the moment I first saw you, Danny, we locked eyes and we both knew, though how can you know, some would say, how can you know immediately like that. But we did, there was no explanation. We just did. We moved nearer and then further away in fear, but all the time we waited we were heading for this moment, like we were on some kind of fatal course. And the first time you touched me you put your hand on me and it was like a surge of electricity and neither of us said anything but all night I felt it. I would have stayed close, couldn't bear to be separated until we had to be. Until we had to go home alone.

I looked up at James and I felt the world beneath my feet starting to tilt, sliding away until I felt like I was falling.

'This is you, isn't it? All this time you said your writing was work but it's not. It's been really happening, hasn't it?' His eyes were glazed and black, like he'd been drinking or snorting something. He'd lost all rationale; he was spitting with fury. 'You fucking bitch.'

He slapped me so hard I fell backwards off my chair. I didn't see it coming; I was too unprepared to save myself. I went crashing into a crate, trying to protect my face as I went.

And as I fell, it seemed like it was in slow motion. As I fell, all I could hear around me was the sound of breaking glass.

PART TWO

Chapter Nineteen

Remember tonight . . . for it is the beginning of always.

Dante

I move through the room like a ghost. I *feel* like a ghost, though I know I must have shape and form because people seem to see me; they smile and greet me and I smile back. I keep moving onwards and I smile over and again, I pour the wine and our guests are laughing, kissing me, touching my bare arm. 'Congratulations!' someone says with enthusiasm, and I nearly say 'For what?' but I don't. I don't question it: I just thank them quietly instead.

I spot Alicia – she is there before me – and then almost as quickly she is gone. She flits in and out of the crowd in her green dress with all the ruffles: in the shop I thought it was too old for her but I caved in too fast. I keep finding that my resolve to fight has fled. Alicia is overexcited, a small wraith pulsing with the exhilaration in the air, so much her father's daughter, her dark hair falling against her pale face. Her friend Holly follows faithfully behind, carrot-coloured plaits bouncing on her shoulders – and then there is Effie, trundling through, struggling to keep up with the older girls. Her solid little limbs so plump you could take a bite out of them, her tongue stuck between her teeth in concentration as she hunts for her big sister, her round cheeks pink with effort and excitement.

'Effie.' I shove the wine into someone's hand – Xav's I think. 'Do you mind?' I mutter absently, and he grins and says, 'Mind? A Clos des Papes '07? Are you insane, darling?' I release the bottle and quicken my step to catch up with my smaller daughter as her gaze darts from side to side, as she realises she's finally lost the trail. My heart aches, and I reach her with a rush of something like relief, scooping her up, pressing Effie's face into my neck, the smell of her always like being home. The short bunches she insisted on tickle my nose, her shiny blonde hair blending into mine, and for one moment, Effie relaxes in my grasp. She lets her weight go and rests there, small and sturdy in my arms, and for a second I feel safe. Not even safe, in fact, but actually – sane.

And then Effie starts to wriggle. She's spotted Alicia and Holly now. They are rapt with concentration over by the ice sculpture of a couple subtly screwing that James had insisted on. 'It's art, Rosie,' he'd said with a grin when I demurred. 'The kids'll think they're hugging.'

'I doubt it,' I muttered, but I acquiesced, because after all it was his big night.

I watch Alicia and Holly now, wide-eyed as the MP Eddie Johnson flips his fingers behind Holly's freckled ear and retrieves a shiny coin. I wonder why he is here – but then, I'd given up any control of the guest list, apart from Hadi Kattan. I'd told James I didn't want him near the house – but Xav said he'd heard he'd returned to Iran anyway.

I'm reminded painfully of Effie's presence as she kicks me in the ribs, struggling to get down.

'Let *go*, Mummy,' she demands at the exact moment the band strike up, a handsome group of swaggering twenty-somethings, darlings of *NME*, The Hothouse, about to become huge. To my relief Alicia flashes through the fishnets and stilettos, the ripped Levi's and the Prada dresses. Star is in a dress so ripped and tiny it's like a teabag, black leather bondage boots up to her thighs, and the pop star Domino McFadden's even wearing wet-look PVC, of course she is, and I allow myself a wry smile. Once I might have worn it myself, but not tonight. Not any more. Instead, for J's sake, I chose a demure Chloe dress, grey wool, so very grown-up. Just like me these days. I've lost a tiny bit of weight through misery, but I am still curvier than I used to be. I am new Rose. Undesirable, it seems. Not the old Rose – the Rose who for a time was shameless in bed, full of confidence. I am Rose who has three children, whose body is marked irreparably by motherhood, who has lost the defiant confidence that came after Dalziel, the confidence that came despite the implosion of Society X, that has finally dissipated for ever. I touch my bruised face, now covered by make-up.

Alicia is by the stage now, Holly in her wake like a small tug – and Star is about to dance. She waits for the music to reach the climax, swaying gracefully. Below her, at the foot of the stairs, a boy stands, almost a man, and he is quite beautiful, with white-blond hair and dark skin, and he reminds me of someone. He reminds me of Dalziel, I realise with a sharp pain, he reminds me of the friend I loved so much and lost.

'Mum-*my*,' Effie puffs, and I come back to the present and I lower her. She slides to the ground and I watch her small figure stomp through the adult legs until she reaches her sister's side and slips her small hand into Alicia's slightly bigger one. I look for the boy again, but he has his back to me now; he's talking to a couple of young women in matching backless dresses, who look at him rather adoringly and keep laughing silly tinkly laughs.

'Oh, Charlie,' they keep saying, 'you *are* funny.'

I think of myself aged eighteen and I shiver.

Instinctively I start to move towards the stairs. I want to check on Freddie; he's had a temperature and is tucked up in bed. The band are playing 'Suicide Blonde' as I climb upwards, my feet sore in my Louboutins, and then the song is climaxing and I hear Liam's voice, thanking everyone for coming, and I'm up on the first floor, looking down on them. How absurd, I think absently, to live in a house so old and grand there's actually a minstrels' gallery. I hear my name as Helen Kelsey comes out of the guest bathroom, blotting her scarlet lipstick on a tissue, her small prim mouth overpainted, her auburn bob coiffured to within an inch of its life. She starts when she sees me by the pillar.

'God, Rose, you scared me.'

'Sorry,' I smile automatically. I wonder if she's looking for my husband.

'Fantastic party, darling,' she purrs, but I sense her fighting to keep the malevolence from her tone. 'This wallpaper's new, isn't it?' She waves a manicured hand at the golden caged birds on the wall.

'Yes,' I agree.

'It's Nina Campbell, isn't it?'

'I think so.' I shrug. 'I'm always a bit rubbish on names.'

'Who did you use this time then?' Her face is rigid with unspoken emotion.

'Oh, some new mate of J's.' I lean over the parapet and look down at the many coloured heads below me, the cigarette smoke forming wreaths in the air.

'Who, though? I'd love the name.'

'I think he was – he's called Gilbert.'

'Not Gilbert Donaldson? Did Madonna's place apparently? Oh God, I'd just die!'

'Oh well, you know what J's like,' though I doubt very much she does. I remember his words about her crush. 'Always got some new celebrity friend in tow.'

I look down for my jolly husband. Last time I saw him he

was in the middle of an anecdote about a very famous rock star and his predilection for being spanked with hairbrushes, and everyone was roaring appreciatively. Now he has vanished too. Helen's gaze stings me.

'God, Rose,' she says, and she can't hide the envy this time. 'You really *do* have it all, don't you?'

'I'm very lucky,' I intone politely. 'I know I am.'

As I move off I think I hear a sigh – more than a sigh, a moan. Someone is in the blue bedroom. I hear the bed creak and a murmured 'Oh *fuck*,' the vowel sound drawn out languorously in pleasure, followed by a more violent sound. The crack of the antique headboard against the wall, I guess, and I sigh myself. At least the kids are oblivious and out of earshot, I think as I glance down to see the girls still hand in hand waving at their uncle Liam on the stage, waiting for the magic they've been promised.

And I creep down the gallery, away from the couple presumably entwined, away from Helen Kelsey's false smiles, and down the thickly carpeted corridor, because I have a craving to see my son; I imagine him asleep in the bed, his fists curled above his head, his sleep-soaked face utterly peaceful in this madness.

I sit on the window-seat in his room and I realise with a crashing certainty that the only person I want to see right now, apart from my kids, is never going to be here, and I feel such sorrow; such anger with myself for having chosen so badly. I fooled myself I could do sex without emotion: I was horribly wrong. I am riven with desire and I can't seem to fight it. I bite back the tears. I waited so long for him and yet I chose so badly; he only made me feel worse. And everything is falling apart and I can finally see my life for what it is: the fact that in Paris eight years ago, I mistook my shared guilt with James for our destiny.

Freddie murmurs in his sleep as I hear the drum-roll begin downstairs, and when I come out again, as if on cue, I hear my name as James cries it from the stage where he has just replaced

Liam. I lean over the balcony and James looks mussed and sweaty and larger than life in his slightly overtight T-shirt. In this light it looks like he has glitter on his face.

'So, people,' (I groan inwardly. I do wish he wouldn't say 'people'), 'you all know I couldn't have done any of it without my rock.'

I cringe inside.

'My mate, my lifelong companion.'

Outside, I force a smile.

'My beautiful wife, mother of my three pride and joys – I know you'll excuse my poor English – Rosie has ever since our student days, eh, petal?' Everyone laughs indulgently. I wish he'd hurry up. My face is as rigid now as Helen's Botoxed one as the glasses are all extended towards me, and I search the crowd for one single upturned face that I recognise. For one I actually like. My eyes settle on Jen, standing beside Xav, and she winks. I feel so flat, I cannot return the smile properly, although I do try.

'To my petal. My Rose!'

'To Rose,' they parrot, and then, thank God, James is on to the next thank you, his partner, Liam, and I exhale, pushing down the feeling, thinking, oh God when will this ever end? Then the lights go down and a thousand fairy lights flicker across the room, and for a split second there is silence, and then a whoosh of air.

I feel my hair flutter against my cheek as the girl in silver spangles sweeps above everybody's heads. There is a collective gasp as she gracefully arcs above them, one foot extended in its sparkly shoe, the other leg tucked neatly behind her, and then she is standing on her trapeze, her peroxide hair short as a boy's, her face pale and her mouth red, her eyes huge and dark, dusted all over with some kind of shimmering powder as she spins and arches elegantly above the room. The band begin to play again, a sad kind of rocky ballad, and slowly the crowd get used to her being there and begin to drink and talk again, although many are transfixed.

And for a moment, I feel a kind of jealousy for her freedom as the ethereal form turns upside down effortlessly, and then almost immediately upright again on the swing entwined with ivy leaves and tinsel, answerable to no one but herself. Her gaze seems to be fixed on someone – though from this angle I can't quite tell on whom. There's another smaller gasp as she hangs precariously by one foot, and all eyes are back on her. I think I hear a kind of banging outside but it is drowned out by the music and I am almost mesmerised. I enjoy watching this supple girl as she passes before me and then back again. Then suddenly I become aware of some kind of commotion in the corner by the door downstairs: raised voices. I look over, I see James there fleetingly and then he's gone again, and standing in his place is a small cluster of men whom I don't recognise, stocky, all in casual jackets and jeans, and Liam is trying to placate them, and I suppose I'd better see what they want – and then there is a scream.

I turn; I see the girl grappling with the flimsy trapeze – and I watch as if it's slow motion as she twists desperately through the air – as her hand clutches emptiness. The band breaks off and the crowd are realising that the figure who moments ago soared above them like some bird of paradise has in fact lost her footing and has tried and failed to hang on but now is falling, is plunging upside down, is spiralling like a heavy feather on the breeze.

There is no safety net, of course – J wouldn't have thought of such a thing. And I realise the girl is lost; there is no time to save her. She is lost. And the silence is broken only by a crunch, the hideous thud of a body crumpling on the floor.

I wake up. I run down the stairs, my heart beating frantically, tripping in my high shoes.

'Ring an ambulance,' I yell at someone, and I see Alicia's great eyes wide with shock.

I push through the crowd to the girl and she is not moving, though her eyes are open and she is still alive, I think, thank God. One leg is tucked neatly behind her again, the other out at a horrible angle that I cannot bear to look at, and two of those stocky men are pushing towards us. Holly's mother offers a pink pashmina to place below her head.

'Don't move her!' another voice says.

I look at that leg and I grab Effie, who is round-mouthed with horror, and shove her into the nearest arms, which are Jen's, hissing. 'Take her away, get her away, please. And Alicia and Holly.' Jen nods dumbly, the colour draining from her face, and grasps Alicia's hand. Star is so drunk she bursts into tears and begins to wail.

'Mummy,' Effie whispers over Jen's shoulder, 'the lady's not flying more now, is she, Mummy?'

I feel a hot needling in my eyes, and I crouch down by the spangled girl who is breathing shallow rapid breaths, and I say, 'Try not to move, OK?' and I try really hard to smile reassuringly.

'The ambulance is coming,' an authoritative voice says, I don't know whose. I think it's one of those men, he's on a phone, and I take the girl's hand and it's so cold, and as I look up I see the other two thugs escort my husband through the arch, towards the front door. And by the door I think I see Ash Kattan turning away, and the beautiful blond boy. They look like brothers, I think vacantly, though the blond boy looks horrified, truly sickened – and then a voice cuts through my thoughts.

'It was like she threw herself off,' the voice says, 'I'm sure she did.'

'It looked like she did,' someone else agrees, breathy with shock. 'It was like she was – I don't know. Trying to fly.'

I turn back to the silver-spangled girl and I wonder why her sequins are turning darker, and then I realise with a kind of dull horror it must be blood. I see her eyes flutter, reflecting the thousand tiny lights strung up around the room, and she's saying something, something I can't understand. A name, I think. Helen Kelsey's husband, Frank, is heading towards me now and I remember with relief that he's a doctor.

Just as I hear the front door bang shut against the spring wind, the candles all guttering in the breeze, the girl's eyes close; they flutter and they close. The reflections are extinguished; her eyes are shut.

Chapter Twenty

At first they wouldn't tell me about the girl. The nurse at reception established that I wasn't family, therefore I couldn't know, but eventually relented in the face of my evident distress. A harried doctor came to talk to me; wearily he looked at my face and asked what had happened to me. I'd forgotten about my own bruise. I'd covered it so carefully for the party with make-up that had apparently now worn off.

'It doesn't look very hopeful,' he said quietly about the girl, and asked me if I knew how to contact her family. Before I could answer, the crash-cart came racing down the corridor and the doctor went running.

I sat alone in the waiting area, drinking tepid coffee and trying to think straight. I still had no idea who had taken James. After he'd been manhandled out of the house and all hell had broken loose, I'd shooed everyone away into other rooms. I'd quickly seen that Star was far too drunk to accompany her injured friend to hospital, and out of frantic guilt, I'd left the kids with Domino and Jen and ridden behind in the ambulance.

Two hours later, I still didn't know where James was; his phone was ringing out – and now Liam, whom I'd left in charge of the guests, wasn't answering his mobile either.

And then the doctor who I'd just spoken to appeared from behind the rapidly drawn curtains and walked towards me, head bowed in exhaustion.

I couldn't believe Katya had died. I just sat in the neon-lit corridor on an orange chair, in shock, my mind racing. Sparkles from her costume on the corridor floor caught the overhead lights, twinkling incongruously against the well-trodden lino. Rational thought seemed impossible, but I promised the staff I'd get them her details as soon as I could, and then I called a cab and went back to the house; the house that seemed even less like home.

The children were sleeping, thank God, and the guests had all gone apart from the few who'd passed out in drunken disarray. Jen was still up. She grasped my hands and told me there was still no news of James.

'I'm sure he'll be fine. You know James,' she soothed, and made me tea, hugging me for a silent moment before going to bed herself.

I sat amongst the debris of the party, the half-full glasses smeared with lipstick and fingerprints, the overflowing ashtrays; the empty canapé platters and discarded bits of clothing; the paper streamers and the hundreds of crimson roses, and I tried again to call Liam, James, anyone who might tell me what was happening. I was scared that James had been hurt, that he had been strong-armed away by someone he'd upset in clubland. I didn't know who to call but I tried calling them all anyway, until I ran out of options. Eventually I fell into a doze on the sofa, clutching my cold tea.

The phone pealed through the bizarre dream I was having about dancing in the old college bar with Danny Callendar and Dalziel, and I spilled the tea down my leg.

'Rose.' It was James. He said – and he wasn't calm, he was a very long way from calm – he told me he had been arrested. The men who looked like thugs, they had turned out to be police.

'What for?' I asked harshly. A single silver stiletto shoe lay abandoned beneath the coffee table.

'I don't know.' His voice sounded strangely small and high-pitched. 'They just keep asking me where I've been recently and how I met the guys I bought the marble from.'

I stared blindly at the ice sculpture of the couple fucking; it was melting.

'How *did* you meet them?'

'I can't remember,' he said plaintively. 'My head's a mess right now.'

God knew what he had been taking at the party.

'What do you mean, you can't remember? Isn't that why you went to Vietnam?'

'The last few weeks have been so mental, I can't think straight. I think Liam introduced me.'

'Liam did?' I said. I thought of Liam poking round the studio when James was away. I thought of Liam's face on the day he had brought my children home. I thought about the fact that James said he hadn't remembered asking Liam to collect them.

'I need to speak to him,' James said urgently. 'Now. He needs to come down here.'

'I can't reach him. I don't know where he's gone, and Star's out cold.'

'Well, keep trying, can you?' he snapped. 'It's pretty fucking desperate here.'

I saw the trapeze artist spinning in the air; I shut my eyes hard as I heard the crunch and slap of her body hitting the ground. Someone had covered up the bloodstains with a towel; it lay at my own feet now.

'She's dead, James.' My voice was a croak.

'Who is?'

'The girl on the trapeze. She died.' I stared numbly at the towel. 'I went to the hospital with her.'

'Dead?' he whispered.

250

'They couldn't stop the bleeding. She had massive internal injuries.'

There was a silence.

'James?'

Softly my husband started to cry. 'Oh Christ,' he sobbed. 'Oh Christ. I can't believe this is happening.'

'If there's anything you need to tell me, J,' I said, and I felt very cold, 'you should do it now.'

There was a pause. I pulled my cardigan tighter around me but I couldn't stop shivering. The crying stopped. I could sense James pulling himself together.

'I need a lawyer. Ring Ruth Jones. Get her here now.'

In the morning, after a few hours' troubled sleep, I found a bedraggled Liam in the kitchen. Jen had apparently taken the children into Burford for hot chocolate and Star had already left for London. She would contact Katya's parents and the hospital, Liam said, handing me a stewed cup of tea. I looked at him slumped over the kitchen counter.

'What the hell's going on, Liam?'

'I honestly don't know, Rose.' He looked exhausted as he ran a meaty hand through sandy curls. 'I've been at the police station half the bloody night myself with some weasely-faced copper yelling at me to tell the fucking truth.'

'Were you?' I stared at him. 'James didn't say.'

'James didn't know.'

'So why've they let you go and not him?'

'I don't know, Rose. I just know that I haven't a fucking Scooby what's going on myself.'

Of course, in time, that transpired not to be true, either.

Chapter Twenty-One

THE TIMES, APRIL 2008

Millionaire record producer and club promoter James Miller was apparently apprehended by police during a lavish party at his home in Gloucestershire last night. It is unclear at this stage what, if any, the charges brought against Mr Miller are but he is currently being detained at Oxford police station. Mr Miller had considerable success in the late '90s with remixes of various Top Ten dance hits, the most famous being Domino's smash 'Hole in the Head'. Miller is also a partner in the Revolver super-clubs in London, Paris and New York. His business partner, Liam MacAvoy, was unavailable for comment today as was Miller's wife, Rose Langton, the award-winning journalist; she is believed to be at the couple's million-pound home in the Cotswolds, along with their three children.

Slowly, everyone left the house until I was alone with my children. And the scary thing wasn't being on my own; it was that I felt a kind of peace I hadn't felt in years, a peace rapidly spoiled by my own guilt – and the fact that the poor girl had died here.

On Monday morning I took the children into school, valiantly ignoring the stares and whispers. Only Holly's mother

Karen, who'd been at the party, asked if I was all right. The rest just stared, po-faced, beady-eyed – and I had the horrible feeling they were glad; that they felt I deserved it. We had always been outsiders, however 'cool' they thought we were, they didn't really like us. They didn't like our success, hated the fact I'd kept myself apart. But I hadn't isolated myself for the reasons that they suspected. I was just wary of getting close to them; to people who would see the cracks beneath the façade of my life.

When I got home, a car was waiting in the drive, a small dark woman leaning against it in an efficient grey suit. Too efficient to be a journalist.

'Mrs Miller?'

'Yep.' I went to unlock the front door.

'You need to come with me, please.'

'Are you arresting me too?' I swung to face her.

'Not unless you want me to,' she said pleasantly. 'Or you think there's a reason I should?'

At the police station they kept on and on about James's recent movements. I was torn between explaining that I rarely knew what he was up to at the best of times, and playing the loyal wife. I plumped for the latter, but I could sense it was to little effect, mainly because I didn't have the answers they wanted.

'You live an extremely comfortable life, don't you, Mrs Miller?'

'We've worked very hard for it.'

'Really?' She looked disbelieving. 'I thought you were a stay-at-home mum.'

I stared at her. How in this day and age could one woman look at another with such disdain? What happened to the sisterhood?

'I am a "stay-at-home mum", yes. At the moment. Apart from the one day I do at the *Chronicle*. But I was an extremely career-driven journalist before I had my first child six years ago. I had

253

a weekly column; I did a lot of radio. I was doing well, financially.'

'So you don't work? Not really.'

'Not really, no,' I said wearily.

'But still you live in a beautiful and costly home, you drive top-end cars, you employ a cleaner, your children go to private school—'

'I drive a five-year-old Passat. Alicia goes to the village primary. The twins go to a nursery that we pay for, yes. But it's hardly Eton.'

'You have expensive foreign holidays, your clothes are—'

'Sorry,' I interrupted, 'but what exactly are you getting at? My husband set up a record label in the nineties that does extremely well. He also produces artists who are multimillionaires themselves. You might even have heard of some of them.'

'Might I?' Her smile was false. 'Enlighten me.'

'Bono, Radiohead, Coldplay? Plus he co-owns three large nightclubs with a massive turnover. Occasionally we holiday in the towns they're based in, but other than that, we mostly go to the Peak District to stay with my mum and dad. And like I said, I used to be fairly successful myself before I had Alicia.' I drew breath, steadied myself. 'We're doing all right for ourselves, thank you. That doesn't mean we are criminals.'

She changed tack. 'So he's away a lot, your husband. And you keep up with his arrangements, do you?'

'He travels all the time. It's normal in his line of work. We both used to, when I worked full time. It's hard, with three small kids, to keep up with exact schedules.'

DS Montford looked unimpressed. 'Does he often say he's out of the country when he's not?' She peered at me over black rectangular glasses, like an impatient schoolteacher.

'Sorry, I don't follow,' I said, glancing at the clock. 'Will this take much longer? I have to collect my twins soon.'

'Not much longer, no,' she smiled affably, perusing her notes briefly. 'The thing is, you've just told me Mr Miller's last business trip was to Vietnam, last month.'

'That's right.'

'Only, according to all our information, he never left the country.'

'Never left the country,' I repeated stupidly. My mouth was suddenly dry as sandpaper. 'Are you sure?'

'Pretty sure, yes. He never boarded the flight you say he did. He never crossed a border.'

'But I dropped him at the airport. I spoke to him out there and everything.' I thought of the crackly line, the shouted conversation. Helen Kelsey's smug little face reared into my mind. *I saw him driving yesterday.* I looked at the policewoman. 'As far as I know, he was abroad.'

'He wasn't, you know.'

'Well, where was he?'

'As his wife, Mrs Miller, I was hoping that you could have enlightened me on that one.'

I felt a tightening in my chest. I didn't answer.

'As it is, we're just trying to ascertain exactly where he was.'

'Are you enjoying this?' I asked her flatly. 'Because you look like you are.'

'Just doing my job, Mrs Miller,' she smiled grimly, and pushed her glasses back up the bridge of her nose. 'Just doing my job.'

They wouldn't let me see James that morning. I knew that they probably couldn't hold him much longer without charging him: the lawyer said they still hadn't. But they also wouldn't free him.

I drove home through hedgerows still bursting with spring. Unbelievable that in the midst of this burgeoning beauty my life had just turned on its head; I feared it was not about to turn back soon. I was just grateful that for now, the children were still oblivious to the situation.

255

A white butterfly fluttered across the windscreen – but when I glanced again to see it fly to freedom, it had disappeared. I had a horrible feeling that I had just destroyed it. Annihilated for simply being in the wrong place at the wrong time. I was starting to realise this wasn't all just a horrible mistake.

Chapter Twenty-Two

That night, after I'd read stories, sung songs, warmed endless milk and kissed fat cheeks, trying desperately to pretend everything was absolutely normal, that Daddy was away for work again, that I was actually sane, I wrapped a blanket around myself and went alone into the dark. I sat on the bench beneath the magnolia tree, now bare of its petals, and listened to the gentle popple of the pond as the frogs broke the surface; I thought that this night-time peace was one of the things that had made my isolated life here worth it.

I had been so lonely recently in the presence of my husband. I thought about the fact that now he was not here, it didn't feel wrong.

There was a soft crunch of gravel underfoot; my head snapped round. And then he was there, stealthy as the cat he had entered the garden without me realising; he was standing to my left.

He stood beneath the stone archway where the roses grew in summer. My breath caught in my throat and my heart began to race until I had to forcibly quell it. There were so many things to say and yet nothing at all. I didn't want to sound recriminatory and yet there were only recriminations. I was stupidly glad that he had come, although I knew I shouldn't be; and yet so hurt and confused that I didn't know where to start.

Why did you vanish? Why did you threaten me? Why did you come near me in the first place?

Questions flooded my head and yet I stayed silent. I stared at him as he leaned back against the wall, contemplating me. In the half-light it was hard to see him properly. With a pain like a hammer striking home I realised the only thing I wanted to do was reach out and touch him – and yet I was still so angry I wanted to scream. Worst of all, I was furious with myself for feeling like this.

In the end I said, 'Have you come to hurt my children? Because you'll have to hurt me first.'

'I'm sorry.' His voice was low and hoarse, and he seemed more unsure than I'd known him before.

'Great. Thanks for the apology.' I stood up. 'Please, will you go now?'

My legs were unsteady because I'd been sitting for so long. He crossed the gravel in two strides and I stepped back quickly, out of his reach, almost overbalancing in my haste to get away.

'Please, Rose. I am really sorry. I just can't—'

'What?' I put my hands up to ward him off although he had not touched me yet. 'What, Danny? Sorry that you slept with a married woman? Sorry that you threatened my kids? Sorry that you just disappeared?'

'I would never have hurt them, you must know that.'

'How do I know that? I don't know you at all, that much is clear.'

'I can't explain, not now.'

'Why not?'

'I shouldn't even be here.'

'Why shouldn't you?'

'Because. I can't explain. Not now.'

'Right. Well, don't then.' I slipped out of his shadow and

moved to step into the house. But before I could, he pulled me back.

'Don't,' I croaked, but found I couldn't stop him. I just wanted to not think, to lose myself for a while.

'Rose,' he whispered, 'I'm so sorry,' and then he picked me up and I let him; he carried me into the house and I was crying tears of sorrow, anger and frustration, and I wanted to pummel him with my clenched fists but instead I wrapped my legs around him and kissed him back until my mouth hurt. I felt his warm skin beneath my splayed fingers and he held me so tight I felt he could crush me and at that moment it would have been all right, because I sought oblivion.

Afterwards we lay on the floor beside each other and listened to the sounds of the night outside. I looked over at him. He had a scar on his face that somehow I had never noticed before, a small white nick below his left cheekbone. He looked back and then he stroked my face, my sore cheek where James had hit me, only now the bruises had faded.

'God, Rose,' he muttered.

'What?'

'Just . . .' He ran his hand through his hair distractedly. 'You.'

My heart caught on itself, but somewhere deep down I didn't believe him any more.

He felt for his tobacco. 'Want one?'

'I don't smoke. Don't you remember?' I rolled away from his warm arms. I lay on the bare floorboards and I felt like an island floating alone, and then I thought, I must get up and put some clothes on before one of the children wake up. Only I couldn't move, not yet.

'I do remember, aye. I was just being polite.'

'Well, don't be polite. You've never bothered before.'

'I'm sorry,' he said equably. 'Sweet then?'

'I don't want a sweet.' I was being petulant, I knew. 'Why do you always eat them?'

'Trying to give up smoking. I got hooked on both instead.' He ran a hand over the floor. 'Home improvements?'

'I tore the carpet up.'

I hadn't been able to bear the bloodstains any more, so I'd hacked at it last night. The only time I had cried since James's arrest; I'd sat amidst underlay and tacks and wool pile and sobbed.

I looked back at Danny. 'Why are you here? I still don't understand.'

'Because I wanted to see you.'

'Where've you been?'

'Here and there.' He looked at his watch. 'I'm going to have to go, Rose. I'm sorry.'

I felt numb, like my soul was being sucked out, like I'd finally lost all sense of levity and joy. I knew we did not belong together. That much had become clear.

'Danny?'

'Aye.'

'Did you know James has been arrested?'

He sat up and felt in his discarded jacket for a light. 'I had heard, aye.'

'Ash Kattan was here.'

'When?'

'The night James got arrested. Do you know why?'

'Nope.'

I wanted to touch him and yet I couldn't.

'Can I ask you something else?' I said quietly.

'Go on.'

'Was it because of the children?'

He lit the roll-up. 'What do you mean?'

'Did you vanish, did you hate the – the idea of me in the end because of the children?'

'I don't understand.' He ran a hand through his hair; he looked tired. He rubbed his face as if to rouse himself.

'Because I was not just me?'

'Rose, it was nothing to do with your weans, I swear. Or you. Not in the way you think.'

'What then?'

'One day you'll understand, pet.' Danny inhaled deeply. He stared at the ceiling. Car headlights moved across it, two white discs sliding down the shadowed wall. 'I promise you that.'

'So why did you come back?' I whispered. I would not cry again.

'I came to find you – to tell you.' He reached out and ran a hand down my ribcage. My stomach contracted. 'I came to tell you that I was sorry.'

'You came to find me, to say sorry,' I was parroting again. 'And that's it?'

'I'm good at finding things.' The end of the roll-up was a tiny firefly in the darkness. 'That's what I do.'

I rolled back to him and stared down into his face. 'Just not so good at keeping them.'

'That may be true, Rose Miller. It may well be true.' He looked up at me, the blue of his eyes doused by the dim light; and then he ran one finger down my cheek. I could feel the heat of the cigarette on my skin. 'I wish I could stay.'

'But you can't.'

'It's not something I'm glad about.'

I moved my head away. 'What *are* you glad about?'

'Right now,' Danny stood up fluidly and walked to the window, buttoning up his jeans, 'not much.'

I watched him wordlessly.

'I'm flying out to join Kattan tomorrow.' He looked down the drive. 'I just wanted to say goodbye.' He drew the blinds.

'Where is he? Kattan?' I stared at Danny's naked back. He was lean in the moonlight, the well-defined muscles, the dip in the small of his back, the black dragon on his shoulder shadowed and smooth, another smaller tattoo on the other bicep, some kind of flag I didn't recognise. 'Where is he now?'

261

'Abroad. On his way home, I think.'

'And you're not here any more either, are you? In spirit, you're not here?'

'Not in the way you want me to be, no, I suppose not.'

I wanted to scream 'Don't go!' but I couldn't speak. I took a deep breath.

'I think you should leave now, Danny.'

He swung round. 'I *can't* be here, Rose. It's not that I don't want to be. It's just – I can't.'

'Whatever. It's fine.' I stood quickly and pulled my old sweat-shirt back over my head, scraping my hair angrily back from my face. 'Please, just go.'

How easy it is to say in love the opposite of what is actually meant.

'If that's what you want,' Danny shrugged. 'I guess you're right.'

How hard it is to confess what we really feel. To lay ourselves open, on the line.

I stared at him. 'Could you not even argue?'

He didn't answer, just got dressed silently. When he left he leaned to kiss me on the mouth, but I moved my head so that his cool lips landed awkwardly on my cheek. He stared down at me and in the half-light I could see the piercing blue of his eyes again, and I felt despair.

And when he left, slipping out of the back door like a furtive lover from some bad farce, I felt so much worse than I had before. I stared out into the dark.

When I went back into the living room, I saw he'd left his old jumper on the sofa, and a stupid lemon sherbet sweet had fallen from his pocket. I picked them up and carried them into the kitchen; I held them above the bin.

I despised myself for wanting him. I despised myself for wishing he had stayed. I hadn't meant to let him in but he'd got in anyway, like a fine layer of sand beneath my skin, he was there, hurting me because I couldn't have him and couldn't rid my head of him. And perhaps I had been greedy and bad, perhaps I deserved the pain. Whichever, I was sure as hell paying for it now.

I felt dead inside; I had lost any vestige of hope I had left. He might have said I was beautiful but still, he left. And I was a bad, bad woman who had cheated on her husband; who yearned to run away, who had, at one mad moment, forgotten she was a mother and only remembered that she was full of lust and longing and – love.

I carried his jumper upstairs and I breathed in its smell, just once. Then I tucked it into my bottom drawer, beneath my old pyjamas.

Chapter Twenty-Three

THE TIMES, MAY 2008

Record producer James Miller has reportedly been granted bail. He is at home in Gloucestershire awaiting the outcome of an investigation conducted by the Met, apparently in conjunction with drug trafficking. As yet no charges have been brought. Thirty-nine-year-old Miller declined to comment, although friends say he is fully intending to prove his innocence, should there be any need to.

They sent James home the next day. He was exhausted; hadn't slept at all, he said, and he looked thinner already, though he surely couldn't be.

'I've been fucking set up, Rose,' he kept saying. He sat at the kitchen table and drank a bottle of heavy burgundy, glass after glass of it. 'He set me up.'

'Who?' I couldn't bear it. 'Do you mean Liam?'

James stared at me, his mouth stained red. 'No, not bloody Liam. Of course not Liam. The bastard who did the deal on the importation. He set me up.'

'Who was he, though? Who was it?'

'He never told me his full name. Saquib something.'

'You must have had an idea, though, James, of who you were

dealing with?' I was nonplussed by his apparent denseness. He must be lying again, he had to be. 'Surely?'

'I met him in London before I went,' was all he would say before he drank himself to sleep.

And I watched him and I thought perhaps I should feel real guilt about Danny, but I knew that I didn't. Not really. I had lost James long, long ago.

In the morning over breakfast, I asked James why the police had said that he had never left the country.

'Because they're out to fucking get me.' He slammed the chair against the kitchen wall so hard it dented the paintwork, his plate of toast flying to the ground. 'They're all out to get me. Don't you understand?'

He yelled so loudly that Effie began to cry.

'It's OK, darling,' I crooned, cradling her to me as if she was still a baby. She looked up at me with woeful eyes.

'I want Daddy to go away again.'

All morning James rampaged through the house shouting and cursing until he wore himself out, just like his three-year-old son on a bad day. He yelled at me about the torn-up carpet for ten minutes until I quietly explained why I'd done it. Then he slunk off to the studio and slammed the door.

After school I took the children to the playground behind the church and then to The Copper Kettle for cheese-on-toast and lemonade for tea. I watched the little bubbles crowd round the glass that Effie held, and I craved peace for them; for their innocence. I listened to the women behind the counter moan about the Poles in Witney taking over their clientele.

'Bloody foreign muck,' one said, and I looked at her thinning crown, her baby-pink scalp, as she wiped the table next to her and I tried not to despise her fear.

I was sure people were staring at us as I watched the children laugh on the climbing-frame, screeching down the slides.

People who didn't know us were busy making judgements, and I thought that I wanted to leave this place now, this place that had never welcomed me. All I wanted – as was my habit, my oldest trick – all I wanted was to fly.

Later James was calmer. He'd spoken to his solicitor; Liam was coming up tomorrow.

'I'm sorry,' he apologised. 'I'm just under a lot of stress.'

I said of course I knew how hideous it must be, and I understood – but actually I didn't. I concentrated on the children because I didn't know what else to do.

As darkness fell, Helen Kelsey arrived on the doorstep with a basket full of charity, but I didn't let her in. I watched her from the upstairs window; I knew she had only come to delve and then impart the gossip to the village. I was quite simply done with being nice for the sake of it.

'Rose,' I could hear James calling me as I turned away from the window and drew the curtains, 'have you got a number for Hadi Kattan?'

My heart thumped painfully. 'Why?'

'I need to speak to him now.'

'Why?'

'Have you got a number or not? The one I've got doesn't seem to work.'

'Somewhere, I think. But why do you need him?' I said carefully, coming down the stairs.

'Because the furniture guy, I've just remembered. He was recommended through the Kattans.'

James went through to the studio and I followed. I was shocked at the tip it had become; he had pulled every file and box and folder from the shelves. There was paper, CDs, album artwork everywhere, the floor was covered. He was never usually the tidiest man, but James was extremely house-proud when it came to the studio.

'What do you mean you've just remembered?' I said, stepping over Mick Jagger dressed as a wizard. 'How could you possibly not remember before?'

His eyes were blazing with something. 'It doesn't matter, does it?'

'But you were banged up for three days and you didn't remember—'

'Shut up, Rose. I've remembered now.'

'Remembered *what*, though?'

'When I spoke to Kattan at his house, at that party he had. He offered to put some money into Revolver.'

'Yes, I know that. But what has it to do with – to do with—'

'And then we were talking about decking it out, the new club. I was admiring some of his furniture. All that gold-inlaid marble. I thought it would be classy in the new VIP. He said he would put me in touch with someone who imported it.'

'James, *please*. Be straight with me about everything now.' I sat heavily.

'I am.'

'You're not. You went back there, to Albion Manor, and I saw you, and you lied about it.'

'When?'

'You know when. What else are you lying about?'

'Nothing.'

'James! Were you really in Vietnam? Come on, J. Be honest.'

He was about to argue – and then suddenly he shrugged. 'I didn't want to worry you.'

'About what?'

'Stuff?'

'What kind of stuff?' God, he was infuriating.

'I had so much to sort out here and I – I *was* going to go, really, only then—'

'But I dropped you at the airport and everything.'

267

'Yeah. Well, I was going to go and then – they rang me, asked me to meet in London before I went away.'

'And what did you talk about?'

'When?'

'At this meeting when you were meant to be in Saigon?' How could I have been so slow? Marble wasn't even a Vietnamese product. 'Was it – was it heroin, J?'

He stared at me and I waited, hand outstretched to him, frozen. Finally he was going to tell the truth, I could tell. The computer pinged suddenly, announcing an email, and the spell was broken. He turned away.

'That bloke sorted it. The meeting in London.'

'What bloke?' I said carefully.

'You know, that Scottish geezer. The tall quiet one. Callendar. He arranged the meeting – about the furniture. I didn't trust him then. Never trust the quiet ones. I think – Christ's sake – careful, Rose.'

'Ouch.' I sliced my finger on the silver knife he used to open his post. 'Sorry. You think what?' I fumbled for a tissue to stem the blood; it dripped down onto the snowy paper I'd been assembling.

'I think he's fucking set me up.' He pulled another in-tray of stuff from the desk; it swirled through the air. 'Where are their fucking numbers? Why does everyone move my fucking stuff?'

My blood flowered onto the white tissue; a deep deep red.

That night James had another nightmare, the worst since we'd left university. He kept screaming a name over and over, a name I couldn't make out; he kept screaming it and moaning, 'Sorry, sorry, sorry . . .' When I eventually managed to wake him, his eyes were wide with fear. He said he couldn't remember anything, but his distress was tangible.

*   *   *

The next morning I drove to Albion Manor but it was boarded and shuttered – no cars, no horses in the field. I took a deep breath and rang Danny, but his voicemail was always on. I tried to call Hadi Kattan, as James already had, but his number was unobtainable. I tried Maya too, several times, but although it rang, she never answered her phone or returned my calls.

At night James paced the house, too frightened to close his eyes in case the nightmares came again; in the day he dozed on the sofa. Liam came and went, they spoke to endless lawyers, they muttered to one another – but they never really told me what was going on. However hard I tried to get it out of James, he was constantly vague. 'Set up' became his mantra; deep down I was terrified he was guilty.

I couldn't shake the feeling that Liam knew more than he was admitting, but he was at great pains to avoid being on his own with me at any time. I'd still never understood why he'd collected my children that day, and I'd lost my trust in him. My paranoia was growing, I was aware of that, but our world was falling apart and my reason was following close behind.

At the end of that week, one morning around dawn, the police came and took James away again – and this time he looked broken. Fred woke up crying with all the noise and confusion, and I scooped him out of bed and carried him downstairs. He was too heavy for me these days to hold for long, but now I held him tight in my arms, his head heavy on my shoulder, blinking and bewildered, tears like dewdrops on his lashes. We stood on the doorstep in the early morning mist, the distant hills wreathed as if in dragon's breath, shivering in our pyjamas.

I watched DS Montford escort my husband into the back of an unmarked car: I thanked God at least two of my children were still sleeping. James stared out at me, and he looked just like his son, like a little boy – and my heart went out to him.

He looked like someone who had lost his fight. I held Fred's hand up to wave to his father.

And later the expression on James's face – oh God, it haunted me. I'd seen that look before. The same look he wore the day that Dalziel tried to kill his own brother.

Chapter Twenty-Four

THE TIMES, MAY 2008

Record producer James Miller has been rearrested and is now apparently being held at London's Pentonville Prison. There is still no news of the exact charge, but it's understood that bail has been refused on the grounds that he might flee the jurisdiction, unusual in a case as high-profile as his, and worrying indeed for Miller.

When everyone starts lying, how do you ever know whom to trust?

The one person I needed to speak to most had completely disappeared. His phone was never answered, and then the number stopped working altogether. Like a mighty slap in the face, finally and irrevocably I realised I'd been played for an utter fool. I blocked the pain of rejection from my mind as best I could, busy with the salvation of my family, but the knowledge that Danny could never have cared at all nagged at me until I felt dust-like. Until I was nothing. The ridiculous longing dragged at me, scraped its rusty fingernails across my self – until slowly I realised this was the price I must pay for daring to look outside my life for happiness; for the lust that meant I'd forgotten I was not just me, I was many. I was not me; I was my children too.

But there was no space for self-pity and heartache. I had to figure out how to keep my family together the best I could, before we lost everything.

The week after James's second arrest, I took the children out of school for a few days and we went down to stay with Jen in London. I had people to see and questions to ask.

Liam wasn't expecting me when I buzzed at his door. He answered it in a pair of cut-off jogging bottoms, sporting a small paunch I'd not seen before. He was obviously hungover, his pale skin unhealthily pallid, his sandy curls on end. He looked not unlike the derelicts who lived at the bottom of his stairwell.

'Rose.' Was it my imagination or did he seem apprehensive?

Liam lived in the penthouse of a converted button factory in Hoxton – the apartment all shiny floors and James Bond posters, Nintendo Wii's and BMX bikes that Liam never rode unless he'd been partying all night. He was the archetypal London geezer, full of charm and exclusive drinking clubs and expensive dinners, until his women fell for him and began to dream of wedding dresses and chubby babies. Then Liam would turn into the proverbial 'toxic bachelor' – in short, his duped girlfriends wouldn't see him for dust.

'God, Hoxton's a dump,' I said, dumping my bag beneath a leather chair shaped like a vagina. 'I'm gasping for a cuppa, Liam. I'm having the worst week.' My chattiness was designed to disarm him. I sat on the vagina. 'Make that the worst year, actually.'

'No kids?' Yawning, Liam put the kettle on, rubbing his eyes blearily.

'No, Jen's babysitting. You remember Jen? I finally got my visitor's order to see James.'

'That's good.' He yawned again, so wide I saw his fillings.

'I'm sorry,' I said drily. 'Did I wake you?'

It was two in the afternoon.

'No. Just a bit of a late night.'

The detritus strewn across the flat spoke volumes: empty bottles, fag ends, rolled-up notes. An electric-blue bra hung from the lampshade over the table. The matching pants weren't visible.

'Who's there, Liam?' The little voice came from the mezzanine.

'No one. Just Rose.'

The kettle snapped off.

'Hi, Star,' I called. I'd hoped to catch him alone.

'So what can I do for you?' Liam tried a strained smile. He sounded rather like my bank manager.

'Oh, I'm sorry.' I was taken aback by his terse manner. 'I didn't realise you were – I mean – I – I won't take up your time.'

There was an infinitesimal pause whilst he hung his head. 'Sorry, Rose,' he said sheepishly. 'I don't mean to sound—'

'Unfriendly?' I met his eye. 'Because you do, a bit.'

'I'm really sorry.' He flushed. 'I'll do anything to help, you must know that.'

'Thanks.' But I didn't know that, I realised. What did I really know about Liam at all? I wasn't even quite sure why I had come. I had no plan formulated, nothing more than these nagging certainties that James's own partner *must* have known something was wrong; if James was guilty as charged. If James *hadn't* been set up, as he so vehemently insisted that he had. Right now, I wasn't sure what the lesser of two evils was.

'Liam, do you *swear* you don't know what's going on?'

'I swear I'm as flummoxed as you about the drug thing.' Liam had read my mind. 'I swear. It just doesn't seem like James's style.'

Didn't it? What was my husband's style? The things that had attracted me in the past were his gung-ho spirit; his restless, reckless lust for adventure. I stared at my hands. My inevitable attraction to the proverbial bad boy. How pathetic.

'It's not the only reason I've come.' I took a deep breath. 'Not to put too fine a point on it, I'm broke.'

'You can't be.' He stared at me uncomprehendingly. 'The house, the flat, the—'

'No, I mean, broke right here and now.' The blood suffused my own face. 'I can't get my hands on any money. They've frozen the credit cards, there's nothing in the bank accounts. Everything's in James's name. I've been a bit dozy, I suppose. Baby brain for too long.' I took another breath. 'I've been wondering, can you help me? Sub me some cash against the club or something? Something from your shared account.'

I realised slowly he was looking aghast.

'I wouldn't ask . . .' My voice trailed off into a trickle. 'Only I'm starting to feel a bit desperate.'

'It's a bit complicated.' His voice seemed harsh. 'We keep our money very separate, James and I.'

I looked at him in surprise.

'Really?' It made no sense to me. But how could I challenge him? 'I'm sorry. I guess I – I shouldn't have asked.'

'Rose, it's just – it's complicated.'

'Really? Complicated like when you took the kids from my mum's?' I held his eye; he flushed unattractively. 'Just tell me the truth, Liam. I'm so tired of all the bloody lies.'

'OK.' He took a deep breath. 'I took them to scare James. I'm sorry, Rose.' He saw my furious face and held up a hand. 'Look, I know it was shit, and I should have thought harder about you. But I was fucked off with him, so fucked off with him, and I was panicking. I couldn't get through any other way.'

'To scare him?' I was confused. 'Why?'

Star appeared at the top of the stairs dressed in an electric-blue thong and little else, her brown-tipped bosoms too big and pendulous for her tiny frame, a gold crucifix dangling between them like a third eye. I averted my gaze.

'All right, Rose?' She seemed uncomfortable too, although not about her blatant nudity. 'I'm sorry about . . . you know.'

'Thank you,' I said to her feet. 'And how are you?'

'OK.' She shrugged and yawned like a small cat. 'Bit tired. I'd love to chat, but I'm gonna be late. I'm going for a bath.'

I thought of something. 'Star?'

'Yeah?' The girl turned, her bosoms swinging softly.

'Did you – did you see Katya's parents? The other day. Are they all right? Do you know when the funeral is? I'd like to send something.'

'Her parents?' She wrinkled her brow. 'No. Why would I have seen them?'

'Go and put the bath on, love,' Liam interrupted quickly. 'I'll bring you a cuppa up in a sec.'

''K.' She wandered off, tiny buttocks tight like halved peanuts.

'Liam, what . . . ?' I shook my head in confusion. 'You said Star was going to let them know, didn't you?'

'Yeah.' He busied himself with tea leaves. 'God, I never know what you do with all of this. Star insists on the bloody green stuff but it's so foul.'

Through the open window a girl's laughter floated in from the street below, a carefree kind of laugh. I felt a stab of jealousy.

'Liam! For God's sake!'

'Star didn't know Katya,' he said flatly. 'I just – I was trying to make you feel better.'

'About what?'

'About a girl dying in your front room.'

'But I thought she was Star's friend?'

'Nope. That's just what James wanted you to think.'

'I can't – sorry, but this isn't going in right.' I stood, then sat again heavily. 'So who the hell was she then?'

Liam looked at me very directly for the first time since I had arrived. 'You're going to find out anyway, I guess.' He submerged the leaves in boiling water.

'Find out what?'

'She was—' He stopped.

'Go on, please, Liam.'

'She was one of James's girls.'

275

'One of his—'

'One of his girls. That's right.'

'You mean, like a girlfriend?' I was surprised at how calm I felt.

'No, I don't mean like a girlfriend. I mean, like a—'

We stared at each other; this man whom I had been friends with since James and I met up again; since before my marriage. Something else in my life I knew nothing of. My life was apparently a house of cards that couldn't withstand the pressure of the gentlest breeze, let alone the gale that was now blowing.

'You mean – like a – an escort?'

'If you like.'

'An escort like a – a whore?' I whispered.

'Yes, Rose. I'm really sorry, lovey. I mean, like a whore.'

Chapter Twenty-Five

After leaving Liam's flat, I got the tube to Pentonville Prison. I felt anxious and strung out, thoroughly overwrought.

All this time I had longed for the city, but here and now, amidst the fumes and grime, the drab grey uniformity of the architecture, the boarded-up shops and smelly kebab houses, I found myself craving fresh air and space, just to be. Ruefully I shook my head. Why is the grass always greener?

At the entrance to Old Street tube I passed a girl on a mobile phone, speaking a language I couldn't place – Polish, possibly. She looked tired and cross, her long hair tied back, a waif-like body, slanted eyes, smoking furiously, jabbering into her phone.

'You will be sorry,' she said suddenly in English to the person on the phone, and something in her face made me pause. I imagined Katya twisting through the air; I heard the—

I closed my eyes and hurried down into London's bowels.

On the tube I studied the women in my carriage: ordinary women reading papers, fiddling with iPods, napping, eyes shut against the world. How did they make their living? Did they spend their days cleaning, filing, striking million-dollar deals or selling their own bodies? How did we ever know what lay beneath someone else's surface, unless they wanted to share it?

Suddenly I felt overwhelmed by life, by the fact that everything I'd counted on was being dragged slowly and relentlessly from beneath my feet.

The prison was deceptively white and grand from the street, but the air inside was filled with a lacklustre kind of dread. The visitors' hall was a large soulless place full of hollow-eyed men – but somehow their female visitors seemed sadder, like they'd given up hope. Blank-faced or tearful, accompanied by curly-headed toddlers sucking thumbs or plastic dummies, and babes-in-arms thankfully oblivious to Daddy's new home, they were world-weary beyond their often youthful years; the older women apparently exhausted by their lives.

James was seated already, unshaven and black-eyed, wearing a yellow tabard, and Diesel jeans that were baggier than a week ago. We hugged briefly above the wooden divide that separated us, presumably so I couldn't pass anything beneath the table.

'Did you bring me something?' he whispered hoarsely. For the first time since I'd known him I could feel his ribs.

'What kind of something?' I sat, feeling like an innocent, as nervous as if we were on a first date, only without the nice bits to look forward to. I'd visited a few prisoners during my reporting years, but this was entirely different.

'Fags? Money? Dope?'

I looked at him stupidly. 'Am I allowed—'

'Of course you're not allowed. But next time, bring me some dope, OK? A lump of hash, yeah? Stick it in the fag packet. No one will check, apparently. And some money, yeah?'

'OK,' I said quietly. 'If it helps.'

'Nothing helps.' To my horror, his eyes began to fill. 'Fuck, Rose. I'm not sure I can do this.'

'Of course you can. You're tough as old boots,' I soothed, taking his hand. But he didn't look very tough. I eyed his shaven-headed neighbour, a large overweight man who sported a missing front tooth and a serpent tattoo that slithered up his windpipe.

'It won't be for long. You'll be out soon, I'm sure. You've got to hang in there, OK?'

'I don't understand why the fuck they won't bail me now. This crap about "fleeing".'

Nor did I, that was the problem. Ruth Jones, James's solicitor, said it was because the CPS thought there was a substantial risk James might 'flee the jurisdiction'. Why, I wasn't sure; no one would tell me.

I squeezed his hand. 'They seem to think you might do a runner. I don't know why. But we'll keep trying. I spoke to Ruth earlier. She's pulling out all the stops, I promise.'

A blond-haired toddler was crying in the play area as an older child snatched his action figure. The mother hushed him quickly.

'Will you bring the kids in? Please, Rosie. I need to see them.' James stared at me with beseeching brown eyes. 'They'll make me better.'

'I can't, James,' I said quietly. 'Not yet. Let's see what happens, shall we?'

He pulled his hand away. 'I need to explain to them I'm not bad,' he muttered. He'd been biting his nails again, a habit he'd kicked long ago.

'Don't be so silly, J. They don't think that, and they don't even know where you are. I just don't think— They're so little, James, they wouldn't understand. I don't think we need to tell them.'

Yet. The unspoken word whirled heavily between us, like a spinning plate on a stick.

I clasped my hands on my lap. I took a deep breath. 'I need to ask you something, James.'

The couple next to us started kissing hungrily, the burly man holding the girl's dark ponytail and twisting it round his hand. There were scratches and nicks all over his bald head. From the end of our row, the warder spotted them.

'What?' James muttered, biting his thumb-nail. His knee tapped incessantly, nervously, against the divide beneath the table.

'The trapeze artist, Katya . . .'

'What about her?'

'Who was she?'

'Just someone I hired for the party. She worked in the Paris Revolver, then in London, on the trapeze. She was good.' He tore into the skin around his nail. 'I can't believe she's dead,' he muttered.

'I thought you said she was a friend of Star's?'

'Did I?' He met my eye. It was a direct challenge.

'But she wasn't, was she?'

'I dunno.'

'James,' I felt the first flickers of anger, 'that's not good enough. We talked about this before. All this not remembering. I don't believe it. You've got to be straight with me.'

'I *am* being straight.'

I grabbed his hand. 'You are not. You're lying through your bloody teeth. After everything we've been through, I do know when you're lying.'

He tried to pull his hand away, looked at his lap.

'James, it's not fair. Think of the kids. Think of what this is doing to them. The better idea I have of what's going on, the better chance I have of helping you. Surely you can see that?'

He looked at me venomously. 'How the fuck can you help? Can you get me out of here? No. Can you make it go away? No. So how are you going to make it better, eh, Mummy Rose?'

I swallowed hard. I pinched the skin on my hands. It hurt but I hardly felt the pain.

As quickly as James lost his temper, he saw the error of his wrath. 'Sorry, sorry.' He put his head in his hands. 'I don't know what's wrong with me at the moment. It's like I'm in one of my bloody nightmares and I just can't wake up.'

'Well, start by telling me the truth. Who—'

'Five minutes for all visitors,' the Tannoy announced flatly.

The guard pulled our neighbour back from his girlfriend. 'You know the rules, Rigger,' he said.

'Yeah, all right, geezer.' The man winked at me and stretched leisurely. 'You can't blame a man for trying.' I saw he had LOVE and HATE tattooed on his plump inner arms.

'Bastard,' the girl said, just loud enough for the warder to hear, tossing her hair over her shoulder. The warder squared his shoulders, choosing to ignore her.

'James, tell me.' I looked back at my husband. 'Who was Katya?'

James gazed at me and in that moment I felt the years drop away and I saw the boy I had met at university, that hopeful lively boy with a sense of fun, a graffitied guitar slung over his back, and I fought down a sudden urge to rail against our situation. I saw the emotions fighting across his face. There was so much I obviously didn't know about my husband, so much I hadn't looked for or he had kept hidden; and I saw that he looked young and vulnerable and almost like he used to. Like I could put my trust in him again.

'I'm sorry, Rose,' he whispered, and his voice cracked.

'So . . . ?' I held my breath.

'So – so she was my girlfriend. Well, not girlfriend.' This time he reached for my hand, but I moved too fast for him. I couldn't bear his touch right now. 'Lover, I suppose.'

'How romantic.' It was too late for recriminations. I took a deep breath. 'Liam says she was a whore.'

'He did, did he?' James sat back. His face closed up again. 'Well, he would. He was jealous.'

I looked dispassionately down on James, as if I was out of my body. How bizarre our life had become: my husband and I sitting in prison, discussing whether his business partner was jealous of the girl James had apparently been sleeping with.

'Why jealous?' Liam might not be the next Brad Pitt – 'Liams are always mingers' was the joke between us when we'd met first – but he had no trouble whatsoever attracting women.

James shrugged. 'I'm sorry, Rose, but she was gorgeous. You saw that. Any bloke would . . .' He caught my eye and trailed off. It only affirmed everything I'd guessed James felt about my exhausted body since I'd had the kids. I stayed at home, he cavorted with young dancers and the like. I looked back at James, who seemed utterly bashful. 'Well, you know.'

And yet – Danny had made me feel beautiful. I pushed the memories away. I thought back to Katya. I hadn't taken much notice of her, to be honest. I had been caught up in my own well of misery, busy with the arrangements. She'd turned up the night before the party and I stayed hidden in my room after James had hit me, with ice on my swelling eye, praying it would go down by tomorrow.

The next day she and Star had gone shopping in Oxford, then they'd played with the children for an hour whilst I ran around tweaking things. I remembered her painted face as she flew through the air, the thick black eye make-up, lashes like spider's legs, silver glitter on her cheeks. I remembered the oxygen mask clamped over her white face whilst she lay dying. But I couldn't recall much else.

'Time's up. Come on, Miller. Say your goodbyes.' The lanky officer stared at me.

'But, James, why would he say that?' I leaned forward urgently. 'He meant she was a proper whore. Like a prostitute. I know he did.'

'Shut up, Rose,' James hissed, standing now. 'You don't know what the fuck you're talking about. He was just jealous because he wanted her and she preferred me. And I'm sorry, Rose, I'm sorry that I slept with her. It was only once or twice.'

'Oh. Well, that's all right then,' I said flatly. For who was I to judge now?

'Come on, Rose. You haven't seemed bothered for years.'

I opened my mouth in incredulity, but nothing came out.

'Don't deny it, Rose.'

'You're talking rubbish, James.' I stood too. 'I can hardly remember the last time you actually came to bed with me. Probably when the twins were conceived.'

'I did try.' He was unconvincing. 'Once or twice.'

I thought of the night Liam had brought the children home. We stared at each other across the table until James was led away. 'Don't forget the fags next time, OK?' he muttered over his shoulder.

I nodded.

'And kiss the children for me, please. Tell them Daddy loves them.' There was a break in his voice.

'I will.'

But he was gone.

And he was lying, that much was clear.

Chapter Twenty-Six

TIME OUT, JUNE 2008

Get down to the Revolver relaunch tonight and shake your thang to some of the best tunes in club-land. Don't miss British hot-shot DJs Nathan Coles, Terry Francis, Beth B.B. and the altogether nu-wave Tig-Tig . . . And don't say you haven't been warned: the queues will be massive, the floors will be jumping, the bass will be pumping. 11 p.m. – 5 a.m., Smithfields. £10 on the door, £8 if you email Marsha@revolver.uk. Be there or be very very sorry . . .

If it had been a story I'd been chasing in my old life, I would have visited the London club immediately; jumped straight on the Eurostar and gone to Paris to find out about Katya – I would have begun delving into her life until I found the answers. But I had a different life now, so I went home for tea instead.

'Mummy, Freddie pinched me on the tummy,' Effie told me crossly as I walked through the door.

'Effie's a bum-bum,' Freddie said, and pinched her again.

She screwed up her face and burst into loud and dramatic tears.

'Freddie,' I pulled him away from his twin irritably, 'that's naughty. Say sorry to your sister.'

'Don't care,' he said, and stuck his tongue out at me. His eyes were full of fear though; he knew he was pushing it.

'You will care when I make you sit in your room until bedtime.'

'I won't. I'll – I'll sneak out again like Wolverine and then I'll . . .' he said, but his little voice wavered now. It was hard to be cross for long with such an angelic-looking child. He thought of the worst thing possible. 'I'll chop your tummy off.'

'Really?' I bit my lip. 'That's not very nice, is it?'

'Where's Daddy?' Alicia said quietly from the doorway. My heart went out to her as the twins began squabbling again.

'Come here, Lissie.' I held my arms out, but she just scrunched up her anxious little face as the twins began to fight. 'Get off me,' Effie squawked as Jen appeared behind her and quickly assessed the situation. She gathered the terrible two up.

'Bath-time, kiddiwinks,' she said, and I shot her a grateful look.

'Praise be for tolerant and childless godparents,' I said, and she laughed. 'I owe you one, Jen.'

'You owe me more than one, lady,' she said, and scooped the still sobbing Effie up. 'Come on, you two. Shall we have bubbles?'

'I can put my head under water. Is my goggles here?' A now placid Freddie trotted off behind Jen. 'Shall I show you?'

'I said where's Daddy?' Alicia looked on the edge of tears herself.

'He's still away on his business trip, darling.' I reached out my hand for her, but she ignored it, eyeing me suspiciously.

'Why doesn't he ring us up like normal?'

'Because he – the phones don't work where he is.'

'Why didn't he take his phone?' she said, scowling. Her small forehead was knitted furiously: I wanted to smooth it out. I didn't know how much longer I could keep the truth from Alicia. She might be young but she obviously sensed something was deeply wrong.

'He did, darling. It's just – you know, sometimes there is no reception. Mobile phones are funny old things.' I imagined the police had confiscated it when they arrested him. 'In the old days—'

'He didn't take his phone actually,' she interrupted.

'How do you know?' I said tiredly, flopping on the sofa to take my shoes off. Guilt and anxiety and twenty questions were on the verge of making me tetchy.

'Because it's here.' She held the small black phone up triumphantly. My heart flip-flopped.

'Oh,' I hedged. 'He must have just forgotten it. Silly Daddy. Come here, baby.' I grabbed her. 'Come and give your mummy a cuddle.'

I buried my face in my daughter's slippery hair, savouring the warmth of her bony frame. The truth was, I was frightened. I had no idea how I was going to keep their world from collapsing completely – but I knew I had to keep trying.

'What would you be achieving, trying to find out more about this girl?' Jen asked, licking the last of the curry from her fingers. 'So he slept with a dancer. I mean, it's depressing, but are you really that surprised?'

I was shocked by her words. 'Yes, I am actually.'

'Oh.' She went quiet. 'Sorry.'

'But you're not.' I took a sip of my wine, wrinkling my nose against the unwelcome acidity. 'So what are you saying? That my husband's an old philanderer?' I tried to laugh but somehow I just couldn't manage it.

'No, of course not.' Jen still looked uncomfortable. 'But given his lifestyle, the temptations, well—'

'I get the picture.' I held a hand up. 'Enough said.'

Perhaps I had been stupid, trusting and patient. The truth was I had been so immersed with the children in the past few years, there was little time for anything else. Infidelity hadn't been one of my worries. For all his faults, it was drugs and drink that were James's downfall, not women. But Liam's harsh word was hard to erase.

'Whore,' went the whisper in my ears, over and over again until I wanted to plug them with my fingers like the children did.

I tossed and turned on Jen's lumpy sofa-bed, my body exhausted but my mind racing. The noisy city kept me awake, a helicopter beating the air overhead over and again, the sirens, blaring car stereos. I imagined Danny – God only knew where he was now. I scribbled him out in my head. I turned the pillow over, looking for the cool side. I thought of James confined in his cell.

Suddenly I had a flash of inspiration and fumbled around in my overnight bag until I found James's phone, switching it on. Of course it was dead. I scrabbled around for my charger and plugged it in.

Frantically I scrolled through the text messages. Nothing.

I searched for Katya's name in the contacts. Nothing there either. I flung the phone back down in frustration.

I desperately wanted to know who she was and yet I was terrified of finding out. I picked the phone up again and scrolled through the whole contacts list from the top. My heart stopped at Danny's name. I thought about Danny apparently setting up the meeting for James. I stared at the number for a second. I didn't recognise it; I was sure the last four digits were different from the one I'd had. For a second my finger hovered over the call button.

I moved resolutely on.

Finally – a number listed as 'Angel', with a London code.

My hand shaking, I rang it. A girl answered, bored and foreign. ''Allo?'

'Is this Katya's house?'

There was a long pause. 'Who is this?' the girl asked in heavily accented English. 'What do you know about Katya?'

'Is Katya there?' I persisted.

'Fuck off,' came the retort as she hung up.

I pulled on my jeans and slipped out of the flat, hailing the first taxi I saw. Arriving at the club, I asked the exotic doorgirl for Liam. With her tiny leather hotpants, glossy blonde bob and legs up to her armpits, she looked dubious about my casual clothes, my unmade-up face. I doubted she would know I was James's wife, and I chose not to mention it now, but her eyes flickered uncertainly. She licked her pillowy lips and made a call.

'Twice in one day,' Liam tried to joke as he unclipped the red rope. 'I'm honoured.'

'No', I said drily as I walked through, 'you're cornered.'

He took me upstairs to the VIP bar where he ordered us champagne cocktails until he saw me pull a face.

'I'm not drinking, thanks. Bad for the brain. I'll have a Diet Coke.'

He shrugged. 'Your choice.'

'You need to cut the crap, Liam,' I said. 'This is me, remember. Rose. And I've had enough of all the subterfuge. I need to know what the hell's been going on.'

Wryly he looked at me. 'Yes, you. Award-winning and all that jazz.' He sighed. 'OK. What do you want to know?'

'Everything.' I swigged my Coke. 'Money, girls, heroin, the lot.'

'Heroin – first I've heard. Would swear on my mother's life.' Liam adored his mother. 'Girls, James's thing, not mine.'

'But what kind of thing? He says Katya was a girlfriend. Lover.'

'Not girlfriends, no. He loves you.'

'That's sweet, Liam, but we've gone beyond that point. He's already admitted screwing her.'

'Really?' He narrowed his eyes.

'Yes, really.'

'It all comes down to money, I think.'

'Money?'

Liam took a great swig of his drink, rubbed his head until his hair stood on end. 'This is hard, Rose. This is utter shit.'

'Just tell me.'

'I feel like I'm grassing on my best mate.'

'Well, don't. To help James, I need to know the truth.'

'He'd fucked up. I caught him . . .' Pain crossed his face.

'What?'

'Embezzling.'

'Embezzling?' It was hard to hear him above the banging house music.

'Yes. That's why we fell out.'

'I thought it was you.'

'Me?' He stared at me. 'Why?'

'Because you were creeping around. And I heard you arguing. That day you had the Oasis tune in the studio. And because he said – you messed up once before, didn't you?'

'When?'

'When the record label nearly went under.'

'Is that what he said? I was trying to help him, Rose. He'd screwed up so badly.'

'That's why you took my kids?' I said slowly. 'For leverage.'

'No.' But his pale skin was blotchy now. 'To shock him.'

'To shock him? What about shocking me?'

'I didn't think it through. I was so angry with him for risking everything. I'm sorry, Rose.'

'It's a bit late for sorry, Liam!' I tried to push down the fury again. I needed cold hard facts. 'So where did the money go?'

'He's got extravagant tastes. He's been gambling again. You know what he's like.'

'Gambling?'

'And playing the stock market. Bad timing,' he said ruefully. 'Tens of thousands. More.'

'More?' I was aghast.

'Spread-betting. Putting money into young ventures that went down. He'd been fucking up all over the show. And he's been hit like the best of them by the bloody recession that's coming. Look at the US. Nomad going down was the final straw. I think he lost a million that day, at least.'

I remembered that spring day in the kitchen, Radio Four's bleak announcement. The hidden bank statements; the rejected credit cards. How could I have been so blind? I'd stupidly just put it all down to James's normal relaxed attitude.

'But I thought you were doing so well.'

'We are. But James – he's been getting out of control. He just won't listen, that's the bloody problem.' He waved a gurning DJ away who was trying to high-five him. 'In a minute, mate. I mean, that party, Rose. How the fuck much did that cost?'

'I don't know.' Forlorn with misery, I'd hardly batted an eyelid as the costs mounted. I'd assumed James had it covered. I hadn't cared, that much was true. I'd simply been limping through the days since Danny disappeared. 'I thought the party was both your idea?'

'No way. It was so stupid. We'd just lost a backer because he saw James get so fucked up at the club.'

'How?'

'Too loud, too drunk. Snorting coke blatantly off the seats. He'd met that girl, Katya. There was something about her. Something that really bothered him. Like he was drawn to her but not; like some . . .'

'What?'

'I really don't know. It sounds stupid, Rose, and I hate to say it, but like some kind of fatal attraction. He wouldn't talk about it but he started – all the drinking again. He said something about some grand scheme, some old friends. And then this big cheese pulled out. I was so pissed off.'

'And that's when Hadi Kattan got involved?'

'If he did, I never saw a penny from him. I only ever met his son once when he came down with some friends for a night.

I know James was trying to appease me with the promise of money, though.'

Liam's attention was distracted by something and I followed his gaze. Star appeared up on the podium opposite the VIP bar. In her thigh-high boots and slinky magenta dress she looked amazing; I saw Liam's smile spread across his face. I'd never seen him like this before.

'You're really quite taken, aren't you?' I nudged him, and he blushed like an overgrown schoolboy.

'Guess so.' He took my hand. 'God, Rose, I'm sorry. And I'm sorry I was so shite earlier. I was just hungover and—'

'And embarrassed,' I finished for him.

'I s'pose. Look, let me sort you out some cash. Give me your account details, I'll get it transferred.'

He looked round at the jumping crowd beneath us, boys whistling, girls spinning, everyone sweaty and ecstatic as the music throbbed through the packed club. I thought of that night in Oxford lifetimes ago, the night I had first had sex with James, the night our toxic relationship really began, the music banging through my body in a way I had never known. I felt so tired now – like I'd never washed the guilt away, the dirt of that first night.

'I'd appreciate it, Liam,' I said quietly. 'I really would. Just till I get sorted.'

'And you will, my lovely, I know you will. And James will be just fine.'

I slipped off the stool. 'And Katya?'

He sighed. 'I'll think on it, Rose, I promise. See if I can come up with some info.'

As Liam stood to hug me, my eye was caught by a couple behind him at the bar. The blond boy from the party, sweaty pale shirt undone almost to his waist, clinging to him like a second skin, arm draped round a young black girl in slashed leggings. He raised an indolent hand to Liam and then he caught my eye. We gazed at each other for a moment, and then, bored, he leaned down to kiss his companion's glossy pout, his lashes sweeping down to veil his eyes.

'Who is that?' I said, my heart racing suddenly.

Liam raised a hand back. 'That's Charlie. He was at your party.'

'Yeah, I recognise him. Charlie who?'

'James knows him. Charlie Higham. He's a right little toerag. Trust-funded up to the hilt. Got all the girls falling at his feet.'

I stared at the fine-boned face, the dyed blond hair falling just like his elder brother's had as slowly he kissed the girl who clung so hard to him. I heard a rushing in my ears. I saw the bed in that hotel room, the carnage around it. I felt dizzy and sick. This could be no coincidence. I had to get out of there immediately.

I walked back to Jen's flat. I needed to clear my head desperately after the heat and noise of the club, after Liam's words. Nothing made sense: no one was being completely straight with me, not even Liam. I had to get back to see James, to make him tell me the truth.

Just past midnight in central London, the streets were still busy; streets I'd walked alone happily at all hours since moving here after college. I turned into the square where I'd once lived. Quieter here, I slowed my pace. A rattle of a bin, a fox, perhaps. The shadows drew in; it was dingy, not so many streetlights, the small private green in the centre in complete darkness.

I thought I heard a step behind me and turned quickly, but there was no one. Still, Jen's warm flat seemed appealing now. Another noise; a door slamming somewhere. Someone running.

And then a low mournful whistling; it turned my stomach inside out. I was obviously delusional. Why would he be here now?

I paused. The whistling stopped.

My heart aching, I walked on, quickening my step now. My

mind was playing tricks on me. Longing can do terrible things. I thought I saw something and I slowed for a second, and then I hurried past a shadow in a doorway.

Too late. I was pulled into the arch. I could smell sherbet.

'What do you want?' I said, but I was shaking. I hated him and myself for it, for my weakness. And yet I was overjoyed too.

And all these weeks I'd prayed I'd see him and all these weeks I'd imagined him so fiercely; imagined him in crowds, on buses, in fields, in my house. I'd projected us into a healthy future where we had been together . . . but he had never come.

And yet now here he was and I was rigid with something – fear perhaps. I was struck dumb . . . My mouth couldn't catch up with my mind to form words. What to say and how to act when all I wanted was to crawl into his arms and find the peace I craved. The peace I'd never really had since adulthood. I stared at him blankly.

'I came to say goodbye,' he said quietly.

'Well, you've said it now.' I pulled my arm free but his grip was too tight. Not for the first time I felt frightened of him, of this man I knew so little of; this man I had awarded my trust so carelessly.

More than my trust.

I swallowed hard. 'Where's Kattan, Danny? Where has he gone?'

'Abroad.'

'Where?'

'I can't tell you.'

'Why not?'

'Because.'

'Because what?' My voice was rising.

'Because it's more than my life's worth.'

'What about my life, Danny? What about my children's?'

'Why do you want him so badly, Rose?'

'Because he's involved with my husband's arrest. And so are you.'

Danny relit his roll-up. 'What makes you think that?'

'Because James told me so.'

'And you trust your husband, do you?' He inhaled, narrowing his eyes against the smoke. 'The husband who's banged up. The husband who hits you.'

'He only hit me once,' I lied.

'Oh good. So that makes it all right then?'

'No, I'm not saying that. The point is, you need to –' I was blustering ridiculously – 'you need to hand yourself in.'

'And what would that achieve?' Danny actually grinned. 'I'm sorry for you both, but I don't much fancy doing time, if you don't mind.'

'Don't laugh at me.' Tears of frustration filled my eyes.

'I'm not, Rose, I promise.' He stopped smiling. He reached a hand towards my face, and I ducked, banging my head against the wall. 'Don't cry, baby.'

'I'm not your baby.' *However much I might want to be.* 'I am very much not your baby.'

'Fair enough.' He sighed. 'But still, don't cry.'

'Why not? I feel like crying, to be honest, Danny. Everything's turned to shit. My husband's in gaol for God knows what, my kids have got no father, you screwed me and left me. I can't believe my own stupidity.'

'Are you angry with me, then?' He looked down at me calmly, unblinking. 'Or yourself?'

'Both.' I dashed away the threatening tears. 'Both. I don't know what the hell's happening from one minute to the next.'

'I went because I had to.'

'Had to what?'

'I only left you because I had to.'

I absorbed his words. I felt a grain of hope. 'Why did you have to?'

'You're a married woman, for starters.' He looked at me blankly. 'What did you expect?'

I'd never known him to be so loquacious. I stared at him. 'Is that the truth?'

'Of course it's the bloody truth.'

'You would have stayed—'

'If I could have done. God, Rose. And I didn't set James up, I swear. I just arranged the meeting with Kattan's importer, as James and Kattan requested. That's all.' He took a final drag, trying not to burn his fingers. 'Whatever you might think of me, Rose, I'm not a bad man.'

'Really?'

'Really.' He chucked the roll-up in the gutter. It sizzled in the damp. *We are all of us in the gutter*, I thought absently. I wished he wasn't so near me.

'Like you care what I think,' I said quietly.

I wished he was nearer.

'What do you reckon?'

My mind wheeled furiously. 'And why hasn't Kattan been picked up then, if he's the other end of the deal? Or has he?'

'Of course he hasn't,' Danny said wearily. He pulled his zip up to his chin, the gesture I'd come to recognise as a nervous tic.

'Why of course?'

'Because he's done nothing wrong, doll.'

'For fuck's sake, Danny. Does your loyalty know no bounds?'

'And,' he lowered his lids, until his eyes were slits, 'because he has diplomatic immunity.'

'What?' I whispered.

'Surely you knew that, Mrs Rose Miller. You, with all your training and your contacts.'

It started to rain, big heavy raindrops plopping onto the dusty pavement.

I opened my mouth to say something but before I could speak he pulled me towards him, unbalancing me so I fell into him. He kissed me so hard and deep that I forgot about everything for a second, burying his fingers in my hair, holding the back of my head so fiercely, as if he could crush it easily if he tried. And without meaning to, I kissed him back. I didn't care any more; for a moment I lost myself, my insides liquefying, the smell of him, the smell I'd dreamed of, his skin, his hair beneath my own fingers. I held on to him like he was my salvation.

A police car blared past at the end of a road and as quickly as he had grabbed me, Danny let me go.

'Rose.' He looked down intently at me.

'Yes?' I mumbled and I knew I was crying properly now, my tears mixed with the driving rain.

'I've got to go.' He wiped my eye with a gentle thumb. My face was soaking with rain, and tears. He muttered something I couldn't catch.

'What?'

'I can't – I won't see you again. I think it's for the best.'

It felt like a skewer through my heart. I clenched my teeth.

'I see.'

'But I won't forget you, I promise. I'll think of you, Rose.'

'Thanks,' I said shakily. 'But hopefully I'll forget you.' I stepped backwards into the street.

I wouldn't let myself look back. I got round the next corner; saw Jen's mansion-block ahead but I didn't want to go there yet. I wanted to be on my own; I wanted to crawl into a corner and die. The tears coursed down my cheeks. I bent double in the road and I sobbed and sobbed, feeling like someone had just sliced my arteries open. How could it hurt this much? I told myself over and over again it wasn't just him, it was the whole situation, but it didn't help.

A young woman on a bicycle stopped to see if I was all right but I held my hands over my face until she went away. I sat there on the pavement, leaning against the railings, and I cried until I could cry no more.

Inside my heart was breaking; and inside I was thinking that

I'd known it would do all along; that I deserved no better. And I realised finally how dangerous it had been to let myself fall when I had not been ready; when there was no one there to catch me.

It rained so hard that all the flowers in the pots by the front door were bowed and broken when I stood again.

Chapter Twenty-Seven

THE *TELEGRAPH*, JULY 2008

Bright young Tory hope Ash Kattan today joined David Cameron and Baroness Warsi at the Young Muslim Association for a talk on racial harmony. Both are Oxford alumni – although Kattan once publicly criticised the infamous Bullingdon Drinking Club that Mayor Boris Johnson, Cameron and close ally George Osborne were all members of – the pair seem to have ironed out differences now with the announcement that Kattan is standing for a seat in Berkshire. Son of international banker and art dealer Hadi Kattan, Ash is the face of 'a new and excitingly diverse Britain', according to the Tory whips.

'There's a girl called Star on your phone.' Jen pulled a face at the name, extending my mobile towards me. 'Tea?'

'Oh God, yes, please.' My eyes still felt swollen and sore as I pushed myself up off the sofa-bed and took the phone. 'Hi, Star.'

'Morning, Rose.' Her voice was absurdly cheerful. 'Good night at the club?'

'Oh.' I thought about it, my brain fuddled. Next door I could hear the kids discussing Scooby snacks. 'Well, you know. Different circumstances, it would have been great I'm sure.'

'We'll have to have a night out one of these days. When your – when it's all sorted.'

'Yes.' What did she want? I looked at London's hard water scum floating on my tea. To chat about evenings out? Surely not. 'Star, I—'

'Rose,' her voice dropped suddenly, 'listen, the reason I'm calling you so early –' it was 9 a.m., 'is 'cos Liam's still asleep. He told me you want to find out about Angel.'

'Angel?' I repeated stupidly.

'Katya. Angel. Whatever you wanna call her.'

'Yes of course. Katya.'

'I can give you an address. She lived with this foreign bird somewhere south of the river. Pole dancer, I think. Bit moody, Lana, but she's all right. I expect she'll know a bit more about her. Right pally, they were. Have you got a pen?'

I wrote the address down.

'Only, Rose,' Star was whispering now. 'Can you not tell her, or Liam, who gave you the address?'

'Why don't you want him to know?' I asked slowly.

'Oh, you know,' she was still so upbeat, 'he don't like me getting involved with the club. You know, business affairs, and that.' She yawned. 'Right then. I'm off to bed. Night night.'

'Last favour, Jen, I swear.' I wrapped the bobble round the end of Alicia's plait, and kissed the back of her head. She was so skinny, her little shoulder blades jutted like the stubs of angel-wings from her narrow back.

Jen sighed. 'It's not that I mind having them.' She widened her eyes, subtly indicating the kids. 'I love it. Not least because it reminds me why I'm not ready to have any of my own.'

'Jen!'

'Joking, obviously.' It wasn't obvious. 'But I just wonder – I mean, do you know what you're doing?'

'Of course.' I didn't. 'You're talking to the woman who staked

299

out Arafat for a week until he gave me an interview, remember? This is just – stuff. Trying to help James.'

Trying to help myself too. Needing to know the truth.

'It's fine. Really. Just be careful, for God's sake.'

'It's London, Jen, not Gaza. And when I get back,' I looked at the twins' blond heads, faces turned up like flowers to the sun of the television screen, where the immortal Scooby Doo ran from the baddies as he had done since my own childhood, 'we'll go and get pizza, shall we? My treat.'

Gaza it might not have been, but this part of Brixton was a dive. The road was run-down, bins overflowing, several buildings with smashed windows badly boarded. The house I needed was smart by comparison, the first-floor flat sporting beautiful window-boxes filled with violets and daisies, though the wheel-less pram in the front garden slightly ruined the effect.

I rang the doorbell insistently, but there was no answer. A middle-aged Rasta with an enormous hat and a small mongrel in tow rounded the corner. 'She never up before midday.' He winked at me. 'Fancy a brew while you waiting?'

I looked at him, at his calm face, and I smiled. 'That's really kind but I don't have much time.' I buzzed again.

A cross voice suddenly floated out of the intercom. 'Yes?'

'Lana? I left you a message this morning. Rose Miller, the – er – the club gave me your number.'

There was a pause.

'Please, Lana. It's really important.'

A sigh. 'Hang on.'

The Rasta sucked his teeth. 'She got a temper, that one.' He shook his head ruefully. 'I hear her shout many a time at them bad men on the corner. You come see me if you get scared.'

The flat was immaculate but homely, kitsch even. The girl had long fair hair scraped back very hard from her bony face. She wore a kimono covered in delicate butterflies, out of which her

300

long thin hands protruded like small spades, too heavy for her wrists. The coffee that was brewing smelled delicious and I realised how hungry I was.

'Thank you.' I took the scalding cup. 'Nice place.'

She yawned widely. 'What do you want?'

'So you were friends with Katya?'

'Katya?' She looked at me and her tone was accusatory. 'She died in your house. That is strange, no?'

'Not really strange. Tragic, I think is probably a better word.'

'Are you saying my English is not good?'

'God, no, not at all.' I was flustered. 'I just – it was a terrible accident.'

'Was it?' she said flatly.

I stared at her. 'What do you mean?'

'I knew something like this would happen.'

'Did you?' My heart was starting to race painfully. 'How? I mean, we just hired her for the party. For James and Liam's party.'

'And you, you are married to James Miller?'

'Yes,' I mumbled. She made me bizarrely nervous, this thin, cross girl.

'Well, you should ask him then.'

'He's in prison. That's why I'm here. He's in a lot of trouble, and I'm trying to understand why.'

She sniffed disdainfully and spoke in a language I didn't understand.

'Look, please.' I put my hand on her arm. For the first time in a long while, I felt like maybe I was near the truth. 'Please, you must tell me what you know. I don't even know where Katya came from. What country, anything.'

'What country?' She screwed up her face. 'What do you mean?'

'Was she Polish, like you?'

'I am from Russia, *actually*. And she – she was from your country.'

'What?' I stared at her without comprehending. 'My— But, her name and—'

'Kate.'

'But I thought—'

'Katya is just for the act. More – exotic, I guess. Katya the Flying Angel.'

Kate, from my country. Alarm bells began to ring somewhere far off. 'Christ. You're sure?'

'Sure I'm sure.' On the shelf behind Lana was a photo of her and another woman, arms round each other, smiling into the camera on a summer's day. Katya was older than I'd realised; I'd only really registered her in all her stage finery, thick make-up slathered on. I looked closely at the wholesome scrubbed face, the cropped pixie-cut, the beaming smile and my world suddenly seemed very small. I felt my chest constrict until breathing seemed difficult.

'And I tell you something else.' Lana looked at me again, her grey eyes full of sadness now. 'She loved your husband very much. Only one other man she loved that much before. I think maybe she give her life for James Miller.'

I felt a terror that I hadn't since the night Katya died. A small pain, a nut of something rattled in my gut. I remembered the horrified guests whispering as she lay dying. *She fell on purpose.*

'Died for him? Were they . . .' I cleared my throat. 'Did they see a lot of each other?'

'You mean was she his mistress?' She lit a cigarette. 'No, but she wanted to be.' She exhaled the smoke in a perfect plume. 'She was confused, though.'

'Confused?'

Lana stood with a swish of her kimono and a trail of smoke. 'Follow me.'

I did as I was told, following her down the dark little hall. She opened a door: Katya's bedroom. The bed was neatly made, stuffed toys and a china doll on a heart-shaped pillow, a table full of glitter and gloss, lights round the mirror like Judy Garland's dressing room. On the shelf by the window were framed photos, the biggest of a face I recognised immediately from last night. Charlie Higham, lying on a bed, propped on one elbow, smoking, naked to the waist, staring affectedly into the lens, big brown eyes narrowed slightly against the smoke, looking very much like he was making love to the camera.

'You know this boy?' Lana picked up the photo. 'This boy, he is trouble. This is boy she was in love with. I say, be careful, but he breaks her heart. Then your husband, he get involved.'

'Get involved with what, though?' I was more than confused myself.

Lana slammed the photo down so the glass rattled; pushed me out of the door again and shut it firmly behind us, stalking down the hall back to the kitchen.

'I warned her.'

'About what?' I followed in her wake.

'When your husband took her to that man, I knew this would – how do you say here? – be in tears?'

'End in tears?'

'Yes.'

'What man?'

'The big man.' Again she spoke in Russian.

I stared at her, lost.

She relented. 'Always these guys. You cannot trust them. Ever.'

'Sorry, what guys?' My heart was beating so fast it felt like it was going to explode. 'Why did James take her to a – a "big man"?'

'Why do you think? Money,' she said grimly. 'It always comes to money, no?'

'And who was this man? Was he called Hadi Kattan?'

'She would not tell me exactly who. But I know he is – very powerful.' She ground her cigarette out so hard that it was pulverised. 'She goes to him and asks for money – and one month later, she is dead.'

Lana's phone began to ring. She looked at the curly pink clock on the mantelpiece and stood. 'I have to get ready. There is nothing else I can tell you.'

'Do you – did she have family?'

'Her mother. She is very sad now, I think.'

'I'm sure. Do you know where I could find her?'

'Her mother?' Lana shrugged. 'She lives in that old place.'

'Where?'

The girl clattered the coffee cups into the sink. 'Where all the clever ones go. I can't think – how is it called?' She swung round triumphantly. 'Ah yes. Oxford.'

Before I left London I went to meet Xav. I got a taxi that passed through Parliament Square on the way to the City; I stared out at the fairy-tale turrets of the building that housed our government and it jogged my memory.

I sat up straighter, thinking of Danny's words last night. How could Kattan possibly have diplomatic immunity? It made no sense. I'd turned up so little when I was looking into him earlier this year; I'd found no mention of any kind of diplomatic status. I wondered about the secret service rumours in Iran: he'd obviously had some connections in Iran in the eighties or nineties but if anything, that surely made him a bigger threat here.

My meeting with Xavier was so tense, though, that I forgot all about Kattan. We met in a fashionably white restaurant in busy Spitalfields, the kind where children are not welcome and celebrities pretend they don't want to be seen. From the very start, it felt uneasy. Xavier was preoccupied, but I didn't know why – the abiding theme of my life at the moment.

'You look very pale,' he said accusingly after we'd ordered.

'So do you, actually,' I batted back. 'Burning the candle, my dear Xav?'

The cash Liam had eventually sorted would tide me over for

a while. But I needed to start earning again, that was quite apparent. The obvious solution was to go back to work full time, and Xav's offer now made sense. I'd pack up the house and rent it out; move the children back to the flat in London for the time being. I wouldn't be sorry to leave our stifling village, especially since the story of James's arrest had broken. I needed to be near my old friends right now.

'So when do you want me?' I finished my chicken and wiped my mouth on the pristine napkin. 'I'm going to move back in the summer holidays. But I can start from home sooner. I've got to get the cash rolling in pronto or we'll be living in a cardboard box soon.'

Xav summoned the waiter and ordered an espresso. He buttered his bread roll, then abandoned it; added salt and then pepper to the tomato salad that he hadn't touched. He did everything but look me in the eye or respond.

'Xav. Did you hear what I said?' I smiled at him but my heart was sinking. 'I can come back?'

He looked at me, then away again. My old friend, so gaunt and strained.

'Can't I?'

Xav picked up his BlackBerry, turning it over and over on the white linen tablecloth incessantly until finally I laid my hand over his to stem the fiddling.

'Stop, Xavier.'

He looked down.

'I see.' I felt the clench of nerves in my stomach. 'So it's a no, then?'

'Rosie, it's not me, darling.' He sighed long and hard. 'I'd have you on the staff in a shot, you know that. It's – well, orders from above.'

'Higham.'

'No.' he took a gulp of his water.

'Xavier! At least tell the truth.'

'I – oh, I don't know, Rose. Things are changing radically since the downturn. Budgets have been slashed. And I have so little hiring power at the moment. My hands are tied.'

'Not literally, I hope,' I tried to joke. But I felt the thud of the floor come up and hit my feet away from me. I was diving through thin air, spinning away from my own world in freefall.

'And to be honest, Rose, I'm stepping back a bit anyway. I've not – I can't live for work any more.'

'I see,' I said slowly. 'Well, that's good, isn't it? To take some time out?'

'I guess.' He drained the espresso that the waiter had just put before him and gestured for another one.

'Is something wrong?'

He gazed into the middle distance like the answer to all our woes lay there.

'Xav?'

'No, no. Of course not.'

'Are you sure?' I felt a cold wave of fear. 'Xav—'

'I'm fine,' he snapped. 'Just leave it.'

'Right. OK. Good. Look, I've been thinking. The Kattan story—' I began.

'Rose, for Christ's sake. You've got enough on your plate.'

'It's just – he's involved with James's case.'

'Are you mad?' Xavier stared at me. 'Or just paranoid?'

'Both. Neither. I don't know, Xav. We met him and then – well, James swears Kattan introduced him to the guy who organised the shipping of the furniture. Only he's disappeared off the face of the earth.'

'Christ.' Xav rubbed his eyes; they were already bloodshot.

'And now – now someone's told me he's got immunity. The police aren't interested in him apparently. Someone's hiding something.'

'Who?'

I felt my frustration mount. 'Actually make that, *everyone's* hiding something. I want to find out the truth. And I want to bloody well know where he is.'

'But you've got no evidence?'

'What am I going to do, Xav – just lay down and die? And, Christ, let Higham ruin me professionally now because of some old grievance?'

'What old grievance?'

'Never mind. Something that wasn't my fault.'

I thought of the picture of Charlie Higham in Katya's room – debated whether to mention my new concerns to Xav, but it seemed pointless.

'Look, I'm not going to just walk away from my life.' I was more emphatic than I had been in months. 'Not because they want me to.'

'But you'd walked away from it anyway, hadn't you? Your career, anyway,' he said tiredly.

'Not really. I was just . . . changing priorities.'

'They're good priorities to change,' he said quietly. 'Putting your kids first.'

'Yes, I know, they're the best priorities. But it doesn't mean it's OK for them to tarnish my reputation permanently. And to be honest, Xav, I *need* to work right now.' I pleated my napkin into angel wings. 'It's the only thing I know how to do.'

'Rubbish,' he said vehemently. 'There's loads of other things you could do.'

'But I don't *want* to do anything else.'

'Because you are addicted. You always were. That's what gave you your edge in the first place. You were like a bloody Jack Russell down a fox-hole.'

'Well, there you go. And now I need to ferret out this bit of truth.'

'You'll be sub judicious if you even try to write about James, or Kattan, if they're investigating him too. Plus, you're married to the defendant.'

'I could do it under a false name.' I knew I was desperately grasping at straws now. 'Anonymously.'

'Just leave it, Rose.'

'But I *need* to know the truth. James is looking at prison, Xav, that's become very clear. I don't know what the hell is going on, but I'm sick of doing nothing. I'm just sitting here letting it all happen, and I haven't got a clue what reality is any more.'

Xav took my hand. I looked at his face and I felt a plunging in my stomach.

'What is it?'

'Sometimes – sometimes, angel, the truth is just too painful to know.'

Before he could say any more, his phone rang. He paled visibly when he heard the voice on the other end.

'I've got to take this, Rose,' he said, moving away from the table to stand in the window. I sighed. Something told me I wasn't going to get anything else from Xavier that day – other than a free lunch.

Chapter Twenty-Eight

Of good and evil much they argued then,
Of happiness and final misery,
Passion and apathy, and glory and shame:
Vain wisdom all, and false philosophy!

The Devil's Council, *Paradise Lost*, Milton

I packed up our overnight bag and took Freddie to Hyde Park whilst Jen took the girls shopping for clothes. I pushed him on the swings and held him tight on the see-saw to stop him bouncing off through the air, whilst he giggled raucously, and all the time my mind rattled back to Lord Higham. Why this vendetta now? Where did this all link up? I had done nothing to hurt Dalziel; I'd loved him very much, adored him even. So why did I feel now like I was being held accountable for the past?

Something had happened somewhere, and I was missing the obvious clue. I needed to speak to James again, but there was no chance of that for at least a week.

'Which superhero do you want to be, Mummy?' Freddie said as I lifted him to ring Jen's doorbell.

'Batman?'

'No. I'm Batman.' He considered me kindly for a second. 'You can be Under-woman if you like.'

'Under-woman? OK.' I kissed him and plopped him down on the pavement again.

'She wears big pants actually. And a cake.'

'Big pants and *cake*?' He meant cape. 'My type of lady.'

A man suddenly stood behind us, too close. 'Mrs Miller?'

My scalp prickling, I glanced round, clutching Fred's hand tighter.

'Would you accompany me please, Mrs Miller.' It didn't sound like a question. Quickly I pushed Fred between me and the front door.

'Sorry – who—'

'Lord Higham would very much like to see you.' He was politely unsmiling. 'Now.'

'Now?'

'It's important.'

'I'm sure it is, but as you can see,' I picked my protesting son up again, 'I'm busy right now.'

Jen opened the door, Effie in her wake.

'I'm sure your friend can help out,' the man said. He had a very faint accent and greasy pock-marked skin. 'Can't you, madam?'

Jen's eyes flicked anxiously between us. I hesitated, rapidly weighing up my options. Then I pressed Freddie into Jen's arms, kissed Effie's head and turned away. A black limo purred at the kerb, the windows darkened.

'I'm really sorry, Jen. I'll explain later.'

'Are you sure this is wise?' She looked worried. 'Where are you going?'

'Take down the number-plate,' I muttered into her ear, 'and if I'm not back by six, call the police.'

I followed the man to the car. 'See you for pizza in a minute, kids,' I called, waving cheerfully. 'Do what Auntie Jen tells you, OK? And no fighting.'

The man didn't quite push me in, but his hand was merciless, and when he slid into the front, he locked every door.

In an alleyway somewhere between the Houses of Parliament and Victoria Station, I was led past great stinking bins through a cramped and sweaty kitchen into a tiny dark restaurant.

A group of men, some of whom I recognised, were hunched over a table apparently finishing a meeting over a meal, papers and dispatch boxes strewn between carafes of wine, half-empty glasses, bits of bread and reeking, sweaty cheese. At least one was a Tory ex-cabinet member whom I had investigated in the past. I ducked my head instinctively, wondering what they were discussing now. How best to explain their latest expenses maybe, after the Conway and son scandal. Whatever it was, the tension was palpable in the small hot room.

The driver signalled our presence to Lord Higham, who sat in the middle of the table, calmly holding forth about something, the men at either end arguing and gesticulating. When Higham saw us, he quickly made his excuses to the other men, moving down the back of the room to greet us, brandy balloon in hand. His half-moon glasses gave his rather lugubrious face a professorial air.

'Welcome to Pandemonium,' he said wryly, and I stared at him in disbelief, the eerie echo of his son's words from years ago in my ears. 'You have caught us at a precarious time.'

The other politicians hardly glanced round, so immersed in their discussions, and I had a sudden ghastly vision of Lucifer's council: *Vain wisdom all, and false philosophy.* Dalziel had been obsessed with the rebel angels.

'Or possibly our last supper,' Higham smiled wearily. He was older, of course, and thinner than I remembered from our brief acquaintance after Dalziel's death. More stooped; more avuncular, somehow. I thought again how he looked nothing like his son. His face was much broader, the features cruder than Dalziel's

311

finely boned beauty, his skin now folded in on itself as if it had been neatly creased in the middle of his cheeks.

'So good of you to come.' His mellifluous voice was assured as he removed his glasses now, courteously inclining his grey head. Instinctively I crossed my hands before me.

'I'm not sure I had much choice.'

'Well,' he smiled. 'I should apologise for asking you here at such short notice.'

'I'm not sure *ask* is the right word, but I'm intrigued, Lord Higham,' I said casually. Inside I didn't feel the least bit casual, but I couldn't let him see that.

I followed him upstairs to another dining room, most of the tables upended, red velvet chairs against the wall, one young waitress busy folding linen in an office at the far end. The walls were dotted with framed photographs of politicians and singers, many signed to someone called Mario, interspersed with small watercolours of Italian and English countryside.

Higham indicated an unlaid table in the corner, the white tablecloth ringed with old wine stains.

'Can I get you something?' he asked, offering me a chair beneath a watercolour of the white cliffs of Dover. 'A glass of Chianti? A brandy perhaps?'

'I'm fine.' My heart was beating uncomfortably fast. 'I don't have much time. The children, you know . . .'

'Of course.' He inclined his heavy head. 'How many do you have now?'

How did he know I had any at all?

'Three.' I prayed my calmness belied the turmoil inside.

'Three.' He smiled and smoothed a hand across the tablecloth. He wore a heavy gold signet ring that looked like it should weigh his little finger down. I tried to remember the family motto. Dalziel had had a copy of the crest hanging in his hallway; something about Truth and Fortitude.

'And you?'

'Oh, you know.' He met my eye, and the sheer insouciance gave me a sudden flash of his son. I dropped my gaze. 'I lose count sometimes.'

I felt my past galloping at my heels; a faint sweat broke out across my top lip. I stared at the tired white rose in a small green vase on the table between us. I forced myself to speak. 'So, Lord Higham. What did you want to talk about?'

'I've been thinking . . .' He gazed at the painting behind me for a moment. 'There's a nice little spot coming up on one of the red-tops. A kind of upmarket gossip column, if you like. More classy than those silly 3 a.m. girls. Do with it what you will. Make it your own.' He looked back at me, reached into his inside pocket for something. 'Might that appeal?'

'That's kind,' I muttered, 'but I'm not sure it's really my field.'

'You could make it your field, of course. If you so chose.'

'I'm more current affairs, you know.' I thought of Xav's discomfort earlier. 'Why are you making this offer now?'

'Why not?' He brought a cigar out now, rolled it between thick fingers. Each one sprouted a patch of springy hair. A goat, I thought, he's like a large apparently benevolent goat. And then I thought of Azazel, devil goat; horrid Brian in that nasty mask bending over the insensible Huriyyah. I shuddered involuntarily.

'I've just—' I didn't want to mention Xavier's name. 'I know there's no place for me on the *Guardian*. So why now?'

'Is it not good to have friends in high places, Rose?' he smiled. But the smile went nowhere near his eyes. 'And current affairs, well. There's a time and a place. And this is most definitely not the time.'

'High places?'

'I imagine you've heard the rumours about the party. There's likely to be an election soon; the government can't possibly keep up this ridiculous charade. It's time for new blood. Or rather,' he tapped the cigar hard on the table, 'old blood.'

'What kind of old blood?' I frowned.

'Our own kind. Far too much new blood in this country. And so you see, well, we know, Rose – may I call you Rose? – we know there are some things that need to stay in the closet, as it were. And of course,' he took my hand. I felt a wave of nausea, 'of course, I like to take care of my own.'

I couldn't suppress the sound of disbelief. He looked at me, his eyes steely, and the fatherly air dissipated.

'I'm so sorry about your husband's arrest.'

'Oh.' I stared at him stupidly. 'You've heard.'

'Of course. I met young James at Oxford, you remember. He's done well, I believe. A great entrepreneur, no doubt. But – prison, I believe . . . not fun.'

'No. Not fun.'

'Poor man. Oh dear, Rose.' Higham let go of my hand as quickly as he'd taken it. He turned the vase around until the flower drooped its weary head towards me. '*O Rose, thou art sick!* I remember that poem from my schooldays. Pretty creepy, I always thought.' He smiled at me, a rather ghastly smile. 'Are you the sick rose, Mrs Miller?'

'I don't think so,' I mumbled.

'And if so, who, I wonder, is that nasty little worm?'

'There isn't one.' Panic was building slowly but inexorably in my chest. I felt like I was headed into a tunnel and I could just about see the light at the end.

'Isn't there? You're a fan of Blake, I suppose?' he said.

'Not really.' And the end was about to be blocked before I reached it.

'My son liked his later work, of course. All the nationalistic stuff about poor Albion. I have great sympathies for that, especially today.'

'Why?' I held his gaze.

'Who would ever have believed the BNP would be ascending as they are now? Such oiks really, which is a shame. Still, overcrowded and buffeted Britain.' Higham downed the last of his brandy. 'We have to make a stand, don't you think, Rose?'

'Against what?'

'Immigration? Integration?'

'No, actually.' I felt sickness in my craw. 'I really don't.'

'That's a shame.' He sighed deeply. 'But I digress. And I'm forgetting how well you knew Dalziel. You would remember all his little foibles.'

'I'm not sure that I did actually.' I looked at his father. 'Know him that well, I mean.'

Where was this all going?

'Dalziel loved all those dreadful flouncy angels flapping about in Blake's art.' He tapped his cigar on the table again. 'Before he became obsessed with bloody Milton, anyway. Ridiculous obsession. I never understood it.'

One of the cream petals had a tiny stain of burgundy on it. Like wine. Or blood. I stared at it.

'Dalziel once told me,' I cleared my throat, 'he once said he thought his mother was a fallen angel.'

'A fallen angel?' Higham let out a short bark of laughter. It had less joy or mirth in it than any laugh I'd ever heard. 'That bloody lunatic? Christ. Poor misguided boy.'

'I think he identified with something in the poem – in *Paradise Lost*,' I said quietly. 'The moral choice between heaven and hell. He was really struggling at the end.'

For a moment we gazed at one another, and I knew we recognised our mutual shame, shame for the roles we had inadvertently played that cold spring evening so many years ago.

'I still miss him, you know,' I said. 'I really do. He was – he was amazing. Despite what happened in the end.'

Our gazes locked. There was no place to hide.

'He was flawed,' Higham said coldly. 'Deeply flawed, poor boy.'

Downstairs the guffaws grew: presumably indicating the

meeting was drawing to a close. Higham checked his watch. 'So – the job?'

'And what's the condition, Lord Higham?'

'Straight to the point. I like that in a woman.' The waitress appeared at his elbow now with a lighter. She was very young. 'Come now, Rose. You must know what the conditions are.'

'Must I?'

'Oh, I think so, my dear Rose. I mean, you're a bright girl. You must know what serves you best. Especially with your husband so far out of reach.'

'I think I'd better go now.' I stood.

'Must you?' He pulled the waitress's hand down to cigar level. 'Got to sort out the little worm, eh? I must say, it's really not a good idea to send people in to threaten me.'

'Sorry?' I felt wrong-footed suddenly. Scared even.

'Have you met my youngest? Charlie?' He changed tack abruptly, dropping the name in like we were at some kind of social gathering.

'Not really.' My stomach clenched. 'He came to a party at my house, but I didn't know who he was.'

'Charlie is my latest worry.' He gazed at me. His eyes bulged unattractively, like congealed aspic. 'Despite a brilliant education, he's gone off the rails. I've had to cut the ties for a while. Financially, I mean. I fear – I fear he might be going down the route his brother did.'

My mind was racing, trying to make sense of his words.

'So you understand me?' Higham smiled a grim smile. 'Sending people to extort money is never going to be wise.'

'You've lost me.' But with a sinking heart, I remembered the photos in the cupboard. 'I don't know what you mean,' I lied.

He stared at me. And his eyes, they suddenly reminded me of someone else – I just couldn't think who. Not Charlie with his limpid dark eyes. Not Dalziel, whose amber eyes had been slanted and beautiful. Someone I'd seen more recently.

316

'Well, it's been delightful meeting you again, after all this time.'
He was still holding the girl's hand. 'You know, I have such little
time now for R & R. So little time for family. Though of course,'
he let her go now, 'I do what I can to protect them.'

'I guess everyone has to make sacrifices,' I said. 'Sometimes.'

'Sacrifices,' Higham said slowly. His eyes were blank now; blank
and staring like the dead. 'Not one of my most favourite words,
Rose.'

I thought back to Oxford; to the little boy in the bed. The
little boy Charlie. I wondered exactly what he remembered today.
Christ, what a family. What a mess.

'Really?' I looked back: I held my nerve.

'Think on the job. You've a few days to decide.'

We both knew that I would never work for him. I turned
towards the stairs.

'Oh, and, Rose?'

I turned back.

'Dear sick Rose. Do send my love to your children. Hadi Kattan
told me they were delightful.'

'Mr Kattan? He never met them,' I stammered.

'Oh – didn't he?' Higham stood now, brushing imaginary
crumbs from his trousers, cigar clamped between his teeth. 'I
must have got him confused with someone else. Easily done.'

'When did he say that? What's your link with Kattan?' I asked.
'Are you friends?'

'All these questions, my dear. Anyone would think you were
a journalist.' His tone was mocking.

'Just answer the question, please.' I bit the inside of my lip.
'Please, Lord Higham.'

'I'm not sure "friends" would be quite right, my dear. We've
known each other – well, for ever, it seems.'

I thought of Peggy's cuttings. 'Because of the oil embargo?'

'Maybe. I knew his wife, Alia, briefly. A long time ago. And
her son, Ash.' Higham smiled again now, his arm around the

317

young girl who blinked impassively. I hated him at that moment. 'Actually, Kattan rented my Cotswolds house recently. Perhaps you know it?'

My skin crawling, I paused for a second, looking down the stairs, racking my brain.

'Do you remember the end of Blake's rose poem?' I pulled myself up tall. 'If my memory serves me right, it's: *And his dark secret love Does thy life destroy*. Pretty apt, I'd say.'

Then I ran down the stairs and out of the restaurant. The driver opened the passenger door of the car as I passed.

'I'll walk, thanks,' I said. The evening was clear, the sun a dusky pink orb just dissolving behind the city's skyline. I knew I was setting off into my own howling storm.

Chapter Twenty-Nine

When a man is tired of London, he is tired of life.

Samuel Johnson

I took the children home the next day. There was nothing for us here except immediate danger and I couldn't see James again until next week. I knew I'd never work for Higham; I feared I might not work again at all right now. I was exhausted by everything and utterly confused; unsure which way to turn.

I'd spent hours making calls – and frighteningly, I'd found the same story all over town. Ex-colleagues weren't answering; no one was hiring because of the 'global downturn'; no one was posting abroad. Higham's name resounded round my head; somehow it seemed his tentacles had crept into my life and were strangling it. I could only think that he was punishing James and me for knowing Dalziel – and I'd always known that I would pay for my mistake. I just didn't realise the banker would claim everything at once.

In the past when things had got tough in any area of my life, I'd run. I'd follow a story until it unfolded as far as I could take it. If I was unhappy or anxious, I'd bury it beneath work. I'd jump on a plane, I'd live out of a suitcase. I was addicted to moving on. Everything that happened to me at college had shaped me, made me reckless in a way I hadn't been naturally. Later, when I found that I was pregnant with Alicia, I weaned myself off the danger and took different assignments; I stopped running and settled down to domestic bliss.

But now I wanted to run again. I wanted to scoop up my children and disappear them to safety. I was facing the truth head-on and it was this: I wanted out of me and James, I wanted out of the Cotswolds and, for the first time, London was no longer an option. I'd loved it for so long, but now I was tired of the buzz and adrenalin of a city that suddenly seemed mired in corruption. I craved sanctuary, although I knew now it didn't lie with anyone apart from myself and my family.

But for now, our little village would have to suffice. Jen and I hugged goodbye outside her flat.

'You be careful, Rose. No more funny business,' she made me promise, and we set off for home.

'Cor, who's been eating garlic?' Alicia wrinkled up her nose and opened her window. 'It smells.'

'There's a garlic in *Doctor Who*,' Freddie said solemnly. 'A bad garlic what will explode you.'

'Dur,' Alicia said. 'Dalek, dummy, not garlic.'

'It's not, Mummy, is it, it's a garlic.'

'It isn't.'

'Is.'

'Isn't.'

Freddie began to wail as Alicia began to chant, 'Isn't, isn't, isn't.' Freddie hit her; I nearly hit the car in front as I turned to restrain Freddie's flailing arm. In the midst of the chaos, Effie read her *Charlie and Lola* comic calmly, sucking her thumb, wisely ignoring her siblings.

*   *   *

'I spy with my little eye, something beginning with – motorbike.'

'*Beginning* with motorbike? Er –' I tried for solemnity. 'Motorbike?'

'No.' He was triumphant. 'It's – motorbike.'

'Fred-die!' Alicia kissed him affectionately. 'Silly!'

'This isn't our house.'

'This is a funny place.'

'This is – where is this, Mummy?'

A group of children kicked a ball against the wall of the last square house in the cul-de-sac.

'I'll only be a sec. Stay here and listen to *Winnie-the-Pooh*.'

'I'm bored of *Winnie-the-Pooh*,' Alicia moaned. 'It's for babies.'

'I want to play football. I can do really high kicks,' Freddie said, watching the big boys reverently. 'Shall I show you?'

'Look, we'll be home in half an hour, I promise. Then you can have footballs, telly, and –' I floundered, bit the parental dust – 'ice cream.'

'OK,' they sighed in unison.

Bang, went the ball. Bang, went my head.

I rang the doorbell. The PVC front door bore an intricate pattern of gold leaf in the thick frosted glass. A middle-aged woman answered, gingham tea-towel in hand. She looked droopy and sad; pretty once, washed-out now. Even her frizzy hair was limp.

'Hello.' I offered her the bouquet of rather pathetic carnations I'd just bought at the petrol station. 'I just came to say – I'm so sorry about Katya.'

'Kate,' she sniffed. 'Her name was just plain Kate. None of that fancy foreign stuff.'

'Of course,' I agreed quickly. 'Kate.'

'Not Angel either. Just Kate.'

'Sorry. Yes, Kate. It must be awful for you.' Effie and Fred's voices were rising querulously behind me. I tried hard to concentrate. 'Such a tragedy. She was so young.'

'She looked young for thirty-two, I know that. She always took such pride in her appearance.' I could feel her need to talk about her daughter. She looked down at the flowers, and then eyed my car parked at the edge of the postage-stamp lawn. 'Do you want to come in?'

'Oh, I won't.' I did badly want to go in. 'I've got the kids. I don't want to disturb you. We're— I just wanted to say sorry.'

I just want to know how your daughter knew my husband. What they had planned together.

'Bring them in,' she said, peering over my shoulder. 'I'd be glad to see some little ones.'

I felt sick with guilt and duplicity. This woman's daughter had died in my house; this was dishonest and— I hesitated. But I desperately needed to know why she had been there in the first place.

'If you're sure.'

She gave the children flapjacks she'd made herself and glasses of florid orange squash, and they ran down the tiny garden, two immaculately matching beds striping either side, a swing hanging from the cherry tree at the end.

'My only grandchild lives in America now,' she said sadly, watching them run to the swing. 'My son, well, his marriage broke down. It's so common these days, isn't it? His wife went back to Texas. And now – well, now Kate is gone.' Her eyes filled with tears. 'How did you know her?' She turned to me abruptly.

'We— From the club. You know.'

'Those bloody clubs. I never wanted her to do all that circus stuff in the first place.'

'She was brilliant, though.' For the first time since I'd arrived, I wasn't lying. 'She had a real talent.'

'She loved it, she did, flying over people's heads. You should see their faces, Mum, she used to say. All turned up to me. And so peaceful up there.'

'I'll bet.' I had an image of her twisted body on the floor and clutched my teacup tighter.

322

'And she met all sorts. Rich boys who promised her the world and never stuck around.' I thought of Charlie Higham. 'I wish she'd stayed here. There was always a place for her here. With us.'

'I suppose – the clubs were very glamorous.'

'It was him that did it. He came into the café, all smiles and charm. He offered her a job. And now look. So much more fun than a café in town,' she muttered. 'That's what she said.'

'Who is – who is he? Was he called Charlie?'

'No, it wasn't Charlie, though he was good for nothing too. It was that bloody man. He broke her heart once. Then he came back. And now look. Look where he is too.'

My stomach lurched. I watched Freddie trip and fall on the grass, Alicia help him up. Effie clambered awkwardly onto the swing.

'You've got a café?' I tried to smile.

'Yes, in town. It was my parents' before mine.' She sat wearily on the beige armchair in the corner, the fussy lace antimacassars over the arms, reminding me of the ones my grandma used to have. 'The Tea Room, on the High Street.'

I was in that tunnel again.

'We're going to change the name now.' I realised she was still talking. 'My son's arranging a new sign. We're going to call it Kate's Teas.'

The tunnel's end was coming up too fast; I was going to smash into it. I blinked.

'The Tea Room beside Blackwells?' My voice was strangely hoarse. 'Where all the Magdalen and Jesus students go?'

'I don't know which colleges use it, love. They're all the same to me. Lots of foreign students too, these days.' She looked at me again. 'How did you say you knew my Kate?'

'I – we met in London.'

'And where do you live now? Did you come all this way to see me?' Her forehead creased. 'It's a long way to come, with them.' She looked out at the children again.

'Oh dear, I think – oh poor Fred. He's hurt his knee.' I put my cup down too quickly, it spilt on the table, next to the bowl of pungent pot-pourri that looked like bits of dead skin.

'Kids, we're off now.' I quickly slid open the glass door. I was suffocating in here.

'Have we met before?' She was standing now, staring at me. 'You look familiar, now I look at you again.'

'No I don't think so. I'd remember, wouldn't you?'

I ran out into the garden, and plucked Effie off the swing.

'Mum,' Alicia whinged. 'We only just got here.'

'And now we're going home. Now. Hurry up.' I should never have brought them here. Such a bad mother. Such bad parents. I grabbed Alicia's hand. 'Bring Freddie. Hurry up.'

I got them to the car, apologising profusely, Kate's mother standing at her door, nonplussed. I couldn't tell her the truth, though I'd done nothing wrong. I couldn't admit I'd seen her daughter dying at my feet. Not now, I couldn't. I had to make sense of it.

'What, by the way,' I croaked, as I shut the back door. 'What was the man's name?'

'The man?'

'The man you said she loved.' Though of course I knew the answer. But I had to hear her say it.

'Oh.' She stared at me. 'It was that bloody James. James Miller. He broke her heart when she was a teenager, and then he came back, and he broke it all over again.'

Chapter Thirty

Love Is the Drug

Roxy Music

We settled down to our routine at home. Even without James it wasn't very different from how it had been before. The children readily accepted that he was working abroad. Until his trial came up, I didn't want to scare them; I thought they were too little, and when he was acquitted, well, they could wait until they were older to know the truth. Whatever that might turn out to be. *If* he was acquitted . . . I pushed that thought away.

James was able to speak to them on the phone once a fortnight and somehow he managed to keep up a convincing front. I visited him without them, studied the case with the lawyers. But there didn't seem much to know. The police had impounded a huge amount of heroin that had been contained in the shipment of furniture – and that was that. James swore at first he didn't know what Lana meant about the blackmail, but he did eventually admit that Kate was the same girl from the café all those years ago, that cold morning in Oxford. The waitress who'd stolen my scarf.

'I bumped into her,' he said when I confronted him about it. 'I went to the bank and it was opposite the café. She recognised me from Facebook.'

'So you *didn't* just bump into each other? Make up your mind, J, for God's sake.'

'We'd emailed a bit on Facebook last year,' he scowled. 'But we had no plans to meet. It was just – oh God, Rose. Whatever. We met, we went for a drink.'

'And?'

'And one thing led to another. She'd trained at the circus place in London, but she still helped her mum and dad out when she was back in Oxford. I got her a job in Paris.'

'Very convenient. So why – what happened?'

'Nothing happened.'

'You fell in love,' I said sourly.

'Not love, no. Just—'

'What? Lust?'

'I suppose. It was nice to feel wanted. But it was only once or twice, Rose, I swear.' He took my hand. 'I want to make things work.'

It was too late for us, though. I knew that much. Only – what do they say? Don't kick a man when he's about to go down.

'And the money thing? The big man thing? Kate's flatmate, Lana, mentioned a big man – and she means Higham, I know she does. He hauled me in to see him. He was threatening me. Trying to buy me off.'

'There *was* no money thing.'

'James, I know you were in trouble financially. What were those photos doing in the cupboard? The photos of Higham?'

'They were his son's.' James wouldn't meet my eye now. 'Charlie Higham's.'

'When did you get involved with him? Why didn't you tell me you'd met him?'

'Why would I?'

'Oh, come on, James. The kid who Dalziel tried to get us to kill. Why would you not mention him?'

He dropped my hand.

'I felt bad when I first met him, I admit it. I gave him free entry, VIP membership, free drinks – but he's just an arrogant little fucker who thinks the world owes him a living, Rose. Just like Dalziel, in fact.'

'I don't think Dalziel really thought that,' I said quietly. 'I think he was desperately lonely and unhappy.'

'Yeah, whatever, Rose.' James raised a sceptical eyebrow. 'Why the fuck you're still defending him, I don't know. But actually it was Charlie that Kate really loved, not me. They were his photos. Not mine. He gave them to me, and they added up to precisely nothing.'

'James,' I sighed. 'You're not being honest.'

'I've done nothing wrong, Rose.' The shutters came down. 'Other than fucking up a bit financially. How many bloody times do I have to say it, Rose?'

He wasn't budging. He was innocent; he was set up. He was the eternal child, the petulant little boy whose friend had stolen his toy. I gave up. Not knowing what to believe any more, I treated it as I would have done a news story and kept impartial. Of course I would try to support him – he was my husband, father of my family – but I no longer trusted him.

Eventually they moved James to a prison on the Isle of Wight, where Liam or I visited him once a week. He adapted to his environment, growing stronger and more determined he would get out. I encouraged him, but deep down, I feared he'd done something he still wasn't admitting. I waited for the day it would all come out.

And the loneliness I'd felt when James was around faded into a kind of peace. I was questioned again by the police; I still knew nothing. I kept writing for the *Chronicle*, thanks to Tina. I started to earn again, writing features for various glossy magazines;

slowly work came through from the nationals. Xavier sent whatever he could my way. He came to stay occasionally and I loved having him there. Our old friendship cheered me beyond belief. One cold autumn weekend as we tramped along with the kids deep in the Cotswold hills, he finally admitted that he was ill. His penchant for naughty boys and early morning clubbing had apparently caught up with him. I held his arm firmly, feeling a profound grief for my dear friend, although he was remarkably cheery about the prognosis. 'Amazing what drugs can do these days, darling.' He patted my arm sagely as I wiped away my own tears.

I watched Ash Kattan rise through the party ranks and win the Tory seat just before Christmas, not Eddie Johnson's, but snatching a Labour one in Berkshire, much to the *Telegraph*'s delight. There was never any mention of his father in the British press, although one night I thought I caught Hadi's name on the radio, a report on the World Service about a party for the Saudi royal family who were visiting Tehran. I wondered what Kattan was doing in Iran now. I imagined that, though on the streets chaos reigned as the people started to fight hard for democracy, Kattan would rise above it all as ever, enigmatic and mysterious. And in his wake, would Danny be following?

I had pushed all thoughts of Danny as far from me as possible, until sometimes it all seemed like a dream. There were many nights when I couldn't sleep, his face spinning through my head, but I was no longer crippled with yearning as I had been at first. The sickening pain dulled to a monotonous ache. The drug that had filled my veins ebbed away, the fear that this was my one last chance for happiness faded. I accepted my lot, but it was a long and torturous path, considering the brevity of our relationship, and one I struggled to comprehend. Only I could have chosen someone who, rather than rejuvenate my flagging self-worth, actually plunged me deeper into despair. And yet, I started to think now, was it more to do with the place I'd been in, than the man I had chosen?

Whatever the answer, I had fallen too fast, too hard; irrationally, illogically. Now I had to get back up again.

Most frightening though, Lord Higham's newly formed party, the UK National Party, was being greeted by the British public with an alacrity that was entirely alarming. As charismatic as smooth Robert Kilroy-Silk but not as oily or overly earnest as the new UKIP lot, Higham spoke with such charm and fervour that he whipped the proletariat up into a frenzy of desire to be British, to unite, to see the nation return to its 'on the beaches' mentality, accompanied by the trusty bowler hat or knotted head-scarf. Occasionally Higham would mention the scourge of Muslim terrorists, the rise of divisive faith schools, immigration gone mad – but he tucked these subjects carefully into his speeches between the other more noble kind.

'He's a dangerous fucker,' Xav sniffed at the television we were watching with the sound down, gorging ourselves on the champagne truffles he'd brought with him.

'I'll say.'

I looked at those protuberant glacial eyes and I thought of my friend Dalziel. I remembered the way his father had covered the crisis up; how a fatal situation had been made slick after Higham's hand carefully smoothed it over.

Who knew what lay beneath?

PART THREE

Chapter Thirty-One

Our pleasures in this world are always to be paid for.

Northanger Abbey, Jane Austen

THE TIMES, APRIL 2009

The notorious Revolver trial of James Miller finally began today at London's Old Bailey. Mr Miller, the millionaire club promoter and record producer, is accused of smuggling heroin; the consignment police seized holds a street value of £2.5million. The drug was allegedly contained in a shipment of marble and wooden furniture bound for Miller & MacAvoy's new super-club Revolver, based in Smithfield. A last-minute development means Miller will now stand trial along with co-defendant Saquib Baheev; both men are said to be pleading not guilty. Miller's wife, Rose, formerly Rose Langton, was at the court today, although his business partner, Liam MacAvoy, is still out of the country; there has been no suggestion of MacAvoy's involvement in the case.

Prior to the birth of her three children, Mrs Miller enjoyed an award-winning career as an investigative journalist, but she declined to comment outside court today.

The Sunday morning before the trial finally began, I awoke to find Effie staring at me.

'Open your eyes, Mummy,' she was saying, squishing my cheeks between small hands. I opened and shut them again quickly. I felt vertiginous: like I was at the top of the ski-jump in Innsbruck where James and I had gone when we still did things like that, the Christmas before Alicia was conceived.

I screwed my eyes up tight; saw myself as a minute speck waiting at the top of the mighty white expanse – about to hurtle off the end into oblivion.

'Open,' Effie insisted. Reluctantly, I did. She stuck a small finger in my eye.

'Ow!'

'I want a biscuit, Mummy,' she guffawed with delight. 'Now.'

It had been the strangest year of my life. A year of guilt and unrest. A whole year after the party where Katya had fallen to her death and my world had finally split open like someone had cleaved it clean down the middle.

As soon as the case was over, whatever the outcome, we'd move from the Cotswolds. I'd relinquished the delusion that I could ever make it home now; valiantly I'd endured the gossip and the stares until finally everyone got tired of us and forgot the scandal. Surprisingly, a few had shown true friendship; even Helen Kelsey had insisted on making me a weekly casserole, for which my kids were eternally grateful. Properly cooked food, made with care – unlike my burned offerings. I realised James's story about her crush had probably been a downright lie.

My mother packed the children into the car that breezy April afternoon and took them up to Derbyshire. For the duration of the trial I'd stay in London with Jen or Xav, and see the children at the weekends.

I kissed them bravely and then my mother hugged me. 'Good luck, Rosie. I hope it goes all right.'

My parents had been mortified by the whole situation, I knew, but stoically and with absolute loyalty, they had never once mentioned their embarrassment, though my own guilt was immense.

I waved the car off, tears springing to my eyes as Effie blew me kisses through the back window. As they turned the corner, I saw Freddie stick his light-saber up Alicia's nose.

After a year of indrawn breath, I was waiting to exhale again.

I got up at dawn the next day and drove into London beneath speckled mackerel skies. As I sped down the Westway, my phone rang.

'Rose?' It was Ruth, James's solicitor. 'I've got some bad news, I'm afraid.'

'What?' Fear gripped me; for a moment I felt light-headed. The van in the lane beside me blasted his horn as I swerved dangerously.

'We've only just heard. The Crown want to call you as a witness.'

'I don't understand.'

The van driver was mouthing at me, jabbing his finger at my mobile. I ignored him, tucking the phone under my chin. 'What does that mean?'

'It means you'd be a witness for the prosecution.'

A motorbike flashed by, the driver crouched like a bat out of hell.

'God,' I mumbled. 'And what does *that* mean?'

'It means, Rose, that you will be called to give evidence *against* James.'

Given the massive media interest in James, I was unsurprised by the amount of press as I arrived at the Old Bailey that first morning – but still I nearly turned back. The hounds were baying for blood as I put my head down, hiding behind sunglasses although the day was dull and grey, the sky overcast.

Still, I recognised faces I'd known for years, more that I hadn't; TV crews, even paparazzi in some vain hope that a real celebrity might turn up (some hope; James's famous friends had proved fair-weather so far).

Every fibre of me screamed 'go back' as I broke through their ranks. It was utterly alien for me to be on this side – but I had no choice. Suddenly I knew how the fox felt.

'Give us a break, guys,' I muttered. A few stood back to let me through.

The first four days, I just waited around. As a probable defence witness I wasn't allowed to enter the court whilst the Crown case proceeded first. But I felt it was my duty to be near James, despite not being able even to see him. I sat in the corridor or the canteen; I read gossip magazines and drank a lot of tepid tea. I taught myself Sudoku. Occasionally I tried to write something, but my concentration was shot. And all the time I was waiting the refrain played through my head: if James gets out, I have to tell him I'm leaving anyway.

I watched families come and go, crying, ashen-faced, complacent. I watched the defendants who swaggered and those who'd bought a new suit for the occasion. I watched those shaven red-raw for the judge, white shirts still showing the creases from their M&S packet. I watched nervous girl-friends called to give evidence. One tall thin girl stuck in my mind, biting her nails as she waited to speak in an assault case. I watched the innocent and the guilty, and try as I might to discern which was which, I rarely could. Did people wonder the same about me?

Each night after court adjourned, Ruth would patiently run through things with me. I read the witness statements. The Crown were alleging that James had known about the heroin; it had entered the UK inside a massive furniture shipment. They said that James had long been part of the team to mastermind the operation. The drugs had been inside hollowed-out furniture – garden tables, statues – and they believed that he had used the clubs as a front.

Another man was on trial too, a British-Pakistani called Saquib Baheev. I vaguely remembered James mentioning a Saquib, but the fuzzy little head-shot they showed on the one news bulletin I saw meant nothing to me. The prosecution alleged the two men had worked in conjunction with each other, but James had made the initial contact. There was never any mention of Hadi Kattan.

'He's slipped the net on this one,' Ruth had said when I pressed her. 'Even if he *is* involved – and the CPS have no evidence apparently to say he is – I'd guess he's being protected by someone. I don't know. We have no extradition treaty with Iran. Even if he was charged, they'd never be able to bring him in.'

Danny's words echoed in my head: diplomatic immunity. He was like a phantom, Hadi Kattan, like the Scarlet Pimpernel. *They seek him here, they seek him there.* Somewhere, someone was protecting him. I just didn't know why.

And then it was my turn. I took the stand on the Friday morning, feeling under-prepared, trembling with nerves. I'd tried so hard to be calm and collected but I even fumbled my swearing in. It was the first time I'd seen James in a week; he looked thin and anxious as we smiled at each other shakily across the room. And then I looked at the other defendant seated next to him and I felt nausea rise quickly in my gullet.

Saquib Baheev was Zack from Albion Manor: the heavy who had been part of Kattan's entourage.

Cold sweat broke out under my arms; I grasped the card I was reading from so tight I left shiny fingerprints on it. Saquib looked over at me and I could have sworn he winked.

The barrister for the prosecution, Janet Leen, stepped up. Leen's face was clay-like, raw and ill-defined, like someone had forgotten to finish it. She moved uncomfortably in her smart clothes; her wig was tatty and trailing hairs; she stamped across the court. But when she spoke, she was sharp as a cut-throat razor.

'So your husband was experiencing severe financial difficulties?'

'Not to my knowledge, no. His income was considerable.'

'But we know he was; his accountant's already told us. And his spending was out of control.'

'Not really, for someone who earned what he did.'

'But the money had dried up.'

'Not as far as I was aware.' I had to be honest now. 'He was in charge of his business affairs.'

'Ah,' Leen sniffed disdainfully. 'The dutiful housewife taking the back seat.'

Christ. What was it with these bloody women and my domestic life?

'Hardly. But James dealt with his business income himself. I mean, why would I get involved?'

'Why would you indeed, Mrs Miller, apart from to spend it?' She smiled a horrible *faux* smile.

'I'm not some sort of WAG,' I retorted. The jury smiled and I relaxed a little. 'I had a successful career myself before having my children.'

'Really? Doing what?'

'I was – I am a journalist.'

'A journalist.' Leen spat out the word as if I had just professed to being a child killer. 'So how did you feel when you found out he was having the affair?' Slowly she drew out the syllables of 'aff-air'.

The head of John Huntingdon, James's barrister, snapped up. There was a murmur through the jury. My stomach plunged.

'I didn't know anything about an affair.' I tried to keep my voice steady. I hadn't; not when James was arrested, so I wasn't lying, I told myself.

'Didn't it start whilst you were at university?' Leen said calmly. 'When you were involved with the ghastly Society X.'

James and I glanced at each other; I tried to hide my shock. There had been no indication that this would be brought up; we had not talked about the Society to Ruth and she had never mentioned it.

'Objection, Your Honour.' James's barrister shot to his feet. 'What bearing can university shenanigans possibly have on this case?'

The judge looked down from her position of gravitas. 'Expand, please, Ms Leen.'

'I just want to explain that Mr Miller is far from the blemish-free character that has been suggested so far.'

'That's absolute rubbish,' I expostulated. 'Society X—'

'Mrs Miller,' the judge said quite gently, 'please. Wait until you are asked to speak.'

'Sorry,' I mumbled. James's legal team were looking vaguely horrified, muttering to one another. I stared at Janet Leen. She stared calmly back. Her nose looked like someone had given the clay a sharp twist.

'I believe your husband was actually arrested and charged in 1992, was he not? Accused of intent to harm after an incident in Oxford's Randolph Hotel?'

'For about an hour. All charges were dropped. It was a mistake.'

Leen looked at me and then she turned to the jury. 'Ladies and gentlemen, I would just like you to take into account that James Miller was a member of the notorious Society X, whose pranks ended in the tragic death of at least one member.'

'Objection, Your Honour! This is inadmissible.'

'For Christ's sake!'

'Mrs Miller, please!'

'Well, honestly.' I ignored John Huntingdon's desperate gesticulating. 'We were kids. Really. We were eighteen, nineteen. We thought we knew the world, but we didn't, and we didn't know any better. We were just trying to have fun, to be a little outrageous – and it went a bit wrong. It's got nothing to do with this. Nothing. James doesn't have any sort of criminal record.'

The judge banged her gavel down. 'The jury will disregard the allegation just made by counsel for the prosecution.' *Like hell they would.* 'And Mrs Miller will refrain from using the stand as a soap-box.'

I gave her a sheepish look.

'We'll adjourn for lunch. And, Mr Huntingdon,' the judge turned her gaze to the barrister, 'I suggest you get the witness into line over a plate of something light.'

A titter rippled round the court. Huntingdon smiled a pained little smile.

'You can't let them rattle you, Rose.' Ruth took me to task over a stale ham sandwich in the canteen. 'You've got to appear calm and maternal and sensible. And you certainly can't speak out of turn like that. It just makes you look hysterical.'

'OK.' I abandoned my unappealing lunch. 'But it's hard. They really do twist everything, don't they?'

'Of course. That's their job. Now,' she looked tired and for a moment, I thought, defeated, 'is there anything about this Society X that I need to know?'

'No. It was just a silly secret society at university that ended badly.'

'Badly?'

'Someone else got carried away with a silly ritual. The police got overexcited and charged James: it was dropped within two days.'

'Are you sure? What's the death thing?'

'Lena Latzier overdosed,' I said quietly.

'The opera singer's daughter? Bloody hell.' Ruth drained her can of lemonade. 'Anything else?'

'Dalziel St John killed himself.' My voice was smaller now. 'Lord Higham's son.'

'Tell me you're joking, please?' Ruth stared at me. 'Higham, as in the UKPP?'

'Yes. Dalziel was the – the ring-leader, if you like. And some overzealous police got involved, and tried to make a case against some of us when he died. But honestly, the charges were dropped as quickly as they were brought.'

I didn't mention that I was sure Lord Higham had had a hand in making it go away; that he had obviously wanted no mention of scandal around his name if he could possibly help it. As it was, he had resigned from the cabinet the following year.

Ruth looked at me sadly, rather as if I had let her down. Then she left me there alone and went to talk to James.

James's barrister, John Huntingdon, was grave and sincere. I had been alarmed by his youth, by his ruddy complexion and air of suppressed bon viveur – but I had been assured he was the best.

'Your husband is a family man, Mrs Miller? He worked hard, created everything from scratch?'

'That's right,' I said. 'He is extremely hard-working. He was – sorry – he *is* a dedicated father. His children need him at home.'

'Of course. And would you think there was any reason for him to put this at risk?'

'No,' I said honestly, 'I don't. He was extremely successful. His businesses were doing very well. He is very well respected as a music producer. Why would he need to smuggle drugs?'

I talked some more about him being an upstanding pillar of the community, employing lots of people, giving today's youth a chance with various schemes at the label and the club, contributing to charity. The jury looked reasonably impressed, I thought, but they were a motley bunch themselves. One thickset middle-aged woman in the front row looked like she might combust from disapproval; another folded her arms every time I spoke. James studied his hands.

Janet Leen started on about Katya and James; fortunately she

341

didn't mention Society X again. As she droned on and on, I looked up and I saw Kate's mother sitting at the edge of the gallery, holding on very tight, and I cringed inside. She would know now that I had lied on my visit to her house. I tried very hard to not catch her eye at any point. I couldn't look at James at all.

At the end of my questioning I sensed movement at the other end of the gallery and I glanced up to see a tall figure in a long black jacket heading for the stairs. For a second, I thought it might be Charlie Higham.

Then Leen took a final swipe.

'Were you ever aware that your husband was using his clubs as a front for something else?'

'No, absolutely not.' I dragged my eyes back from the gallery. 'He just loves music; he lives for it. He always did. It was a dream come true to make such a great career out of it.'

'And drugs and partying, with lots and lots of girls?'

'Objection, Your Honour.' Huntingdon shot up like a jack-in-the-box. The usual toing and froing began again between the lawyers.

I glanced back up, but the figure in black was gone.

Chapter Thirty-Two

The following Monday, I sat outside the courtroom with a newspaper and a cup of tea. Waiting, again – this time for Liam, the first defence witness. The Crown were nearing the end of their case; apparently they only had a few more witnesses to call, and Liam was coming in from France where he'd been sorting out some problems with the club there.

To my surprise, DS Montford suddenly arrived and sat opposite me at the end of the corridor, staring at her navy court shoe, swinging it on and off her foot like it was the most interesting thing she'd ever seen.

'You've given evidence, haven't you?' I asked eventually. There was a small ladder in the heel of her tan pop-sock.

Montford nodded. I'd read her statement. She'd wielded the knife against James like a deranged teenager.

'So?' She'd obviously come to freak me out. 'Why are you here?'

'I'm waiting for someone,' she said, pushing her glasses up her nose.

'Who?'

'No one you know,' she said crisply.

After a while, I couldn't bear the tension any more and went outside to look for Liam but it started to drizzle.

As I walked back into the building, the clerks were ushering someone into Court Number Two – the one beside our courtroom, the wooden doors swinging shut behind him, DS Montford in his slipstream like a small blackbird.

I stopped a court officer who was following them.

'What's going on?'

'Anonymous evidence for the Miller case.'

'Why are they going in there then?'

'They'll video it and transmit it through to next door.'

Twenty minutes later, Liam arrived, sweating profusely. He kissed me on both cheeks, his great hulk squeezed into a navy suit that was a size too small.

'I've put on some weight,' he said ruefully, as I patted his tummy.

'It's all that loving, baby,' I tried to joke. It was too oppressive to joke, here in the corridors of fear. 'Or too much foie gras.'

'Both probably. Sorry I'm late. Christ, I'm nervous.'

'There's no need to be, is there?' I said, eyeing Liam carefully. We'd seen little of each other recently; we'd kept in touch on the phone or by email during the past few months. He had sorted out the finances with Revolver's lawyers and I received a monthly sum that at least paid the mortgage – the enormous mortgage I'd never realised James had taken out to finance the club in Bangkok he'd dreamed of.

'Guess not,' he shrugged.

'You've just got to tell the truth, the whole shebang.'

'I bloody hate lawyers, though.' Liam ran a finger round his tight collar; the shaving rash on his neck looked red and painfully raw. 'So smarmy and smug, always out to trip you up.'

'Liam?'

'What?'

'You know Lana mentioned some kind of blackmail, and Lord

344

Higham accused me of trying to extort money,' I muttered. 'Then the prosecution just started on about the club being a front.'

'Lana?'

'Kate's flatmate. And James said Charlie Higham was involved in something dodgy.'

'That doesn't surprise me. But it's the first I heard of blackmail.' He looked at me levelly. 'And I can assure you the clubs aren't a front. You know that. I tell you, they've been through bloody everything with a fine-tooth comb.'

Ruth was bearing down on us. 'Liam, we need to have a quick chat.'

I couldn't decide whether to go in and listen to his evidence. I was so sullied by the whole affair; every day it seemed more hopeless. I thought longingly of my children: I missed them desperately. I went outside to call them.

I was at the tea machine when Liam appeared again in the corridor.

'That was quick,' I said, surprised.

'They sent me out again. Big old kerfuffle in there. Some copper's giving evidence anonymously.'

'What policeman?'

'Dunno. Never actually saw him.'

My plastic cup dropped down from the machine with a clunk.

'And they only used his Christian name anyway.' Liam leaned against the machine.

'John?' Dully I watched the cup fill with tepid water, idly plucking names from the air. 'Peter?'

'No. David. No. Not David. Dan!' He looked triumphant. 'Yeah. Danny – that was it.'

Chapter Thirty-Three

Every ounce of adrenalin I possess crashes through my body; I'm shaking with rage. I will find him if it kills me. I smash open the doors and run into the court. He is here, so near and yet still so bloody, bloody far. Further than he's ever been.

I look up, across – and I see him. It takes me a second to absorb the fact – and then I can't believe it. I can't believe Liam was right.

You are in the wrong place, absolutely the wrong place, I think. I see him and for a moment I think I am surely mistaken.

He stands to leave the witness box; he hears the commotion and he turns. Our eyes meet across the courtroom.

'You can't be in here,' someone says.

'Please,' the court officer is speaking, 'can the ushers . . . ?'

Her voice fades. Everything fades as he looks at me across the empty room and it all falls into place. How could I have been so very, very stupid? Of course he is a policeman.

Someone in uniform holds my arm as I just stand there, immobilised by shock.

It's as if my whole life has been heading inexorably for this moment: like the moment when you switch off the television set and the tiny white light dies, the moment you are alone in the darkness.

The officer takes my arm. She is trying to remove me, push me back outside, back into the corridor. There is a furious whispering, a room alive with the excitement of the case, of my misdemeanour. But they are light years away; I don't hear them any more because we are staring at one other, our eyes locked.

There is only him – and my heart, it actually stops; it feels like it stops so I gasp suddenly with the shock of it. I think I even stagger. I feel a pain, a real pain deep in my belly, as visceral as if my insides are tearing away from themselves. I want to bend myself double, to curl up and hide – but how can I here, where I am watched? I am trapped.

And then he looks away.

So this is it, I think. There is just white light and noise around me that makes no sense, and then eventually they succeed. They get me back outside again.

The doors close in my face, and he is gone.

So this is what they call it. It is worse than I imagined: it is worse even than heartbreak and, God knows, I've felt that too.

This is worse than heartbreak. It is infinitely worse.

This is betrayal.

And then they were hustling me out and he was being led the opposite way. I tried to turn to see him but I couldn't twist my head far enough as I was marched out, and the door was firmly shut behind me.

Where would they take him? Where would they try to hide him?

After a couple of false starts, I found an alley that led to the back of the court-house. I saw DS Montford come out and

347

get into an unmarked Rover, and I guessed he'd be somewhere there too.

I ran across the car park and a security guard was calling, 'Miss, miss,' behind me in a strong Nigerian accent, but I ignored him and pushed the fire door open, almost falling as it took my weight.

He stood there, leaning against the wall quite calmly just inside the door, rolling a cigarette, and when he saw me, he narrowed those unreadable eyes at me. Blue as Hockney's swimming pool; blue as Turner's skies.

'Hello, Rose Miller,' he said, and my world crashed again. Blue as forget-me-nots.

He just stood there rolling a cigarette like he had no care in the world, not one.

The security guard lumbered up behind me. 'Please, miss.' He had a shiny bovine face. 'You can't be—'

Danny flashed something that he pulled from his jacket pocket, some kind of badge. 'It's OK. She's with me.'

With me! I nearly laughed – except it would have killed me.

The reluctant guard sized us up. 'OK, sir. If you are sure.'

'Sure I'm sure. Cheers, pal.'

The guard lumbered off again.

'You're going to say, what am I doing here,' Danny said quietly. He was wearing a grey suit and a dark shirt. He looked smart, handsome, his hair less dishevelled than usual. I'd never imagined him like this.

'Yes I am. What the fuck *are* you doing here? Oh God. I can't believe it.' And I slapped my palms against my own forehead so hard it hurt. 'God God God,' I intoned. 'You bastard.'

He grabbed my wrists. 'Don't.'

'Fuck off,' I hissed. I didn't ever remember feeling this angry. Ever. Fury made me strong, strong enough to get out of his grasp this time. I lunged back from him. 'How could you have done that? How could you have?'

'Calm down, Rose,' he said.

'Why? Why would I calm down? You bloody bloody liar.' I stared at him. He dropped his gaze first.

'Just wait a sec.' He leaned over me and pushed open a door. It was some kind of waiting room; he manoeuvred me in.

'What the fuck are you doing here? Where's—' I gazed at him. 'Is it true? Are you really a policeman?'

We looked into each other's eyes; the eyes that once I could have drowned in.

'Aye.' Slowly he nodded. "Fraid so.' Then he bent his head to light his roll-up.

'So.' I was trying to catch up, to get my brain to catch up – but I was so shocked I couldn't work it out. 'So what, Danny? Or – I guess that's not your real name.'

'Rose,' he came nearer, 'I never meant to lie to you. But my hands were tied. I *couldn't* tell you the truth.' The Scottish burr suddenly sounded stronger than it ever had. 'I didn't have a choice. I really didn't.'

'You played me,' I whispered, and I felt sick to my core. 'You just used me to get to James. Oh God, oh God.'

'Listen to me.' He grabbed my wrists again and the smoke from his cigarette made my eyes water. 'It was nothing to do with your husband, I swear. I wasn't interested in him. No one was. He just got in the way, that's all.'

'So who were you interested in? Kattan, obviously.'

'I'm not at liberty to say.'

'Liberty? Are you taking the piss?' I glowered at him.

'Please, Rose.' He dropped his hands. Did he look a little sad? 'It's so complicated.'

'You know, when you ran away from me, I thought that hurt. But this, this is worse.' My eyes filled with tears of rage and pain. 'I thought – I thought that you quite liked me.' I heard my pathetic plaintive tone and I despised myself.

'I did. I do.' He reached out to touch my face, but I ducked like I had in the rain that evening last year, turned away.

Slumping down at the bare table, I hid my face in my hands. 'You don't know what you've done to me, Danny Callendar. Or whoever you are. You have no idea.'

Everything I thought I knew had gone now; the ground beneath my feet was disintegrating. James and I were finished and though I knew he'd deserted me already, I suppose I'd held on to some vestige, that somewhere deep down, Danny had really cared. He must have loved me: he had come back to see me that night. But now, now I realised it was all just a game; that it had meant nothing. Worse than a game, even. Just a job.

'Rose, please,' Danny's voice was tense. 'I tried to stay away from you. Right from the start. I tried, and I know I fucked up, and I failed you. I couldn't stay away. I tried.'

The tears were streaming down my face. 'Why me?'

'I couldn't help it.' He threw his fag on the floor and he walked towards me and he held my face between his hands. 'Listen to me, you daft woman, I didn't lie to you, not about my feelings. I was doing my job, but – and it'll be fucking curtains for me,' he had never sworn, I realised, normally, 'it'll be over for me if they know, but listen, listen to me, Rose.'

'I'm listening.' I breathed deep, trying not to sob.

'It was just about you.' He leaned towards me and he was almost whispering. I could see the tiny freckles on his nose now. 'That's all. Just you and me.'

And, oh God, I wanted to believe him; I needed something to hold on to as the world kept tipping on its head.

'I've got to go, Rose. But listen . . .'

Tipping until it would throw me right off.

'I *am* listening,' I said fiercely, wiping my face.

'I'll find you again, I promise. Afterwards. I'll come and explain properly.'

'And James?' I croaked.

'Kattan had some kind of grievance against James that he never shared with me.' Danny leaned down and gently wiped

350

my face; just like he had once before. My skin felt like butter, like it would hold the imprint he lightly made.

'Grievance? Over what?'

'I don't know exactly. He was settling scores for his son, I think.'

'For Ash?'

'Something to do with that secret society the barrister mentioned. Does that make sense?'

'But –' my mind was reeling – 'but whatever, if huge drug deals were happening, why is Kattan not implicated? I don't understand.'

'Just because, Rose. He's wanted for far bigger things. And James was stupid, he was tempted by greed and desperation. He should have stayed away from them. It was always going to be bad business.'

'Are you saying James did it?' I whispered.

Danny shrugged. 'What do you think?'

'I don't know what I think, Danny. Or – or whoever you are. I don't know anything any more.'

'Listen, Rose. There's nothing I can do to help him. He might get off, there's a chance. But I swear, it was nothing to do with me; our paths just happened to cross. I've told them what I know, and the rest is down to the court. And I know I did the wrong thing with you, and I'm sorry for that. I swear.' He hugged me. 'I should never have come near you, Rose.'

He pulled me close and I clung to him. I knew he had betrayed me, but for a moment I clung on like my life depended on it. He kissed me once, on the lips, and this time he felt hot. His skin was hot, and somewhere, faintly, the lemon sherbet tasted bitter-sweet.

'I shouldn't have come near you,' he murmured into my hair. Then he opened the door. 'I shouldn't – but I had to.'

'Danny,' I said urgently, and he turned. 'What's your name? Your real name?'

'They call me Cal.'

'Cal?'

'I was born on the banks of the river Callendar.' He smiled at me. I'd so rarely seen him smile. 'That's where we stayed. My family. Ma was a bit poetic, you see. Just call me Cal.'

And then he was gone. Somewhere deep inside, my instincts screamed; I knew I'd never see him again.

Chapter Thirty-Four

'That fucking barrister,' Liam kept saying. 'Fucking ugly bitch.'

I clinked the ice around my glass, round and round it went. I tried to concentrate on Liam's words as a group of laughing men came through the pub door. I turned abruptly at the sound of a Scottish accent. It wasn't him; of course it wasn't. Danny was long gone. I bit my lip hard. The pain took my mind off him for about a minute.

'It was a fucking set-up, James was right,' Liam was slurring in the background. 'They fucking massacred me. That fucking bitch barrister made it sound like we're just a pair of lightweights messing around with drugs and ravers.' Liam slammed his glass down on the table and almost missed; it nearly fell onto the floor. 'How fucking dare she?'

'What did you expect?' I said wearily, pushing the glass safely home.

'I don't know. Not that. Poor bloody James. I can't believe how shit this all is.' Liam clutched my hand. He was drunk, really drunk. He swayed forward alarmingly, until gently I pushed him back. 'He's going to get off, Rose, I know it. He'll be home soon.'

I patted his hand. 'Let's hope so, lovely. Let's hope so.'

*　*　*

The next day they called Saquib Baheev to the stand. I sat in the public gallery, thanking God for the small mercy of Kate's mother not being here today, of her reproachful gaze. I listened as Saquib insisted he'd only done what he had been told, according to him: meeting people, couriering, driving for the Kattans. It all sounded very respectable at first.

'I'm not trying to say I'm blameless, yeah? But I was just a soldier, right? Nadif, he was the man. I did do a bit of heavy stuff for him, for my sins.'

I sat up, alert suddenly. Trying but failing to win the jury over, Saquib blamed the entire thing on a man called Nadif Mosa: he was the mastermind, apparently.

'The boss's daughter's boyfriend. He infiltrated the family through poor Maya.' Saquib tried an eyebrow-raise that meant *Women, eh?* 'Well clever, that one. Fooled us all.'

Nadif. Maya's boyfriend, who had died. The man I'd seen Saquib smash down in the gravel. He was obviously lying.

'And what happened to Nadif Mosa, Mr Baheev?'

Baheev made another ill-judged attempt at conspiracy with the jury. He was not an attractive proposition right now, sweating and nervous, a false smile like a tic that he kept flashing at them in some kind of delusional hope. They stared blankly at him.

'Let's just say it ain't wise to get high on your own supply. Know what I'm saying?'

'Meaning?' The barrister was brusque.

'Meaning he majorly overdosed, yeah?'

This was borne out by a written statement from the coroner, and the court was adjourned for lunch before Baheev was questioned about James. I thought I'd better tell Ruth what I knew about Nadif, but she was nowhere to be found. I felt really shaky today; my appetite was shot and I'd hardly slept. Facts that made no sense pursued one another relentlessly round my head. I wished desperately that Danny were here; I wished desperately that I could stop thinking of him. He wouldn't be the answer, I had to remember that.

Outside in the street, I leaned on the railing, glancing down the road. A group of barristers checked their BlackBerrys and smoked by the revolving doors, their robes flapping out behind them like clipped crows' wings. Beyond them, a woman was on the phone beneath an elm tree. I looked again as she put her hand up for a black cab.

'Excuse me.' I began to walk towards her.

She was getting in the cab now, still on the phone.

'Wait.' I was hurrying now. 'Please, wait . . .' But too late. The cab was pulling off now into the busy lunch-time traffic.

I was sure it was Maya Kattan.

Slowly I walked back to the Old Bailey. Ruth was waiting for me outside the courtroom. She looked slightly feverish.

'Something's happened.' She took my arm. 'They're adjourning the trial.'

'What? Why?'

'Some kind of new evidence has come to light.'

'What does that mean?' I was confused.

Was it my imagination, or was there a strange light in her eyes?

'I don't know. All I know right now is they're adjourning the case for a few days.' She clutched my arm. 'Keep everything crossed for your poor husband.'

'I am,' I smiled shakily. 'Believe me, I am.'

Chapter Thirty-Five

The moon was a chalk circle etched on the pale sky as I walked through the dusky city. Dodging tourists still snapping St Paul's, I felt confused and washed out. My exhaustion was immense. At least now, I thought, trying to fix on a bright spot, at least I can go back to my parents and be with the kids. We might have to wait some more, but at least it's nearly over.

Outside Jen's flat, I was searching for the doorkey when my mobile rang.

'Hello? Rose Langton?' a creaky voice asked. 'I saw you on the news at lunch-time. It jogged my memory.'

'Sorry,' I couldn't place her, 'who is this?'

'I found something a while back, but I have to be honest, it's been sitting in the in-tray.' Peggy from Cutting Out. 'Getting a bit forgetful, if I'm honest. You'll have to come back if you want to see it. The fax is broken.'

The fax had been broken as long as I'd known her.

'It might be tricky right now.' I'd lost interest. I'd lost my fight. 'I'm a bit tied up.'

'It's up to you, dear. I think you'll be interested but – your choice. I'll be here until seven.'

I hesitated on the corner of Jen's square, and then a black cab trundled past. I took it as a sign, though this time I didn't bother with the Pernod.

'Sorry, dear,' she said unapologetically as I walked through the door. 'You slipped my mind, if I'm honest.'

'Nice suntan.' I admired her deep mahogany colour, against which her orange lipstick was more alarming than ever. The smell of cats was even stronger today in the fetid basement.

'Yes, well, I popped over to see my dear friend the Sphinx. One never knows when it might be the last time, you know.'

'Don't say that, Peggy.'

'Well, it's true. Time waits for no woman, as they say, my dear.' She rummaged through several wire trays, muttering to herself constantly. 'I know it's here somewhere.'

I turned over a copy of today's *Telegraph*, a flurry of cat hairs wafting into the air as I did so. The front page bore a big picture of Lord Higham shaking hands with Boris Johnson outside City Hall.

'UK Nationalists stride towards Westminster,' the headline crowed. I shuddered.

'One giant leap for racism?' the *Guardian* asked. Thank God for Xav.

'Aha.' Triumphantly Peggy handed me a cardboard file. The first piece was on Kattan and his polo team in the late eighties, a very young Ash proudly wearing polo gear. I saw the insignia, the monogram, and I remembered the sign from the horses Dalziel and I had ridden at midnight such a long time ago. They had co-owned a polo team, Kattan and Higham, but I'd learned that much already. I felt a crash of disappointment.

'Is this it?' I said. 'You're so kind, but – I'm not sure – I think I've seen it.' It was one of the pieces I'd found last time I was here.

Impatiently Peggy pulled something from behind it, pushing her raffish glasses on top of her head to peer at it.

'You did say Huriyyah, didn't you?' She jabbed a gnarly finger at a tiny face. 'I wasn't going to forget that name in a hurry.'

On a rather crumpled piece of yellowing A4, there was a tiny photo of a glamorous young couple, an article from the society pages of *Harpers & Queen*, marked 1990, the bright colours faded, the edge slightly torn.

'It means Angel you know, in Arabic, Huriyyah,' Peggy said conversationally.

Huriyyah, wearing a midnight-blue evening dress, mouth wide and broad in a great smile of happiness. And with his arm around her proudly, head slightly tipped towards his lover, the look on his face unmistakable, straight-backed and debonair for one so young, Ash Kattan. Behind them a group of people, laughing, drinking cocktails.

And then a tiny article clipped from one of the broadsheets, dated December 1994.

Omar Rihad and his family have left the official residence in Kensington and returned home after the tragic and sudden death of eldest daughter Huriyyah, 24. Mr Rihad has worked as a diplomat in London for the past 7 years for the Emirate government. British envoy Lucas Johns extended his deepest sympathies, and in an unusual move, Lord Higham attended the funeral on behalf of the Prime Minister. It is his last official engagement before he also leaves British shores. Mr Rihad's successor has yet to be announced.

Nothing was mentioned about the way she'd died. I felt an intense wave of nausea.

Huriyyah Rihad, dead at twenty-four, Christmas 1994, two years after the implosion of Society X. I would have been in India by then, sweating in Goa, planning my trip up to Rajasthan, newly graduated. I was busy finding myself, setting out on my new adventure . . . and she was lying cold in a morgue.

Peggy jabbed at the page again with her cerise fingernail.

'They tried to cover it up, but it was suicide or drug over-dose, I'm fairly sure of it. I remember it now from the *Express* news-desk.'

'Really?'

'No one really covered it, though. If you look at this,' she handed me a photocopy of that week's headlines, 'Lord Higham announced the changes to Poll Tax that week, I think. Then he resigned.'

I shivered in distress.

Huriyyah 'Angel' Rihad. The girl in Dalziel's house. The girl on the divan. I looked back at the smiling couple, obviously besotted. I looked at the group of people in the background. I thought one might be Higham.

She had been Ash Kattan's girlfriend all the time.

Chapter Thirty-Six

I was climbing into the bath when Jen came home. 'I got ravioli and Häagen-Dazs,' she called. 'There's a letter here for you, by the way.'

She handed me an expensive cream envelope with my name handwritten in thick black ink. I opened it with wet hands, trying not to smudge it. The note inside read:

> Like David, line 1, Psalm 32.
> I hope this is enough, Rose. You deserve more.
> From a friend

When I turned over the postcard, it was a picture from the British Museum of William Blake's *Albion Rose*, the pale figure slightly plump and girlish before the flaming sun.

I climbed out of the bath and sat, dripping wet, wrapped in a towel in front of Jen's battered old PC. I looked up Psalm 32. The first line read: 'Happy are those whose transgression is forgiven, whose sin is covered.'

The handwriting of the postcard was unfamiliar. I turned it over in my hands, searching for another clue, and then I made a call.

* * *

'You back then? Doing a Russell Crowe?'

Pat and I hadn't spoken in over a year, but he sounded unsurprised to hear from me.

'A what?'

'You know. A maverick truth-seeking journalist on a quest.'

'Oh, I see,' I grinned. 'I'm slightly more svelte than him, I hope. No, I'm just trying to help my husband.'

'Yeah, sorry about that.' He sounded uncomfortable.

'You still in Miliband's office?' I changed the subject.

'By the skin of my teeth,' he laughed ruefully. 'So what can I do for you?'

He gave me the address I needed, a road near the Oval Cricket Ground. 'Just don't let on it was me,' he murmured. 'All right, sweet pea?'

'Would I?' I murmured back. 'Same bank account, is it?'

'Don't bother. Save it for something bigger. I might need it one of these days, the way this lot are going.'

'You are a star, lovely Pat. Thank you.'

'Cocktails on you, though, all right, Langton?'

'Soon, Pat, I swear. Soon as I move back.'

I waited outside the great house in the Oval for what seemed like eternity. I used to love this side of my job – the inexorable journey to the centre of the story – but now it just felt depressing, sitting here in the car with a cup of cold coffee. A Filipina maid left and returned with a shopping trolley that she could barely get up the front stairs, just as a group of hooded black boys swaggered down the road. The handsome leader caught my eye, his eyes narrowed, his diamond studs flashing beneath the street-light. I debated getting out to save her. Then he turned to the small puffing woman and carried the trolley up to the top stair for her in one hand.

There was hope here, somewhere, I felt it. These shores were wide enough for all of us, weren't they?

A black Mercedes pulled up outside the big house on the end of the row. I got out of my own car now and moved into the shadows.

A slim woman, all long hennaed hair and high heels, got out – and then a man.

'Ash,' I stepped forward. 'Do you remember me? I wonder if we could have a quick chat.'

'I'm busy, Mrs Miller. I've got to get back to the Commons in an hour.' His handsome face was set grimly – he didn't look pleased to see me at all. Gently he pushed the woman towards the house. 'I'll see you inside, Laila.'

Out on the pavement in the humid street, we eyed each other carefully. I took a deep breath.

'Please, Ash. I need to know what's going on.'

'What do you mean?' he said diffidently. 'Where?'

'I know about Huriyyah,' I said quietly.

A siren wailed in the distance. Ash stared at me.

'What do you know?' he snapped after a long minute. 'Another scoop?'

'That you and she—'

'That your stupid society ruined her?' He took an infinitesimal step towards me. 'That she was drugged and raped and that she never was the same again? That she became a junkie afterwards, that she never regained her honour.'

'It wasn't my society,' I said, but I felt my skin burning with shame. 'And I only ever saw her once. She looked like— I didn't think it was rape.'

'Oh, didn't you?' he spat. 'And what does rape look like exactly, Mrs Miller?'

'I don't know,' I mumbled. 'But at the time, she looked like she was . . .' I couldn't say enjoying it exactly, '. . . complicit.'

Had she though? At the time, maybe, but I remembered my doubts afterwards. My hesitant enquiries into her welfare, enquiries that had come to nothing.

'A little heroin can help a lot, can't it, Mrs Miller?' He glared at me.

'I wouldn't know.'

'And then a little *becomes* a lot.'

'But what has any of that got to do with James, Ash? He didn't give her heroin, I swear. He didn't have sex with her. I know that for a fact.'

'I don't know what you mean.' He slammed the car door so violently that I flinched. 'It's nothing to do with me, your husband's mess.'

'It *must* be linked. The coincidence is too great.'

'All I know, Mrs Miller, is –' and I felt him set his teeth – 'all I know is I need to be back in the Commons for a vote at ten – and you need to go. I don't know anything about your husband, and Huriyyah, well, she died a long time ago.'

'You must have been very sad. I hadn't realised she was your girlfriend.'

He glowered at me. He was imbued with utter rage, I could sense it, palpable in the air between us. But I stood my ground.

'Is your father here?'

'My father?'

'Yes.' I narrowed my eyes. 'Mr Hadi Kattan.'

'No. He's in Iran. And I wouldn't believe anything you hear about my father, you know. He's a chameleon. A shape-shifter.'

'Really? You sound angry with him.'

'Mrs Miller, I really am not going to discuss the complexities of my family with *you*.' He was disdainful, rattling the keys in his hand impatiently. 'So if that's all—'

'It's been adjourned, you know. My husband's trial,' I said.

'Really?' His surprise was unconvincing. 'Why would that be?'

'I'm not sure yet. You wouldn't know anything about it, I suppose?'

'Don't be stupid,' he spat. I took a deep breath. I had to press on.

'So, you buried Huriyyah? Poor girl.' I was emboldened by his rudeness.

'Much as I esteemed her, she was weak in the end. Weakness never pays. Look at your great friend Dalziel,' he sneered.

Unconsciously I clenched a fist. I remembered the Lucifer debate, I remembered the crackling animosity between the two boys.

'And you, Rose Miller, you need to decide what your path is.'

I was surprised. 'What do you mean?'

'Are you trying to save the world? Or are you just trying to find a story, a headline where there is none?' He pocketed his keys and stepped towards the house. 'A terrorist – or an innocent Muslim? A sad drug addict – or an imprisoned daughter?' He turned away from me, so I could see the beauty spot on his cheek, the elegantly curved nose. 'A true reporter – or latching on to a *cause célèbre*? Go home, Mrs Miller. There's nothing for you here.'

He was so angry that he no longer looked handsome, his face so taut, pale eyes wide, and I suddenly realised who he reminded me of. I thought of the first cutting in Peggy's office. I thought of Lord Higham standing behind Alia Kattan in that early photo, their hands brushing.

I stood watching him as he climbed the front stairs. At the top he turned. 'You may feel guilty about Huriyyah, though, peace be with her. You may feel that guilt for ever.'

'But I—'

He slammed the front door in my face.

Wearily I drove back to Jen's for the night. Crossing the river, Parliament silhouetted against the night sky, I supposed it was Lord Higham who had sent the note, although I guessed I'd never know for sure. Atoning finally for his sins.

Chapter Thirty-Seven

Long is the way
And hard,
that out of Hell leads up to the Light.

Paradise Lost, Milton

I was sitting in my mother's garden when Ruth rang to tell me the news. As quickly as it had started, it was over. Three days later, a mistrial was declared. One of the jurors alleged he had been approached by an anonymous source to sway his verdict. At the same time, Saquib Baheev had apparently confessed that he had been coerced to point the finger at James – and suddenly, all charges against James were dropped.

My husband was coming home. I put the phone down and just sat for a while, watching the children finish their tea on the tartan blanket laid on the lush emerald grass. It was a warm, rather sultry evening, given that it was May.

'You've got tomato ketchup on your forehead,' Alicia was telling Effie. 'Wipe it off.'

'Where?' The little girl put her hand up and smeared the sickly red sauce into her hair. 'I haven't. Have I?'

'Have I got a forehead?' Freddie said. 'Where's my five-head?'

I watched them, feeling such incredible love that I could hardly believe there had been a day when I had even thought I could have run away from them, from my life. The madness had truly consumed me for a while, but now I was calm again.

Calm – but without hope for myself. I had seen hope in Danny, I'd grasped it between my fingers, that was what he had brought me. It kept me going for a while during bleak days, that tiny scrap. But in the end it had got so tattered, so dirty and mauled and torn that there was really nothing left.

My only hope now lay in the children. My one wish now was that their lives would be carefree and easy for as long as I could make them so. They would be enough for me.

I sat numbly in the evening sun, knowing now that James would come home and the children would be ecstatic. Gingerly I pressed the small lump beneath my eye, the lump that had never quite disappeared, vestige of the last back-hander James had given me that cold spring day a year ago. Soon I'd have to tell him that I wanted to leave, that I was taking the children too – and how much longer could they be carefree then?

And all I could think was, tonight is my last night of freedom.

The doorbell rang. My heart leaped. Danny's final words stayed with me however hard I fought them. 'I'll find you, I promise.' That tiny shred of hope still flickered then, despite my flat despair.

I heard voices, excited, and then my father called out, 'James is here. Daddy's home.' The kids stood as one, screaming with excitement and confusion, and went running inside, tumbling over one another to reach their father first, my mother's dog barking in frenzy.

For a moment I didn't get up. I looked down at my hands, at my wedding ring, and I saw the storm clouds reflected in my teacup.

We went back to the perfect house in the country. All this time I had been running, and now I saw there was nowhere left to go.

The children were happy here, settled – and I was about to pull their life apart again. For years I had been championing the outsider without realising that I was deliberately making myself one, and slowly I'd begun to realise, too, that it wasn't the place as much as me. I was rejecting safety, not location. And my children needed safety; so here, for now, we would stay. It finally felt more like coming home; and although we wouldn't stay in this house, the children and I would stay in the Cotswolds.

From the day we arrived back in Gloucestershire, James and I slept in separate bedrooms. He threw himself into his work and I prevaricated about telling him that one of us had to go. It bubbled unsaid beneath the surface: I figured I'd wait until the end of the long summer holidays, then at least the children could have some time as a family before it was finally torn asunder.

James was different, humbled perhaps. I felt that he too knew that it wasn't going to work, but he wasn't going to be the one to broach it. We skirted round the subject of his guilt; I built myself up to confront him finally about it.

And then one morning the phone rang.

'Let's just say you've got a special friend, darling,' a woman's voice said quietly, giving me a time and place to meet. I thought I recognised her but before I could question her, she had hung up.

Chapter Thirty-Eight

The light shines in the darkness and the darkness
has not overcome it.

John 1:4, 5

All the way to London, the woman's words circled round my head like carrion crows. She'd hung up before I could ask more; that silky voice echoing down the years, a voice I was sure I knew and yet couldn't quite place. One more piece from the nightmare jigsaw the last year had become; one more piece nearly slotted back in.

Off the motorway, the traffic snaked back solid to the Blackfriars interchange. Frantically I watched the clock, creeping forward incrementally, until I could bear it no longer. Abandoning the car on a broken meter I sprinted through the rush-hour fumes, dodging swearing cyclists and the motorbikes that sneaked down the middle, stumbling over the kerb on Ludgate Hill, until I was falling in panic, unable to right myself. A double-decker bore down on me, horn blaring; a builder in a yellow hard hat snatched me from its path in the nick of time, his calloused hand warm on mine. I was too stunned to do much more than blink at him and run on.

They were closing St Paul's Cathedral to sightseers as I finally reached the great stone stairs. For too long now my life hadn't made any sense; I had to know the truth. Someone, somewhere, had to know the truth.

Inside, the internal gate was shut.

'Please,' I gasped at the curate, closing up. 'Please, I have to – I've come so far.'

That someone might be here.

'You look pretty desperate,' the jolly curate relented, his chin resting on his collar, waving me through with his walkie-talkie. 'Last one in. This one's on God.'

'How do I get up to the Whispering Gallery?' I wheezed gratefully, leaning on the barrier for a moment to catch my breath.

It took me ten minutes to climb up, and my heart was banging so hard by the time I'd reached the gallery in the huge dome that I had to sit down as soon as I got there. I'd passed a gaggle of Italian tourists coming down the stairs, but otherwise the space was empty. I thought he hadn't come, the anonymous writer – and I heard my name said softly, and I turned and saw him.

They say that when you're drowning your whole life flashes before your eyes – though it seems unlikely that anyone could confirm it. True or not, I felt like I was falling backwards now, splashing messily through my own life.

He walked towards me, thin and no longer elegant, wiry-limbed and crop-haired instead.

'Hello, Rose,' he said and I tried to find my voice.

'I thought,' it came at last, 'I thought that you were dead.'

Lord Higham had let it be known that his eldest son, Dalziel, had taken his own life, permanently scarred by the tragic and sudden death of his girlfriend, Lena. There was never any formal announcement of the death and the funeral was said to have taken place quietly and privately on the family estate in Scotland. And of course, that suited them just fine.

How could Higham ever admit that, actually, one child of his had attempted to murder another? One child of his, high on the drug PCP – or angel dust – had tried to coerce a 'friend' – the bullet-headed Brian – into raping another child, his own half-brother, in front of an audience. One child of his had encouraged his once-girlfriend to use so much heroin and Xanax that she had overdosed and died, gurgling at our feet.

And so all this time, James believed that he had effectively murdered his best friend after they had tussled with the knives. Dalziel had been removed in an ambulance, bleeding, taken to a private hospital after the horrible scuffle whilst I still lay unconscious. I'd been hospitalised myself; James had been briefly arrested along with Brian whilst the police tried to ascertain what had happened.

Enquiries I'd made later to the family about Dalziel had been politely rebuffed. They were mourning their dear son; they didn't want strangers' eyes on them, and I accepted that. Brian had disappeared into the navy, I found out later. James and I returned to our lives, separated – scathed and saddened but ultimately the apparent survivors. We had been utterly brazen in our ambition to show no one could restrain us – and our ambition had exploded in our faces.

All these years, James had endured the pain of thinking he'd murdered his friend; that his fatal blow had killed Dalziel. We'd believed that Higham had covered up the death to prevent a scandal; that James had been saved by the lies of the father for the death of the son.

But Higham had been covering up something very different indeed.

I sat beside him, staring, staring, and I was eighteen again, back in Oxford. My hands were shaking. I kept looking up at him to check that I hadn't gone mad.

'Where have you been?' I said, and he smiled slightly, and I saw a glimpse of the old Dalziel, the boy I had once known. Although now I looked closer, I could see that his beauty was quite ravaged.

'Here and there, darling, here and there. South America, mainly.'

'But how can you have just disappeared like that? You can't have just vanished off the face of the earth.'

'I can.' He put his hand in his pocket. 'Although obviously I didn't.'

'Well, where—'

'There are plenty of places to hide, Rose, if you don't want to be found.'

'So your father . . .' I said slowly.

'Has forgiven me? Just about.' Dalziel tried to smile, his teeth bared briefly. They told the tale of past addiction and indulgence; no longer perfect and straight and white. 'As long as I do what my father says, I'll be all right.'

He spoke differently, no longer with the louche drawl I remembered, more clipped as if there were no words to spare, and he held himself as if he was so tense he might never relax. Once willowy, now he was wiry, the veins on his arms too pronounced. And he didn't look well, I thought suddenly. He was too thin and his eyes seemed to be blazing with something, though the dim light made it hard to tell. I felt a shiver. It was hard to imagine Dalziel ever growing old. In my mind, he was twenty-one for all time, gone for ever, having lived fast and died too young. I'd always thought he was like Dorian Gray. He would never age, never grow old or ugly or fat. *It is better to be beautiful than to be good*: Wilde had written it, Dalziel had lived it. But now, here he was. Severe and somehow rather monk-like.

Slowly it began to tumble into place. The reason Higham had tried to buy me off. And now apparently, why he had stepped in, involving himself in something on a far bigger scale.

A little girl in polka dots entered the gallery, dragging her mother behind her.

'You've got little ones then, Rose?' Dalziel watched the couple as the girl leaned precariously over the barrier. I imagined I saw a shadow of something flit across his face. 'With the lovely James.'

For the first time, I felt anger flare. 'You nearly destroyed him, you know.'

Dalziel bowed his head.

'He still has nightmares now.' I had never spoken up against Dalziel, not once during the days of Society X, not until that fateful final night, but now I could hardly bear to summon the filthy terror he'd put us through. 'James thought he'd killed you. He's been haunted by what happened. How could you let him think that for all this bloody time, Dalziel?'

'I didn't have much choice,' he said flatly.

'What do you mean?'

He sighed, and the thing in his pocket that he fiddled with rattled. 'Let's just say I haven't been master of my own ship for some time. And I promise you, I'm haunted too. Utterly.' He slumped back against the bench. 'I'm ruined for all time. Though I must say, James did have a pretty good go.'

'That's rubbish and you know it. He just tried to stop you doing –' I paused – 'doing whatever it was you were about to do.'

We sat there for a second in quiet contemplation. Did either of us even know what Dalziel had planned?

'I still bear the scars, you know.' Dalziel pulled his black shirt aside at the neck to show me the fine puckered line of a wound I'd never seen, a wound that travelled from collarbone to breast, that had missed his throat by centimetres. But James had no intention of killing Dalziel, that much I knew. He was struggling with him when the knife in his hand had slipped and gashed his friend.

Slowly Dalziel did the buttons back up, right up to the top so no flesh was exposed. 'I guess it was no less than I deserved.'

'It wasn't about what you deserved. It was desperation.'

'I was mad, Rose.' His voice was a monotone. 'I didn't know what I was doing.'

'Christ, Dalziel. Why didn't you tell us, though? We thought that you were dead.'

'Let's not bring Christ into it, shall we?' He tried to smile that confident smile that I remembered so well, but he was hollowed, a shadow of the boy I'd known. 'That's where the trouble started, I seem to remember.'

'So what happened?'

'I was incarcerated for a while.'

'A while?'

'A few years. A special hospital in Buenos Aires. I have to take a lot of meds today.'

'Medicine?' I said. 'For what?'

'Depression. Schizophrenia. You name it, Rose. But I'm fine. Really. Don't be scared.'

'I'm not scared of you, Dalziel.'

'But you're angry.' It was a curt statement.

'No. I don't know. It's been so long. It's such a bloody shock.'

Two portly Americans entered the gallery and began to search for the Whispering Wall. I thought of how Dalziel had opened up my narrow world. For all his madness and grand designs, he had lent me a lust for life that I hadn't had before I'd met him, an enthusiasm that had led me to places I'd never have seen if I hadn't known him.

'Why now?' Dully I watched the Americans. 'I mean, why are you here?'

'I came to pay my dues.'

'What do you mean?'

'To help get James acquitted.'

'How the hell could you do that?'

'I think that's a question for James, dear Rose.'

'But James isn't here, Dalziel. So you'd better tell me.'

'I only know the bare facts. She tried to blackmail him, you know.'

'Who did?'

'I came back to see a doctor a few years ago, at the London Clinic. I spent a bit of time in town before my family corralled me again. I fell into some of my . . . of my old habits, shall we say. And that girl who had got involved with Charlie recognised me.'

'What girl?' I stared at him. 'Kate?'

'The silly waitress who loved James.'

'Yes, Kate. And?'

'And she tried to blackmail my father. Last year. My little brother put her up to it, though, I fear.'

'Why?'

'My brother hates my father almost as much as I do. And he admitted to Kate – Katya – that I was alive when she asked. She put two and two together: she saw that my father was on the political up and she threatened to expose the fact that his son was a mad ex-junkie, still alive. Amongst other things.'

So Lana had been right. But that would mean James had known Dalziel was alive . . . Panic rose in my belly.

'What sort of things?'

'Things she had on my father.'

'How did she know your father?'

'Don't be dim, darling.' For a second, he sounded like the old Dalziel. 'Because she was a whore.'

So it had been true all along. I thought of the photos of Higham, taken at three in the morning. The pictures of scantily clad women entering the house earlier. Some kind of posh brothel, presumably.

'And then she paid the ultimate price.' His voice slowed. 'She died, didn't she?'

I realised the thing in his hand was some kind of worry beads.

'Yes. In my house. But it was an accident.' I tried to keep up with what he was saying.

'Really?'

'Yes. It was, definitely. Or, at worst, it was some kind of stupid noble suicide.' I saw James being hustled out. I saw Charlie Higham chatting up the girls who'd adored him. 'It wasn't murder. She fell.'

'I see. Well. That's one relief, I suppose.'

'But – hang on. The trial. It was your father who got it stopped? Is that what you're saying? And James – James knows you are alive?'

'I guess so. And I don't doubt my father had some hand in it once I'd applied the pressure.'

'But he's not that powerful, Dalziel. Not even Lord Higham could halt a trial.'

'Never underestimate the old school tie, darling. The firm grip of the odd handshake. The power of the politically corrupt.'

'And why would he?'

'Because my father knew I'd come forward. Because he wants me back out of the way before the media cotton on. He plans to take over the world, you know,' his eyes blazed, 'and he doesn't want his lunatic son emerging from the grave.'

Nothing made much sense right now. We sat in silence again, listening to the Americans bounce their shrill voices off the walls, giggling at each other like small children.

'And the Kattans?'

He shrugged. 'We were always going to pay, my darling, I guess, for our iniquity. Ash never forgave me for – for screwing with his girlfriend.' I felt him hesitate on the harsh word. 'Though she was already screwed, shall we say. Beautiful angel. Beautiful lost woman.'

'Why did you do it? Why her?'

'Because,' and his face took on a blankness I remembered for a moment, 'I suppose, if I'm honest, because he humiliated me in front of all those people. At the Union that night. And she was around, abandoned by Ash, most of the time, for all his anger – at all the parties in London, hungry for oblivion, already an addict. Easy to persuade.'

I remembered her, utterly insensate, I remembered Brian between her legs. I felt like someone was scooping out my insides.

'And my father liked Ash, too much,' Dalziel muttered. 'My father and Hadi were in cahoots for most of the eighties – till it all went wrong over the oil deal. And my father's undying bloody respect,' he was paler now than before, 'his respect for the high-achieving Ash? Well, that hurt.'

'Is Ash –' my brain was whirring – 'is Ash your brother too?'

For a moment I thought Dalziel might cry. 'What do you think?' he whispered.

I thought of those eyes, the steely ambition, the photo of the parents. 'I'd say it was quite likely.'

'And you'd be right, my Rose.'

'And so the whole Huriyyah thing? Was that just to get at Ash – at your own half-brother?'

'I suppose so, yes. But, look, *she* was as lost as me – Huriyyah. As lost as I was, before I found God.'

'Oh Christ, you didn't.' I stared at him. In the old days, he would have laughed, but his face was still blank. 'Have you really?'

'I always knew I would, I think. That was my path. There is such a thin line between Lucifer, the light bringer, and our Maker. It's been my salvation.'

I looked at him carefully, still expecting him to turn and laugh at my naivety.

'That's why I thought we should meet here, Rose. At Heaven's gate.'

I thought of the psalm on the note. *Happy is he whose transgression is forgiven, whose sin is covered.* Atonement for his sins. He was deadly serious, I realised. Not worry beads in his hand, but a rosary. I found it painful to hear him now.

Downstairs, Evensong was beginning. We would have to leave soon.

'Where do you live?' I still couldn't believe he was here. 'Back in London?'

'What, with my dear father? Hardly, Rose.' He leaned back and looked up into the great dome. Into the void. 'I live in a mission in Caracas most of the time. Occasionally I retreat to the family farm. My father wouldn't have me, to be honest. Not here. Not any more.' Dalziel looked so sad. So sad I had to turn away. 'I wasn't allowed near the kids. Far too untrustworthy. That was the deal.'

That bed in the hotel room was vivid in my mind now. The snowy pillows, the small dark head. 'I suppose,' I murmured, 'I suppose that's understandable.'

He looked at me. 'Is that what you suppose, my lovely Rose?'

'Well, you – you weren't very well, were you?'

'No, I wasn't very well, for a long time. I . . .' he paused. 'I think I'm a little better now,' he finished quietly. 'I've certainly paid the price, I hope.'

'Do you live alone?'

'Yasmin comes to see me. She stays for weeks at a time, quite often. So it's not all bad.'

Yasmin. The stepsister he had loved so much.

Dalziel, my tragic friend. Born into such privilege and wealth, given everything except proper love. Left with nothing but an empty life. The iconoclast turned conformist.

'It's nice to see you,' he said quietly. 'It really is, Rose. The girl with the sad mouth.'

The voices rose and swelled below us as we sat in silence. I thought of that cold October night so long ago, of the two of

377

us running laughing from Oxford's cathedral, trailing champagne and pink feathers, without a care in the world.

After a while, I slipped my hand into his cold one and we sat some more. We had come full circle, it seemed.

UNIVERSITY, CHRISTMAS 1991

*Yea, he had power over the angel, and prevailed: he wept,
and made supplication unto Him.*

Hosea 12: 4

I had caught them together, although they didn't know at the
time. It was an icy December night just before we broke up for
Christmas, and I'd bought Dalziel a present. I'd saved the rest
of my grant and all my dad's allowance, and travelled up to
London specially to buy him a rare recording of Maria Callas
that he'd told me about one night, and I was so proud of myself.
Exhilarated, I rode my bike very fast from Magdalen to his house,
almost falling on black ice by the Bodleian Library.

At Dalziel's I rang the doorbell several times but he didn't
answer, though I could see light creeping round the curtain in
the bedroom and when I peered through the letterbox, I could
hear opera playing softly from somewhere. Dalziel was probably
comatose on the sofa, or soaking in the bath. Leaning my bike
against the front porch, I let myself through the side gate into
the back garden.

They didn't see me. They didn't see me as I stood by the

French windows and stared in; finally things began to fall into place: the reason the girl had been so angry with me in the pub the week before. The connection I had always felt between them; the tension, the look on his face when she wrapped herself so deliberately around another boy in front of him.

Drunk and naked, they lay entwined on a great white blanket on the floor before the fire, as if they had just made love. A great painting of an angel leaned against the wall, an angel apparently holding a man tenderly. Later I learned it was a Rembrandt, the angel wrestling with Jacob who was pleading for forgiveness for his sins.

And for a moment I was simply entranced by them, the pair on the rug in front of the fire, because they were beautiful together; his long slim body, her tiny slender frame, they were like something Biblical. Oh, the irony. And as she turned over, yawning and purring almost, I saw that her face was made up like the angel in the painting.

Dalziel stood now and stretched as she relit a joint. He wrapped a towel around his narrow hips and walked over to the fire, where I watched him take something from the mantelpiece. He tested it on his finger. I stepped nearer: realising with horror it was a knife – and she hadn't seen it, that was obvious. For a moment I thought I would rap on the window to stop whatever he was about to do. But I saw she was smiling, sleepily, reaching up to him with peaceful languor.

He sat down again beside her and he took her hand and laid it in his lap. And as I watched, he began to carve something into her wrist: so tenderly he held her and the blood dripped on the white fur she lay on and when she winced a little, he lifted her arm to his mouth and sucked the blood away. And then he laid her down again and arranged the blanket beneath her until it looked like she was wearing wings, great white feathery wings that soared and arched behind her. And then he climbed over her, astride her, and leaned to kiss her.

You shall not make for yourself a carved image – any likeness of anything that is in heaven above, or that is in the earth beneath, or that is in the water under the earth.

I was freezing now, my fingers numb in the stinging cold.

I watched them for a minute more as they kissed slowly and then began to make love again – and I was jealous and I was moved. Eventually, I turned away, disturbed, and I pocketed the prettily wrapped CD of Maria Callas, and I cycled to James's house instead. I craved company and human warmth, and I spent the night with him.

Later, I realised it was the second commandment Dalziel was breaking that night. Making and worshipping a carved image. The knife had fooled me at the time: later, I knew he wouldn't have hurt her – he loved her too much. And the sex hadn't shocked me, though it had stabbed me to the core, despite our own asexual relationship. But it shocked me later, when James told me, that night at the Randolph, that they were siblings. Stepsiblings, whatever. It seemed indecent somehow; dirty and spoiling the beauty I'd seen.

The day Dalziel finally went mad and tried to kill her little brother. The brother who was like a piece of Yasmin. Dalziel had loved her and he wasn't allowed her – so he hurt himself instead. He turned himself slowly mad, I realised much later, through love of her.

Chapter Thirty-Nine

GLOUCESTERSHIRE,
SUMMER 2009

So heavenly love shall outdo hellish hate.

Paradise Lost, Milton

Summer came. Tractors traced lanes through the fields like finger-trails through sand. Rabbits sat, fat and free, birds rose in waves from the hedgerows beneath the sun.

We put the perfect house on the market. It was a beautiful family home, waiting for the right family. We just weren't it. James went away on business: we didn't talk, not really. It hung over us, but it wasn't time – yet. Slowly I began to pack up.

A week or so after his release, I started to box up my books, and I found a copy of my university diary wedged between Coleridge and my Shakespeare's Sonnets. I flicked through it, feeling unexpected tears flood my eyes. How much hope and how much expectation I'd had. How nearly it had ended in disaster.

'Penny for them.' James stood behind me. He'd arrived back from Paris that afternoon.

'God you scared me.' I turned quickly. He took the book from my hands; I pushed down the instinct to grab it straight back. Why did it matter if he read the ramblings of an eighteen-year-old, unsure whether she should carry on seeing him at all, secretly in love with his best friend? But James wasn't interested in reading it anyway. He'd never really cared about my writing.

'I'm sorry, Rose,' he muttered, staring at the faded blue cover. It bore a yellow smiley-face sticker and my name doodled in biro round a badly drawn rose. 'I've been an utter bastard. I'd –' he looked up at me now – 'I'd really love it if you could forgive me.'

'For what exactly?'

'For – everything.' He gave the book back and slumped onto the sofa. 'For hitting you, first and foremost.'

'Oh.'

'And for – for Kate.'

I thought of Danny. I hadn't even felt guilty about him, I realised now. I'd felt a lot of things, but guilt wasn't one of them.

'Thank you,' I said quietly. 'Of course I can forgive you. I guess – I guess we haven't been good for each other for a long time now.'

'You must have been so pleased, the day I got banged up.'

'Are you joking?' I shook my head at him. 'It was hideous.'

'I didn't do it, you know.'

'Didn't you?' We stared at each other. I felt like I was slipping back into the yawning black hole. I had been so unsure of the truth for so long, I wasn't sure I could bear it now.

'Did you honestly think I had become a drug baron?'

This man I knew so well and yet didn't know at all. I gazed at him in silence. Behind him on the wall a print of Lautrec's cancan dancers kicked out their delicately heeled feet, faces mischievous, their skirts primrose-yellow froth. So much history – and yet . . .

'Come on, Rose. Don't act dumb. I thought . . .' He trailed off.

'What?'

'I thought it was you that shopped me.'

383

'James!'

'I thought you were so angry, you wanted to shock me.'

'Christ, James. Why would I want that?' I felt wearied, a thousand years old. 'Don't be ridiculous.'

But I saw myself tearing round his studio the day that I'd caught Liam there. I had doubted James severely, that was true. I'd pulled things down, I'd opened drawers, files, I'd gone through his emails. I'd sat numb and dazed, knowing my life no longer stacked up, and had assumed he was up to no good.

'I thought about it, you know.' He read my mind. 'When they offered to cut me in on the deal; when they asked if I wanted to take over running one of their operations.'

I saw the vortex now; I saw my chance to climb back before I was sucked through for ever. This was the chance to scramble out. 'So you were tempted?'

'I was desperate.'

I put all the books down and sat on the sofa next to him.

'Desperate?'

He put his head in his hands, staring at his feet. At the new carpet. 'I'd fucked up so badly, financially. I was terrified. I panicked. For a moment I saw it as a quick fix.'

'A quick fix?'

'Do you have to keep bloody repeating me?' James snapped. He stood and walked to the drinks cupboard, pulled a bottle of whiskey from the shelf.

'Is that why you tried to blackmail Higham?' I asked him drily.

He put the bottle down with a bang and swung to face me.

'That wasn't me.' His forehead wrinkled into a deep frown. 'That was Kate's idea. Kate and Charlie. I swear.'

'Did you know Dalziel was alive?'

He stared at me, his skin blanching. 'Alive?'

'Yes, J, alive.'

We hung over the lip of our life. The moment that finally cracked the final vestige of trust between us.

384

'I had an idea,' he muttered in the end.

'I see.'

'Only very recently, though, I swear. And I figured . . .'

'What?'

'He owed me.'

'You? You specifically?' I felt that familiar flicker of anger now. 'Not all of us? Just you?'

'It was me that thought I'd killed him. And it wasn't my idea. It was Kate's. She saw him, a few years ago apparently, off his face again.'

'So she *was* a whore?' I said coldly.

'She was . . . let's just say she was a good-time girl. Whatever. She was in love with Charlie Higham, and he had some kind of revenge up his sleeve. When Lord Higham appeared again – well, she knew Higham was struggling for political power. She did it all, I swear, Rosie.' He grabbed my hand, my hand that suddenly felt terribly cold. 'I swear it wasn't me.'

'And the heroin?'

'I thought about it.' He poured a few fingers of whiskey and downed the glass in one. 'He made it sound so bloody easy.'

'Who did?'

'Kattan.'

'But I still don't understand. If it was him, if you knew he'd set you up, why didn't you implicate him in the trial?'

'They weren't interested. They literally ignored me every time I mentioned his name. Jesus, Rose,' he slumped again, his head in his hands, 'I was just a pawn in something else.'

For the first time in a year, I realised I believed him. The relief I felt was immense. He was telling the truth. I put my arm around him, felt his solid warmth through his sweatshirt. I felt sorrow for what he'd endured; but most of all, I felt relief for our children, that their father had not veered as far off track as I'd feared.

'I think he wanted me to go down.' James stared at the wall. 'But I don't know why.'

'Who did? Hadi Kattan?'

'No.' He gazed at me. 'Not Hadi. Ash.'

In the end, who knew? Who knew whether the Kattans came to wreak revenge or whether they just happened to be in our path when we stumbled so clumsily across them? But Maya apparently recovered, and for that I was truly pleased. The photo in the paper at the Islamic protest; it turned out to be a photo taken from the wrong angle, an image from a set snapped by one of Xav's staff photographers that proved Maya and Nadif were part of a peaceful protest all along – against the fundamentalists, not for.

Some time in the autumn I caught Maya's appearance on Channel 4's News, talking passionately against her brother's involvement with Higham's party.

'No comment,' said Ash Kattan icily, outside the House of Commons, pushing past the TV crew.

'He is betraying himself,' she said, back in the studio, and she seemed almost regal, and silently I cheered her. 'Just like his father too.'

I began to accept the facts would never add up neatly. Life didn't work that way. Not mine, anyway. I told James that I was leaving him; he wasn't surprised. I rented a small cottage outside Stow-on-the-Wold. Alicia wouldn't have to move school, and the twins would join her there in the autumn. James was going back to London, to stay with Liam until he'd sorted himself out. He'd keep a flat in Oxford, he said, and he'd see them in the week, after school; he paid half the rent on the cottage and that was fine by me. The children seemed largely accepting. They'd got so used to him not being around, and we'd managed to separate without the acrimony that could have ruined us all.

One Monday morning in September, Mrs McCready arrived early, looking terribly pink, clutching the *Daily Mirror*. She hovered by the kettle for a moment, finally thrusting the paper almost violently into her shopping trolley. For the first half-hour she puffed around the small kitchen, tidying things that didn't need tidying. Eventually, after she had wiped the counter for the fourth time, I looked up from the computer.

'What's wrong?'

'I'm – I really don't think it's my place to say,' she mumbled, her mouth setting in that familiar line.

'What isn't?'

Reluctantly she retrieved the newspaper from the trolley. A broad and rather repellent face stared from the front page, cheeks angry with something red like acne rosacea. Hair like a brush, head like a bullet.

'*My life in the den of devils: Sex, drugs and Lord Higham's son.*'

For a moment I just gazed at the headline, at Brian's ugly face, and then slowly I grinned. 'Brilliant.'

'It's all about sex!' McCready stared at me like I was mad.

'Are you horrified, McCready?' I stood and put my arm round her, scanning the front page. A small mention of James and me – but no new scandal involving us. And since the trial, it was all out there already, as far as we were concerned.

'Please don't abandon me now,' I murmured, scanning the page. 'Not after everything we've been through together.'

'As if,' she sniffed. 'Rotten little liar, I expect. All that stuff about opium. It's Chinese, that poison. And such horrible skin.'

'I expect that's true.'

She gazed at me, soft cheeks trembling. 'What?'

'That it's Chinese.'

I was simply exalting in Lord Higham's shame. There was a small photo of him, stern-faced, getting in a car outside his house; one of Dalziel, smirking mischievously, taken at a May Ball in 1990. And a picture of Charlie Higham outside a club called Bungalow 8, wearing a bowler hat and a fur coat, smoking from a holder, eyes caressing the camera.

I couldn't help thinking Lord Higham had got exactly what he deserved. It would be forgotten in a week, anyway. Tomorrow's chip paper, no skin off his back. I gave the paper back to McCready.

'I got you some more Pledge by the way. The eco kind.'

And Danny never came.

I waited, but he never rang the bell. Ours was not a love story. For a moment I'd believed it would be, but then he went, retreating from me so far it was like he had never existed. The only reason I knew he had was the pain he'd scored on my heart; right through my very soul. And the fact that whilst he'd been here, so briefly, I'd felt alive for the first time in years. One morning I received a small parcel in the post, an old copy of TS Eliot's *The Four Quartets*, with a single rose pressed between two pages: the lines about doors not opening into the rose-garden underscored. I lifted the book to my face and breathed in the old leather: it smelt somehow of Eastern bazaars, and I thought of my lover, watching Kattan, like a cat about to pounce, and I tried to staunch my tears.

I'd confused him for the real thing: he'd masked the pain of my own life with James, and it was all too easy to let myself go. He lit me up and I believed in him, so I came forward to where I thought I would meet him. Only by then, he was gone.

After a while, a very long while, I stopped waiting altogether.

UNIVERSITY, MAY 1994

When no fair dreams before my 'mind's eye' flit
And the bare heath of life presents no bloom;
Sweet Hope! Ethereal balm upon me shed,
And wave thy silver pinions o'er my head.

To Hope, John Keats

On the May Day before I graduated, I rose at dawn. I walked over the bridge with hundreds of others, above the brightly coloured punts bobbing in the water, and sat outside Magdalen chapel. I listened to the young choristers sing '*Te Deum Patrem colimus*', and I cried and cried.

I knew that I'd managed to successfully salvage the time I'd spent here, but inside I carried the most immense sense of loss. Loss and something stronger I couldn't quite describe. Gratitude, perhaps.

We had been the lost kids, the ones Dalziel had rounded up, the shy or the sad or the misfits. We had fallen from our nests, pathetic fledgeling birds – and he watched, and he collected us. Carefully he picked us up, and we were so grateful for being rescued by him that we forgot to question what it was he wanted.

389

Perhaps, more simply, we were merely the outsiders.

And in my joy at being accepted, of being desired in this strange form, I had temporarily chosen to ignore the whisperings, whisperings that later I supposed were always in the ether. I chose to believe that others were jealous, of him, of us. I couldn't see the truth until long afterwards. Until it was almost too late.

And yet somehow, I'd stepped back from the brink in time. Somehow, I'd made it through.

I sat in the chapel, the sun rising in a pale washed-out sky, tears streaming down my face, and I thanked a God I didn't believe in for a chance to start again.

Points for discussion on NEVER TELL

- Consider the role of truth within the novel. How much of the action would be irrevocably altered had people chosen to tell the truth at all times?

- Can any of the characters be described as wholly 'good'?

- Discuss Rose's ready acceptance of Society X's more salubrious actions, such as group sex or drug taking. What do you think she found in the group that was lacking in her own life?

- Is Rose always in control of her own destiny?

- Consider why secret societies seem to proliferate in elite learning institutions – both here and in the US. Do you believe that participating in these clandestine groups has any bearing on the members' success in later life?

- Discuss Dalziel's assertion that 'you can have free will ... and still live in the confines of civilised life but outside organised religion.' Do you agree with Rose, that it was 'far more about decadence and doing exactly what you liked' than any aspect of religion?'

What's next?

Tell us the name of an author you love

Claire Seeber   Go ▶

and we'll find your next great book.